SAIGON ROUST

"So what else is buggin' you, Harry?"

"Were you with the 716th when Mark Stryker was an MP here?"

"Oh, sure. I remember Mark went into Special Forces or some spooky-tunes outfit. Wasn't content with our occasional sniper and slash-happy hookers. Wanted to jump out of perfectly good airplanes and have 'em pin silver jump wings on his son's chest and all that macho stuff."

"Well, he's a private investigator living in Saigon now. Over at the Miramar. Major Phuong has filed a complaint against him."

"Phuong?"

"Yeah. Says Stryker has been putting pressure on the ARVNs to help him solve some missing persons cases."

"Phuong's full of it."

"Perhaps, but I want your Decoy Squad to roust Stryker every chance you get."

"What?" Richards' jaw dropped as he stared at the C.I.D. agent.

"You heard me. Put the squeeze on Stryker. I want his ass out of Saigon."

THE SURVIVALIST SERIES
by Jerry Ahern

SAIGON COMMANDOS

BY JONATHAN CAIN

ZEBRA BOOKS
KENSINGTON PUBLISHING CORP.

ZEBRA BOOKS

are published by

KENSINGTON PUBLISHING CORP.
475 Park Avenue South
New York, N.Y. 10016

First printing: November, 1983

Printed in the United States of America

Dedicated to Angie H. L. Lu, the girl from Saigon, who helped me make it through the nights and the nightmares, and saw us both back from Vietnam safely.

SAIGON COMMANDOS is a novel based on several true stories the author swapped with other MPs at Mimi's Bar in Saigon where he was assigned to the 716th Military Police Battallion.

"Saigon Commandos" was a derogatory term invented by infantrymen in the field to refer to any soldier stationed in the "rear." But some of the military policemen—fighting snipers, sappers, and other hostile hooligans across the Saigon underworld—affectionately adopted the title, proud to be lawmen battling crime in the toughest beat in the world.

Jonathan Cain
January, 1983
Singapore

I. JUNGLE JUSTICE

His cat-green eyes, squinting against the sizzling Asian sun, scanned the rice paddy panorama as the helicopter dropped from the belly of the storm clouds, descending heavily, circling the landing zone. A soldier below had popped purple smoke, signaling wind direction for the pilot, and he felt the hair rise along the back of his neck as the ground rose up to meet them. Out of habit, he smacked the thirty-round clip in his M-16, testing its seal, then superstitiously rubbed the tiger claw on the gold chain around his neck.

The Cobra gunship lurched to one side as the skids tested the flooded swampland, finally setting down after half the men aboard had jumped off.

Keeping his head low, he followed the man in front of him down onto the sinking skid and plunged waist deep into the muck. Despite the younger, more agile troopers struggling past him on both sides, his spirits remained high and he made his six foot, stocky frame keep up with them. Even with the swirling twigs and shreds of bamboo striking his face, he caught sight of the Special Forces combat patch on the man beside him, and that rush of pride and fearlessness surged through his gut again. It was all he lived for now. The lush jungle closing in on them, the heat, the soldiers. All of it.

Searching the distant treeline for movement, he imagined a

future mission where the men wore their green berets. That made him smile.

The team encountered no hostile fire as they entered the treeline, but beyond the hills the gunship was diving abruptly up and down like an enraged predator, its doorgunners showering the rain forest with machine gun fire. Briefly, the men looked back at this sudden, distant firefight, then ignored it and continued into the jungle.

Within minutes, the sound of battle faded away as their brisk trot forced them down through a tropical valley, across a burned-out plateau, then down again, to the banks of the murky Mekong River. Despite the sweat rolling thick down his chest, burning salty in his eyes and coating the hair of his legs, he cherished these patrols across the steaming highlands of Vietnam. Imagining it to be gun oil, he carefully wiped the sweat in his hands across the black plastic of his rifle, covering all the dry spots and feeling the hot surface bite back at him as he did so.

They walked along the banks until they found a curve in the river that suited them. And then they settled down, behind the reeds and bamboo, to wait.

He felt disappointment that they had not yet engaged the Cong, but he knew that, this time, contact was not in the plan. He immediately reprimanded himself mentally: he was lucky enough they had let him back in the Green Berets, had let him return to the 'Nam. They rarely allowed that.

He thought back to his first tour in Vietnam, as an MP in Saigon five years earlier, in 1962. He spent twenty-four months policing the drunks, watching the addicts overdose, and locking up AWOLs from combat zones. They gave him an Arcom medal, then shipped him off to freezing Korea, where he battled the race riots for three years.

The mockery of the court-martials soured him on police work quickly enough, and at age 35 he went through Airborne and Ranger training again, despite it having almost killed him, and volunteered for the 'Nam. Again. They could have the

8

brief enjoyment of the stick-time that always ended in brutality complaints. The high speed chases that always ended in twisted metal and broken bones. The shoot outs that ended in the suspect's family suing you for your house and ten years' worth of your salary.

"Heyyyyy . . . Mark. . . ." One of the men was whispering over to him, breaking the spell, and he instantly fell into phase red: ready to lunge from the reeds and kill beast or man.

Another soldier, with the slightest flick of his eyes, directed everyone's attention upriver.

A long, thin sampan, its passengers in the center shielded from the sun by a roof of thatched palm fronds, appeared around a bend in the Dak Ba River. Seconds later, the boat's noisy, gas-powered engine could be heard above the startled cries of parrots high in the trees overhead.

Quite suddenly, as the sampan drifted into the range of the canyon ambush, the protesting birds fell silent, as though conditioned to expect hostilities in this bend of the river.

A dull thump announced the blast of an M-79, and before the grenade could explode beside the craft, sending a geyser of splashing waves upon the passengers, the other men in the squad unleashed a fury of automatic weapons fire that tore the Viet Cong officials to shreds. Some of the muddy river ran red with their blood even before the sampan and lead sank to the river bottom.

One of the cadre survived the initial ambush, and the cop-turned-Green-Beret brought his sights to bear on the man's back as he swam, terrified, for the opposite shore. Two rounds kicked up, zinging splashes on either side of the swimmer's face, and as he buckled his shoulders to dive, the American placed the third round at the base of his skull. The impact tore the back of the man's head completely off, sending scalp and grizzled bone and meat scattered along the opposite bank, to which the wild parrots eagerly flocked.

The current caught hold of the Cong's body and began to take it downstream, rolling it over as it did so that the empty,

9

bloodied eye sockets where the shattered bullet had exited stared back at the American for several minutes before it drifted out of sight and sank down to the muck.

He should have swum out to retrieve any identification papers and documents, but he just sat behind his reeds and bamboo, grinning. I relished that kill, he thought, amazed at the job satisfaction he suddenly felt.

While the others dove for the sampan and the documents it was rumored to carry, he maintained his position on the bank, watching over the weapons, gently squeezing a slimy frog beneath the tread of his jungle boot. "I'm actually a very gentle person," he told the frog, smiling, resisting the impulse to squish it flat and instead releasing it to hop off into the elephant grass. His attention then focused on a black water snake, slithering back and forth just under the surface of the river, its head poking out now and then as it grew nearer his men. He brought up his rifle sights again, then lowered the weapon and giggled out at the serpent. "Better turn back, boy! They gonna eat you for breakfast."

Minutes later, they had returned to high ground to await the helicopter gunship that would extract them from this mission. And soon, right on time, the dull beat of rotors flapping against the hot, sticky Asian air could be heard in the distance. He loved that sound. He clenched his fists in ecstasy, thinking maybe he loved that sound even more than his tribeswoman groaning beneath him at night in their little bungalow on stilts back in Pleiku.

One of the wild parrots, its bright white feathers stained red from picking at the scattered meat of the dead Cong, had followed them back to the landing zone and now squawked down at him. "Mocking me, you overweight canary?" he wondered aloud.

He resisted the impulse to raise his rifle and make the noisy bird just so much floating feathers, and instead concentrated on the living, breathing, imposing rain forest that closed in on them. Its snake-infested, canopied ceiling radiated mystery

10

and challenge. Life and death. He held himself back from jumping for joy at the savage feeling deep in his soul, and searched instead for the approaching chopper. God, it felt good to be back in the Orient. In the jungle he feared yet needed. He was home.

She was singing softly in her childlike singsong voice when he climbed the steps to their bungalow, kicking off the green canvas boots just outside the door. Brushing aside her long, black silky hair, she quickly rose from scrubbing the polished teakwood floor and ran to greet him, her full, bare breasts swaying wildly as she jumped into his arms and wrapped her legs around his waist.

She ignored the rifle, tossed past her onto the bed. Her man was home from work.

II. INCIDENT AT 541 THANH MAU STREET

It wasn't unusual for him to miss them, lurking in pre-dawn, back-alley shadows, down the street from his apartment. Even at that hour, merchants were setting up their sidewalk cafes and corner vending stands, ignoring the soon-to-expire martial law curfew. Within minutes, downtown Saigon would become a noisy, bustling, smog-engulfed mess—once the police barricades, roadblocks and overnight checkpoints came down.

He brushed the dust off his laminated, black MP armband and shifted his web-belt around so that it centered properly. Out of habit, he gently pressed the clip of his .45 automatic with his middle finger, checking that it was locked in tight. He forced open exhausted eyelids that deserved much more sleep, then braced himself against a lamppost and waited for the first blue and gold Renault taxi to venture down his street. He checked his watch; with luck he'd make it back to MACV compound in time for guardmount inspection.

He bought a thin roll of hot, buttery bread from a passing *mama-san*, checked it briefly for razor blades or glass, then looked back over his shoulder and up at her. She stood on the third-floor balcony, waving down at him and smiling. So beautiful, in her purple *ao-dai*. So innocent and trusting—the gleam in her eye. Still a schoolgirl.

He resisted the urge to chuckle, aware of his good fortune in

13

having found such a loyal, naive lover, and just smiled back at her instead, nodding his head slightly as he did. Sometimes she was just like a little puppy—always waiting for him to come home from the streets, faithfully preparing his meals. And his bed. Massaging him late into the night. Talking little, except when it was to teach him another Vietnamese word. Or to tell him how lazy she became when he was gone—how she thought of him all the minutes he was away, and how her energy died when he left, to be revived magically only upon his return.

Yes, so lucky, he repeated to himself as he ducked down into the taxi and handed the driver a card on which she had written the directions in Vietnamese back to Pershing Field compound. Despite all the street instinct he prided himself on, and all the police training they had drilled into him back at the MP Academy in Georgia, he failed to spot the two American deserters standing silent in the distant doorway. Even though they carefully studied his departure, then shifted their gaze up toward his woman.

Halfway through his shift he fought the urge to leave his patrol district and visit her. His partner was a by-the-book buck sergeant who wouldn't have any of that. He was too busy checking ID numbers on the military vehicles, in between the burglary and larceny calls.

He missed his old partner. The private with the Brooklyn accent. Now, *they* had raised some hell together! Broken many a night stick at the best of the bar fights. Even jailed a colonel or two. But he had rotated stateside, and hadn't written in months. Was gonna be a New York City cop or die trying. Claimed that was where the action was.

A wall of billowing, dark gray, castlelike clouds was slowly rolling into Saigon, and with it you could taste the change in the air, the anticipation, the potential for excitement. Even the electricity in the air, the masses scattering for cover as the first giant raindrops splattered down, the sights changing before his eyes as a distinct wall of showers obstructed the sun and its rainbows, was different than in any city he had ever lived. He knew he had found his new home. Ever since he had witnessed an Army chaplain catch a sniper's bullet between the eyes he stopped believing in God, yet every night, as the flares ringing Saigon drifted along the edges of the city, he found himself praying they would never make him leave Vietnam.

"MP needs help! MP needs help!" the call crackled over the jeep's radio; instinctively he pulled to the side of the road, out of the congested motor scooter traffic, straining to hear the location. "North wall of the American embassy! Partner's shot! Suspects eastbound on foot! Two Victor-November Nationals, armed with revolvers!"

The dispatcher at Pershing Field hit the emergency tone scrambler, in order to grab the attention of any beat-walking MPs within fifty feet of their units. Then he calmly solicited more information from the excited cop. "Clothing description, gimme a clothing description."

"Both in jeans, tire-tread sandals, one with a white T-shirt, the other a red muscle shirt! In their twenties! Man with the gun wearing black glasses . . . has a mustache."

Other police units were cutting in on the transmission: "Car Ten responding from the Rex theater." "Car Twelve from the MACV commissary."

"Jesus, I can't stop the bleeding!" the excited MP was yelling into his mike. "Get me a dust-off! Repeat: I need a chopper!"

"Stupid fucker!" the buck sergeant muttered as he whipped their jeep around in a screeching U-turn, activated the siren, then grabbed for the microphone. "Pursue those suspects, Kruger!" he directed over the radio to the MP who was then stuffing a blood-soaked T-shirt into the gaping hole in his partner's chest. It had been drilled into their heads over and over back at the academy: if a two-man unit got ambushed, or a car crashed during a chase, you ignored your dying brother and continued the pursuit. At all costs, the first priority was the

15

capture of the cop killers.

There was no response on the air, then: "Car Thirteen, on the scene! We've got suspects in sight, headed southwest down . . ." The rest of the transmission was garbled.

"Good ole Mather," he thought as he cut another corner, crashing through a vendor's display, sending melons rolling across the street. "He'll get their ass!" Sergeant Mather had volunteered for the Car Thirteen designation, a call-number most superstitious cops shunned. In most metropolitan departments, a code thirteen was an "officer down" code. But Mather relished danger and the slightest chance of conflict. That was why he was still a buck sergeant after twelve years in the MPs.

Sirens soon filled the air, competing with rolling waves of thunder that sent uneven sheets of rain down across the city. As they pulled up to the scene, his sergeant directed him to jump out and apply first aid to the injured MP, and before the jeep had rolled to a stop, he was leaping through the air, seeing the crowds of Vietnamese civilians closing in on the man down, watching the sergeant slide sideways up the flooded alley as he raced in the direction of a sudden flurry of gunshots.

A woman in the crowd was weeping as he pressed the bandages down onto the sucking chest wound. There were none of the hostile eyes glaring at him that he had expected. Only helpless, sympathetic embassy workers.

Additional units were now skidding up through the rain-drenched crowds, but there was no pulse beneath his fingers as he pressed against the blood-soaked throat. The man's heart was no longer forcing a fountain of red spray up through the grisly hole into the misty air. The sucking chest wound was no longer sucking. Another eighteen-year-old military policeman lay on his back in the street, dead.

He released the scene to one of the senior MPs that had arrived, then ran several blocks, gun in hand, past terrified pedestrians to where more MPs had the two suspects face-

16

down in a puddle. One cop was jabbing the Vietnamese with the red muscle shirt repeatedly in the rib cage. A shattered pair of glasses could be seen crumpled beneath one of the MP jeeps.

Sergeant Mather, who had been calmly standing over one of the suspects, observed the commanding officer's jeep careening around a distant corner on two wheels. Before the captain arrived, the sergeant pretended the semi-conscious suspect was a football and with all his might kicked a perfectly placed field goal through the man's mouth, smashing his teeth and snapping his neck so that all could hear the sickening crunch of sudden death.

Sergeant Mather smiled at each of his men individually, making a point of meeting them eye to eye so there would be no misunderstanding.

"Such are the hazards of war." One of his privates grinned in reply.

"This was not war," Mather said seriously. "This was a cop killing. There's a difference." The rainfall grew more intense, and most decided they were too wet and miserable to ponder what that difference was.

Several hours later, after all the paperwork had been completed and the investigators from C.I.D. had interviewed him and his partner, his taxi, the same blue and yellow Renault that picked him up every morning, coasted up to his apartment building. But the access road down Chi Hoa alley was cluttered with police jeeps and Vietnamese ambulances, making it difficult for the driver to pull directly into the courtyard. "Wonner was up?" the cabbie asked him, motioning to the several policemen clustered around the private security guard's shack, but he ignored the question, handed the driver a carton of Salems instead of Piasters, then slowly got out of the taxi.

One of the policemen noticed his cautious approach, recognized him to be one of the American MPs from Pershing Field, and started toward him with an outstretched hand. He immediately detected the nervous expressions on the faces of

17

the other policemen, and he instinctively looked up to his third-floor balcony, where she should have been smiling down at him, throwing a kiss.

Instead, more policemen stood up there, stern faced, some writing on notepads. The flash from a camera triggered a sudden intense fear inside him and he bolted past the startled policemen, all a foot shorter than him, dwarfed by their huge American revolvers.

He raced through the lobby of the complex, empty but for an ailing *mama-san* who sat in a corner on the floormat, listening to Chinese music on an ancient radio. Her teeth black from chewing betel nuts, she surveyed his passage with a drugged look of bewilderment.

When he reached the third level of the darkened stairwell, he was met by several officers who he recognized from the combined MP-Canh-Sat police patrols he had ridden with. They attempted to slow him down, but he brought his hand to the butt of his holstered automatic and they backed off. His slender frame, clean-shaven face, and the GI haircut that made him look like a thousand other Americans didn't scare the Canh-Sats, but his .45 automatic did, especially the hollow points it was rumored to carry.

At the door of his tiny, one-bedroom apartment, a hand reached out and grabbed his jungle fatigues by the collar. He swung around and stopped just short of slugging a young policeman who had saved his life several times over. "What the hell's going on, Jon?" he demanded of the Canh-Sat, but the officer just put his arm around the MP's shoulder as though to comfort him. He brushed the arm away and charged into the room, its Casablanca ceiling fan still twirling lazily against the heat just as he had left it that morning.

His eyes were drawn to the bed against the left wall. It was now a pool of blood, thick upon the gold satin sheets. More blood was splattered along the wall and across the bamboo curtains—across the huge photo of the two of them posing in front of the Rex theater fountains downtown.

18

The aquarium with her favorite shimmering purple fish was no longer atop the refrigerator. It was lying in hundreds of pieces across the floor—the fish long dead and now dried beneath the fan. Like a magnet, his eyes followed the trail of blood across the room to where the stereo cabinet was overturned, a tapestry of a jungle tiger was torn from the wall, and a body lay face-down under a blanket.

He wanted to scream her name, but it would not come out. His mouth had gone dry. A trickle of blood, like a tiny snaking stream, inched its way from under the blanket toward his boot. His knee went down into it as he forced himself to raise the blanket.

He couldn't even recognize her, so badly was she beaten. Knife wounds were all over her naked body, gushing more blood onto his uniform as he gently turned her over. He could not hold back the tears as he held her tightly in his arms, rocking her like a little, helpless baby. He kissed her cheek, despite the gash that had sliced through her eyes, and looked up at his police friend, blocking the sunset through the doorway.

"Who could have done this to her?" he demanded, puzzled at this tragedy that had struck their simple, quiet life. He was crying now, looking to the growing crowd of policemen in the doorway for help, for guidance. But they just stood there. Silent, like ghosts frozen in a nightmare.

Then his dazed eyes focused on the shattered mirror above the dresser he had given her on Valentine's Day, and the message scrawled across it in red lipstick: "PAYBACK IS A BITCH, PIG!" And he knew. Deep inside he knew who had done this to his woman, but he was still confused by all the blood, and he could hear himself asking the policemen over and over, "Who could have done this to my baby?"

He brought her body home to her family, down in the delta village of Mytho, forced himself to witness her burial, then drank tea with the old man, though this made him uncomfortable.

He stood before the family altar for several hours, looking at the black and white photo of her between the candles and trying to remember her laugh or the way she sounded when she told him she loved him but didn't want to leave her beloved Vietnam.

He always had been a good, dedicated MP. His only weakness had been the woman. Now she was gone, and he was a week AWOL, but it didn't matter. He examined the pictures of her in his wallet: the one of her waving down at him from their balcony, one where she was cooking shrimp soup in the wok. The one where they lay in the flowers next to the river started the tears again, and he abruptly put the wallet away.

He knew it would require several more days for his mind to sort this one out, to become rational again. Then he would do what had to be done.

III. THE DANGER SEEKERS

It was their tenth alley. Three hours past the midnight curfew, several miles of prowling Saigon's sleazier sidestreets, and still no bandits had accosted this crack anti-crime strike force, the latest brainstorm from the armchair batmen at Puzzle Palace, alias the Military Assistance Command Vietnam.

"Whatta ya say we call it a night?" one of the MPs finally requested of the glory-hunting squad sergeant. Membership in this new, "elite" goon platoon was voluntary; its young, energetic cops first had to complete their mandatory twelve-hour shifts in the guard towers at MACV Headquarters, the foot beats at Disneyland East, or the street patrols downtown.

It was drizzling that night. Sudden breezes whipped up gray ash from countless trash can fires along the back alleys, covering their faces and civilian clothes with soot that ran black with white streaks when the cloudbursts rolled in and drenched them.

"Just one more alley." The buck sergeant grinned, patting the .45 automatic in the shoulder holster under his jean jacket. "We need some contact tonight—for the stats."

They were walking the maze of sidestreets that ran off of notorious Tu Do Street, the raunchy and electric bar district.

"Up there!" one of the men whispered harshly, pointing at an elusive shadow racing across the rooftops.

"Just a prowler," the squad sergeant said, dismissing the incident lightly, "or a bedroom gigolo." But the fleeting footsteps seemed to follow them from high above as they made their way through the maze. Twice they crossed into new territory, where the curves and sudden dead ends sent the sweat running down each of their backs. And still the midnight phantom—high above them like an invisible tease—frayed at their nerves, his footsteps fading off into the night, only to reappear as the patrol descended deeper into the heart of the city, around another corner, into another maze of tenements.

"Awright," mumbled the squad sergeant finally, checking the glowing watch dial beneath the black velcro wristband. "Four hours now and no contact. Back to the jeeps."

"Let's get that asshole following us up on the rooftops," one of the youthful troopers suggested, "before heading back." The tension of the last several nights of non-contact patrols was eating at them all. Several American soldiers had met death in these back alleys lately, at the hands of seasoned robbers who lay in wait, ready to ambush them as they staggered drunk from the numerous after-hours bars in the area. It was the mission of this new squad to pose as off-duty GIs, entice the potential bandits into a street encounter, then eliminate them at the first sight of cold steel, and notify the Vietnamese National Police. And the morgue wagon.

The squad was four months old now. Several initial skirmishes brought them medals and some limelight, but the publicity had hurt: the criminals of the Saigon underground were now wary of all staggering Americans. Contact was less frequent. "Negative," the sergeant began.

Then it happened again. Down at the end of the alley, several dark figures appeared under a lone streetlight. And began walking slowly toward the small group of four Americans.

"This is it," the buck sergeant whispered across to his men. "It's goin' down. Make it look good: start staggering." But a warning cry in rapid Vietnamese from high above came accompanied by glowing arcs of red and green tracers

22

descending down on them, turning the street between them and the gang of hooligans into a storm of sparks. The sniper corrected his aim quickly and shifted the automatic weapon's fire so that the stream of sizzling multi-colored bullets appeared to chase after the Americans as they dove for cover.

With hand signals, the sergeant smoothly directed two of the MPs to concentrate on the advancing hoods, while he and the private scanned the rooftops for the spy who had betrayed their mission. It was now obvious to him that not one, but several lookouts had monitored their progress throughout the maze, signaling each new block with an eerie code of bells and gongs the MPs had ignored, thinking them only decorative windchimes, the kind displayed on almost every balcony in Asia to ward off the demons of the night.

The sergeant pulled a small, hand-activated flare from his web-belt, scraped its bottom against the harsh blacktop and watched it swoop skyward like an angry rocket. He was briefly showered with sparks, then the missile, its fuel spent, arced silently over the cluster of leaning warehouses surrounding them and burst in all its fiery glory above the rooftops from where the tracers had originated. At the same time, the sergeant sprayed the area with a submachine gun he had had taped to his side, also under the jacket, its folding stock now extended to full length. The weapon held no flashy tracers, but the roofline erupted into a brief wall of sparks as hot lead impacted on the concrete sides of the huge French building, showering glass and cement fragments down onto the street.

The sergeant glanced to his right and a smile creased his rugged features. His two men were now low-crawling toward the group of thugs, ignoring the sniper above them, attempting to get a better line of fire on the bandits. At the same time, the third MP was firing a set of carefully placed pistol rounds up at the roofline to set down some cover fire. It made the sergeant proud: his men were reacting true to their training.

Even with dozens of sirens screaming against the night silence as police across the city closed in on the rage of the sudden firefight, the sergeant found himself basking in the exhilaration and intense excitement of the moment—at the same time reviewing each of his men's personnel files as though they were lounging back in the poolroom at Pershing Field, beside the shrapnel-riddled TV set that hadn't worked in years, going over evaluation reports.

Pvt. Michael Broox. Age eighteen, fresh from the academy, raised in Trinidad, Colorado. Had a slender build even though he was constantly doing push-ups. Prescription sunglasses hid a set of piercing blue eyes that reminded him of a hawk he had once shot as it glided low over the Sangre deChristo range, not dying until it met its stalker eye to eye. Despite light brown hair that the Asian sun had bleached a dull blond, Broox still sported hundreds of red dots on his exposed arms where mosquitos had swarmed over him his first night in Vietnam.

Spec. 4 Timothy Bryant. Early twenties. Volunteered for an extention of his original tour, which he had also volunteered for. Lean and mean: he stood just under six feet tall and was proud of muscles that were firm and symmetrically perfect—not huge. A real hotdog. Cocky, yet respectful to his sergeant, which was all that really mattered. Had been stabbed by his girlfriend only three weeks earlier when she caught him entering a bar without her.

Pfc. Anthony Thomas. Another teenager, but wise beyond his years. Kept his blond hair shaved short. Boasted a black belt in offensive police jujitsu, but never flaunted it. Had a slight weight problem, despite two-hour workouts, religiously, each sunset, between meditating and attending Vietnamese language classes. Had one goal in life: to screw a whore in every capital city in Asia and not catch the clap.

The sergeant slapped another magazine into his machine gun and sprayed half the clip up at the rooftop, then directed the remaining bullets out over the heads of his men, at the Vietnamese up the street, the whole time grinning with pride at how smoothly his little group was performing. The ammo was running dangerously low, but they needed to hold out only a few minutes longer: already gunships were cruising low over the city, headed for the sound of fighting—marked brilliantly now and then by a lone, stray tracer round that ricocheted off into the night sky like some wild shooting star.

Out of habit, he glanced over his right shoulder—to the rear. It was still clear there. Secured.

Out of the corner of his eye, he caught a brief flash of the combat patch on his shoulder: a green dagger flanked by two gold axes pointing outward—mark of the Eighteenth Military Police Brigade, Republic of Vietnam. It made him so damn proud to wear it, and he marvelled at how he could take the time to admire it in the midst of a street fight.

His mind was racing backwards now, past the two years he had policed soldiers in Saigon and Bien Hoa, past the years he had hunted terrorists in Germany, even past boot camp at Fort Ord, California, to those boyhood days hunting snakes along the Everglades. He found he could review his life in mere seconds. Over thirty now and still a buck sergeant. But the street made it worth it.

"One, two, three . . . motherfuck MP!" The sniper leaned over the roofline to scream down at them during a lull in the shooting. But Buck Sgt. Gary Richards was ready for the mocking, taunting terrorist: he let rip his last thirty rounds of .223-caliber ammo in a zigzag pattern across the wall of the tenement, tearing the sniper's face in half diagonally in a splash of crimson, so suddenly that one portion of the dead man's face still smiled while the other was a gnarled mask of horror. The man's shredded body then tumbled down from the roof, crashed through a parked car's windshield and sent shards of glass flying halfway down the block.

Three MP jeeps, crammed to the hilt with action-seeking cops clinging to the M-60 machine gun support bar in the back, skidded around the corner down the street on two wheels, and the few surviving bandits now caught between the cavalry and the decoy squad immediately rose to their feet and surrendered, hands reaching for the stars as weapons clattered to

25

the pavement.

While disappointed military policemen commenced slamming the suspects face-down back onto the street for body searches, a black sedan rolled past the melee and stopped just short of the buck sergeant's striped tennis shoes. An electric, tinted window slid down, and an American C.I.D. agent poked his bald, flabby head out, instantly recognizing the MP. "Hmph . . . if it ain't Super Sergeant," he muttered while wiping beads of sweat from his forehead. He didn't bother to hide his contempt for Richards. "Should have known you were behind this. Always lookin' to gun somebody down in a back alley somewhere."

"What brings you downtown, Harry? We didn't radio for help."

"You know any 'Shots Fired' calls require C.I.D. response, asshole."

"Well, we're all okay. Not so much as a nick. Naturally."

"Naturally."

"Hey, Sarge, we really brought smoke down on those scumbags!" One of the young MPs—Broox—was running up to Richards, intending to slap him on the back. He pulled up short upon recognizing the agent from the Criminal Investigation Division, but his enthusiasm did not sour: he directed his excitement to the bald, cigar-chomping man in the black sedan. "We really kicked ass, Mister Sickles! You shoulda been here! The sarge blasted that VC up on the roof right outta his socks! Damn!" The young MP was now walking around in circles, trying to shake off the flow of adrenalin, then he was heading back down the street to where the prisoners were being handcuffed. "Damn!" he repeated. "I eat this shit up, yes, I eat this shit up!"

C.I.D. agent William Sickles tossed the cigar butt out the window and into the gutter as he sized up Sergeant Richards. Sickles' first name was not really Harry. The sergeant just called him that to irritate him when he was in the mood to ride the warrant officer about his bald head. "Hairy you ain't,"

26

he'd always crack. Sickles was sensative about his crown. Blamed it on the helmet he was forced to wear for three years during the Korean war.

"Never happy unless you're in the shit, are you?" Sickles challenged him.

"It's where the action is, Harry." But Sergeant Richards' smile had faded instantly, and he was thinking back to what his life had amounted to. "It's what I do, brother. The streets are all I got left."

IV. GOLDEN LOTUS PETAL AND
THE PLEASURE PALACE

The blue-striped water snake had no trouble skimming up the canal. The surface was smooth as glass, quite silent and unmoving, and heavily polluted. A rocket attack weeks earlier had sent a bridge crashing down into the canal, damming it completely several miles downstream, and it now backed up into the center of the village-on-stilts, making the nights unbearable because of the vast swarms of breeding mosquitos.

Fourteen-year-old Pham Thi Vien sat balanced on her haunches on a flimsy plank above the canal, watching the huge snake approach. She had been washing laundry in the murky water for two hours, but she froze when it became evident the serpent had not seen her yet. All its concentration centered on the small clouds of mosquitos hovering along the banks of the canal. Its slender forked tongue slithered rapidly in and out as its head darted back and forth, inches above the water, snatching up dozens of the insects at a time.

When the snake was but a few feet from the girl, a frog leaped over its scaly snout and plopped in the middle of the canal. It began flapping its webbed feet frantically for the opposite bank, the snake in pursuit. As they approached, the girl, who had been watching intently, reached down suddenly, snatched up the snake and snapped its head off.

Pretty little Pham Thi Vien giggled as the serpent's head

splashed down into the dark canal, its forked tongue still flicking in and out. She tossed the wiggling remainder of the reptile behind her into a fish pail and resumed scrubbing the laundry.

She giggled again when it came time to soap up and rinse the red silk bra she had found in a gutter days before. It had a little gold heart sewn over each tip—the rest was so sheer she could see through it. She wondered about the woman who had discarded it, then giggled again, thinking about how her mother would yell at her for snapping off the heads of slimy snakes and even considering wearing such sexy undergarments —if only she were alive to witness such acts.

The girl wore a towellike sarong from the waist down, and a long-sleeved shirt with the arms rolled up past her elbows, but with the front buttons conservatively fastened all the way up to her throat. The blazing sun appeared as the sheet of dark storm clouds overhead moved away from her hamlet on the outskirts of Gia Dinh, and headed south across the heart of Saigon. Beads of perspiration soon formed above her eyebrows then trickled down along the arch of her high cheekbones. She flicked the long black hair that fell to her belt over one shoulder, glanced about for any passers-by, then unsnapped the top four buttons on her blouse.

A rainbow-colored dragonfly attempted to land on her bare toes, and after she swatted it away and shifted to balance herself on the swaying plank, she noticed how firm and full her breasts appeared beneath the harsh, scratchy fabric of the shirt. She wanted to tear off the cloth and squat there naked so the warm sun could dry the beads of sweat collecting on the upturned nipples, but there were too many old men tending their water buffalo up and down the banks of the canal, and they could appear from beyond the scattering of trees at any time.

After rinsing the bra, she laid it across the plank to dry and started on the last of the clothes before she would return to the bungalow to put the rice on the fire.

Across the water, a man clad in black burst from the treeline, his eyes wide, fear etched across his young face. He glanced both up and down the canal, threw a rifle he was carrying into the murky water, then raced off toward her housing project. The weapon and the unfamiliar face should have been warning enough that she should also flee and hide, but pretty Pham Thi Vien remained squatting on her slender haunches, frozen with indecision.

Within seconds a platoon of South Vietnamese soldiers appeared from different sections of the jungle—most stared questioningly at her. But she misunderstood the look in their eyes and clutched instinctively at her open blouse to close it tight. She didn't answer across the canal to them at first simply because they were too far away to be heard clearly, and after several seconds the impatient infantrymen ignored her and, with their machine guns at the ready, began trotting up the trail toward the village.

After they were out of sight, innocent, naive, little Pham Thi Vien, with her tight muscular thighs and her erect bouncing breasts, gathered up the rest of the wet laundry, slipped on her bamboo thongs and started for the alley down which she had lived all her life.

As she started to climb the steps to her bungalow, there came an excited shouting in the distance—commands in rapid Vietnamese to halt, a rumble of shots, then scattered laughing and cheers from several soldiers. She hesitated briefly at the sound of the gunfire, but resumed climbing when silence again fell over the village. Before she reached the door, a rigid hand clamped down on her arm from behind and she was twirled around to face several angry soldiers.

They began with accusations—something about protecting enemies of the People—then dragged her into her bungalow before she could answer.

The leader of the squad grabbed a handful of her thick, flowing hair, jerked her off her feet and slammed her down onto the straw mat that was her bed. As the other soldiers in

31

the background laughed, he fell down onto her, ripped her blouse open with one quick, tearing pull, then forced his mouth down onto hers. With his left hand he held both her wrists high above her head, and with his right he began rubbing her chest between her taut, quivering breasts. She almost gagged when he forced his tongue deep into her mouth, and then another soldier was dragging her sarong off and pulling her panties down.

She began kicking, not quite sure why they were doing this to her, yet instinctively feeling a strange, woman's fear deep inside her. And then two more soldiers were holding her feet down, by the ankles, legs spread far apart. The sergeant still slobbered all over her face, and her lips were becoming sore, but she could see beyond him—to another man, who now grinned down at her as he dropped his pistol belt to the floor and slowly began unzipping his pants. Tears began to well up in her eyes—she wanted to scream or cry, she was so terrified, but no sound would leave her throat.

When he dropped down onto her and rammed his penis up in between her legs, she felt a searing pain enter her body, and the sound that finally left her throat was an animal sound that she could not control. As he forced himself farther and farther, penetrating to the root of her womb, her mind began to blank out, and she imagined instead that some jungle demon was pounding a hot, burning stick up into a part of her that had always been so secret and private.

As the sergeant began squeezing her left breast and sucking on the other, the man on top of her began thrusting his pelvis back and forth into hers, pushing her buttocks down harder into the mat as his groin grinded down roughly onto her wet mound of jet-black pubic hair. With each thrust, the tight muscles within her yielded more and more, opening her up to him even more than she thought possible, until he seemed to explode against her insides, sending hot semen along the walls of her dry, inexperienced vagina.

The soldier collapsed atop her, brushing the sergeant aside,

32

and she hoped it was coming to an end, but then two men were roughly pulling him out of her by his ankles and tossing him aside amidst a roar of laughing and insults she couldn't understand.

The reflex of sudden pain bent her legs at the knees, up in the air, and she felt the strange, burning liquid begin to drip from between her legs down into the crack between her buttocks. She started to roll over onto her side into the fetal position.

Within seconds, she was again spread-eagled on her back and another soldier was raping her, his meaty penis going in much more smoothly this time, forcing out pools of semen the first man had left behind. But her insides were becoming swollen with the pain, and she brought herself to scream finally, only nobody came. Her chest ached from this warrior biting at her nipples, and then he had his orgasm and another stranger was violating her.

Soon the pain numbed her body and she could no longer move beneath the men to cushion their pounding bodies, so the soldier groaning on top of her flipped over onto his back, pulling her hard against his muscular frame so that she rolled atop him and felt his erect penis stab repeatedly against the membranes beneath her stomach, pushing up higher and higher, deeper within her.

She felt like throwing up, her entire body was tingling as if a million pins were pricking her soft, smooth skin, and as she started to pass out on the chest of her assailant, she felt two soldiers grab her shoulder roughly, sit her up, then bounce her up and down savagely atop the man who now laughed uncontrollably beneath her.

She awoke on her back, alone in the room, the village outside quiet, brightly twinkling stars shining in through the open windows.

Her first instinct was to rush for the door to ensure that it

33

was bolted, but the pain brought her back down to her knees and she began crying. She rolled over onto her side and let it all out, wondering why this had happened to her—wishing she had a god to pray to, or curse at. She ran her fingers down her chest and hips, feeling the bruises, hoping to find no broken bones.

She dragged herself over to the door and locked it, instantly knowing it would not stop them should they decide to return. Then she sat back against the wall and sighed. She stared at the opposite wall for a long time, then started to wipe the sticky juices from her inner thighs with her fingers, shuddering violently when she raised her hand against the starlight and discovered that the liquid oozing slowly from between her legs was a milky film, streaked with blood.

She wanted to go out into the night, to walk down to the polluted canal and bathe the filth from her aching body, but animals lurked in the jungle at night and she was scared of the animals. The thought of calling the police never entered her mind: the soldiers, the police—they were all the same to her. She wondered if the old *mama-sans*, their teeth black with betel nut, ever endured such humiliation, and if it would happen again.

A group of fireflies appeared just outside the window, hovering as if to entertain her, and the smile from her youth reappeared briefly, as though she had forgotten what had just happened to her.

But in a sudden swirling rush, the glowing bugs flew off into the night, her smile faded, and the Viet Cong mortar barrage descended onto her quiet village.

The VC were "walking" the mortars up and down the main path of the hamlet, and when the first explosions tore down two walls of her hut, she barely had time to rise to her feet before another missile detonated right on her porch, disintegrating half the floor. The impact lifted her through the air, twisted her upside down, head over heels, and deposited her with a chilling splash into the middle of the canal.

34

As a legion of VC swarmed across her village right before her eyes, she slowly waded within the deep reeds along the bank and submerged herself up to her chin behind the vines and mosses. As her hut burned to the ground and VC soldiers dragged terrified, screaming girls off into the night, she began to wonder how long her life would go on like this—why was there no one to take care of her and what was a girl her age to do now?

The following evening she was wandering the streets of Saigon in a daze. Somehow she had managed to gather a sackful of what remained of her clothes. She was taken in by a crippled Chinese restaurant owner, who gave her a dingy backroom to sleep in and put her to work washing dishes.

It took several months for her to raise the courage to venture out into the city. She was amazed at all the sparkling lights and crowds of people, and at the smog that made her eyes water, and the clouds of blue smoke that hung everywhere, killing off the tamarind trees that lined the wide boulevards built by the French.

Once, when the old Chinese man who employed her ordered her to drag a large bin of trash out into the back alley, she came across two soldiers dragging a kicking, screaming girl off into the dark, as she had been dragged, and it snapped inside her again. The fear, the pain, the rage.

She threw an empty beer bottle at the men, but they ignored her and she walked back into the restaurant and slammed the door shut, strangely forgetting about the young girl who looked so much like herself.

She was not herself after that. When the greasy Chinaman finally handed over her pay, she left, roamed the fashion boutique on Nguyen Hue, and bought a pair of high heels, black netted stockings, a red satin miniskirt with a low-cut blouse, and a makeup kit.

As she applied the thick gooey lipstick in front of the mirror

35

in the boutique's restroom, she found herself giggling. Her old aunt had always called her "Little Golden Lotus," referring to the beautiful flowers that dotted the banks of the Perfume River. Luckily her stupid old aunt, who had been run down by a drunk taxi driver in Cholon, couldn't see her now. She giggled again, propping her breasts up from the bottoms with her hands so that they swelled forth along the rim of the dress. Should have bought that see-through halter top instead, she thought out loud with a wicked grin, failing to notice the evil gleam glazing her almond eyes.

The blue and yellow Renault taxi pulled up in front of the Purple Dragon Pleasure Palace, and several doormen rushed out to open the door for her. She made sure they saw plenty of leg when she stepped from the cab, and several American GIs strolling down the sidewalk whistled at her and licked their lips.

It was hard to mask her astonishment when she entered the Purple Dragon. Beyond the small scattering of tables, and above the band, running the entire length of the bar, was a fifty-foot-long glass menagerie. Inside, dozens of gorgeous Oriental women, all dressed in white, sat with their legs crossed upon rattan stools. Each had a different number on a large card, hanging from a string around their neck.

As she watched several drunk Americans stagger up to the bar, a waiter, walking with a pronounced swish, placed a small glass in her hand and whispered, "Now go find GI, buy you Saigon tea!" He evidently mistook her for one of the regulars.

He quickly disappeared into the mist of stage lights and cigarette smoke and she walked on across the vast room, frowning when the Americans pointed to two of the little "caged kittens," and the bartender bellowed out over a pager, "Numbers seven and fourteen!"

The women with cards seven and fourteen smiled and blinked their eyes as if they'd just won a beauty contest, then both climbed down from the cage and followed the GIs off into the back rooms.

As she inspected the dark recesses of the establishment, she came upon a room furnished with but a single, large rattan bed in the center. An American in his forties lay on the bed completely naked, his head excitedly twitching from side to side with his eyes tightly squeezed shut while a beautiful Vietnamese woman, naked from the waist up, kneeled beside him, bent over, sucking on his erect penis and slowly moving her lips and tongue along the entire length of the man's throbbing shaft.

Suspended from the ceiling, another gorgeous tart sat in a giant cylindrical straw basket with a foot-wide hole in the middle. This girl, completely naked and eating a banana as if she were bored, sat with her legs spread wide, her crotch right above the hole.

When the American began to groan out of control, the girl beside him slowly removed her mouth from his cock, signalled to the woman above her, then let her lips glide down the entire length of the penis, where she swallowed up his testicles and began moving them from side to side and up and down with her tongue.

At the same time, the girl in the basket, using a complicated assortment of ropes and pulleys, set the huge basket to twirling around in circles and into a slow descent.

By the time it was inches above the American, it was spinning so fast the woman inside was barely a blur of flesh. The girl licking his balls moved out of the way at the last second, and the basket dropped the last inch, plopping the moist, twirling spread-wide-open pussy down onto the man's bulging erection.

The American whimpered in ecstasy and delight as the basket and the woman in it revolved around his cock faster and faster. He grasped at the edges of the bed as the basket, and the pulsing vagina inside, rose up a bit to take in just the enlarged head of his penis, then suddenly dropped back down, engulfing, absorbing his throbbing tool which he now humped with all the strength left in him harder, farther up into the succulent thighs and crotch until he could take it no longer. He ejaculated like he had never come before, and as he fought to smother the yell that signalled his orgasm, the basket lady twirled around him for a few more seconds, then pulled the straw platform and herself suddenly away, rising to the ceiling like the skyrockets blazing in the American's head just then.

Little Miss Pham Thi Vien giggled when she noticed semen dripping down from the hole in the basket onto the man's rapidly-turning-limp dick, but the guy just lay there—his eyes still shut, a smile from one ear to the other. From behind, someone tapped her on the shoulder and she turned to find a Vietnamese soldier waving a roll of bills at her.

She winked at the man, grabbed his hand and the money, then started up the staircase to the balcony, where she tested every doorknob until she found an open, empty room.

The soldier immediately went for the bed, sat upon it, bounced up and down a couple times, then slipped off his clothes and slid under the cool, white covers. She still stood by the door, contemplating whether to grab his clothes and run, slamming the door behind her—or just what to do. The man grinned and motioned for her to join him under the covers and she thought later perhaps it was the grin that caused her to roll down her nylons and unzip the skirt, letting it fall to the floor revealing a slim, hungry body, eager for contact. She wore no panties underneath.

She slowly took off the blouse, climbed in on top of the man and allowed him to unhinge the see-through red satin bra with the gold hearts that covered her wide, upturned nipples. But as the man began sucking on her breasts and slid his hand gently down across her smooth, flat stomach, she began to shiver. When his fingers filtered through her coarse pubic hair, then expertly separated the thick lips of her vagina—allowing his two middle fingers to probe the outer depths of her hot, moist meat—she pulled away from him and started to get out of the bed.

He grumbled something unintelligible, caught her by the

end of her long, silky hair, and pulled her back down onto the bed. He climbed back on top of her, forced her legs apart with his knee and plunged his penis down into her so hard that it made her gasp. He quickly commenced pumping deeper and harder against her flesh, then came after only a couple minutes.

After he collapsed across her chest, she slowly reached down onto the floor, located her purse, then brought out a long, shiny ice pick.

"You damn slut!" he yelled at her in Vietnamese as she brought the pick down square into his back. But she was too weak, and the tip penetrated only an inch or so—enough to send a burst of adrenalin through the soldier and causing him to flip over in time to catch her wrist before she could bring down the weapon a second time.

The man sat up in the bed, grabbed her by the hair again and forced her face down onto his crotch. She held her lips tightly closed at first, but he eventually forced her mouth open and rammed the full length of his sticky cock all the way into her throat before she even knew what had happened.

As she struggled for air, the soldier grasped her head on both sides and forced it rapidly up and down, over and over, dragging her nose down into his pubic hair repeatedly, smashing her lips to the base of his penis, bouncing her chin off his sweaty balls.

When he came in her mouth, the juice—hot, thick and sour—exploded down the tunnel of her throat, and she fought to spit it out, feeling it rush back across and over her tongue, tasting the salty flood as it bubbled forth from the corners of her mouth, escaping from the tiny cracks that were not crammed tight with his throbbing, pulsing cock. She fought to raise her head again, but he slammed it down effortlessly until she could resist no more and swallowed what remained of the nauseating tide.

It was then that the strange force took hold of her insides again, and she was suddenly grabbing the man's balls gently, pushing them up from underneath, squeezing the last of his juices into her mouth. And as he released her head and laid back to enjoy this pleasant change of attitude, she just as suddenly chomped down with all the strength left within her, slicing her teeth deep into the man's swollen penis.

As the soldier began screaming and slamming his fists at her head in a shocked frenzy, she clamped down tighter, locking her jaws, swinging her head wildly from side to side as she tried to rip off his penis by the roots.

As she tried to block his blows with one arm, she reached down into her purse with the other and produced a meat cleaver. She had stolen it from the same cooking board where she had found the ice pick: in the old Chinaman's restaurant, just before she had quit.

Flares drifting across the outskirts of Saigon made the razor-sharp meat cleaver sparkle briefly before she brought it down savagely across the man's throat, silencing his screams, neatly severing his neck to the bone.

V. WILD IN THE STREET

Saigon police private Jon Toi kept one white-gloved hand waving the traffic through smoothly while he wiped the gritty sweat from his forehead with the other. Atop his wooden pedestal in the middle of Le Loi traffic circle, amidst several lanes of jam-packed commuter vehicles, Officer Toi remained calm and professional despite the daredevil cabbies who raced by all too close, ignoring his hand signals and engaging in a foolish game of see-whose-tail-gust-can-topple-the-traffic-cop. Someday he would jail one of those clowns, or maybe even slap them upside the head a couple times to straighten them out, but for now he was content escorting the rush hour commuters out of the heart of the city and into the suburbs.

Officer Toi frowned at those policemen who hid their traffic boxes behind the sidewalk vendors' stands, then manipulated the mechanical signal lights at the busiest intersections so that scores of cyclists ran red lights that mysteriously appeared right after the green. What had happened to the yellow lights? they wondered, astonished at this bit of "magic" as the corrupt "white mice" of the Vietnamese National Police pocketed their bribes in lieu of issuing a hefty ticket. Officer Toi couldn't understand why they didn't enjoy regulating the hordes of motor scooters and Renault taxis with expertly directed hand signals and coded blasts from their official police whistles.

41

Even though it was unusually hot across Saigon this day, Officer Toi didn't mind the stifling heat waves rolling across the boulevards. They were a part of the intensity that was his world. It didn't matter—sun today, rain tomorrow. It all paid the same. And he loved it on the street.

Officer Toi didn't miss much. Not the rare gust of wind catching the streetwalkers' skirts, not the known black marketeers smuggling tarped crates into their secret warehouses, not even the alley children swiping bananas from the sidewalk vendors. But Officer Toi especially did not miss the burly punk darting in and out of traffic on foot several blocks down the street, a briefcase in one hand and a .45 automatic pistol in the other. Officer Toi raised himself up on his toes atop the traffic pedestal, ignoring the honking throng of cars that immediately jammed up the intersection without his guidance. He squinted against the clouds of blue smog that clung to the heart of the city, and followed the progress of three Vietnamese MPs as they chased the thug with the weapon, unable to use their own slung submachine guns because of the masses of pedestrians sidestepping the hordes of noisy, puttering motor scooters.

The MPs, their shiny black helmets bearing the white "QC" letters, were losing ground on the suspect. Fear often did that to the hunted—granted them that extra surge of adrenalin needed to outrun the poorly paid, poorly motivated policemen across the globe. Officer Toi slowly stepped down from his box in the middle of busy Le Loi traffic circle, ignoring the protests of several irate motorists, dodging the squealing skid of a troop lorry that narrowly missed him. He took off his police cap, tucked it under his left arm and unstrapped the holster on his right hip, all the time moving closer, slowly closer to the gunman who unknowingly ran straight for the cop hidden in heavy traffic.

The man running from the QCs, a huge Chinaman with swollen biceps bulging beneath a yellow muscle shirt, was toppling vendor wagons and storefront stalls in an attempt to

42

slow up the men behind him as he vaulted the obstacles lining the narrow sidewalk. Perhaps that was why he was so surprised when Officer Toi stepped out in front of him from between two parked Saigon metropolitan buses.

Officer Toi extended a polished, spit-shined boot and tripped the goon to the ground. The thief's briefcase clattered across the gutter and slid out into the street, but he managed to hold onto his .45 despite skidding across the sidewalk on his nose and knuckles.

Officer Toi had his revolver out even before the suspect made eye contact with him, and he brought the sights down on the man's gigantic frame, all along listening to the QCs halfway down the block yelling something about the suspect having blasted an American businessman and robbed him of his briefcase—use caution, don't take any chances, waste him!

But Toi was mellow this morning. In his eleven years as a Saigon policeman he had dusted four criminals. He had smoked dozens while in the South Vietnamese Rangers, but the death lust of his youth was gone. No more satisfaction in saving the courts and the government money. Or the jails, for that matter. Too much paperwork.

That was why Toi hesitated shooting the man, though it would definitely have been a justified kill, clearly a righteous police shooting, the phrase all the younger members of the force had picked up after some new T.V. series had hit Saigon. It wasn't because Toi dreaded cleaning his service revolver afterwards. He broke it down, swabbed and oiled it religiously twice a week anyway. No matter to him some of his fellow officers had cobwebs in their barrels. They had cobwebs in their brains too. His revolver was to him what a saw was to a carpenter or a calculator to an accountant—it was his equalizer, an important tool in his profession. Invaluable.

The suspect looked up to face Toi and showed no shock at the sight of a policeman's uniform. Toi found himself concentrating on the blood now covering the man's nose, clotting in his mustache, streaking his large white teeth as he

43

breathed heavily through his mouth, and Toi laughed to himself at how much this badass looked like a clown from one of those traveling Burmese circuses, but Toi didn't miss the movement of the man's gun hand as the .45 quickly came up and leveled at Toi.

That's it, you crossed the line, chump, Toi thought to himself in English, and he began to squeeze down on the trigger, watching the whole scene pass before him in a kind of slow motion, his mind's eye critiquing everything about the subject: how he held the automatic, how its hammer was already cocked back, how it was almost up past Toi's beltline, how Toi's weapon was planted firmly between the man's eyes and how Toi would easily paste the first killing round whereas his opponent would only cripple Toi at most if he got off a shot. All these things flashed through his mind as his finger squeezed tighter on the trigger, and just as he was wondering when the goddamn hammer would fall, discharging the revolver, someone was hitting him in the back of the head with a heavy board.

Officer Toi went down face first, the board knocking him off balance, the impact from behind bringing instant waves of pain across his neck and skull, forcing darkening shades of black across his eyes. His weapon finally discharged as he fell limp across the ground, the round exploding on the sidewalk, shards of lead ricocheting back into his thighs and forearms. The suspect blasted away simultaneously, missing Toi by inches but catching the old *mama-san* behind him with two hollow-point rounds that took off her arm at the elbow and shattered her lower jaw.

The senile old woman, angered by this intrusion into her quiet, routine existence as a sidewalk vendor, hysterical at the rude toppling of her jewelry table, had taken her rage out on the closest man involved in the foot chase and began slamming an old plank twice her weight against the back of Toi's skull, ignoring the police uniform. The gunman spun around on the ground like a wild cartwheeling fireworks fountain, trying to

44

regain his footing, shooting into the sky as the QCs arrived.

One of them let go with a wild burst from his submachine gun, but the flat-nosed rounds bounced harmlessly off the side of a dump truck parked in a nearby alley, forcing several curious spectators to dive for cover under nearby vehicles.

Toi could see from his peripheral vision that the old *mamasan* was still conscious, behind him, sitting on the ground in a cloud of dust and gun smoke, her wrist dangling from mere shreds of meat, her face a mask of horror at her inability to scream: her lower jaw was all but gone, bits of mandible hanging from bloodied strands of gristle and shattered bone.

She stared back at Toi, the glare and mixed terror in her eyes sending a chill down his spine, spurring him to move, pulling him from the daze. He felt the left side of his face against the harsh ground, knew he had to whirl around and face the gunman if he were to survive, knowing he might summon the strength to turn his face only to have the suspect fire into his head, point blank. Visions of the Chinaman thrusting that ominous .45 into his face then pulling the trigger—the powder burning into his face as the flash seared his skin, opening the way for the hot lead to crash through the front of his face, burrowing with explosive force through the bone, expanding as it tore into meat then brain, penetrating into his mind of memories, knowledge, secrets. Painfully severing nerves, swelling the shell of his skull to its limits until the now-deformed projectile exploded out the back of his head, sending gobs of matted hair, chunks of brain matter and pieces of bone out into the freedom of the sky beyond, suddenly relieving him of all the pressure of his life as he sailed from his body, free of gravity, hurtling skyward through the fortresslike clouds that changed to cotton. . . .

But Toi turned to his left anyway. The gunman was gone. He was limping away, down a back alley. Toi rolled over, watched the man fading off into the distance, ejecting an empty magazine from his .45, dropping the full clip and fumbling for it on the ground then clumsily inserting it and slamming the

45

slide down on a fresh round. Toi leaned onto his left elbow, brought his revolver up and jerked off a round down the alley, striking a trash can several feet from the suspect with a dull thud. An old man delivering rolls of bread on a bicycle jumped from the ancient contraption and dashed into a doorway, ignoring the rolls as they splashed down into the stagnant gutter. The gunman turned to return Toi's fire, but refrained at the last moment and hobbled off down a second intersecting alley, nursing his sprained ankle.

Toi struggled to his feet and started after the gunman, briefly feeling the knot rising in the back of his head, almost running into the old man who had reappeared and was gathering up the soggy loaves of thin, buttered bread from the puddles of polluted rain water, diesel fuel and dog piss.

Toi was wondering where the hell those QCs had disappeared to, but his attention turned to the hunt as he rounded a corner and descended into a maze of alleys that fell away, down into the bowels of the city, deep within the inner kingdom of underworld characters: the pimps, the gangs, the scum of Saigon. Toi grinned—it seemed such characters could now be found on every street corner in the capital.

Toi entered the alley in a crouch, his gun arm extended, left hand cupped under the right fist, fanning the revolver slowly, left to right. The alley was vacant, silent. Toi didn't like it. There should be children scampering about, women beating rugs against balconies, mating dogs stuck together.

He instantly regretted entering the alley in such a careless manner. Presenting such an easy target. Ignoring all he had learned in the last twelve years.

In a few seconds he had surveyed everything before him. A shiver ran the length of his spine as a hot gust of wind swirled past his face from down in the alley's depths: this place breathed danger.

Two reports followed the fetid breeze and Toi hugged the blacktop just as the two bullets smacked into a support beam

46

beneath a balcony to his left, splitting the board nearly in half and sending little shavings of wood floating to the ground. Toi brought up his revolver and fired one round on single action up the alley, blowing up a vase for lack of any other visible target to shoot at—he could not see his assailant.

Toi got back to his feet and zigzagged twenty meters down the alley to the nearest doorway, firing only once to conserve his ammunition. Breathing heavily, he flattened himself up against the tin walls of the tenement that towered beside him, hoping that no one was on the roof waiting to drop garbage down on him. Toi checked the cylinders on his revolver, annoyed he had forgotten how many rounds he had fired, worked to control his heavy breathing, decided then and there against waiting for reinforcements that might never arrive, then darted around, back into the alley and charged forward.

At the same moment, the gunman leaned out from his hiding place and aimed down at Toi, but the policeman was firing again, hitting the wall beside the man and sending chunks of brick into his face, blinding him temporarily, forcing him to duck back for cover.

Toi raced the last thirty meters up to the suspect, fired his only remaining bullet into his chest as he crashed into the startled figure cowering in the doorway, then smashed the barrel of his revolver repeatedly down onto the man's face.

The gunman desperately popped off three rounds into the roof overhang above as Toi wrestled his weapon from him, kneeing him in the groin, pounding him to the ground with flailing fists, kicking viciously at the man's face after he crumpled against the blacktop, twisting his wrist harder and harder until the muscles tore loose and the .45 clattered to the blacktop, its slide locked back on an empty chamber.

Toi holstered his revolver then pulled out his handcuffs while the man was still dazed. He kicked him over onto his stomach, forced his arms back and snapped the bracelets on.

That's when the catcalls began. From the balconies, from

47

the rooftops, from behind barred and shuttered windows. People who knew nothing about Toi or his prisoner unleashed a torrent of insults, challenging the policeman to free his prisoner or perhaps be taken captive himself by this hostile block of renegades.

Toi could have stood his ground. He knew none of the hooligans screaming down at him would dare face him in the street, but he was too exhausted to take on an entire neighborhood. All he needed was a few minutes to get his breath back. Then he'd escort his prisoner back to friendly territory—if such an area existed in lower Saigon—and flag down the first passing police jeep, or phone for a squad if he could find a beat phone that hadn't been ripped from its moorings for sale on the black market.

That's when the first beer bottle flew down from the rooftops, splattering only ten yards away. Toi swallowed hard—he didn't need this crap. Five hostile faces suddenly appeared along the edge of the roofline across the alley, scowling down at him from behind broken bottle halves that had been inserted in the building's walls when it was constructed, supposedly to protect against cat burglars.

A shower of bottles and bricks began to rain down around Toi and his prisoner and as the Chinaman chuckled defiantly at the policeman's predicament, there came a sudden flurry of shots from down the block that sent the rooftop prowlers scattering as slugs ricocheted about the tops of the buildings. Toi could not control the smile of relief that creased his features at the sight of the squad of QCs rounding the corner.

The grin faded from the face of Toi's prisoner as several jeeploads of Vietnamese MPs pulled in behind the beat cops to supplement the cavalry. A brave or stupid bargirl, obviously awakened by all the commotion as she slept late into the day in preparation for another night of tricks, yelled down at the jeeps that had arrived with sirens blaring, but she quickly disappeared behind the barred shutters when several dismounting QCs turned back to look up at her balcony with

48

hostility in their eyes. You just did not fuck with the cops in Saigon.

The door to Toi's seventh floor apartment in the police family barracks on Tran Hung Dao Street flew open suddenly and Toi's seven-year-old son Nang raced from the unit and jumped up into his father's arms as Toi reached the top of the concrete stairwell. Nang clutched a plastic baggie filled with iced coffee, sealed at the neck with a rubber-band wrapped around two straws, and he brought this to his father's parched lips just as Toi's wife, Lan, appeared in the doorway with their daughter of ten months, Diep, cuddled tightly in her arms.

"How many cowboys you shoot-'em-up today, Papa?" Nang giggled with boyish enthusiasm as he took Toi's drooping police hat off his head and placed it on his own.

"Nang!" his mother scolded good-naturedly, but there was a troubled look in her eyes as she carefully surveyed her husband's face as he gently lowered the boy to the floor and unlatched his gunbelt.

Toi smiled at his wife as she shook her head in mild irritation at Nang's behavior, but then the child had disappeared back into the apartment and Toi had to face his wife. She stood there patiently, her brow creased with worry and genuine concern. "You know?" he asked casually, wondering if the incident with the Chinaman had made the radio news which Lan listened to religiously whenever her husband was away at work.

She merely nodded her head again slowly, this time in the affirmative, and Toi draped his arm protectively around her shoulder then led her and his new daughter back into the modest apartment.

They had been together now eight years, yet Lan never once complained about Toi's intense honesty. While most of the other policemen they knew lived in plush homes outside the inner city, paid for with the bribe money brought in hourly at

49

traffic stops and storefront shakedowns, Toi insisted on surviving on the government salary paid him by the National Police Force and the now-and-then payments the foreign newsmen gave him for snapshots he took at the scenes of bombings and terrorist acts with the little pocket camera one of the American MPs had given him. Lan had never complained that Toi's meager income forced them to live in the barracks set aside for police families only. Lan didn't like the tall fences of concertina wire that ringed her family's home, but she refused to complain. After all, rent was free and those Vietnamese who hated the Canh-Sats could not harm her or her children here—all her neighbors were also police families. And anyway, life in Saigon was much safer than in Mytho, her hometown. The Delta was becoming more dangerous as the years went by.

Toi kissed his little daughter on the forehead after Lan placed her in the tiny hammock swinging mere inches above their bed, then he walked back into the connecting room where he kept the family's possessions. A small table, with two metal chairs, was the only furniture in the room. It was cleared off except for some old newspapers, neatly stacked to the side, and Toi unfolded one of these while his wife opened a can of Saigon "33" beer. Toi thanked her as he always did, then drew his service revolver, emptied the cartridges from the cylinder onto the table, then reached under his chair for the old shoebox that held gun oil, patches and cleaning rods.

The sound of the bullets bouncing atop the table immediately caught young Nang's attention, as it always did, and he rushed into the little backroom and sat across from his father patiently, waiting for Toi to hand him the hardwood grips from the .357 Colt Python. Toi slowly unscrewed the grips in robot-like fashion without paying attention to what he was doing. His eyes scanned the countless photographs that adorned the walls of the room as he finally handed Nang the gun handles and the young boy smeared them with oil, then briskly set about rubbing the fluid into the rich rosewood until the friction

50

caused his hands to heat up and the room filled with the rich smell of the liquid merging with the odor of gun smoke and cordite that still lingered on Toi's uniform.

"You used some, Papa!" Nang gasped in rapid Vietnamese, pointing to some of the empty bullet holders on the officer's gunbelt, but Toi didn't hear his son's exclamation. His mind was far away as his eyes scanned the photo enlargements that covered the walls like scenes from his past: overturned sedans with arms and legs dangling from shattered windows, bombed-out restaurants with charred corpses staring back at the photographer, Buddhist monks setting themselves afire after pouring cans of gasoline over their orange robes, suicide victims hanging in abandoned pagodas downtown.

Lan avoided the room except to straighten out the table now and then. She was deeply superstitious and felt pictures of dead people only invited ghosts and goblins to their dwelling, but she endured Toi's macabre hobby because it kept him at home and not out cultivating a harem of young mistresses like some of the other policemen living in their housing project.

Toi set about cleaning his revolver with a sudden urgency as a police siren in the distance began to grow closer. He swabbed the barrel of the Python fourteen times with solvent then followed the same procedure with the six cylinders quickly, out of habit.

Toi normally repeated this method of removing the particles of spent powder and lead from his weapon three to four times before drying it out with a rag and applying a protective coat of oil, but now, as his mystified son watched silently, he slipped six fresh rounds back into the revolver while it was still wet, hastily slapped his gunbelt back on, and rammed the pistol back into its holster.

Several other sirens had joined the first and they were closing in on his neighborhood. He was sure, for some reason felt it in his bones, that they were headed for the Purple Dragon bar two blocks over, and that they would need help.

As he raced out the door and headed for the stairwell he

expected Lan to complain about "getting involved when he was off duty," but she didn't say a word—only frowned at his departure and dumped the bowls of rice back into the cooker, the lines of worry creasing her young forehead once more.

Toi made it down the seven flights of stairs and had sprinted across the street through the heavy traffic even before the green and white police jeeps skidded onto his block. He hopped a cement fence without tangling his uniform in the single strand of barbed wire running the length of it, and landed within sight of the Purple Dragon. Three excited waitresses stood jabbering at high speed at the main doors of the establishment, pointing at a slender woman with long, jet-black hair who had run from the swinging doors of the bar out into the street, flagged down a taxi, and was now disappearing down the block.

Toi drew his revolver and ran with all his might toward the approaching cab, but the driver only stomped down on the gas pedal and swerved around him—Toi had neglected to put his police shirt back on, and the cabbie wasn't about to stop for a man in khaki pants and a soiled T-shirt, wearing a holster and waving a magnum revolver at him.

As the taxi breezed by, kicking up dirt and gravel as its tires screeched around the corner, Toi observed the woman in the back seat to be unusually beautiful, wearing a red satin mini-skirt and matching blouse. A very low cut, form-hugging blouse, Toi noticed, but it was the woman's eyes that really caught his attention. They stared back at him confidentially, almost mockingly, as the cab raced by. The look in the woman's eyes sent a shiver down Toi's spine and he was almost relieved she had eluded him.

Toi could not force the image of the woman's face from his mind as he ran back to the main entrance of the Purple Dragon. At the time he did not know the memory of woman's piercing eyes staring at him above the wicked, sardonic grinning snarl would haunt his dreams for several weeks to come.

"What happened?" Toi demanded of the girls crowding the

52

front doors of the bar, but they could only point into the establishment, speechless. A young shoeshine boy appeared suddenly in front of Toi and, not intimidated by the officer's gunbelt or appearance, grabbed his free hand and dragged him into the smoky bowels of the gambler's den.

Toi, once his eyes grew accustomed to the gloom clouding the bar, saw that more employees—waitresses and a bouncer—crowded outside the doorway to one of the rooms up in the exposed upper level of the building, and Toi broke free from the excited youth and leaped several steps at a time up to the dimly lit corridor.

"Cahn-Sat!" Officer Toi identified himself confidently as he strode past the group smoothly and entered the dark room. He reached for the light switch but the bulb in the ceiling had been smashed out. Flashing rays of electric neon outside the window filtered in to reveal a scene that brought Toi to an immediate halt and melted his aplomb: the officer didn't hear the bouncer explaining that the maid had entered the room to change the sheets when the closet door slowly creaked open to reveal its contents. A Vietnamese soldier, his arms outstretched like a giant bird, was nailed by the hands to the inside of the closet door. Sitting in a neatly carved-out hole where the man's stomach had once been, was his severed head. And dangling from the mouth that was contorted grotesquely in horror hung his testicles, the jagged and torn stump of scrotum stuffed in backwards.

VI. THE HUNT BEGINS

The door to his apartment was slightly ajar when he finally returned to Saigon. There had been no signs of police activity in the area, but he drew his .45 regardless, cautiously nudged the door open with his right boot, and entered slowly.

One of the old *mama-sans* he had so often passed in the courtyard below sat on her haunches in the corner of the living room, scrubbing the dry, caked blood from the teakwood floor with a sponge. She looked up briefly as he entered, ignored the huge pistol pointed at the ceiling, nodded slightly as she recognized him, then continued scrubbing at the thick layers of blood. He holstered his weapon beneath the jean jacket and surveyed the room quickly, without moving another step. He sighed . . . the closet still held his clothes, the desk those possessions he didn't keep at camp. His extra pair of jungle boots were still lined up beneath the bed—someone had changed the satin sheets from crimson red to midnight blue. That made him smile, though the pain he felt inside killed the smile immediately—they had left her belongings alone also, acknowledging he had paid the twenty-dollar rent through to the end of the month.

He forced another smile, this time for the old woman down at his feet, but she only nodded her ancient, drugged head back, repeating the Vietnamese words for "sorry" several times as she cleaned the lifeblood of his woman off the bamboo drapes. He had hoped they'd be done by this time—he was gone over a week in Mytho—but he remembered the Vietnamese to be lazy about such matters, even death and the mess it left behind, and he was just glad they had not permitted the small apartment to be looted by the street scavengers.

A jeep passed by below on Thanh Mau Street, and he brushed the drapes aside hoping it wasn't an MP patrol—surely he'd be on their AWOL roster by now. But the vehicle was only an old surplus crate, now used by the manager's errand boy. He watched a blue and yellow taxi cruise past below slowly, the driver's skinny left arm hanging out the window, playing with the cool morning breeze. A second cabbie followed, his head poked out the window, inspecting the top floors of the complex for late-rising GIs needing a lift back to camp. His dark face sported thick black sunglasses that made him look like the pimps down on Tu Do Street—the sight of this taxi driver reminded him of all the tours she had taken him on from the rear seats of the Renaults, showing him Saigon, her Saigon. He let the drapes fall back against the shuttered window and he walked over to the wall switch that activated the ceiling fan.

The old woman started to scold him softly when he failed to leave his boots outside, but he ignored her and walked over to the desk and began going through the mementos: the tabletop pictures of them in front of the Rex cinema fountains, the delicate glass dragon ships from Thailand, the photo albums and faded visa applications.

He unlocked the desk and brought out her jewelry: seven of the ornately carved gold bracelets all the Saigon women owned (she would switch one from each wrist to the other on a daily basis—much better for good luck throughout the week), a pair of jade earrings, some pearls he was not sure were real. He placed the jewelry and some of the photos in a shirt pocket and snapped it shut, then froze.

Something was missing.

He glanced to his right—the tiger and elephant tapestries were back up on the wall, even straightened.

An unexpected voice at the door first startled, then angered him. "Hey, Jeff! Where you been?" It was one of the girls from the second floor, Kim. Always nosy, stirring up the gossip. Always overly friendly with the Americans. He slammed the door shut in her face.

"So fuck you, MP!" she yelled back, somewhat embarrassed, yet intent on ensuring the rest of the apartment house heard the commotion. But Jeff ignored her antics, and soon the building, isolated from other dwellings on Thanh Mau because it sat at the end of the alley, returned to its normal quiet routine.

Jeff resumed searching the small buffet. He noticed the bottle of whiskey neither of them ever touched was still on the fridge. He would have grinned, amused that the old *mama-san* cleaning the apartment hadn't nipped a swig, but the old feelings of humor and resignation at the way of life in Saigon had left him. His woman was dead, murdered. He was sure he could have dealt with it if death had claimed someone other than her. It was not true you grew to love and understand your police partner more than your mate. At least not in Saigon, where he relished the nights in her arms, unsure if a lone, random VC rocket might claim them before dawn. Uncaring, so long as he was with her when death struck.

Saigon. Where your police partners often changed so rapidly, because of the snipers and suicides, you rarely really got to know them well. Where you were afraid to make friendships for fear sudden death would claim your new friends.

He frowned upon checking the far wall—they had cleaned off the words on the mirror. But he remembered them clearly, and surely his friend, Toi the Canh-Sat, would have photographs of the entire place if he needed them later. Recalling the words smeared across the mirror brought back memories like an unavoidable, drowning flood.

57

His mind began flashing back again and he saw scenes from that arrest he had participated in when he first arrived in Vietnam and was assigned to Saigon's 716th Military Police Battalion, Bravo Company. The faces of the six black soldiers they had caught after staking out a complicated black market operation would not leave his mind's eye—how they kept laughing, mocking, spitting at him even as the handcuffs were clamped on. But he shook his head violently, blocking them out—he did not want such visions soiling other, more cherished memories returning to him while he was in this room where she had lived, had breathed, had bathed. Had loved him, cared for him, lived for him, unselfishly.

He wrestled briefly with the stuck cap on the whiskey bottle, then poured some of the harsh liquor down his parched throat and handed the bottle down to the *mama-san* who had been watching his every move.

The aquarium with the strange, purple fish was gone, of course, destroyed during the struggle. But something else was missing. It wasn't the hot plate, or the wok, or the rice cooker. Even the stereo was in place, though splashed with crimson stains. No, the necessities and the furniture were present. Accounted for. "Not AWOL," he thought aloud, wanting to laugh as he said it. "Not AWOL, like me." But the comparison failed to rate even a forced chuckle, and he dismissed any further thoughts of surrendering before the thirty-day deadline arrived and *They* branded him a deserter.

It had to be something small that was missing. Sparkling. A novelty. A decoration . . . or a gift. Something the fish had always concentrated on in the night, silhouetted in their tank of colored water, illuminated by a shaded bulb inside the murky frogman's castle.

Sparkling! That was it, he decided, a macabre excitement growing within him. He turned back to where the aquarium had been and realized the little statue was gone. The temple dancer, with her spired crown and long fingernails, dressed in ceremonial robes, yet barefoot.

58

She had presented it to him on his birthday. Only seven inches tall, made of dark green Siamese jade—the statue of the delicate Thai dancer she had given him after they left the Rex cinema, on their way to the Caravelle for a candlelight dinner. At first he had been surprised, even mildly disappointed. What type of gift was this for a "Saigon Commando"? He had expected a silk shirt with Oriental designs or Chinese script on it, or a Seiko wristwatch with one of those thick leather bands that prevented the motorcycle cowboys from snatching it off your wrist, or even a pair of those Air Force sunglasses that cluttered the black market these days. But she had fooled him again and done something unpredictable. And except for the first wallet photo he had kept after her about, that statue was the only thing she had ever given him. Except unselfishly of herself.

He often ignored the daily rules of military life, shrugged off the disciplines designed to save his life in a tough street situation. But loyalties were important to him. As were mementos—the subtle souvenirs of this, his first great adventure in life: intense, electric Saigon, and graceful, beautiful Mai. This mysterious woman of Asia, the first to call him a man.

The whiskey was slowly taking effect. He lay down briefly on the small bed they had shared for only a hundred nights and must have passed out from the sea of memories swirling like a storm within his head, because he awoke abruptly, drenched in sweat, his shirt off.

The old *mama-san* had summoned one of the housegirls from the courtyard below, where the youngster had been hanging clothes to dry, and she was now walking back and forth on his back, kneading his sore shoulders with talon-like, skilled toes. The massage and the liquor made the stress fade slowly, and he began to muse back to that first arrest, months ago. . . .

They had watched the warehouse for three weeks, on a shaky tip, before the suspects were finally detected. They had been entering from a back alley, dressed in beggar's garb, pulling a little wagon along—quite a daring tactic and a credit to their efforts at disguise, considering all of the suspects were black Americans.

Word had reached them the MPs were probably onto their activities—bringing medical supplies and commissary goods to this warehouse, where they were sold to a middleman and eventually delivered to the Viet Cong or countryside bandits—and instead of abandoning the operation, their greed dictated they try to move the entire inventory to another location. "Stupid," he thought aloud again.

"Huh, Joe? You say what? You no like the way—" the housegirl began jabbing a toe into his ribs. Surprised she spoke English, Jeff motioned toward a sore spot in the middle of his lower back, and the housegirl concentrated on that area, humming in her pleasant singsong voice as she rhythmically kneaded the tense muscles. Her singing voice was so smooth, high and feminine, he thought to himself this time. Such a contrast to the deep, hoarse bargirl drawl she had used when talking English at him. No doubt trying to imitate all the ladies of questionable virtue that rented apartments in the building.

Memories of his high school friends taking him for his first raft expedition down a wild, foaming river in the wilds of Australia intruded upon his thoughts suddenly, and as he noticed that the teenager dancing gently on his back could never match the skill his woman had displayed with her almost magical fingers, he fought to concentrate on the arrests again.

The whole team was apprehended one cloudless day at noon—but not until additional MPs had to be called in to subdue the suspects. He remembered it clearly now. Two MPs approached each suspect and instructed them to spread-eagle on the street. None complied. Sticks instead of guns were drawn and the fight was on.

The suspects, six enlisted men, all went to the hospital for stitches before transfer to LBJ—Long Binh Jail. While at the Third Field Army Hospital in Saigon one of the prisoners—a twenty year old from Oakland wearing the red, green and black patch of the Black Liberation Army—had repeatedly threatened to "pay back" the MPs for going out of their way to jail him. "Gonna blow up your house, rape your old lady!" he had declared. "Payback is a bitch, pig!" he yelled, while the startled physician closed the stitches across his scalp. But the MPs heard those threats every other day. And they usually went unfounded. He still religiously kept a small note book on everyone he arrested—especially all blacks with the BLA patches, and all radicals threatening death to the cops. The BLA had already assassinated a number of policemen stateside, and though all who wore BLA patches or armbands were probably not hardcore members but just sympathizers, it didn't pay to take too many chances.

The stockade guards escorting the prisoners to LBJ where they would await formal court-martials had been mysteriously ambushed by suspected Viet Cong guerrillas, but Army C.I.D. was investigating the possibility a black market kingpin had liberated his friends since only the guards were killed in the attack—both shot at point-blank range in the back of the head with a small-caliber weapon, behind the ear. Ballistics tests inconclusive.

Somehow he would have to get into the MP barracks to retrieve his notebook from his locker. He remembered one of the suspects—the one with the big mouth and all the threats— was named Lance Jackson, wore a First Signal Brigade patch on his left shoulder, and had a jagged scar running across his nose from an earlier scuffle with MPs at Fort Sam Houston, Texas.

The others were a blur, a faded memory in a long history of routine arrests. He'd have to check that notebook for details on them, if the notebook and the rest of his gear were still in his locker, unconfiscated.

Beads of perspiration began rolling down his forehead as the face of Lance Jackson reappeared before him, crystal clear, invoking a latent rage that made his fists shake noticeably, frightening the housegirl that still walked lightly back and

61

forth in circles on his back. Lance Jackson, busted back to buck private—he'd never forget that face. Flaring nostrils, like some berserk Zulu tribesman, head shaved bald, one of his teeth in front silver with a black onyx clenched fist engraved into it.

They had gone underground since their escape. Rumors circulated that the fugitives had resumed wearing GI uniforms—less chance the MPs would take interest in them when they were out on the street. Since martial law went into effect, civilian clothing for soldiers was prohibited in most cases.

He came to suddenly, shaking the effects of the liquor from his system, startling the girl off balance as he realized he had to act fast, before the trail got colder. The housegirl tried at first to keep her footing on his back, but gave up and leaped onto the bed and bounced to the ground, landing catlike on the hard-wood floor.

He went back over to the desk, took a copy of the magazine *Tour 365* from the bottom drawer and leafed through it till he found the colorful pages depicting all the military unit patches worn in Vietnam. He had always valued the magazine—they were almost collector's items now, in league with the malaria, booby trap and VD warning brochures, but he now roughly tore out the example picture of the First Signal Brigade patch and showed it to both women in the room, asking them in his pidgin Vietnamese if either recognized it, had seen any black soldiers wearing it.

But they just stared back at him, bewildered, and he brushed by them, down into the courtyard where he interrupted the old *mama-sans* chewing betel nut and gossiping as they listened to Oriental talk shows on their American transistor radios.

The old women missed little passing by them in their limited, confined world, but none of them had eyesight keen enough to distinguish between the countless shoulder patches that entered and left the apartment compound, or so they claimed. This statement about the abundance of GIs surprised him; he had thought he picked an apartment far enough from

62

the red light district that he wouldn't have to bother with Americans or worry about who knew he wore an MP armband. It didn't really matter though, since more and more he had taken to wearing civilian clothes himself—just another privilege he took advantage of as the Canh-Sat and MP patrols in this sector of Saigon, Nguyen Van Thoi, came to recognize him on sight.

The thought struck him to canvass the sidewalk vendors in the vicinity of the warehouse where the original arrests had been made so many months ago, but as he was leaving the courtyard to abandon the *mama-sans* to their radios (tuned permanently to one friendly government band and distributed by propaganda teams free of charge), one of them mentioned to another that patches meant nothing to her, but teeth certainly did—now they were another thing altogether. And damned if she didn't want a design put in her silver front tooth like that one "dum dum GI" had. Dum dum was Vietnamese slang for the color black, and he whirled around upon hearing this and commenced to question her at length. But she could add little more than to verify his suspicions: the man with the shaved head and the BLA tri-color had been through this compound the morning of the homicide.

The morning of the homicide . . . There he went thinking in police terms again. He would have to get out of that habit. He didn't have the resources of the 716th Military Police Battalion to assist him in this case, or the Vietnamese National Police either. He was alone on this one. And it wasn't business as usual. This was not a case to be filed away after the leads were exhausted in six months. He would close this case. He owed her that much.

As he exited the courtyard through a creaking metal gate, rusted and heavy with crossbars of reinforced steel, he came upon Kim squatting in the shadows, her slender fingers rapidly slicing stalks of sugar cane skillfully into little cubes to be sold at the market. Her dark, almond eyes looked up at him sadly, an expression of extreme hurt across her tear-streaked face. He stopped and squatted before her, trying to keep his heels flat on the ground like she did so he wouldn't start swaying back and forth if they cramped up.

"I'm sorry, Kim." He forced a smile, realizing he needed all the friends now that he could get. A woman scorned could just as well turn him in to the MPs. "I lost my temper. I was wrong."

"One, two, three . . . motherfuck MP," she snarled at him under her breath, never taking her eyes off his.

"Really, Kim. I was wrong. I'm sorry." He held out his hand to her, but she just continued slicing the sugar cane. Finally her eyes drifted from his and scanned the quiet alley that ran the length of the compound's jagged walls and beyond.

"So you want to fuck, GI?" she asked coldly, still avoiding his eyes.

"Kim, I only want to be your friend. To say I'm sorry," he whispered, looking behind him nervously to see if anyone could overhear.

"Your woman, Mai. She dead now only one week and already you want quickie. That what you think I am? A short-time girl?" She raised her voice at him, then lifted her haunches a few inches higher so she could look over his shoulder to the old *mama-san* sitting across the courtyard against the opposite wall, chewing her betel nut in a drugged daze. "He thinks I'm a goddamn short-time girl!" Kim yelled over for the benefit of the *mama-san*, and the old woman nodded back slowly, as if bored, and he knew then that she spoke no English.

"Okay, Kim. Forget it. I'm sorry I bothered."

"Screw you, Mister Jeff," she said coldly, with disgust in her voice.

"Yeah, okay," he mumbled, tired of the quarrel, mildly surprised at the same time as he noticed that her swollen breasts, partially visible through the sheer, filmy *ao-dai*, failed to arouse him. The soft brown whirls of her nipples were taut against the silky blue gown, which was now slightly wet from

64

the steam rising from the cooking plate. Jeff let his eyes fall to the smooth, firm thighs, spread slightly before him but protected by black satin pantaloons and he abruptly got back to his feet and started down the street.

Several taxis began racing toward him from down the block, only to give up just as quickly to the leading sedan, and as Jeff routinely flagged it to the curb he felt a tug at his elbow. He turned swiftly, expecting to fight or flee a policeman, but found only Kim staring up at him, her moist eyes now innocent as a schoolgirl's.

Her hand was outstretched. "Friends?" She smiled, her shoulders swaying a bit from embarrassment.

He grasped her hand gently, ignoring an icy feeling that engulfed him as memories of a little shoeshine boy, also reaching to shake hands but with a razor blade taped between his fingers, raced back at him from his past. Left handed, he had drawn his .45 and shot the fleeing youth in the back, separating his shoulder blades down the middle and plopping most of his intestines out across the filthy sidewalk. Jeff returned Kim's smile, but they were not grinning about the same things.

He had been standing in the rain almost two hours now, watching the skinny Puerto Rican kid across the street outside the Mississippi Soul Bar. But the rain didn't bother him. He savored the downpour, telling himself the thick sheets of warm water trying to pound him into the gutter beside that concrete light pole actually helped to cleanse him of the filth of the city.

This thought immediately puzzled him for he knew he loved Saigon. He smiled sadly: he had to love this city, since it was all the home he had now. Now that he was AWOL over a month and classified a deserter.

He thought of Mai. The rain making its harsh tapping noise as it pounded the sheet metal roofs of the tenement behind him reminded him of her, of how she loved the storms that swept over the city each night, the thunder slapping harmlessly at the windows as they lay snugly in each other's arms beneath the wispy layers of tinseled mosquito net.

He found Saigon colder now, as the loneliness set in, but it was still the most magnetic city he had ever traveled to. Even with all its sinister sidestreets and the maze of endless back alleys, the city breathed an impatient rush of life at him he had experienced nowhere else: the air and sky mingling, moving about heavily, almost aggressively, oppressively, as the mountainous black clouds gathered on the horizon ahead of the monsoons and their thunderclaps rolled in over the city. The heaviness of the night moving in on him until he could breathe the excitement, feel the danger amidst the bustling crowds overflowing from the sidewalks into the streets as they rushed about before the curfew was clamped down on the city. The merging of minds before the words when he spoke with Mai in the night, lying awake after making love, their bodies glistening with a thin layer of sweat despite the slowly twirling fan above them in the ceiling. Listening to the bombs rumble in the distance and trying to distinguish them from the thunder. Watching the flares drift past the drawn curtains outside, suddenly wanting to make love to her again, urgently, always fearing that solitary rocket falling randomly somewhere across the city. But this time forcing her to look into his eyes as she came—to see the love, to see all his emotions fill her soul, her mind, to exchange the love and the loneliness and not just the physical feeling. And never forgetting about the rocket. . . .

The Puerto Rican kid stood in the rain also, but he paced back and forth impatiently and kept unfolding dry pages of the Saigon Post over his head until they fell apart, soggy and shredded, to the ground. Several times he watched in anticipation as the doors to the Mississippi swung open and the loud soul music flowed out, followed by small groups of blacks, their arms tangled in endless rituals of greeting or farewell.

He watched the Puerto Rican grow irritated when the contact he awaited failed to show up, and Jeff spat against the warm drizzle as he recalled cold cocking a black rookie MP he was once breaking in who had started to "dap" a black suspect they had just arrested for burglary. The spittle was forced back by the rustling breeze and narrowly missed his leg as it splashed soundlessly into the rushing torrent overflowing from the gutter.

Finally, a taxi pulled to the curb halfway down the block and a black soldier with a crew cut and wire-rim glasses got out and started walking with an exaggerated skip toward the Puerto Rican. Jeff didn't recognize the black to be one of the group his squad had arrested earlier at the warehouse operation, but he was wearing a tri-colored BLA wristband and—yes—he had a First Signal Brigade patch on his left shoulder.

He watched the Puerto Rican look around cautiously, then hand the other man a roll of greenbacks, who inspected it briefly, then pulled from a thigh pocket of his fatigues a small package wrapped in old newspapers. Without so much as a word, the Puerto Rican turned and walked off down the street away from the Mississippi, and the man who had just sold him illegal narcotics started off casually down the alley that circled back behind the club.

He watched the black disappear in the gloom of mist, then Jeff crossed the street and headed for a collision course with the Puerto Rican, who was busy untying the wrapper enveloping the heroin. As they passed each other, Jeff kneed the doper in the groin and with a quick succession of blows, pummeled him down into the gutter.

The Puerto Rican started to protest as the ex-MP snatched up the man's parcel, and he managed to reach up and resist slightly despite his surprise and the intense pain wracking his body, but Jeff rammed a shard of broken brick into his mouth till it lodged in his throat, then kicked the protruding edge in another inch and started off down the alley.

Luck had been with him so far, but he knew chances were the black dealer had disappeared into the back door of the Mississippi. He was surprised and suddenly charged mentally to see his man still sauntering off into the dark, down the alley, adding even more jive to his gait as he inspected the money roll more closely.

The next thing the black deserter knew, two steel-soled jungle boots had connected with his spine from behind, knocking the wind out of him and tumbling him face first into a mud puddle. He cursed himself mentally at his carelessness but felt a sudden intense bolt of fear replace that irritation as a choke hold brought him out of the water and a long, narrow commando knife was placed across his throat roughly.

"Hey, brother! Be cool!" he stammered, feeling the razor-sharp blade slicing slightly into his skin, allowing thin rivulets of blood to slide down over his Adam's apple as he wondered which shipment of dope he sold must have turned up bad. At his feet, his money roll lay untouched, ignored by the man on his back.

"I'm arresting you, asshole!" came the smothered reply from behind him. "But first I want to know where your pad is—where your buddies are staying."

"Sure, sure brother! Whatever you say! Just don't cut me, man. Please, just don't cut me!"

Jeff replaced the dagger in his calf sheath, then pulled the slender black man off balance, up onto the balls of his feet, with his left hand while he frisked him with his right.

He started at the top, the way they had drilled it over and over into him back at the MP Academy in Georgia, tossing the man's cap and long, steel, spiked comb onto the ground. He quickly ran his finger tips through the deserter's bushy hair, then, finding no hidden weapons, checked beneath his collar, in the armpits, under the belt, in the small of the back, against the crotch, inside the boots.

"I ain't carryin' no heat, brother!"

"I'm not your brother!" Jeff growled, keeping his voice threatening but low as he applied pressure on the choke hold. Denied oxygen for mere seconds, the black man grew faint and his knees started to buckle, but Jeff held him up and dug into a

68

rear pocket for a wallet. With his free hand, he unbuttoned the photo section of the wallet and glanced through it quickly, ignoring a flattened roach that fell to the ground, stopping briefly to inspect the only picture inside: a pose showing three men, arm in arm, in front of stateside scenery. "Where's your ID?"

"Don't have none. Just the driver's license—California. Don't do me much good here in this lousy cesspool."

Jeff couldn't locate the hidden license with only one hand, so he reached for the man's dog tags dangling across his chest instead. Narrowing his eyes to catch beams of moonlight, he read the blood type, religion, service number and name: "STUBBS, CLARENCE."

"Private Clarence Stubbs," Jeff repeated under his breath several times, allowing the name to sink in, hoping it would match those scattered throughout his mind's memory files, mixed up as they were. "Private Clarence Stubbs . . ."

"Do I know you, bro?" the other man asked, grasping at hope that didn't exist, and when he struggled to bring his eyes back to look at Jeff's face, Jeff tightened the hold again until he blacked out, then flipped him roughly down onto the ground.

Within seconds Stubbs regained consciousness, and as he shook his head from side to side and raised himself up on one elbow, Jeff asked him, "Where is your friend, Mr. Jackson?"

"My friend? My who?" He looked up at Jeff, astonishment in his eyes. It was good acting, but Jeff didn't hesitate to kick the drug pusher square in the mouth, knocking him down onto his back with such force that he was stunned again momentarily.

"Jackson," the ex-MP repeated, more slowly. "Lance. Private E-1. U.S. Army, deserter. I want to know where he is staying." Jeff unbuttoned his windbreaker and drew his holstered .45, snapped off the safety with his thumb, then pointed the pistol at the man's face.

But to Jeff's surprise, the man just grinned back at him, looking up with bright, gleaming eyes as he balanced himself on both elbows casually. "Eat shit, white boy," he said, flashing immaculate white teeth.

"What?" Jeff asked incredulously, betraying some of his shock.

"Go fuck yourself, honky! You're gonna have to shoot me—" But Jeff had already brought the automatic down to point at the man's left knee, and he cooly popped off a round that shattered the man's kneecap and nearly severed his leg.

As the man started screaming, Jeff felt the adrenalin replace the uneasiness he had felt, and he went down on one knee and grabbed the violently thrashing gunshot victim—the top half of his body achieving all sorts of contortions and twists, while below the belt his legs remained frozen because of the intense pain. Jeff rammed his pistol into the man's shrieking mouth, cutting the sound down to a tortured whimper as the cold steel forced teeth to break inward. "I said, where does Jackson stay?" Jeff repeated loudly, jerking the gun back out before Stubbs could even begin to answer, rapidly placing it against the man's other knee and jerking the trigger, this time twice.

The shock of the bullets disintegrating Stubbs' kneecap all but flipped him upside down this time, and as Jeff struggled to stuff his pistol back into the man's bloodied mouth he demanded again, "Where does Jackson stay?"

Stubbs' eyes almost popped out of their sockets as Jeff this time jerked the .45 back out and placed it against the man's groin.

"42 Tung Chou! My God, man! He lives at 42 Tung Chou!" he cried, lapsing into hysterical laughter as Jeff holstered his weapon without firing it again. "Man, you done blew my legs away! You done blew my legs away!" the man babbled incoherently, lapsing back into drowning sobs then insane laughter again. But suddenly he fell silent, as if a rush of heroin had raced through his veins, deadening the pain, and he just stared up at Jeff, eyes wide, lower jaw agape for several seconds. Then he just said, "Why?" drawing out the word as if there could not possibly be an answer.

70

Jeff started to respond, then decided against enlightening the dirtbag. Instead, he pulled the bag of heroin from his pocket and jammed it halfway into the man's mouth. Then, with all his might, Jeff slammed his fist at the man's face, bursting the plastic on the other end and forcing choking amounts of the fine, white powder down Stubbs' throat.

Unsure what the results would be, Jeff was upset when the black man simply rolled back onto his side and started to fall off into unconsciousness instead of screaming wildly in pain.

"Shit, this is like giving morphine to a battlefield belly wound," he decided, regretting the move, and he immediately grabbed Stubbs by the collar, jerked him into a sitting position, then slapped him viciously until he came to again.

As their eyes met, Jeff whispered, "This is for Mai," placed the .45 against the man's forehead, pulled the trigger several times, then walked off down the alley in the opposite direction from which he had come.

VII. A CASE OF WAR CRIMES AT DUC CO

With all of Sgt. Mark Stryker's combat experience, despite the
dozens of HALO (High Altitude—Low Opening) parachute
drops he had made into undeclared war zones and all those
other bizarre escapades that had sharpened his survivor's edge
to the point where he knew a soldier's inner workings with that
first handshake, he still registered only puzzlement as he
surveyed the blank faces of the Green Beret troopers looking
up at his rapidly descending helicopter as it circled an
unnamed hamlet two kilometers west of Duc Co. The dazed
look of shock and despair masking their features was
something he hadn't seen in years—not since the two hour
firefight at Gia Long Palace in Saigon that culminated in the
bloody coup of 1963 and the assassination of President Diem.
Stryker, then thirty-one and completing his first thirteen-
month tour in Vietnam with the 716th MP Battalion, had
extended a second year of his enlistment to remain with the
"Saigon Commandos," and had been promptly assigned to the
joint U.S.-Vietnamese police patrols. He was with one of
the first patrols that swooped in on the besieged palace in
an attempt to restore control, and the faces of the ARVN (Army
of Republic of Viet Nam) Special Forces soldiers resembled
those of the Americans scrambling beneath his landing gunship when the Vietnamese learned their commander, Colonel

Trung, had been executed and the men under his command ordered to surrender their weapons to agents of the new regime.

The village of twenty bamboo-and-palm-thatched huts was encircled by twelve-foot barbed-wire fences topped with rows of sagging concertina wire and interlaced with trip wires that activated flares and claymore anti-personnel mines in case of enemy attack.

Stryker could feel the layer of heat that hugged the marshes and rice paddies of the land creep into the chopper as it made its final approach turn and lowered its tail two dozen feet above the huts before plopping down onto the red clay. His tired eyes had scanned the treeline that closed in on the strategic village as they circled prior to landing, and as the endless shades of green mirrored the jungle in those eyes, he searched for any signs of suspicious activity beyond the perimeter. A deep moat, constructed by his "A" Team before he joined them months earlier, also encircled the village, and he knew that long bamboo spikes, called punji sticks, soaked in water, buffalo urine and excrement lined the bottom of the moat, their tips bristling just below the stagnant water's surface.

This was just one of the estimated thousand or so "strategic hamlets" left over from the Saigon government's project of housing ten million of its fifteen million peasants in fortified villages by 1963, but it was the village topping Stryker's humanities-assistance list, and he was determined to make the best of a bad situation.

Even before the chopper had touched down he had jumped off its skids to the ground and was running to the nearest American NCO.

Several soldiers started for the helicopter, passing by him almost zombielike, responding to the LZ only because they were conditioned out of habit to off-load valuable supplies quickly—before that inevitable sniper took a bead on the Cobra gunship. This time, at least, there appeared to be no wounded soldiers awaiting medical evacuation (medevac).

Stryker stopped in front of a squad sergeant he knew from previous missions and dropped a packload of medical supplies at the man's feet. "A week's worth," he smiled at the stocky, short-haired soldier whose six-foot height put his clouded gray eyes on an even level with Mark's.

Two Vietnamese strike force tribesmen, clad in baggy tiger-stripe-camouflaged fatigues and with BARs slung over their shoulders, appeared from a hut twenty yards away and began walking casually toward the two huge Americans that dwarfed them. Stryker noticed they also wore the traditional toothy smile from ear to ear, but a pained expression in their dark, childlike eyes betrayed an ominous fear of tragedy that was settling over the village.

Stryker pulled a wrinkled and sweat-smeared manifest from under his green T-shirt and began reading haphazardly from it, "Smallpox, cholera, tetanus, typhoid vaccines, something-'malarial,' penicillin cubes, twenty jars of multicolored chewable vitamins, and a batch of sugared placebos." Stryker shook his head in mild disgust then voiced a question to no one in particular, "Why sugared? Gonna rot out what teeth they haven't already filed down for their beauty contests."

Stryker looked up from the manifest, but the American in front of him was ignoring Mark, staring out over his shoulder at the distant hills and Mark wondered if the other Green Beret sensed a mortar barrage in the air or an incoming rocket. "Damn it, Sergeant! What is it? What is going on around here?" Stryker gently grabbed the other NCO by the shoulders and started to shake him, but the man immediately broke his grip and led him behind the hut from which the two strike force members had emerged. Stryker was becoming more irritated by the second . . . Special Forces soldiers just did not act this way. He never saw them let anything faze them, especially a resupply chopper that was only a day late.

Stryker immediately felt something terribly wrong in the air after the NCO grabbed his shoulder this time and with his free hand, pointed blankly to a mound in the center of the small

75

village. Stryker looked to his right carefully, then to his left: all vegetation except a small community garden had been cleared inside the confines of the fenceline. The flesh-colored hill, taller than a man, had become the eerie focal point of the entire hamlet. As Stryker started walking toward it, almost fifty yards off now, he heard a child's muffled cry from within one of the huts, followed by hushed whispers, then a return to that same deathly silence again, broken only by the distant rhythmic thumping of the helicopter as it idled, rotors swishing through the hot, sticky, heavy onrush of air that preceded high noon.

It wasn't until Stryker got closer to the grisly mound that he suddenly realized what it was. The NCO assigned to the region as a village strike-force advisor had followed a respectable few steps behind him. "The VC came in right after we left yesterday," he informed Mark in a calm, matter-of-fact voice, "hacked off the left arm of every baby we innoculated and threw the severed limbs into a pile. Told the villagers anyone approaching the mound would be cut down by snipers. Told them anyone cooperating with the Imperialist running-dog Americans from now on would have their huts burned to the ground, among other things."

Stryker, finding unannounced shock waves beating at his temples like ancient Chinese gongs, continued walking up to the pile of mutilated arms. His eyes, squinting against the flat orange globe sizzling midway up the eastern sky, scanned the hostile treeline from beneath agile fingers that worked rapidly at massaging away the migraine. *Damn, I haven't had such a splitter since I was a cop,* he thought to himself, aware even then that he was not hearing the cloud of buzzing flies that swarmed over the pile of tiny limbs, their miniature fingers now curling up and drying out, leatherlike, under the merciless Asian sun. Even as he reached the huge mound, and the wild flies the size of cockroaches began bouncing at his face and arms by the hundreds, he could not hear them, although a clear picture of the scene twenty-four hours earlier was re-enacting itself across the screen of his mind's eye. He could see the dreaded

76

black-pajama-clad squad entering over the wire at dawn.

"One of the strike force members, Quoc, was VC," the NCO advised, attempting to break into his thoughts as they both stood before the buzzing mass of insects, each man seeing something totally different. "That shocked me, because—well, as you know, these 'Yardes don't cotton much to the Viet Cong. Consider them Vietnamese, body and soul. And you know these highlanders don't get along with the folks in Saigon, or Hanoi. Just can't understand how he got by us. How he fooled the villagers especially. Old Quoc was born just over in Duc Co, for Christ's sake. Must've been a latent commie or something. Maybe they blackmailed him, kidnapped his old lady or something. We're checking that angle."

But Stryker wasn't digesting the man's account of the atrocity. He was in a daydream, seeing the terrorists breach the wall of barbed wire with the long bamboo ladders they had used to cross the saber-laden moat. He saw them round up all the sleeping kids, gunning down some terrified parents who had refused to surrender their children. He saw them drag the screaming infants out into the middle of the village, where they then forced the adults to attend an hour-long political lecture as the VC waited patiently for the sun to drag itself up off the scarlet horizon. He saw them take the first child, a four-year-old girl with long, black hair braided down to the small of her back, and sit her atop a stool for all to see. As the girl, held in place by a mean-looking female cadre on either side, screamed helplessly for her mother with bewildered, innocent eyes, the leader of the squad, a man in his forties with a patch over one eye and a jagged scar running the length of his right cheek, extended the little girl's left arm out to its full length then swiftly sliced it clean off with a razor sharp, shiny machete.

"Quoc made his nightly rounds, right on schedule," the NCO continued, "and knocked out the perimeter guards with the butt of his carbine."

Stryker wasn't thinking of Quoc just then. He was watching the expression on the little girl's face as she witnessed her tiny arm part from her shoulder, saw the blood gush out until one of the women VC slapped a dirty rag to the wound, felt the rush of pain sweep through her as the one-eyed monster tossed her twitching limb into the dirt five feet away. Stryker saw the terror race from face to face of the other children lined up alongside the little girl as they realized they were destined to suffer the same assault.

Stryker could see other members of the squad applying crude tourniquets to the wounded infants—it would simply not do to have living examples of collaboration with the round-eyed white devils die from loss of blood. He could see the children struggling with their captors as they waited their turn to have their recently innoculated arms chopped neatly off—it just would not do to have these innocent Vietnamese endure vaccination scars for the rest of their lives.

"I don't know how them bastards made it over the wire without tripping even one wire or booby trap," the NCO admitted.

But Stryker was watching the one-eyed leader, immersed in all his revolutionary enthusiasm, hack off one tiny arm just a little too hard. The machete smacked with a sickening thud deep into the stool supporting the screaming child, shattering the handle of the weapon, and the remaining babies were subjected to a much duller, rusted meat cleaver that required several messy hacks before the arm could be torn off.

"The other members of the strike force were rounded up without much resistance," the NCO continued dryly. "Several of the teenaged girls were raped. All in the name of Uncle Ho, of course."

"Do we have a positive ID on the one-eyed asshole?" Stryker finally asked, forcing the vision of the young, sodomized virgins from his mind and instantly wishing he'd rephrased the question. There he went thinking like a cop again. He was surprised he hadn't let "positive ID on the suspect" slip out.

"Ngo Van Nanh. Hardcore cadre. Got a file on him this thick." The NCO was holding his fingers up for Stryker, indicating the folder was a couple inches deep. When the other Green Beret sergeant finished speaking, Stryker became attuned to the uneasy silence that had fallen over the village again. It was not exactly a hush enveloping the entire area, because birds still screeched now and then off in the jungle beyond the polluted moat, and here and there, inside darkened huts, armless infants cried anew, but Stryker felt a macabre lack of motion about him—there was no movement in the stifling air, no swirl or gust of breezes. In fact, the air seemed as stagnant as the oiled surface of the moat surrounding the hamlet.

It was a feeling he had experienced in the past, on the edge of steaming battlefields years before, and he involuntarily fell flat on the ground, propelled by a primitive instinct he had not mastered yet, just as an AK47 round whizzed by where his chest had just been. It was that sudden silence freezing events and the passage of time between him and the sniper, that minuscule pause in the whirling of life around him that signaled his subconscious into action and saved him once more.

The soldier behind him had taken cover with the first of three rapid shots and were already peppering the treeline with M-16 fire before Stryker could drag his own rifle up from the dust under his chest. Twigs and clods of dirt kicked up all about him as the sniper tried to center his out-going rounds on Stryker's green beret.

He began rolling to the left as he sensed the bullets impacting closer and closer, and as his back smashed hard against a section of the fenceline ringing the village, he bolted to his feet and fired a half clip of fifteen cartridges from the hip, fanning the rifle from right to left in the general direction of the gunman.

A dull *whump* signalled that one of his men had let loose with an M-79 grenade launcher, and as he hustled back toward the other Special Forces soldiers he was overjoyed in his panic to see how quickly the shock of the VC atrocity had been pushed aside so that their training and inbred professionalism could take over.

As Stryker trotted back toward a partially buried bunker, firing three-round bursts backward over his shoulder the whole time, he started laughing at the stupidity he had displayed walking up to the pile of limbs despite the warning of a possible sharpshooter camping out in the treetops. *Yes, you had to be psyched half crazy to fight in this war as a Green Beret,* he thought as he raced back through the billowing clouds of gunsmoke floating out from where his defenders lay prone in the dust. To survive, you had to already have accepted the possibility of the most painful kind of death. That firm belief that you were prepared for the worst—eager to sacrifice yourself for what some saw as only a giant ant hill with a numbered designation attached to it. That was the edge you needed.

As he felt the rifle's bolt lock to the rear on an empty chamber, one of the sniper's impacting bullets tore the M-16 right out of his powerful hands, and a second later he felt hot lead sting his left ear like an angry burrowing hornet, then pass through and continue out ahead of him, beating him to the bunker as the sizzling red tracer, glowing like a fiery poker, impacted on a sandbag and exploded into tiny, sparkling fragments.

"Jesus Christ, Stryker! You got zapped by a goddamn tracer round!" One of his fellow Green Berets stared on in disbelief, still hugging the ground, as two other soldiers continued to return the sniper's fire. "It looked like that bullet hit you from behind and exited your face. Brother, that was close!"

"I never seen such luck," one man lying beside a steel conex crate ten feet away paused to reflect loudly as he looked up briefly, ejected a spent magazine and slammed in a fresh thirty-round clip then returned his concentration to the shoot out.

"Yeah, you okay Mark?" the third Green Beret, the NCO that had just briefed Stryker on the VC atrocity, asked seriously. "Hell, you're bleeding all over the goddamn place!"

Stryker felt his ear for a second then stuck his pinky finger through the new hole plugged neatly in the center of the earlobe. Despite the searing pain, he forced the finger all the way through until it came out the front, then wiggled it at his friends mockingly and asked, "Anybody got a spare earring?"

Semi-automatic fire continued to rain down on the men, then the noisy reports ceased abruptly and the NCO was rising to one knee. "I got that son of a bitch!" he declared and everyone nodded in agreement as the sniper was catapulted backwards out of the highest palm tree by several .223-caliber rounds that stitched across his chest diagonally from liver to clavicle. The guerrilla refused to cry out and silently fell the fifty feet to the hard ground, landing with a dull thump between the treeline and the dark moat.

Even before the Green Berets had risen from their refuge, several villagers had unlocked the main gates to the hamlet, lowered their makeshift bamboo bridge across the murky moat, and rushed out to surround the fallen guerrilla. They immediately commenced pummeling him about the head and shoulders with spades and clubs.

"Get out there and stop them!" Stryker commanded one of the village militiamen in Vietnamese. "Or we won't have a prisoner to interrogate!" But the Viet Cong had died long before his body crashed to the ground, and his scant clothing carried no identification or documents that could be of any help to them.

"Maybe this really *is* a friendly village!" the other Green Beret sergeant conceded as they rushed out of the compound toward the unruly mob gathering about the crumpled body. A young mother, her child still bleeding through hastily administered bandages following the crude amputation the day before, continued kicking at the guerrilla's mangled face long after the dust had settled, and Stryker had to gently pull her aside and instruct one of the strike force members to escort her from the scene so they could inspect the body.

* * *

The Cobra gunship had been sitting idly by on the far edge of the village when the sniping broke out. It had quickly taken to the skies at the first sound of gunfire and returned shortly thereafter with three more choppers. For nearly a half hour they swooped down on the tangled terrain concealing an abandoned tunnel system Stryker's men had stumbled upon, unleashing several rocket-pods' worth of explosives that streaked into the trees and uprooted several palms and collapsed a number of spider hole escape routes, but did little other damage.

Volunteers among the Vietnamese strike force entered the extensive tunnel system with pistols drawn, in an unusual show of bravery, but the seek-out-and-destroy operation was called off after no enemy forces were located and two militiamen wandered into a decoy tunnel avoided by the VC, designed to blow up when discovered and searched by American or South Vietnamese tunnel rats.

In the meantime, Stryker called in a fleet of dust-off choppers, loaded down with medics, who set about treating and evacuating the kids.

That evening, after a ten minute post-action critique, Stryker wanted to know more about "that little bastard Ngo Van Nanh."

"Lost his eye at Dien Bien Phu, fighting the French in '54," the Vietnamese interpreter from Duc Co explained. He had arrived with the last of the assisting gunships, carrying an intelligence packet hastily compiled in Pleiku the night before. "Sustained the scar to his cheekbone two years ago. Members of Ngo Van Nhu's Secret Police, the So Nghien Cuu Xa Hoi Chinh Tri, had him cornered in a Cholon back alley, but he escaped with that bullet 'scrape' that has marked him to this day. He's no relation to Chief Nhu, of course."

"How long has he been harassing this village?" Stryker asked calmly, still thinking about the painful treatments the tortured children were undergoing at that very moment back at the Evacuation Hospital.

"Seven months . . ." the scout began, but he was cut off by the sergeant Stryker had fought beside only a few hours earlier.

"The damn ARVNs had him in their hands several times," he muttered sarcastically for the benefit of the interpreter, "but their commanding officer bugged out when it looked like it was going to come down to a shoot out. And of course his men, who are already unmotivated because their commander keeps a large percentage of their salaries for his private bank account, aren't going to risk unnecessary bloodshed when they can't even get enough rice for two meals a day." The NCO tossed the agency folder back to the Vietnamese and strode out of the room in disgust.

"Were you sure to get photos of those children for distribution to the news media?" Stryker asked the interpreter.

"I didn't think to . . . I mean, it's not really my—"

"What about the piles of arms stinking up this village?"

"Well, I really can't see where that's my job, Sergeant."

"Damn it, what kind of intelligence man are you?" Stryker fumed.

"Well, Sergeant, I just don't feel propaganda is—"

"Propaganda?" Stryker interrupted him. "The atrocity happened, my friend! We didn't make it up. And now it's history."

"Never fear, Mark," the Green Beret sergeant had returned to the room, a large manila envelope in his outstretched hand. "Perkins snapped off these photos with his pocket camera. Just got 'em back from a little camera shop in Pleiku. Some old Vietnamese man on the agency payroll developed 'em on short notice. After he vomited, he guaranteed us prints would reach all the Saigon papers by morning."

The interpreter added dryly, "It's doubtful the papers will publish them. They would make Vietnam appear primitive to the outside world."

"We've got a team chasing this one-eyed Nanh character,"

the sergeant advised Stryker, "but the trail has cooled and we weren't very successful in getting the ARVNs at Duc Co to help. They don't go out on patrols after dark, you know."

After Stryker flipped through the glossy eight-by-ten black and whites, he removed two and placed them inside his shirt, then handed the rest back to the sergeant. "See to it copies find their way to newspapers stateside." A grin then creased Stryker's deeply tanned features. "Write on the back 'COURTESY OF PRIVATE SNIKREP, SAIGON.' Nothing else." And as the Green Beret hustled out of the building again, the Vietnamese interpreter smirked back at Stryker and nodded his head slowly back and forth.

"Snikrep," he muttered. "Perkins, spelled backwards. Not very brilliant, if you ask me." But Stryker was already headed for the door, intent on ignoring the interpreter for the moment.

A lone candle flickered in a window of Stryker's bungalow when he arrived home.

A smile instantly took hold of him as he started up the steps to the hut on stilts which he had spent weeks fortifying with sandbags and the little luxuries of life: a cheap stereo system, hot plate, and even a miniature refrigerator. The fridge only worked when electricity found its way to this distant housing project on the outskirts of Pleiku, but that was not what caused Stryker to smile.

He prided himself on constantly remaining in phase yellow. That was what he called it, anyway. It was more a kind of military survival than religious enlightenment, because you always practiced it—unlike the Buddhist meditations which you could play with only if you were in the mood. Phase yellow required that he always be aware of his surroundings. Even when he returned to familiar locale, such as home. It was not so much like the alertness practiced on the jungle patrols. That was phase red, prowling on the offense, expecting to make contact with unfriendliness. With phase yellow, you just refrained from daydreaming or whistling at the flowers and made damn sure you anticipated all that could go wrong between point A and point B. Be it ambush, potential bandits, an unexpected dog eager for the chase, or even those wily pythons slinking about in the grass.

That's why, being in phase yellow as he had been, and having eyeballed his hut while still a hundred yards away, he had taken to smiling. It was because the candle had not been in the window when he first entered the housing project.

The candle was their little game. If it glowed in the window, then Stryker was to wake her up. It meant she was eager for contact—her loins were restless. If the window was dark, Stryker entered as silent as a cat, careful not to wake her. The signal was not foolproof, however. Sometimes the candle burned completely out before Stryker made it home. On those nights, dawn was usually cracking before he made it into the sack.

This sudden appearance of the candle told him that she had been waiting up all night again. When finally she spotted his elusive shadow floating pantherlike into the compound, she would have quickly lit the wick then scrambled under the covers to pretend she was in a deep sleep.

That was her simple game: act like she was too tired to wake easily so he would have several minutes to kiss, lick and massage the most sacred portions of her young, ripe body. It would just not do to have a proud Montagnard maiden grinning and groaning with such pleasure unless she did so in her sleep. It was allowed to have dreams where these huge foreigners tickled and aroused her helpless body—treating it as their personal plaything.

Stryker's night vision remained acute in his left eye as he started up the stairs. A routine flare had drifted across the edge of the compound earlier, and he had kept his left eye closed as he proceeded through the orderly rows of huts, using the other to briefly check the shadows he came across for any sign of intruders. When the flare eventually burned out, its plastic "invisible" parachute still drifting lazily against the dark clouds, Stryker opened the protected left eye and closed his right. He was then able to see through the darkness as if there had never been a flare, while his right eye began readjusting its purple cones to counteract the night blindness which the flare's white-hot light had inflicted.

As he entered the one-room bungalow he could see a slender ankle protruding from the covers of the bed. He wasn't really in the mood for romance after the incident near Duc Co, but he refrained from the impulse of running the barrel of his M-16 along the rough edges of her foot. *That would sure wake up her horny ass!* he thought to himself, grinning again as she shifted lazily onto her stomach. Suddenly aroused himself by the sensuous curve of her buttocks beneath the sheet, he quietly undressed and slipped in beside her. He slowly pulled the sheet down, surveying the smooth, dark features of her back, then began kissing the back of her muscular thighs, above the knee. As he began to spread the thighs apart, he felt the firmness that ran along her entire body as he moved his fingers beneath her flat stomach up to the swell of her breasts, pressed unyielding against the hard mattress.

Her nipples went taut instantly as he caressed them, protruding through his fingers until fully erect, but as she ended the game by turning over onto her back and opening up her legs to him he discovered he was still soft as the pillow, unable to force visions of armless children from his thoughts.

"Damn," he whispered, surprised at himself, even embarrassed, as he rolled over onto one arm, wishing he had a cigarette to light up even though he did not smoke.

"What I do wrong?" she asked meekly, the fear in her eyes forcing a rare crease along her high, pronounced cheekbones. "You want I should leave?"

Where the hell would you go, he thought instead of answering her immediately. *Now that you shack up with a round-eye who would have you?* "It's not you," he finally admitted. "It's

86

something that happened today at work."

"Ohhhhh," she whispered in relief, drawing the word out so that she reminded him of a waitress in Tokyo he once met. She had gasped at him in almost the same way when he explained to her what "sodomy" meant. "You talk 'bout Duc Co."

"Jesus. You already heard?" He raised his eyes at her. "Radio?"

"No," she replied, sounding bored now as she got up to walk over to a large plastic bowl near the toilet drain. "It is the gossip now of the old women of the market," she explained matter-of-factly.

He watched her silently as she squatted there naked, facing him as she pulled a wet washcloth from the bowl and began wiping the sweat from between her breasts. She grinned impishly up at him as she spread her legs again, this time to wipe away the wasted juices, but Stryker just got to his feet and walked over to where his fatigues were draped over a chair. He pulled the two pictures from inside his shirt and returned to the bed. After lighting a small camping-type lantern, he propped up the pillows and laid back to inspect the scenes of the atrocity again.

"The old women talk about other things," she added, a look of hurt making a frown wrinkle the edges of her mouth. "They say when Americans leave next year, VC sneak in and cut off the breasts of all women like me."

"Don't worry about it, Lai," he muttered as if she were distracting him. His eyes were riveted to those of the girl that stared back at him from the photograph—tears ran down her face and her mouth was contorted in horror at the sight of shreds of muscle and bloodied skin hanging from where her tiny arm once was.

"The old women say the VC come for sure—march me naked through the streets with their bayonet in my back! Then I disappear for good!" She threw the sponge floating in the bowl at him suddenly. "You hear what I say? You listen?"

"Christ, Lai! It's only 1967! The South Vietnamese Army

won't be ready to defend this country for at least two years. Nobody's leaving next year." Stryker stared one last time at the photograph depicting the severed limbs. He snarled mentally at the wild dog in the corner of the picture trying to drag off one of the tiny arms, then put the prints down and looked over at Lai. Her usually narrow eyes were now large and dark with worry as she stared up at him.

"Will you take me back to the stateside with you, Mark," she asked uneasily, a tear sliding down her cheek, "when you go from the 'Nam?"

VIII. FLOORSHOW, PLEIKU STYLE

The military police jeep carrying the somewhat notorious Decoy Squad cruised Saigon's Nguyen Hu Street like a silent hawk gliding just above a canyon floor in search of rats. It was now well past curfew, but the Canh-Sats were behind in erecting their roadblock barricades across the major intersections downtown, and nervous bargirls were still hustling intoxicated GIs out through swinging nightclub doors to the few brave taxis still prowling the city. Nguyen Hu (pronounced Win Way) was perhaps the most rowdy street patronized by the Americans, next to Tu Do and Le Loi.

Ever since the commander of the 716th MP Battalion had authorized the Decoy Squad to paint their jeep entirely black, as opposed to the customary olive-drab green, the men had taken to attacking their mission with unusual zeal. Patrolling the city in previously planned routes that rotated nightly and covered those areas most rampant with violent crime, they even began plotting their assignments and arrests on a huge cardboard map, using bright multicolored plastic pins.

Several times the driver of the black jeep—the MPs affectionately called it "the Beast"—would pull up behind one of the blue and yellow Renault taxis just as a dainty, painted prostitute struggled to lift her drunk and dazed American trick into the cramped back seat.

"Need any help, ma'am?" Pvt. Michael Broox would always ask, exaggerating his courteous tone. The hooker would always respond with mild shock, betrayed by her bewildered frown and wildly racing eyes that searched for an escape route she would never use.

Broox would still be directing his accusing stare with piercing blue eyes from just above the rim of prescription sunglasses when Pfc. Anthony Thomas went into action, hopping from the rear of the jeep and pulling the GI out of the door opposite the one the girl had just forced him into. While Spec 4 Tim Bryant waited patiently for the lady of questionable virtue to produce her government-regulated VD card, Thomas went through the soldier's pockets in search of his military ID.

"Congratulations, honey," Specialist Bryant smirked sarcastically as he inspected the small, pink folding card. "You haven't had the clap in a couple months." The little booklets had weekly medical stamps affixed to them—in black for a clean medical exam, red for a diagnosed VD infection requiring a shot of penicillin.

"Are you finished?" she snapped, swallowing the humiliation as she grabbed the card out of Bryant's hands.

"Jacobson, Clifford. Lieutenant, Signal Company," Thomas began reading from the drunk's wallet as Broox, still sitting behind the wheel of the jeep, took notes. Just in case the soldier turned up dead in a back alley later, without any identification on the body.

"Get his officer ass off the streets, honey," Sergeant Richards suggested to the woman politely. "It's after curfew." She smiled at the sergeant, winking seductively, then frowned over at Bryant again before speaking in rapid Vietnamese to the cabbie. She climbed over her GI into the back seat and the taxi soon sped off down the street, disappearing in a squeal of tires around the first corner.

"You shouldn't be so hard on those chicks," Sergeant Richards advised his men without looking at them after they had hopped back into the rear of the jeep. "Most of them wouldn't trick for a living if they weren't forced into it."

"Aw, gimme a break, Sarge," complained Bryant defensively.

"No, he's right," added Broox, "there's over thirty thousand war-orphaned prostitutes trying to survive in Saigon right now."

"Jesus H. Christ," chimed in Private First Class Thomas.

Broox turned in his seat to look back at the two MPs and continued, "and I emphasize the words 'war-orphaned.'"

"Who appointed you statistician, Mister Bleeding Heart?" Thomas laughed, slapping him good-naturedly up the back side of his head, "I mean, if you ask me—"

"Take us down to that alley!" Sergeant Richards interrupted, pointing to where two figures darted through the shadows.

"What the hell . . . who the hell was that?" whispered Bryant, bending forward to squint against the dim yellow street lamps.

"I'll be damned if it didn't look like a white guy chasing a black dude," decided Broox as he gunned the accelerator and steered for the sidestreet, leaving the headlights off.

"Naw, you're full of it."

"Screw you, dickhead!" he growled at Thomas. "I saw what I saw. And that guy was waving a butcher knife over his head!"

"Can we get this dickhead transferred to the DMZ, Sarge?"

"Really!" Thomas agreed jokingly with Bryant although he spoke in a serious voice. "The ol' Black Syph has finally affected Mikey-boy's excuse for a brain!" and he lightly tapped his clipboard against the side of Broox's MP helmet.

As the Beast rumbled down into the maze of tenements rising beside the revered Le Loi square, an uneasy tension settled over the Decoy Squad. Word had reached them through the GI grapevine that one of their own fellow MPs, Jeff Rodgers, all-around Good Guy and dedicated cop, had flipped out after arriving home one morning to find his girlfriend raped and murdered. He had gone AWOL, or so they had told the men at briefing. But what they didn't tell the men was that Private Rodgers was now a one-man revenge squad, out to kill the black deserters suspected of the brutal homicide. And that in the last two weeks, eight innocent servicemen, all black, had turned up floating down the Saigon River and Rodgers was suspected of the executions.

The alley had taken a downhill turn, and as the Decoy Squad coasted silently along, their jeep's engine now off, nervous whispers were exchanged.

"I hear they found one of the suspects last week. His knees shot all to hell and a bag of dope stuffed down his throat."

"Yeah, a deserter from the First Signal Brigade. Jeff arrested him a few months ago, too, when he first arrived in Saigon."

"Serves the punk right."

"Righteous on!"

"Don't you mean, 'White on!'" More subdued giggles followed.

"Knock it off." Sergeant Richards gave all three men a dirty look. "Boy, some nights you guys are real pros; other nights you're a definite pain in the rectum."

For several silent minutes the team cruised the back alleys running off the old Rue Catinat.

"We musta missed 'em down one of these corridors running open air between the buildings," Broox muttered, straining through the prescription sunglasses against the dark.

"You'd think that black dude would be screaming bloody murder if that was really Jeff chasing him down the street."

"Yeah, I'm sure word has spread thru the soul network like wildfire that some mad dog honky killer was on the loose, offing the brothers." That brought another round of laughter that broke the unnatural quiet riding with the patrol.

"Now look, you guys, nobody has proven yet that Jeff killed anybody," Bryant added in defense of his friend.

"True," whispered Sergeant Richards, the level of his voice an indication the men were showing lax discipline again. "But they found an arrowhead necklace at the scene of that one kneecap murder. Now who else do you know wears a damn arrowhead necklace?"

"Lots of guys!" Bryant's voice rose dramatically. His hand now rested on his gunbutt as the walls of tenements on either side of them rose up to hide the moon and its silver beams.

"With the initials 'JKR' monogrammed on it?"

Bryant had little more to say as the Decoy Squad continued to prowl the back alleys of Saigon without results.

Two hundred miles north of the capital, Warrant Officer William Sickles, Army C.I.D., stepped from the single engine Air America Cessna and planted both feet firmly on the ground before surveying the terrain about him and formulating an opinion on Pleiku. As he swayed back and forth slightly, his knees buckling and his stomach still swimming, Sickles wondered whose toes he had stepped on to warrant this mission. Within seconds two other passengers had deplaned the aircraft behind him. One, a chemical defoliant expert in his late forties sporting a flat-top haircut and stooping his almost seven-foot frame to talk to the C.I.D. agent, wore black subdued captain's bars on both his collar and the helmet tucked under a hairless, bony arm. The man had chewed Sickles' ear on the entire flight and wasn't about to stop just because they were safely on the ground. After lecturing him on the finer points of their new secret weapon, Agent Orange, the captain then spent an hour pumping him for information: he just had to know why a C.I.D. agent was hopping a flight to Pleiku City. Who had he come to take back to the Monkey House?

As Sickles took a Pepto-Bismol tablet from his brown safari shirt pocket and squeezed it from its plastic wrapper into his dry mouth, the captain came up from behind, slapped him on the back with unrestrained enthusiasm and said, "Bet your original flight from Oakland didn't take as long as this one, eh, C.I.D. man?"

93

A squadron of low-flying fighter jets roared past overhead as he spoke.

"Eh, what's that? Say again!" the captain leaned over even closer to Sickles until they were almost nose to nose. "Speak up, son!"

Sickles wiggled a stubby finger around in his ear as though such was remedy for the sonic boom explosion that still ringed in his head, echoing back and forth between the ears. "I said, yes, it did take a couple days to obtain a seat north from Saigon." He wished he had a glass of water to wash down the pill now lodged in his throat.

"Ah, bullshit," the captain laughed heartily, "there's always flights to Pleiku City. It's just that the damn VC been mortaring the place regularly this week. Been Off Limits to you sightseers." The captain grinned at Sickles surreptitiously. "Come on, Mister, what brings a straight-leg like you north into Injun country?"

"So tell me about this mortaring business," Sickles changed the subject.

"Oh, apparently some VC went into Duc Co last week and rounded up all the pregnant women in the village. Made their families watch as they sliced open their swollen bellies and jerked out the unborn fetuses then threw them down in the dirt."

Sickles felt suddenly nauseous again as the captain imitated a football player spiking the ball after a touchdown.

"The usual stuff. So the ARVNs went out and tried to capture some VC but only succeeded in killing a couple teenagers and in retaliation the Cong have been mortaring us all darn week." The captain began playing with the rank insignia on his helmet which had come loose during the flight.

The sound of something twirling and flapping through the oppressive midday heat overhead caused the captain's face to turn white, and as a jeep raced by with its passengers yelling "Incoming!" at the top of their lungs, the captain flattened his giant frame against the earth.

Sickles also dove for the ground, and in his haste landed half submerged in a puddle of red clay and mud.

"Damn bats!" the captain was saying, already on his feet and dusting himself off as two of the mammals fluttered briefly above his head then disappeared into the distant treeline.

Damn bastards, Sickles thought as he looked back at the jeepload of practical jokers. There was one at every airport, he decided, intent on razzing the new arrivals incountry. Still lying half in the puddle, Sickles pulled out a stained and creased pocket notebook and jotted down the registration number stenciled to the rear bumper of the rapidly fleeing vehicle before it disappeared in a cloud of dust.

"Damn bats!" the captain repeated, now grabbing one of Sickles' elbows to help him up. "Thought they only came out at night."

Sgt. Mark Stryker sat alone at the table, tossing his prized collection of Death From Above playing cards into the overturned beret. His seventh bottle of ba-mui-ba beer was having the desired effect—he was missing most of the throws.

The laminated cards, all black aces, were designed to be left in the open mouths of dead VC by American airborne troopers, and these were discarded leftovers he had found through the years scattered about the jungle floor of silent battlefields. If you happened to come across the cards hanging from the lips of an enemy body you left them there, in place, so Charlie's buddies would eventually come across the stiff and have their whole day ruined—the superstitious Vietnamese dreaded the ace of spades. It was the worst possible omen, especially when discovered sticking out of a dead comrade's shattered mouth, the reddish pulp and spittle coating the plastic covers.

Yes, laminate the cards with two thick layers—what a brilliant idea, Stryker decided, toasting the unknown inventor with another beer. So much harder to destroy the card. Maybe they should just drop a batch out a plane window, he thought

95

harder on the subject, but no—that would ruin the fun of killing the Cong first. Not to mention how it would lessen the value of the much sought after cards if they were made available in larger quantities, as a psyops air drop would require.

Two go-go dancers, their bikini tops flattered by even thinner G-strings that left little to the imagination, gyrated to hard rock on the stage mere feet above Stryker's eyes, but even as one tossed her bra down onto his table he still ignored them, concentrating instead on making just one more card into the beret. Visions of pregnant women being disemboweled danced before his eyes while armless children ran to the aid of their injured mothers.

"Now isn't it sacrilegious to turn a Green Beret upside down?" a taunting voice asked from behind Stryker. He hesitated a second or two as his eyes shifted to the Fifth Special Forces "flash" on the beret's front. No, that wouldn't do to have the flag of South Vietnam lying upside down he decided, even though its gold field and three red, horizontal stripes looked the same from any angle. Bending forward in his chair slightly, he flipped the beret over, knocking several cards off the table, then continued silently tossing more aces slowly onto the righted beret without glancing back to see who had addressed him.

"Do I detect some disenchantment with the legendary Green Berets?" Sickles asked this time, moving around cautiously to the other side of the table, between the Special Forces sergeant and the floor show. "Do I need an invitation to sit down, Mark?" he smiled somberly.

For several seconds Stryker said nothing, but when one of the wildly dancing topless go-go girls began rubbing Sickles' bald head with her flapping breasts (like a cherished Buddha—for good luck), it took all of Mark's self-control to keep from laughing. He forced a grin and gently kicked a chair out.

"Sit down, Harry."

Warrant Officer William Sickles frowned momentarily at

the distasteful nickname, then quickly took a seat, if only to get away from the other dancer who had begun licking his smooth crown to the cheers of the other patrons in the bar.

"That's the first time I ever saw one of those women rotate her tongue around your skull the same way she licks the head of my pecker, Mister Detective-san," Stryker made a face. "Must be your cologne. Christ, Sickles, you smell like a barn."

The C.I.D. agent brushed some of the twigs and bamboo shavings that still clung to his knees from the fall in the puddle at the airstrip. "Aren't you wondering what brings me all the way up to Pkeiku?" he smiled, as if offering a riddle.

"It's a free country . . . for now," Stryker said bitterly.

"Sounds like that VC business in Duc Co has really got you down."

"If it's not one thing, it's always another," he replied matter-of-factly.

"You want to talk about it?"

"So what brings you to Pleiku City?" Stryker changed the subject, feeling the distaste growing in his mouth. A squad of Green Berets, fresh from the jungle, entered the bar at that moment. They nodded curtly and sat at another table after the youngest soldier in the group dropped some coins in the jukebox. Barry Sadler's "Ballad of the Green Berets" began flowing from the huge speakers built into the cinderblock walls, and the go-go dancers struggled awkwardly to adapt their footing to the softer tune.

"I need your help on a case, Mark," Sickles began.

"A criminal case?" Stryker asked, mildly surprised but not yet intrigued.

"A homicide. Double homicide. Shit, triple homicide. And the floaters keep turning up in the Saigon River."

"So what's wrong with all your super cops at C.I.D.?"

"We're up against a very clever and devious personality, Mark. Even demented. One of the most slippery perpetrators I've ever encountered."

"Not impressed, Harry. Stop trying to make this sound like

97

you're hunting a diabolical monster." Stryker took another swig of the Vietnamese beer, washing down the smoke in the room that was now sticking to the insides of his throat. He eyed Sickles with irritation. Stryker had always been instantly distrustful and suspicious of people who called him by name at the end of every other sentence. "I repeat: what's wrong with your elitist C.I.D. geniuses?"

Sickles knew that the Green Beret sergeant actually respected the Army's criminal investigators, despite how he described them, so he ignored the challenge. He was also aware Stryker had spent several months in the less celebrated Military Police Investigations branch (MPI) while stationed in Korea, but had requested reassignment back to patrol division after tiring of the paperwork and follow-up duties. Sickles chuckled to himself silently: this character sitting coiled before him always returned to the street.

"This time our suspect is a cop. An AWOL MP."

"Cops have gone bad before," Stryker said, frowning. "Too much time on the street can turn 'em dirty."

"This ain't your regular beat cop, Mark. His name is Jeff Rodgers."

The name hit Stryker like a thunderclap, causing him to flip one of the Death From Above playing cards several feet over the beret and up onto the stage. He turned to look at Sickles and the C.I.D. agent met and held his stare.

One of the dancers on the stage, now totally naked, squatted lower and lower toward the card, her slender hips sensuously gyrating slowly to the drumbeats of hard rock now blaring from a dozen wall speakers.

"Jeff Rodgers," Stryker whispered beneath his breath and Sickles could see the mind beyond the icy eyes set to work automatically, effortlessly, as it digested and examined this unexpected information. Sickles knew the Green Beret sergeant had been on the list for transfer to C.I.D. but had been passed over because of attitude problems. The C.I.D., a branch of the Army operated outside the Military Police Corps and independent of the Provost Marshal's Office, was to street MPs what the FBI is to county deputies in civilian life. Sickles believed the sergeant never quite got over being refused admittance to the division's ranks. It was his theory Stryker opted for Special Forces because the experience had soured him altogether on law enforcement, but Sickles had never battled race riots day in and day out for nearly a week and would probably never come close to knowing why the former MP had left the street.

"You still with me, Stryker?"

"Jeff Rodgers . . . our Jeff Rodgers?" the sergeant repeated incredulously.

"The same. Was shacking up with some Vietnamese girl down on Thanh Mau. Some scumbags raped and murdered her. Now Jeff is roaming the street on a one-man avenger kick."

"Little Jeff . . ."

"Problem is, we think he's knocking off all the wrong dudes."

Stryker's mind flashed back nearly ten years to when he was an unemployed steel mill worker, returning to California and his hometown of San Marcos, determined to finish college. Jeff had just been a kid back then—hell, he was still a kid now. Stryker swallowed hard, unable to get rid of the distaste rising from his gut.

They had played football on the street back then—the whole neighborhood, though none of them were really athletes and few even played ball in high school. He could not even remember one of them lettering the whole time he was there.

Jeff had always been the eager-to-please sixth grader, striving to imitate the older boys. Always carrying heavy gas cans when the tank ran empty on those river rafting expeditions. Always smuggling the skin magazines up into the treehouse for all to examine. Always skinning up his knees more than anyone else when the bigger boys from the east side tackled him on the blacktop even though they were only playing touch or flag football. Constantly proving to the older boys he could hack the course with them. It was too bad there were no kids his age on the block way back then. Maybe Jeff wouldn't have grown up so mean. But mean in a cunning, controlled manner. It was always better to get even instead of mad he maintained, and that was one of the few things the older boys had learned from little Jeff. Even if few of them ever had to fall back on the lesson.

"We need you, Mark," Sickles insisted, intruding on his thoughts. "You know this Jeff Rodgers inside out. I've got MP patrols down in Saigon stacking jeeps up left and right trying to chase him down. Hell, half the time I think they're just in pursuit of shadows."

But Stryker was thinking back to all the letters he had received from Jeff during Mark's first tour in Saigon. Maybe it was the distance of twelve thousand miles separating them that encouraged Jeff to unload all his personal problems on "the adventurer far off roaming the Orient." Growing up amidst dopers in school, trying to figure out girls, planning ways to raise money for that first car. . . .

When Stryker had transferred to Korea in 1964 the letters continued, but their tone changed dramatically and Jeff now wanted to know how many men Stryker had killed in Vietnam, how much did the prostitutes charge, had he ever caught the clap and did he kill the girl that gave it to him? Or did he even know which one that was, so busy was his nighttime schedule.

They had some great times together when Jeff reached the age where he could join the Army and volunteered for Southeast Asia to the astonished cries of all the sweethearts that tore off nylons and dresses in after-school scuffles, all for the chance to wear his senior class ring. And that crafty Jeff had never even bought a ring to give away. Before and during that period in Jeff's life, they had exchanged dozens of letters, pro and con on military service, and, yes—Mark had come to know little Jeff inside out.

It was that inner, subdued razor-sharp stealth Mark saw in his childhood pal that made him uncomfortable. During a two

100

week R&R to Saigon, before shipping north to Pleiku after that second jump school, Stryker had detected a dangerous, hidden cunning in Jeff that made him uneasy and left him worried. Perhaps it was all the intense questions about the jungle and death that made him click back into phase yellow, but he had quickly dismissed it all as youthful enthusiasm. That was something hard to control in an exotic land like Vietnam, and Stryker had forced from his mind all those bothersome doubts though they returned to gnaw at him now and then.

"So far we can link only one of the murders to Rodgers," Sickles advised him. "A deserter, Negro. Clarence Stubbs. Your friend Jeff plugged his mouth full of H, popped off his kneecaps with a .45, then put four additional rounds into his forehead, point blank. Split his skull in two, right down the middle." Sickles laughed wickedly as he recalled the crime scene photographs and he downed a glass of bourbon to silence his mirth. By then the go-go dancer had managed to clutch the slippery ace of spades in the folds of her crotch, and she proudly tiptoed over to the edge of the stage carefully and rotated it in front of Stryker's face for Sickles' benefit. Again the soldiers crowding into the bar cheered uproariously.

"Let's get outta here," Stryker muttered, abandoning his card collection as he expertly balanced the beret atop his untamed crew cut.

"I can swing it for you so you can transfer back to the good old 716th," Sickles revealed. "I know you're burnt out on all that 'let's go jump out of a perfectly good airplane' crap."

"Worked hard for this green beanie," he frowned over at the C.I.D. agent. "I'm not so sure I want to go back to the street as a flatfoot."

"Okay, big fella," Sickles replied with a compromising grin. "How's about temporary duty assignment change. Until we get this Rodgers mess straightened out."

"What's the M.O. on the floaters?"

"Throats slashed. Then they're dumped in the river."

"What kind of weapon?"

101

"We're still working on that—at the lab in Tokyo. I'll hav you an answer before you get back to Saigon."

"Didn't say I'd take this scab job yet, Harry. Tell me abou the girl."

"The girl?"

"Jeff's woman."

Sickles pulled a soggy notebook from his shirt pocket and flipped through the yellowed pages. "Le Thai Mai. Bor Mytho, 1950."

"Christ, only seventeen?"

"Yeah. Apparently they only stayed together three month —a hundred days exactly. At least that's what the *giay son chung* papers say."

"*Giay song chung?*"

"Yeah, formal engagement license. Enables them to live together and avoid the police raids where the girls usually ge carted off to Chi Hoa jail unless they got enough bribe money."

"Picked up as street whores, you mean."

"Correct, Mister ex-MP. Say, who's asking who the questions here, anyway?"

"You think she was buckin' for a ticket stateside?"

"According to the residents we questioned on Thanh Mau Street, no. The two often argued on that point. She didn't want to leave Vietnam. He wanted to take her home, his new bride."

Stryker wondered briefly about that. Jeff had never written him mentioning the girl. But then he hadn't written, period, in the last several months. "So what connects the shooting with the other murders?"

"Well, so far, just race. All the victims were black. The suspects in the murder of Rodgers' fiancée were all black."

Stryker shrugged his shoulders and made a motion as if he were about to get up and leave. "What kind of evidence do you call that, Harry? You're wastin' my—"

"We found a necklace at the shooting scene. Had the initials JKR on it." Stryker remained in his seat as Sickles went on to describe the crime itself. Two heavily made-up bar girls in their forties sat down at the table uninvited and batted their outrageous eyelashes at the two Americans for a full five minutes, but neither man so much as looked their way and the girls got impatient and moved on to another table. After they left, both soldiers got up automatically and started for the door again.

Sickles read a background synopsis on the six deserters whose arrest Rodgers had participated in earlier, adding that no one was sure yet just how many subjects had been involved in the actual attack on Le Thai Mai.

"Funny thing about that shooting, though. If it really was Rodgers, I think the guy's lost it mentally, Mark."

"And why do you say that, Sherlock?"

"He left a large roll of greenbacks untouched at the scene—over two thousand dollars U.S.!"

"And the others—the floaters."

"Picked clean. No wallets, no jewelry, no nothing."

"Doesn't click."

"Correct. Shrouded in mystery, my friend. Ideal for a sleuth of your esteemed abilities, knowledgeable as you are in the ways of the Saigon underworld." Stryker ignored the bait.

"Do you have the file on this case with you?" he asked and Sickles' dull eyes brightened instantly.

"No, my friend. It's all down in the big city."

"Let me think about it, Harry," he said as they left the bar and stepped down into the street life swirling past the nightclub in a frenzy of beat-the-curfew madness. Even at that late hour, the layer of night heat pressing down on them when they left the air-conditioned world of neon and naked dancing girls was instantly noticeable—depressing for Sickles, who was already wiping imaginary sweat from his brow. Invigorating for Stryker. The warm rush of breeze that swept past them, trying to sneak into the bar, aroused all the senses vital to his survival. Sexual and jungle instinct. *Both primitive*, he thought to himself, smiling. Stryker always noticed the heat chasing the electricity in the air and the constant hum of people

103

crowding the streets. He appreciated all the irritants that other Americans attempted to ignore. Or endure, filling their existence with reminders of America until almost all of Vietnam showed signs of G.I. Joe, poisoning the culture of these Asians and destroying their simple way of life forever. Stryker made a point of it to experience each day in his combat tour to the fullest. Vietnam was all he had left. And he knew that someday it would be all over. When that day arrived, he felt his life would also come to an end.

"Oh, one other thing," Sickles said as they flagged down separate cyclos. "I'm not sure how it fits in yet, but there's a statue of a Thai dancer—some kind of jade lady—mixed in with this puzzle somehow. Rodgers' housegirl says it was missing after the murder. She believes it had a map or something valuable hidden inside. Maybe even drugs."

"I think she's full of shit."

"No, seriously."

"That's a bit melodramatic for Jeff Rodgers, Harry. He didn't mess with drugs. He was one of the rare breed nowadays that doesn't require a morning dose of dope up his arm to feel like a man."

"Asia changes men." Sickles smiled, but it was a sad smile. He knew Stryker was the last man that needed to hear a statement like that.

"Not Rodgers, buddy."

"You said he hadn't written you for several months. That would indicate a change in personality to even me."

"To 'even' you, Harry?"

"Yeah, to 'even me,' Mark," he repeated sarcastically.

"Hhmmm. Well, even a blind cat stumbles over a dead rat now and then," Stryker let that one slip, instantly feeling corny when he said it and knowing Sickles wouldn't appreciate Green Beret humor. *Aw, screw him,* he answered his own thoughts.

"The think tank at C.I.D. has attached considerable importance to locating that jade lady," Sickles continued, holding his arm on the cyclo driver perched up behind Stryker's bench seat on the awkward three-wheeled contraption. Mark kept motioning with his fingers for the driver to leave the gutter and merge into the traffic, but the elderly Vietnamese calmly sat motionless so long as Sickles' heavy forearm remained where it was, body language the C.I.D. man was not ready to see the Special Forces sergeant off. "They think the statue can answer some questions about Rodgers' possible involvement in that black market operation he supposedly busted—the same one conveniently being run in his own neighborhood."

"Gimme a fuckin' break, Harry," Stryker just laughed as his cyclo left the curb. The vehicle, looking like a giant motorized tricycle driven backwards with a customized seat capable of seating two people over the two front wheels, appeared even more absurd when Stryker stood up in it briefly and bared his ass to the C.I.D. agent.

"I think we're talking big bucks here, Stryker!" Sickles yelled after the sergeant, whose bent-over body was quickly escaping down the crowded street. Several couples paused momentarily to take in the spectacle—the men grinning with surprise while the women blushed more than was necessary and hid their eyes in the folds of their silky *ao-dai* gowns.

As the cyclo started to round the first corner, Stryker started to lose his balance and decided to sit down rather than topple out the side with his pants down around his knees.

Sickles suddenly found himself unable to control the laughter building up inside him. "Pull up your trousers, you son of a bitch!" he yelled again, the smile so wide it hurt his usually frowning cheeks, but Stryker's only response was to flip Harry the bird out the rear open window of the canvas sun canopy until the cyclo had disappeared in the misty gloom of night.

Back in the capital, Pvt. Michael Broox pulled the MP jeep to the side of the road behind the Hotel Majestic. The entire squad, exhausted from chasing elements of the city's two hundred thousand gang members all night, struggled out of the Beast and made their way down to the banks of the Saigon River.

After padlocking a thick chain to the steering wheel and brake pedal (Army jeeps did not require an ignition key but had a single toggle starter switch any passerby could operate), Broox grabbed a cooler full of sandwiches and coconut milk and joined his partners.

Though nearly four a.m., fighter jets still raced their engines against the night silence several miles away at Tan Son Nhut airbase, and the glowing eyes of a pack of wild dogs, prowling the other side of the river, filtered in and out of the trees. Above the skyline of bombed out and blackened tenements, rising up behind the MPs, countless flares ringed the metropolis, drifting in and out of the huge castlelike clouds and disappearing beyond the vast rubber plantations surrounding the city.

The restless hush clamped over the capital by the midnight curfew was deceptive. Broox knew that behind the walls of countless French villas crowding the riverbanks life teemed. Their pastel-shaded stucco walls and roofs of red potterylike plates concealed boisterous activity that seldom died before dawn. Now and then the smell of cooking drifted down from a window high in the leaning tenements on the other side of the river, their rin roofs alive with scurrying rats and falling cockroaches.

Occasionally a solitary convoy of military trucks rumbled through the quiet city, but usually Saigon lay silent after midnight. The restrained hum and tingle of energy crawling over the skin was still there, elusive and mysterious, yet powerful as a dormant volcano ready to erupt. He could see it in the eyes of the militiamen standing at checkpoints throughout the city, their faces illuminated by the flickering trash can fires burning at all the major intersections. The fires

106

were there to announce sudden barricades crisscrossing boulevards normally active by day, but they also cast an eerie glow on the features of the unmoving sentries. They never challenged the MPs cruising throughout the concrete canyons on their lonely patrols, but there was always an evil, almost haunting gleam in the bitter eyes of the Vietnamese and they were quick to pounce on any civilians caught wandering the streets at that time of night.

"Hey, MP Joe!" came a high pitched, feminine voice from a dark window behind the Americans.

"Hey, what?" Sergeant Richards called back defiantly, ignoring the code of silence the Decoy Squad usually observed out of the jeep. They considered themselves to be in friendly territory despite the unwritten rule there was no place safe in Saigon after dark.

"Hey, MP Joe!" the seductive voice, barely audible above the sluggish current of the river slapping at its banks, called down to them again. "You want number one quickie?" A chorus of younger, more childlike giggles followed the question.

Suddenly there came a much older woman's voice yelling in rapid Chinese at the tricksters, and even after she slammed the shutters of the seventh floor apartment shut, the MPs below could still hear her scolding her daughters for several minutes.

Broox was beginning to realize how much he was falling under Saigon's spell. The threat of danger in the night alone was enough to hypnotize young Americans patrolling the Orient. Then the hint of adventure, lying in wait down dark alleys, had to compete with the alluring lips and dark almond eyes of an Asian woman spying on you from every street corner, her sensuous miniskirt hiked up above firm, golden thighs as she winked at your passing patrol with those narrow, mystical eyes.

He was beginning to hope the war would never end. He could easily envision a career as an MP in Saigon. He didn't care that he was being selfish with his wishes. What could be more exciting in life?

"What the hell is going on over there?" Sergeant Richards whispered to his men. It appeared the pack of wild dogs on the far side of the river had discovered a dead animal on the wood-littered bank and were trying to drag it from the muck as tiny enraged crabs raced about their feet in the moonlight. Now and then the mongrels would snap at each other and snarl loud enough for the MPs to hear them above the din of the river.

Sergeant Richards took a pair of folding binoculars from his pocket and trained them on the dogs. "Aw, fuck," he muttered, "don't tell me . . ."

After a few seconds, Spec. 4 Bryant got to his feet slowly, as if that would help him see better. "Another body, Sarge?"

Two of the dogs were now fighting viciously over the rapidly decomposing corpse that had floated to the surface of the river at a point only fifty yards downstream from the bridge off which it had been dropped three days earlier.

"Broox!" the sergeant directed, his eyes still trained on the body through the binoculars. "Take Thomas and get back to the jeep. Kick ass up that bridge there and cross over. Check it out. Me and Bryant will remain here and keep an eye on the floater." Richards then pulled a flare from his pocket and scratched its bottom against the whetstone of his survival knife's sheath. The projectile soared skyward like a rocket, showering sparks over the river like a fountain and sending the pack of dogs scattering briefly, their tails between their legs.

Broox and Thomas started up the hill back to the jeep, an urgency in their forced climb they hadn't felt in several nights, but still Michael managed to steal a glimpse up at the balcony where the seductive voice had been. In his mind he saw a beautiful Vietnamese woman standing there, beams of moonlight making her smoothly perfect Asiatic features glow silver as she held out her arms to him. She wore a thin nightgown that had come loose down the middle, and as a breeze swirled about the balcony it grabbed at the silk about her shoulders, pulling it back in a gentle flutter to reveal full,

108

golden breasts—like ripe grapes on a tantalizing vine, ready to burst. The brown, whirling twist of nipples beckoned him with upturned smiles; but they remained soft and dreamlike, waiting patiently for him to lick them erect.

"I don't believe it!" Thomas muttered as they reached the top of the hill, but Broox didn't hear him, seeing instead his maiden on the balcony, a necklace of shimmering gold leaf from ancient temples hanging down between her jutting breasts like ivy clinging to fruit.

The sound of Private Thomas slamming his helmet down onto the pavement jarred Broox back to reality. He couldn't even remember making the long climb up the hillside to the street, the balcony high above him was dark and deserted, and when he turned to look at their jeep he was only mildly surprised to discover it sat atop cinderblocks, all four tires gone and a bag of stinking garbage dumped in the front seat.

"Christ almighty!" Thomas was fuming as he picked up his shattered helmet liner and slammed it down on the blacktop a second time. "I just gotta get the fuck outta this godforsaken country!"

But Broox just sat down resignedly on his own helmet and smiled at the funny-looking MP jeep, its whip radio antenna waving back at him in the breeze like a single blade of sharp elephant grass, out of place so far from the living, breathing jungle strangling the city's outskirts.

"You know, Mikey, this has just got to be the asshole of the whole entire Earth!" Thomas slammed his black helmet with its glowing white letters one last time across the uncaring street.

Broox watched him with a strange rush of intense interest—this crazy man going berserk right in downtown Saigon before his very eyes. This same partner he thought he knew inside out.

The wild dogs down along the riverbank, chased off by the whooshing launch of the flare, had now returned to the corpse. Not impressed by quiet, floating lights drifting so high above

109

them, they had emerged from the dark as the last of the sparks disappeared on the night breeze. Broox could hear the sound of their gnashing teeth tearing the body to shreds again down at the bottom of the hill, and as he watched his partner draw his .45 and walk over to the jeep as if he were going to put it out of its misery, the smile returned to his worried features.

He was beginning to understand what Saigon was doing to him. What she was doing to them all. He waited eagerly for Thomas to fire his pistol because it just wouldn't have been Saigon without the sound of gunfire echoing across the night silence.

IX. SODA POP SURPRISE

Five thousand piasters a month was not a salary to brag about, even in Saigon where life and the cost of living was cheap, but nine-year-old Dong was contented. The wealthy Chinese merchant who so graciously allowed Dong to run the tiny fruit stand at the corner of Phan Dinh Phung and Le Van Duyet maintained no strict standards of employment governing the child's activities—in fact, he even allowed the boy to sleep under the vendor's wagon on rainy nights instead of simply in the gutter . . . so long as Dong was at the stand from dawn to curfew, and no substantial amounts of stock turned up missing when the owner arrived in his supply truck every three days.

Dong received his equivalent of ten American dollars on the first day of each month. The boy's father had been killed five months before his birth when a buried rocket left over from the battles between the French and Viet Minh detonated as he plowed the small plot of desolate farmland cordoned off behind their hut near Dalat.

Even worse, the water buffalo pulling the plow had been killed too, and water buffalo were as valuable as three or four penniless farmers. And of course there was Dong's mother. She had died giving birth to him and, according to the old aunts withering away in Nha Trang, had left him nothing except a bucket full of rice and a battery-operated portable radio that hadn't worked in years.

There were no pictures of his father, but Dong kept in the bottom of his shoeshine box the cracked and faded wallet photo of a tiny, fragile woman in her early twenties, dressed in a light colored *ao-dai* and looking so frightened of the camera she could not even smile.

Dong kept the little black-and-white snapshot wrapped in brittle, yellowing plastic and often dreamed of the woman posing before the serene pond and lifeless jungle although he never knew her. He made a point of it to say a prayer to Buddha every night, asking that good fortune follow the worried-looking woman in the picture on her travels through that faraway land of ghosts and spirits, and that showed unusual discipline considering the age of the youth.

If there was one thing the strict nuns at the orphanage impressed upon him, before he ran away two years ago, it was to be sincere and regimental in his daily prayers to his god. Even if Dong had the last laugh in playing his little joke on the Catholic sisters: he always chanted to Buddha instead of Jesus Christ.

And young Dong wasn't one to take things for granted. He was secretly thankful and appreciative that, unlike most tyrannical storefront managers in Saigon, his master did not object to Dong hustling a little extra shoeshine revenue on the side, so long as he always tried to also sell these customers a banana or two. The easy-going Chinaman frequently drew a giggle from Dong when his jovial, roly-poly figure appeared wobbling around from the rear of the lorry, his flabby arms loaded down with a tall stack of mangos that hid his paunchy face. Yes, Dong was indeed lucky to have this kind old merchant place such trust in him. And it was an added benefit to work for a tradesman who did not tax his laborers to excess like most of the ethnic Chinese running the markets on this side of the bustling city.

A military convoy loaded down with South Vietnamese

112

soldiers appeared up the street that morning and as it rumbled toward Dong's little sidewalk fruit stand, he found himself hoping the long line of escort vehicles would pass by without halting for refreshments. It wasn't so much the clouds of dust following the huge trucks and monstrous tanks which bothered him, even though he often spent an hour after they had passed washing off the moist papaya and sliced tangerines.

It was the soldiers themselves bothered Dong the most. It was not unusual for them to cart off half his inventory without paying, and what was a nine-year-old boy to do against gun-toting men that outnumbered him forty to one? Hadn't it been enough that he already spent all morning carefully watching the suspicious woman in the red dress (a very revealing red dress, he recalled, the likes of which he saw only the classiest bargirls wearing) milling about his fruit collection only to walk off without buying anything when he was busy with a shoeshine customer?

The scowl that made Dong look like an old man appeared automatically as several gunjeeps, laden with QCs, skidded up to his stand. The usual clouds of choking dust that rolled in behind them failed to gag the boy this time as he started into the ARVNs, barely warning them to pay first or he would report their license plate numbers to the Canh-Sat directing traffic down the street. But the soldiers only laughed uproariously, one of them shaking his index finger at Dong in reprimand as he playfully threatened to draft the youngster into the military and send his young ass out into the boonies to fight the VC.

While several of the men started gurgling down the icy bottles of Coca-Cola Dong kept hidden in the bottom of the cooler, another QC reached for an expensive tangerine, bit into it heartily and joined the others in harassing Dong as the juices overflowed from his lips and dripped down over his chin. "You probably aren't even licensed to operate on this corner, now are you, young man?" the QC rattled the question off in a dialect Dong could barely understand, and as the boy reached

113

into his shoebox to produce the legal documents his employer had left with him, the soldier munched down another mouthful of the sweet fruit.

Dong was so startled when the QC began screaming hysterically that he dove right under the fruit stand, convinced a suicide squad of Viet Cong sappers had stabbed the man in the back. Or it could have been any number of other possibilities just as devastating to his business and personal welfare that kept the boy hugging the earth. After several terror-filled seconds had passed, he cautiously peeked out through a crack in the bamboo walls of the wagon and saw the soldier bent over in agony, a bloody razor blade protruding from both his already horribly swollen and shredded lips. Dong, though young, realized he had only a short time to react before the ARVNs came down hard on him. As the man scampered about in little circles, his frantic comrades following close beside him unsure how they could help, Dong took this as his cue to beat a hasty retreat. Scooping up his precious shoeshine box and the day's meager receipts, he crawled down into the sewer drain behind the fruit stand and disappeared amid the confusion.

Across the street, from behind the tissue-thin drapes of a second-story bordello window, pretty Pham Thi Vien had to work hard at suppressing the laughter that seized her tensed, agile frame. She kept long, delicate fingers pressed tightly across her lips as she watched several ARVN soldiers now writhing in agony in the street below. Satisfied with the results of her little escapade, she found herself wishing she had slipped even more shards of glass secretly into the bottles of soda pop when the obnoxious little shoeshine boy was not looking. A couple more razor blades hidden in the tangerines wouldn't have hurt either.

Vien felt her nipples stretch taut against the flimsy negligee clinging down along the curve of her slender body as satisfaction turned into tingling arousal—almost a sexual gratification as more soldiers fell in the street, spitting blood into the gutters.

114

The silky gown covered her only from the middle of the shoulders to a point riding an inch or two below the crest of her shapely hips, the cheeks spread wide due to the relaxed way she leaned against the window sill, kneeling from a chair, catlike, ever watchful of all that transpired outside the misty glass.

The businessman she had been entertaining started to rise from the bed to see what so interested his little short-time girl, but when she noticed this, Vien casually left the window and returned to him, lifting her nightgown from the waist so her breasts jutted out, the already erect nipples brushing against his anxious lips as she plopped down mischievously beside him and drew the sheets up over her face like an embarrassed schoolgirl. Despite her shyness act, the woman in that dimly lit room did not feel the weight of the man as he straddled down atop her. While her eyes stared unblinking at the tiny lizards scurrying about upside-down on the ceiling, her sensitive ears heard not the animal grunting of his lust above her but the birds singing high in the treetops beside a quiet canal that ran through a lonely little village north of Gia Dinh.

Dong never enjoyed roaming the confusing network of sewer tunnels that crisscrossed like ancient catacombs deep beneath the city. Once, when he had taken refuge in the tunnels during a VC rocket attack three years earlier, several huge hungry rats chased him through the dark for miles underground, and the memory had never left him. He often came across the alley children whose lips and eyelids had been nibbled away as they slept in the gutters, and the sight of these outcasts during his daily search for shoeshine customers always took Dong instantly back to that night when rats were hot on his terrified tail, nipping at his feet with their filthy disease-ridden snouts.

Dong was not concerned with pursuing soldiers as he ventured further beneath the city, careful to take only tunnels running uphill, avoiding those that burrowed down into the bowels of the earth—where the dreaded rats lurked. He was confident that once he surfaced several blocks from the commotion he could resume his role as curbside observer, content to watch the impatient Saigonese swarm past him in all directions as they raced against time and the unknown, unsure when their harried life as they knew it might crash to a screaming halt, like so many terrorist rockets, launched outside the city limits by phantoms no one ever saw, their motives completely misunderstood. Yes, Dong was sure other neighborhoods were in need of his renowned shoeshine talents. And in a city with close to a hundred thousand homeless waifs abandoned in the streets—half of them now shoeshine boys like Dong, or child-pimps for other orphans—he felt confident the QCs would not be able to distinguish him from the rest of them.

Dong had pressed his puny shoulders up against several solidly stuck manhole covers before one finally gave way. As he slowly peered out into the wide boulevard, his frail arms shaking as they supported the heavy steel lid mere inches over his protruding head, he spotted the approaching armored personnel carrier just seconds before its giant metal treads rolled over the rusty cover, slamming it back down tightly in place and bouncing the boy roughly onto the webbed floor of the chamber. As he sat there slightly dazed, rubbing the bruise rising on his forehead, he felt a scissorlike attack on the fingers of the hand bracing his limp body. When Dong looked down and saw the cat-sized rat hop onto his hand, a terrible panic seized the boy and he bolted up toward the manhole cover again, forcing it to fly free with the impact of his body.

A second APC tank, its unmanned machine guns swaying from side to side as the vehicle clattered along, bore down upon the boy as he scrambled from the black hole, but Dong had jumped to his feet and dodged from the tank's path right at the last second.

After diving toward the row of parked cars lining the tamarind-shaded avenue, Dong rolled under a delivery van and

116

surveyed the area around him. Through the dust of the last tank in the convoy he could see that this block appeared no different than all the others he had survived on. Old *mamasans* sat beneath huge, brightly colored umbrellas on the hard sidewalk, selling piles of watermelons and pineapples. Storefronts opened entire ground-floor walls, shrouded with iron gates like wide-mouthed shallow caverns, allowing the rush of pedestrians to flow in unobstructed. The shops and pharmacies, running along on Dong's left as far as his tired eyes could see, overflowed with crowds of excited shoppers, some dismounting from the hordes of sputtering motor scooters and creating a massive traffic jam as they paused to inspect something sparkling in the vast sea of wares.

Across the street, beyond the two-way blur of speeding taxis and creeping rickshaws, Dong saw several Westerners sitting along the sidewalk in an open-air restaurant, its chef slicing up fresh shrimp on the grill before them. They applauded as he expertly propelled the prawns across the sizzling plate of black tin, depositing them in the deep frier. The cook was now twirling chopsticks and bits of bean sprouts and celery in the air like some demented drummer to the delight of his audience, but Dong was looking past him, to the towering block-long tent he knew sheltered a portion of the central market. Inside were long rows of stalls selling every variety of seafood and poultry, products which gave the entire block a distinct fragrance.

Dong slowly crawled from under the van and carefully checked his shoeshine box. The different tins of wax and all the brushes and rags were there. And his mother's photograph was firmly planted beneath the small bag of piasters that was his life's savings.

Satisfied he had lost nothing in the sewers except some skin, Dong confidently hoisted the box's sling over his shoulder and headed for the market, hoping to find shelter and a new master.

Officer Jon Toi was not amused when manpower shortages

forced his superiors to reassign him temporarily to unfamiliar parts of the city for traffic control duties at major intersections. The years he had spent learning the faces of crime czars, bordello madams and other underworld figures did him little good ten miles on the other side of town, where all the hostile eyes passing by below his TCP box belonged to strangers.

That was why Toi was not concentrating on the usual things when he noticed a flurry of activity up at the far end of the block, beside a sidewalk fruit stand.

Toi stepped down from his pedestal and started for the commotion, pleasantly surprised when the sound of screeching tires and crashing fenders did not follow the abandoning of his post. The Canh-Sat would have been surprised again to learn the policemen usually assigned to this intersection rarely reported for duty. Instead, they spent their shifts "inspecting" the whorehouses and nightclubs. The drivers on this boulevard were used to navigating the congested traffic circle without the guidance of a TCP officer, and his impressive figure high above the swarm of cars with its swirling white gloves and shiny blasting whistle created more of a curiosity slow down than anything else.

Toi had been spending much of the last month visiting the hotels himself (two weeks had passed since he stumbled upon the body nailed to the closet door). But his inspections rarely went past the desk clerk's station, where he meticulously reviewed the guest roster, searching for a certain name. Toi had responded to several of the recent massage parlor homicides—where a strikingly beautiful woman in a crimson dress had brutally hacked to death her male guests, and the same name appeared in the hotel registry at those crime scenes: Pham V.

Toi had been inspecting several sign-in sheets during his daily rounds, hoping to happen upon this mysterious call girl before she could commit another gruesome slaying. He also made a point of it to reprimand the desk clerks for failing to follow regulations: the majority of them were not requiring

118

that Vietnamese National ID Card numbers be placed after the guest's name, which was necessary under martial law. And that included passport numbers for foreigners. Even Americans with a handful of greenbacks under the table who didn't want their true identity logged for posterity beside that of a hooker had better start presenting valid identification.

Toi's gun hand rested on the butt of his Colt Python as he sprinted quickly into the midst of the wounded soldiers. The sight of several ARVNs rolling around on the ground clutching their throats and a half dozen broken Coke bottles littering the ground instantly told him to beware of a VC ambush, but his alert eyes met only those of bewildered soldiers, helpless to remove the splinterlike fragments of glass imbedding themselves deeper in the victims' throats with each tortured swallow. Ambulances began arriving as Toi fastened the leather strap of his holster back in place over his revolver's hammer. Whoever did this was long gone.

As more policemen pulled up to the scene, Toi directed the mostly young Canh-Sats to commence questioning the sidewalk vendors gathering up and down the curbline. The first thing to do was determine who operated the now-abandoned fruit stand.

Two QCs had the soldier with the razor blade jammed between his lips down on his back in the street. As they sat on his chest and held down his shoulders, a hardened lieutenant reached down and gently grabbed hold of the double-edged razor, ignoring the muffled pleas of the injured man. With one quick motion he jerked the razor from the soldier's swollen mouth and jumped back before any blood could splash across his uniform.

Officer Toi turned away from the ugly mutilation and started for the hotel across the street. There were now plenty of Canh-Sats present—men who knew the territory much better than himself—and he'd just as soon leave the bulk of the investigation to them. He had already seen enough gore since becoming a policeman to last him two lifetimes. He had never been an ambulance chaser though unusual crimes of violence did intrigue him.

As he reached the steps of the parlor, Toi hesitated then turned around to face the wounded soldiers. He glanced about to see if anybody was watching him, then he pulled the pocket camera from its plastic holder on his gun belt. After taking one quick shot of the men still rolling around on the ground, careful to properly position the sea of emergency vehicles with their flashing red and blue lights in the background, he walked up to the QC with the lips split apart and snapped off another photo before retreating to the sidewalk.

"I need to see your registry," he was telling the desk clerk a few minutes later, and just as Toi's eyes struck upon the name "Pham V.," there came a horrifying scream from one of the rooms above—a man's voice, crying out in terrible pain.

"The girl in the red dress!" Toi yelled at the startled desk clerk. "Which room?"

"Eleven."

Toi drew his service weapon and raced up the dark stairway toward Room Eleven, hoping as he moved swiftly down the gloomy corridor that this phantom reeking of evil would not be gone before he got there, instantly disappointed when he kicked the flimsy door in and discovered she had indeed already vanished.

The stocky Vietnamese man who had bedded down this wicked beauty now lay in a tub full of blood in the bathroom—his throat tied to the water faucet with a twisted clothes hanger, and his legs missing above the knees, hacked off with a machete.

X. IN LIEU OF HOSTAGE NEGOTIATIONS

"Listen to this," Private Broox told the other members of the Decoy Squad. Their black MP jeep was parked behind the Hotel Majestic, near the place the vehicle had been stripped only four days before, but now it was four o'clock in the afternoon and the men were joking good-naturedly with each other about the planned May Day celebration that coming weekend. Broox folded his three-day-old copy of *The Stars & Stripes* newspaper and concentrated briefly on an unfamiliar word before continuing, while Sergeant Richards climbed back into the jeep. He was loaded down with small plastic baggies containing iced coffee, purchased at the fruit stand across the street.

"Listen to this," Broox repeated for Richards' benefit. "Says here the Vietnamese are really into celebrating this May Day holiday, and the police chief and the president are arguing about firecrackers."

"May Day ain't even a Viet holiday," decided Spec. 4 Bryant as he curled a cement-filled "barbell" can with his left hand and noisily slurped at the coffee straw with the other.

"The Vietnamese celebrate *any*thing," Private First Class Thomas informed him, "whether it's their holiday or not. You just tell 'em someone somewhere is celebrating and they just feel obligated, out of respect of course, to celebrate too. Hell, nothing wrong with that." Thomas noticed that his belly was sticking out a bit over his customized chrome belt buckle just then, and he hastily drew in his breath and glanced about to see if any of the other MPs had noticed. "Say, anybody know how many calories in this stuff?"

"Whatta you care?" asked Richards, "you work out two hours every night anyhow, right?"

"Don't do the bum no good," laughed Bryant heartily and he leaned over to slap Thomas on the stomach.

"Says here," Broox was still reading the U.S. Armed Forces publication, "the president plans to participate himself in one of the May Day parties at the embassy and is considering declaring it a day off for the working class."

"Tell someone who cares," muttered Bryant as he reached the bottom of the coffee but continued sucking at the crushed ice with the straw.

"Are we part of the working class?" Thomas leaned over toward Sergeant Richards this time.

"Says here the police chief, though, recommends against any displays of fireworks and warns that such activities would invite the Viet Cong to mount a sneak attack on the capital, their initial bursts of rifle fire going undetected because they'd be confused with or mistaken for the firecrackers."

"Ah, that old police chief is a man after my own heart," declared Thomas. "He'll keep the president in line."

"Hey, MP Joe—you want refill?" The young vendor from the fruit stand, a boy of only nine, had walked up to the Decoy Squad with a pile of delicately balanced baggies full of coffee loaded on his left shoulder.

"Refills are on the house, right, kid?" Bryant held out his empty sack. "Just like Dunkin' Donuts."

"On house?" The Vietnamese boy cocked his eye up at the huge MP in a humorous display of puzzlement.

"Free, you little junior VC!"

Young Dong kicked Bryant in the shin and threw him a subdued scowl that made the other MPs laugh. "I no VC! VC number ten!" he declared.

"Jesus Christ, Tim," complained Richards, "give the kid a nickel."

"What for, Sarge?" Bryant stood up in the jeep feigning mild shock. His mouth hung open in mock dissatisfaction. "This coffee's not even warm!"

"It's not supposed to be, you douche bag!" Thomas clamped a heavy forearm down on his partner's shoulder and forced him back down in his seat. "That's why they call it ice coffee."

Richards flipped the boy a dime and reached for another bag. He held it up to the sun briefly, looking for any foreign objects that might be floating around inside the plastic.

"Says here good old Senator Barry Goldwater is talking nukes again," Broox continued scanning the paper as he switched to the last page. "Says we should start defoliating the jungles of Vietnam with low-grade atomic weapons."

"What's low grade?" Specialist Bryant quipped.

"Kinda like your brain," Thomas told him, but Bryant ignored the remark.

"You want number one shoeshine, MP Joe?" Dong was leaning close to Sergeant Richards, his buffer cloth already out.

"See, what I tell you, Sarge?" Bryant nodded his head at Richards. "Be nice to the little squirts, next thing you know they're leaning all over you and you wake up the following day infested with crabs!"

"Christ, knock it off, Bryant!" the sergeant shifted nervously in his seat and began scratching his elbow absent-mindedly.

"Ah, that Goldwater is a man after my own heart," said a smiling Thomas. "Just blow this friggin' country right off the face of the Earth!" He made a loud explosion with his lips and slowly arced his arms above his head to represent a mushrooming radiation cloud.

"*Every*one's a man after your own heart!" Broox added sarcastically. "And speaking of sex, how far are you on that

123

stupid goals sheet of yours?"

"Goals sheet?" interrupted Bryant, suddenly smiling in evil anticipation.

"Yeah, he wants to screw one whore in every capital of Asia without catching the clap."

"You gotta be kidding!"

"Not in every capital of Asia," Thomas corrected him. "In the Orient, my friend. The Orient."

"What the hell's the difference, cunt breath?"

"There's a big difference, you jerkoff!" Thomas brought his fist back to slam one into Bryant. "But a worm of your caliber couldn't be expected to know that."

Sergeant Richards held his arm up between the two MPs, preventing them, at least temporarily, from killing each other. "So how far *are* you?" he asked, a look of genuine curiosity in his eyes.

"Well, Sarge, I hit Taiwan and Hong Kong on my last thirty-day leave. So that makes three countries left. Burma, Laos and China."

"They'll never let you in China." Richards started to explain the drawbacks of holding military police identification, but Broox interrupted.

"Hong Kong didn't count, Anthony!"

"Whatta ya mean it didn't count? It cost me fifty bucks for that piece of ass!"

"Fifty bucks?" Richards asked incredulously. He never knew anyone before who had paid more than five bucks for an all-nighter in the 'Nam.

Broox was now laughing uncontrollably. "And he caught the clap!"

"Did not! Did not!" Thomas was now climbing over the sergeant's lap to get at Broox. "I just had the drips from accidentally drinking some rusty water in Wanchai!"

Sergeant Richards shrugged his shoulders, requesting neutrality as he looked helplessly down at the Vietnamese.

"Dinky dau," the young shoeshine boy concluded, uttering

124

the phrase in his language for crazy as he watched Thomas chasing Broox down the street with a night stick raised high over his head. "Bookoo dinky dau!"

Two blocks away, Saigon policeman Jon Toi was standing in the shadows of an alley doorway, partially hidden from the people scurrying about Quach Thi Trang Square, near the central market. He had been following the girl in the red miniskirt now for several hours, abandoning his TCP box on Le Loi Street just about at high noon, when the midday heat was most unpleasant.

Though Toi would be the first to admit that red was a favorite color among the city's prostitutes, and that more and more Vietnamese women were beginning to wear the Western-style dresses, there was something about this girl that had sent an icy shiver through him when her taxi passed beneath his TCP pedestal in the middle of the intersection.

Perhaps it was the way her dark, unblinking eyes met his and locked on—the same way the woman fleeing the mutilation murder at the Purple Dragon weeks earlier had stared at him, totally unafraid. On both occasions Toi had felt an intense fear of evil settle over him as the woman briefly confronted him, then were gone—the sight of their vicious, mocking sneers remaining for several minutes afterwards. But Toi could not be positive the woman he now followed was the same one he had seen fleeing the pleasure palace. That first encounter had been too brief. So for now he would have to satisfy his anxieties by being patient and practicing the surveillance techniques they had taught him in the training academy, even though he hadn't used them in years.

Toi detected several shades of personality as he trailed the woman. She would summon a taxi that had already passed her by, ignoring closer, more convenient vehicles, then haggle over price for several minutes before pointing her flawless nose in the air and marching off in a huff, mindful to flash

125

some leg at the cabbie as she stepped back up out of the gutter.

As the woman glided into the open-air sidewalk cafe lining the edge of Cathedral Square, Toi jotted down the license plates of all the blue and yellow Renault taxis she had flagged down, and made a mental note to check later with them to see where she had wanted to go.

Officer Toi couldn't help but be mesmerized by the beauty of this woman, her straight jet-black hair falling like strands of reflective silk all the way to her narrow, teasing haunches. Toi had never been disloyal to his wife, but as he watched this tall, slender enchantress slip the thongs off her tired feet and carry them loosely in long graceful fingers, the sensual slap of her bare feet on the hot sidewalk aroused a desire in his loins he had not felt in years.

The woman stopped at a fruit stand midway down the block and selected a large banana which she slowly peeled in front of the storekeeper before paying. Without any words spoken between them, the middle-aged Chinaman, resting his arms on his pot belly as he squinted through thick black glasses, watched with growing excitement as she touched the head of the banana with the tip of her tongue gently, then slowly licked the entire stem down one side and up the other. The fruit vendor, now smacking his lips in anticipation and wonder, jumped back a couple feet when the woman slowly brought her face closer to his—the banana now almost entirely sucked in by her own thick, voluptuous lips—and suddenly chomped down hard on the banana, slicing it neatly in half with her teeth.

Without a word, the woman in the revealing, low-cut dress tossed the leftover peel back onto the fruit wagon and turned to leave, expertly shifting her firm hips in a fluid sway as she walked off down the sidewalk.

The tart never looked back, and after several seconds of watching her float away on the mild breezes swirling about downtown, the Chinaman shook his head from side to side in disappointment and went back to carting his tangerines.

Toi watched the woman approach an American sailor sitting

126

alone in one of the open-air restaurants. The man, in his early thirties with hair cropped close and the traditional seaman's white, floppy dixie-cup-and-bell-bottom uniform hiding an underweight, poorly exercised body, was writing on what appeared to be postcards. At first, he just looked up at the woman's solicitation with mild irritation on his face, then he ignored her totally and went back to his writing.

The woman stomped her foot down one time to get his attention again, and Toi saw one unintelligible word leave the sailor's lips. The woman then yelled some choice Vietnamese insults at the American, called him a "Cheap Charlie," and sauntered off down the sidewalk like an enraged tigress, her step losing little of its enticing bounce.

The sailor paused a few seconds in his writing, finally looked up at the woman as her racy figure began to merge with those of shoppers departing stores and shops along the way. The American abandoned his postcards on the table, hastily left a tip, then hustled to catch up with the hooker and wrapped his arm gently around her shoulder as if they were old mates, simply settling a domestic quarrel.

After a few brief seconds of feigning embarrassment and injured pride, the woman put her arms around the seaman's waist, changed her gait to a more relaxed sway again, and led the American through the doors of the Xin Loi bar. Toi followed at a discreet distance, trying to decide if he should take off his uniform shirt or not. The delay in hiding it might permit the death of the American or the escape of the woman. On the other hand, entry to any bar by a uniformed Canh-Sat not on the establishment's payoff list automatically activated a complicated series of silent alarms designed to shut down the gambling dens, narcotics deals, or unnatural sex shows being performed for private members and their "guests."

Toi had seen those backroom floor shows before. For ten American greenbacks he had been treated to a disgusting "talent show" of several women varying in age from fifteen to fifty, performing acts ranging in variety from whiskey bottles

127

secreted into body cavities to sexual liaisons with excited monkeys or anxious mongrels. The scenes had repulsed Toi at first, but he always found himself drawn back to those shady backrooms again and again whenever word hit the streets a new show had come to town.

Toi elected to leave the uniform on, and after entering the bar, he paused a few moments just inside the doorway to allow his eyes to adjust to the dim light.

Toi breezed past the cramped central bar after determining the couple was not at the counter or any of the tables and headed for the back quickie stalls.

The Canh-Sat scanned the informal registry the manager kept for future blackmailing purposes and observed that the couple signed in as Philip Anderson and Lisa Lee. Toi frowned without knowing it, slightly irritated the woman had adopted an English first name—as so many women who patronized the Americans were doing—but then he thought of his many friends at the 716th MP Battalion and his anger cooled immediately. The registry showed the couple had paid three dollars for room fifteen, though Toi observed the original number had been scratched out. Still, he was not overly suspicious of the change of rooms. Many tenants switched hotel rooms when they discovered too many crabs hopping about or stained sheets that hadn't been changed yet.

Toi quietly drew his revolver, locked the hammer back on single action, then walked softly over to room fifteen. When he reached the partition at the end of the dark hallway he cautiously tested the doorknob and found it unlocked.

Deciding to wait a few minutes to allow the couple to get undressed—that was one of Toi's weak points: he loved busting prostitutes while their legs were spread wide—he retreated quietly and rested his back against the opposite wall. Toi failed to notice that the door behind his left ear was slightly ajar, but he did feel an incredible force in the air, an uneasiness pressing against him in that dark corridor. As the hairs began to raise on the back of his neck, he nervously gave the couple in

128

room fifteen another sixty slowly counted seconds then rushed through the door.

Toi was seized with intense horror as he stumbled in through the blackness and came face to face with the mangled corpse of the nude sailor. He was hanging from a rafter in the ceiling— his throat stretched grotesquely by a noosed lamp cord, his tongue and popping eyes bulging out at him just as they had in the man's last seconds of tortured life. Toi knew instantly that this was no suicide—the man's hands were tied behind his back, as though they were preparing for a sadistic round of sex and the expert with the mysterious almond eyes had pulled a surprise on him. Blood still flowed freely from a stab wound over the heart, and the policeman knew it would be useless to cut the victim down and begin efforts to revive him.

Instead of searching the rest of the room for the woman, Toi's buried superstitions surfaced, got the best of him, and he slowly backed out of the room and into the hallway—praying to Buddha the man's ghost would not choose to chase him. Just then the door from the opposite stall flew open and the woman in the red dress charged out and grabbed Toi from behind. She emitted a blood curdling, deranged scream as she grabbed the policeman's hair with her left hand, jerked his head back and placed a long, gleaming straight razor against his throat.

As he was seized in the clutches of this raving maniac, Toi's revolver discharged accidentally and the bullet travelled across the corridor, back into room fifteen, where it struck the dead sailor in the abdomen with a sickening *thump*. The body swung around slightly with the impact, then returned to its original position, the American's eyes still locked on Toi's. A second later, the corpse, already bloating with internal bleeding and loosened by the shock of the magnum exploding into it, emptied its swollen bladder down one leg onto the floor below in one last act of defiance as the American's soul said goodbye to a hostile land that had yet to show him the slightest kindness.

The sound of the urine splashing down onto the dusty bamboo floor was the only noise on that floor of the Xin Loi "boarding house" until the woman holding Toi spoke. "Why do you follow me all day, Canh-Sat?" she demanded in rapid Vietnamese, the whisper and calmness of the words frightening Toi even more. A killer aware of a police tail who still had the guts to murder again would never hesitate to stab a blundering traffic cop. Toi felt the straight razor digging into his Adam's apple, preventing him from swallowing his panic. "You die today," she decided then and there, not allowing Toi to answer her question.

The policeman looked across at the corpse grinning a grotesque smile of relief across the hall at him, and he closed his eyes tightly, hoping their souls would go separate ways and not clash after the woman cut out his throat.

"Was that a shot?" Private Broox put down his newspaper and perked up an ear dramatically with a calloused hand.

Bryant sat up in his seat immediately upon hearing the discharge on the other side of the fancy Hotel Majestic. "I think you're right," he agreed.

"Aw, cool it you guys," Thomas pleaded. "It's break time. Just relax. Somebody's always shooting somebody in Saigon." But Broox and Bryant had already started off down the street on foot, and they soon came across the shoeshine boy, Dong, waving at them from the steps of the Xin Loi bar.

"Five greenbacks or ten bucks MPC—" Dong was holding out his hand with an amused smirk—"and I tell you where boom-boom come from." But the two MPs brushed past him and into the Xin Loi.

Instinctively, Bryant rushed through the center room cluttered with tables and headed for the boarding rooms the Decoy Squad had often raided in the past.

"Okay, now calm down, lady," the MP was requesting of the woman in the red dress when Broox caught up to him. Toi's eyes darted back and forth between the two Americans, while the restless lunatic holding him hostage pressed the blade in even closer, causing a slight stream of blood to spurt forth.

"Now, honey," Bryant continued with a confident smile across his face. "You want to kill this useless Canh-Sat, that's fine—that's your business. Just give me a second to get a shot of this for my scrapbook!" And to the amazement of Broox, his partner pulled a pocket camera from his thigh pocket and calmly attached a flash cube to it.

As the woman stared with surprise and wonder at the outrageous conduct of the MP, Bryant slowly brought the Kodak up with his left hand, clicked the shutter loose and set off the blinding flash. With his right hand he simultaneously drew his .45 pistol, rushed forward placing the barrel against the woman's unseeing face and popped off one hastily aimed explosive round into her gaping mouth, knocking her body back limp against the wall.

Toi flew like a rocket from her gasp, and as the woman crumpled to the floor, the back of her lower skull torn off by the exiting hollow-point bullet, her shocked and betrayed eyes looked up at Bryant for a couple of seconds, a drawn out, obscure word gurgling in her shredded throat, before she collapsed and died at their feet.

Bryant, still grinning despite the tide of bile rushing about in his stomach, walked over to Toi and playfully forced the camera into his weak arms. "For you, Toi. Stick *that* picture in your collection, brother. We're going to get you a Pulitzer Prize yet!"

"Even if it kills you," Broox added.

XI. JUST POPPING CAPS

One after another, the monsoon storms of spring rolled into Saigon, practically halting traffic in the city for hours at a time and putting a damper on the scheduled May Day activities. Small, scattered celebrations were still held at a few of the plantation barracks and some homes in Cholon and Phuto, but the parades scheduled to crisscross the major boulevards downtown were cancelled for the most part due to the heavy rains. The short notice given the National Police resulted in hundreds of barricades being left up all across town, which caused many of the usually congested avenues to remain quiet and deserted even during the normal rush hours in the afternoon.

Former MP Jeff Rodgers stood beside the flapping tarp hastily erected to protect a section of sidewalk cafe from the blustery downpours, staring at the run-down apartment house across the street.

"Why you no come out of rain?" A chubby waitress with short hair leaned out and looked up at the American quizzically. "We have special on egg rolls today. Today Friday. 50p. We have special on Fridays. You come inside and sit down. Enjoy. Only 50p."

The teenager started to tug at Jeff's arm, but he ignored her. He pulled free and started across Tung Chou Street, failing to notice the thick sheets of rain pounding down on him in separate, wind-swept layers that seemed to snap at the skin and actually stung at times. Rodgers checked the time on his watch: 3:30 p.m. This was the seventh day spent staking out Jackson's apartment and it appeared to be another dry run.

Each time he monitored the compound, Rodgers used different shifts staggered to cover the street an entire twenty-four hour period, since he was unsure when the deserter came and went.

Rodgers entered the building through the rear door like he always did, checked for any signs of activity in the stairwell or hallway, then silently climbed to the fourth floor and tested the doorknob of room forty-two.

Still locked. He had to smile. That crafty Stubbs had told him forty-two Tung Chou, not room forty-two of twenty-four Tung Chou Street. That last act of defiance and plastic loyalty had cost Rodgers precious time, but he had managed to locate the deserter's flat anyway.

He ran his fingers along the top crack of the frame, inspecting the strip of Scotch tape he had placed there a week earlier. Still undisturbed. The door hadn't been opened in seven days. Unless of course Stubbs was no dummy and had noticed the tape immediately—was just replacing it whenever he left the room. *"The dirtball must be lying low,"* he thought out loud, instantly looking about to see if anyone had appeared in the dim corridor that might have heard him talking to himself again. But the building remained quiet. No signs of life whatsoever.

Rodgers slowly took his .45 from the shoulder holster under his windbreaker and pulled the slide back a half inch until he could see that there was indeed a hollow-point round locked in the chamber, ready to go, anxious to do its job, complete its mission. Rodgers laughed again as all these objectives of a simple bullet flashed through his mind and concentrated on not answering the thoughts out loud again.

He twisted the knob, then pressed his shoulder lightly

against the door. Solid. He might not be able to force it open. There would be a lot of racket and he'd probably wrench his shoulder. Breaking down doors was not as easy as in the shoot-'em-up movies. Especially for a man weighing only 160 pounds who now was subsisting on only two meals of rice per day.

Rodgers also pressed against the thick planks supporting the door frame and realized there'd be no going in through the wall. Much more chance of getting hurt that way. *Think it through—what you gonna do?* he asked himself in rhyme, accepting the fact he was too small to crash into the room uninvited, and he wondered why he was so unrealistic about so many other things.

A door slammed down on the ground floor and footsteps started slowly up the stairs. Rodgers holstered his automatic and walked down to the far end of the corridor, away from the stairwell, unscrewing ceiling lightbulbs overhead as he went.

The footsteps stopped on the third floor however, and when a knock was followed by a soft exchange of whispers in Vietnamese, then a door slowly creaking open and slamming back shut, Rodgers went back down the stairs and into the street.

Three days earlier he had felt panic rise in his gut when the possibility that Jackson had fled Saigon surfaced in his thoughts. He hastily checked train, airport and bus depot passenger lists and manifests, despite the danger so much exposure in public terminals created, and it wasn't until he had reviewed hundreds of pages of records that he realized even Jackson would not be foolish enough to use his real name.

Disappointed, he had returned to the open-air cafe across from the deserter's apartment building and spent endless hours in the rain, watching who came and went from behind folded pages of a soggy Saigon *Post*.

Only last night he had taken a cyclo back to Pershing Field, the compound housing his old MP battalion, and had waited outside the barbed fenceline behind the shanty-town walls across the street until when he knew the gate guards would be

135

changing shifts and would be carelessly away from their posts.

Pershing Field was only a little more than one or two square miles in size. Its four-sided complex had sentry towers in each corner, but only two were manned, and these by underpaid civilian PFs (Popular Forces) who usually slept on duty unless a water buffalo or goat got caught up in the crude empty-can-and-trip-flare warning network strung out along the perimeter.

The compound had one main gate on the southeast side and held four wooden barracks for each platoon of the five-company battalion. There was also an NCO club which the enlisted ranks were allowed to patronize so long as they didn't get too drunk and start punching out any of the sergeants. There was even an outdoor theater that showed all the latest John Wayne movies. Vietnamese QCs often were allowed to attend these flicks, mainly because the Americans got a kick out of how the ARVNs always cursed loudly when the Indians appeared on screen and called them "dirty VC."

Dozens of perfectly aligned military police jeeps were parked outside the Orderly Room and between two of the barracks, and groups of the men could sign out one of the few unmarked units to ferry a couple miles over to the larger MACV annex, where bowling alleys, an Olympic-size swimming pool, and more theaters could be found.

Next to the main gate was a huge building known as the meat market where Vietnamese women congregated in bleachers beside the see-through, wire-mesh screen running the entire length of one wall. The girls then waited for their boyfriends or even the rare husband to sign them in on-post to watch the Vietnamese band, CBC, playing the latest American hits at the club. There was also a large number of hookers who frequented the meat market and would let any stranger sign them into the camp. The couple usually then headed for the barracks, which were off limits to the Victor-November Foxtrots (Vietnamese National Females) as the MPs referred to them, for a two-dollar short-time before the midnight curfew cleared the bleachers

136

and the streets.

The two MPs reporting for duty at the main gate beside the meat market were required to show up thirty minutes early so information between shifts could be exchanged, but since little intelligence activity was taking place around Pershing at that time of year, most of the MPs spent the half hour inspecting the prostitutes' VD cards and comparing notes on the girls themselves. This included giving them number ratings in accordance with the success or failure of past dates, and noticing who was new in town and who the regulars were—the girls who had been tricking at the meat market since day one, and would be there long after the present MPs rotated back stateside were to be avoided.

So it was during this quasi-romantic interlude in their otherwise businesslike twelve-hour tour of duty when the usually dedicated MPs were away from their posts that Rodgers slipped through the main gate that night, rivaling the coolest of VC types, posing as just another off-duty soldier with a floppy boonie-hat hiding his face.

He went straight to the fourth platoon barracks of Bravo Company knowing that, unless some unpredicted new policy had changed the scheduling procedures, his old team would be out on the Canh Luc Hon Hop patrols with the Canh-Sats downtown, and that the barracks would be dark. The Provost Marshal, commander of the battalion and chief of police in the military, had the foresight to assign graveyard MPs to one building and daytime cops to another so that mixed rotating shifts would not keep waking each other up. But Rodgers had not anticipated that his footlocker would be empty, the padlock chopped in half with wire cutters and still lying on the floor where it had dropped. In fact, the entire hooch had been moved around, and another man's gear—a new MP—was now neatly piled where Rodgers' had once been. "Should have realized they'd confiscate everything after thirty days." He was talking to himself again. "After I became a deserter."

The sight of the neatly polished brass and chrome webgear-

137

belt buckles hanging from bedposts, and the rows of spit-shined boots lined up beneath the bunks tugged at Rodgers' gut. He really missed these wonderful guys. He missed the pride he felt when he wore the uniform. Hell, it wasn't even work to hit the streets with his buddies. It was—had been—fun, could hardly be considered military hardship or years lost out of one's life.

Rodgers pulled out his wallet like he always did when these guilt feelings over his desertion from the U.S. Army surfaced. He flipped the photo section open to the pictures of Mai and the pang left him. Like it always did. He stared at the photo of them standing before the multicolored fountains of the Rex theater and the hatred toward her murderers welled up inside him again. He glanced over to where his locker had once been and wondered briefly who it was now that had his little notebook with all the information on the six blacks he had arrested five months earlier.

Rodgers folded the wallet back up after the dark, trusting eyes staring back at him brought the tears again, and he walked over to his old cot. He picked up the picture frame lying on the o.d. green pillow. The photo depicted a black woman back in the states with an infant in her arms. She was dressed conservatively in a sweater and slacks, snow falling through the window behind her. In the corner of the frame was a smaller snapshot of an elderly couple, also black. *Probably his folks*, Rodgers decided. *Jesus, they've replaced me with a lousy spade.* He walked up to the footlocker and read the piece of masking tape over the double doors, identifying the owner: "DAVIS, CRAIG. PRIVATE E-2."

A jeep carrying four MPs rolled up, unexpectedly, outside, and Rodgers calmly slipped under the new man's bunk, wondering as one of the soldiers jumped out and started up the stairs whether he'd turn Rodgers in if he caught him.

There were some of the men, he was sure, who'd be sympathetic to his situation, but there were others who'd like nothing better than to blast him out of his boots, ex-cop or not.

"Hurry up, Thomas!" Sergeant Richards called up to the MP racing toward the top floor of the barracks. "We ain't got all friggin' night!"

Rodgers could hear two other men laughing down in the jeep, then Thomas' scuffed up boots ran past his hiding place and stopped across the aisle in the opposite hooch. The EM living quarters were made a bit more private by using bamboo curtains purchased downtown or sliding the tall lockers back-to-back like partitions but there were no walls. Rodgers could see a trunk fly open after his old buddy fumbled with the combination lock for several minutes in his haste.

"Hurry up, douche bag!" came an order from outside, and Rodgers recognized Michael Broox's voice below.

"Come on, Anthony!" Bryant called. "Either shit or get off the pot!"

Rodgers watched as Thomas dug out one of the rare, almost precious spools of harsh, GI toilet paper hidden in the bottom of the trunk, then ran for the latrine at the end of the hallway. "Christ, that's the last time I take one of those lousy malaria pills," he muttered under his breath as he unbuckled his web-belt on the run.

After Thomas had locked himself in a stall, Rodgers got up and walked slowly over to the trunk and peered inside. Right on top were what he sought: several loaded .45 magazines. He scooped them up quietly and placed them in separate pockets for less noise. He pulled a pen from one of the khaki uniforms hanging on a wall nail and wrote a brief note on the back of a loose Vietnamese Cross of Gallantry citation lying atop some souvenir VC battle flags: *I owe you, Tony. Remember Mai. Jeff R.* He dropped the message into the trunk, crawled back under the bunk and waited.

After a few seconds, the toilet flushed and Thomas came running back out into the dark hallway. He entered his hooch, tripped on a stray helmet, uttered some choice profanities, tossed the roll of toilet paper back in the trunk and slammed the lid shut without noticing the clips were missing.

139

"I'm coming! I'm coming!" he assured the Decoy Squad as he rushed back down the stairs, taking several steps at a time.

"Holy shit, Thomas! We ain't got all night," Broox razzed him on. "Get your fat ass down here. Uncle Sam doesn't pay you to have rectal problems on government time!"

"Holy shit?" Sergeant Richards turned to look at Broox. "You *do* have a way with words, Private."

"Did I really say that?" Broox looked wide eyed at Richards, mocking his self-declared innocence.

As Broox spun the Beast in donuts across the gravel parking lot outside the barracks, Rodgers looked up at one of the gleaming belt buckles Thomas had left hanging on a bedpost. The personalized inscription said, "YEA, THOUGH I WALK THROUGH THE VALLEY OF DEATH AND DINKS, I SHALL FEAR NO EVIL. FOR I AM THE MEANEST SON OF A BITCH IN THE VALLEY."

Rodgers smiled upon reading it and he thought back to his own customized webgear, now confiscated by the provost marshal. Two buzzards were engraved on the chrome buckle and they overlooked a rice paddy full of Vietnamese farmers wearing straw conical hats and leading water buffalos. The inscription read, "PATIENCE MY ASS: I'M GONNA KILL SOMETHING!"

After the sound of the four rowdy MPs faded off in the night, Rodgers climbed down out of the barracks and cautiously approached the main gate. To his surprise, the night shift MPs were busy frisking one of the Vietnamese cooks who was notorious for misappropriating pots and pans, and with little effort he slipped out of the installation undetected.

When he had walked several blocks from the main gate, Rodgers flagged down one of the noisy, three-wheeled cyclos and directed the driver, a fifty-year-old moonlighting ARVN soldier wearing cutoff jeans and a British safari pith helmet, to take the roundabout way back to Bis Ky Dong Street. The grizzled veteran chomped down on his stubby cigar, nodded his head with a determined, challenged expression creasing his jaw, then swung the vehicle carefully out into heavy traffic.

They had only travelled a half mile when several sirens sounded just behind the cyclo. Rodgers shifted his hand under his windbreaker and rested it on the pistol under his arm, then looked back through the canvas-covered window between the driver's knees and saw three MP jeeps with their red roof lights lazily twirling against the night, rapidly gaining on the cyclo. He was going to tell the driver to keep rolling at all costs, but the top speed on a cyclo was about twenty-five mph. The patrol jeeps were rushing down on them like gangbusters, and the driver had taken it upon himself to swerve to the side even before Rodgers could draw his weapon.

The MP jeeps split up and recklessly passed the cyclo on both sides then continued racing onward to some distant robbery or assault, paying little attention to the cyclo or its white passenger. Rodgers watched the first unit whiz by in a blur of white and black MP helmets and dazzling red strobes, but the second and third jeeps happened to shift gears just as they were passing the cyclo. They paused in their flight just long enough for the deserter to make out faces on all the men aboard. He knew most of the them, but there were also nervous newbies in the back seat of one. Rodgers watched the veteran cops with nostalgic interest: the driver was laughing at something his passenger had said while managing to steer the vehicle with one hand; his other hand nonchalantly balanced a cup of coffee in its palm, and now and then he would take a gulp out of boredom.

The third jeep was loaded down with four MPs who appeared to be laughing hilariously—one was bent over holding his stomach—at some story the man riding shotgun was telling. Rodgers watched the Vietnamese pedestrians sidestepping the patrols calmly, most not even giving them a second thought though some of the women glanced anxiously at the speeding jeeps to see if their boyfriends might be aboard.

Rodgers missed the street. He missed the action, the camaraderie, the danger. As the three MP jeeps grew smaller

141

up ahead and finally disappeared into a jungle of tenements, Rodgers wondered at what made men learn to love racing past the slow routine of "normal" people, barreling at high speed toward men crazier than them, toward situations that could easily leave them face down on the wet street, dead.

The rain had subsided to a warm drizzle as an accusing finger of the storm pointed down Tung Chou Street at Rodgers, but he ignored the omen and concentrated instead on a double rainbow extending out over the city. It was the afternoon following his near miss with the three MP patrols, but the blur of red lights and tough faces stayed with him as he watched ominous thunderheads approach from the west at a fast clip. Tongues of crackling lightning licked out in several different directions along the edges of the black, billowing clouds, and he could taste the moisture in the air as it swirled down on the city behind the hot breeze.

Rodgers took the book of matches from his shirt pocket and looked over the gold-etched inscription again: "THE SUGAR SHACK, 66 Tu Do Street." The words instantly brought back visions of the black man from whom he'd taken the matches. The visions showed him shooting an American Army deserter in the kneecaps and the face. Then going through his pockets and retaining the book of matches and a wallet photo of three black men posing together.

Rodgers ran his fingers along the front of his neck absent-mindedly—down across the throat and along his chest. He had only just realized he was missing the arrowhead necklace he had bought in Atlanta while attending the MP Academy. The monsoon storm rolled slowly closer, until in its race across the noon sky it blocked out the sun and cast an eerie darkness over the land. He tried to recall where he might have lost it and whether or not having lost it might return to haunt him later.

"Hey, Joe—you want taxi?" A young cabbie with thick, black sunglasses hiding his eyes had pulled over to the curb

142

after navigating the barricades at the end of the block. Rodgers stared blankly at the man for several seconds then got up from the sidewalk coffee table and leaned in the taxi's window. He showed the driver the matchbook.

"Take me to this bar," he said and ran his finger under the Vietnamese and Chinese characters in case the cabbie didn't read English. "Take me to number sixty-six Tu Do."

The driver shook his head eagerly after inspecting the matchbook and waved Rodgers into the rear seat. After a wild, five-minute ride in and out of packs of motor scooters and long convoys of ARVN trucks, the cab pulled up in front of the Sugar Shack. Rodgers knew that the driver had taken him on a roundabout cruise, adding at least two miles to the short trip, but since the meter had never been turned on (he had never seen a meter used since arriving in Saigon), he handed the man an entire dollar and stepped from the car.

The Sugar Shack's outside billboards advertised it to be one of the area's "soul bars," catering mostly to blacks, but Rodgers spotted a group of defiant white roughnecks from the Twentieth Engineer Brigade who didn't allow stereotypes to ruin their parties. Rodgers nodded to the group casually as he passed them, instantly wondering if the PMO had distributed wanted posters on him or if he even rated a reward bulletin. After one of the engineer specialists raised a clenched fist at Rodgers and grumbled, "White on, bro!" in a drunken slur, he relaxed, remembering he had never seen any flyers distributed by the 716th or C.I.D. since his assignment to town patrol.

His eyes locked onto those of a dark-skinned Cambodian prostitute sitting against the far wall at a corner table, and when she smiled over at him with her tongue running the edge of her lower lip he sauntered up and sat down across from her uninvited.

"Chou," he said the Vietnamese greeting to her, mis-pronouncing the tone slightly. He inspected the dull yellow glaze in her eyes and recalled a medic once telling him that that either meant she was a doper or a disease carrier.

143

"Hello, honey." She smiled again; her voice was harsh and nasal. Rodgers wondered if that was a sign she suffered from clap throat and he winced noticeably when she put her warm palms on his hands. "Ohhhh! You're so cold, honey. Been out in the rain? We'll have to fix that, won't we?"

He bought her a watered-down drink then followed her up to a room above the bar, its single window overlooking the street. He spent several minutes looking out onto the traffic passing frantically through the rain below and the woman, who had been standing before a large mirror, watched him in its reflection as she brushed her short, kinky hair.

"What you like from Sally do for you today, honey?" she asked, now sitting on the edge of the bed. Jeff ignored her and continued staring out at the rain. "You like massage, honey?"

The coffee-colored hooker waited patiently a few more minutes for an answer, then walked over to the window and slowly drew the shades so that only a narrow shaft of clouded daylight filtered into the smoky cubicle.

The woman leaned her slender body up against Jeff and pressed the curve of her hip against his side. She expertly slid the zipper of his jeans down and inserted long, probing fingers inside until she had found what she was hunting for. "Maybe you want a number one blow job, honey?" she purred and started to fondle him gently.

Getting no response, she pulled her hand back out, danced over to the bed humming an imaginary tune, and turned the lamp down low. She spent a couple seconds unfastening the hinge on the back of her dress then let it fall to the floor around her ankles. "I really want to love you, honey," she said seductively, "but you have to cooperate a little." She stepped out of the pile of clothes at her feet and laid down on the lumpy mattress. "Maybe you just want a quickie," she giggled and when Jeff finally turned to look at her, she spread her legs open invitingly for the briefest of seconds then closed them back up slowly and motioned with her fingers for him to come to her. "And I only charge you 2500p, white boy," she said

144

with a smile.

Rodgers suddenly sprang across the room and dropped his icy cold military police badge on top of her soft mahoganylike stomach. The badge, called a shield by the cops, was custom-made from solid silver and had gold cross-pistols in the center. They hadn't been issued for wide use yet; MPs in Korea used only inexpensive brass copies, and only armbands identified the MPs in Vietnam, but Rodgers had borrowed Stryker's when he had first seen him in Saigon and had a copy made for souvenir purposes.

The badge had his year of arrival in Saigon and the words, "SAIGON COMMANDOS" inscribed on it, but these unofficial alterations were not noticed by the prostitute. Plopping an ounce of cold metal on her bare skin produced the desired results: the woman's tinted eyes showed that she was terrified.

"Police?" she whispered, fear cracking her voice.

"Yes, honey," he answered softly, drawing his .45 and placing it in the fold of skin between her breasts. "MP. Canh-Sat. Canh Luc Hon Hop. Number ten bad ass! Number ten-*thousand* son of a bitch! Take all whore girls to underground jails and saw off their tits and ram broomsticks up their—"

The woman started crying, but Rodgers only slapped her. "I want information."

"Please," she said, "what I do to you?"

"You're black!" He almost spat the word out in her face. "Not many black girls tricking in Saigon! Many black GIs come to you for boom boom." Rodgers pulled the photo of three soldiers from his pocket and pointed to a short, skinny guy on the end. "I want to know when you last bedded this bastard down."

She looked at the photo but balked. "Lots of bars in Saigon. Lots of soul bars."

Rodgers brought the .45 back as if he were going to pistol whip her and she recoiled automatically, hiding her face behind fingers painted with purple nail polish, as though she'd been beaten many times before. "His friend had a Sugar Shack

145

matchbook on him," Rodgers sneered, placing the .45 in the woman's ear this time. She grabbed the picture from his hand and studied it intently.

"Oh yes, yes. I remember now. This man Nate."

The name set the wheels rolling in Rodgers' head. Yes, that was it. Nathan. Nathan Webb. The little squirt with the scraggly Malcolm X goatee.

Rodgers shook the girl by the shoulders. He had her where he wanted her now. Scared out of her wits. As he pulled her off the bed and stood her roughly on her feet he could see the fear running down her legs. "Where does he live?" He pronounced each word slowly, distinctly.

"He live down the hall!" she stammered, suddenly eager to cooperate now that Rodgers had gotten the initial bits of information flowing. "Now you let me go. Please, leave me alone."

"Where? Which room?"

"Number eight."

"Thank you, honey," he said sarcastically as he brought the heavy .45 down on her temple. The prostitute crumpled to the floor and Rodgers went over to a closet, found some narrow dress belts, tied her up, ankles to wrists, and slipped her unconscious form under the bed.

Rodgers entered the hallway and walked down to room eight. He quietly pressed his fingers against the door, saw that it was as flimsy and hollow as the one he had just closed, and kicked the panel in without any further hesitation, pistol drawn.

He entered with his .45 at arm's length, chest high, fanning the room ready to fire, and his sights came down on Webb's bare back. The man was naked on a dirty mattress on the floor, a girl's skinny, yellow legs spread out beneath him.

Webb froze and slowly turned to face the intruder. "Who the fuck are you?"

But Rodgers didn't answer. He kept the pistol trained on Webb until he was close enough to place the gray barrel against the base of his skull. Then he slowly moved around to the side

146

of the mattress, grabbed the wrist of the juvenile beneath Webb, and dragged her out from under the sheet onto the grimy floor. "How old are you?" Rodgers asked the child, temporarily forgetting he was no longer a cop.

"Thirteen!" she lied, snapping at him defiantly as if that number made it all right. She tried to break his grip on her wrist as she wiped a streak of blood from her inner thigh.

"Get your damn clothes on and split! Beat it!" he yelled at her, and she scampered out of the room without dressing.

"You Nate?" Rodgers directed his glare at the deserter, but he recognized the man immediately.

"Yeah," he answered slyly, masking his anger. "And I repeat: who the fuck are you?"

"I live at 541 Thanh Mau Street." Rodgers grinned. As shock and fear struck the man's eyes, he made a break for the door. Rodgers hit him in the stomach with a chair and the man crashed to the floor. "That was my woman you violated back at 541 Thanh Mau." Rodgers repeated the address slowly, deliberately, as if it were important for the man never to forget it.

The deserter lay on his side, curled up in a ball, the wind knocked out of him. Rodgers took a switchblade from his pocket and snapped it open without ceremony. Then he threw it down so that it stuck in the hardwood floor inches from the man's face.

"Now I'm giving you a choice, Nathan." He cocked the hammer back on the .45 for dramatic effect and, using both hands, aimed the weapon at the man's head. "Either you castrate your black ass with that blade right here and now"— Webb's head shot up and his eyes met Rodgers', stunned—"or I'll pop off your kneecaps with Mr. Colt here and then do it myself!"

Webb rose to his knees and started pleading with Rodgers to let him surrender to the authorities. "I'm sorry, man! I'm really sorry! How could we know? I thought she was just another whore, man! I thought—"

147

Rodgers lowered the .45 to Webb's left foot without warning and pulled the trigger. The impact tore three toes off and spun the man around, throwing blood across the walls as he flipped back onto his side.

Rodgers grabbed Webb by the hair and put the pistol up to his mouth as he stomped down on the man's shattered foot.

"My God, you're killing me!" he screamed.

"The blade," Rodgers said softly. "Pick up the blade—learn to love the blade, Nathan."

Rodgers knew there was a possibility the man would try to stab him the second he picked up the knife, but it didn't matter. Life had become so empty without her. It just wasn't worth living anymore.

Webb was shaking violently now, as he pulled the knife from the floor. His eyes met Rodgers' again after he stared at the sparkling blade for several seconds, and he saw in the white man's face a rage he could not match or combat.

Rodgers could feel his finger pulling tighter on the trigger and Webb could see the ex-cop's fingernail turn red with the pressure and his knuckles going white. He swallowed hard and looked down at the shriveled organ between his legs like it was a dead relative he was seeing at graveside for the last time. Webb briefly contemplated lunging at the crazy man above him but he knew he would die an instant, violent, most painful death, and every second of life was suddenly precious.

He looked into Rodgers' eyes again and felt their almost hypnotic control over him, and he looked back down at the blade then at Rodgers again, their eyes locking for several drawn-out seconds.

"Do it!" Rodgers screamed suddenly, slamming the pistol into Webb's face, and with a terrified, automatic response, the black deserter grabbed the head of his penis, stretched it out and watched his hand jerk the blade down.

His mouth exploded with a scream of agony and regret that seemed to shake the entire room, and Rodgers backed up in revulsion at the sight. As Webb held up the severed organ in

148

one hand, he started toward Rodgers, yelling frantically, insanely, "Are you happy now? Are you happy now? This for a whore? All this for a lousy, stinking whore?"

"Shut up, Nathan," Rodgers muttered irritably.

"Shut up? Shut up?" he screamed. "Look what you made me do?" he screamed at Jeff accusingly, and as the blood in his body found the hole and gushed forth out onto the floor, he collapsed at the other man's feet, pleading for an ambulance. "Here, I want to kiss your boot!" he begged. "Let me kiss your boots! Anything! Just get me some help!"

But the man was just an insignificant piece of scum now to Rodgers. He pointed the .45 down at the man's terrified face, but all he could see was Mai, waving down at him from a distant balcony. He blew the top of Webb's head off. A large chunk of skull slid across the floor and splattered in a crimson mess against the wall.

There just wasn't anything left of his face after six more shots, so Rodgers left, feeling more empty inside than he thought he would, the satisfaction eluding him.

XII. TRUTH OR CONSEQUENCES

"Bao Cao!" the interrogator yelled at Ngo Van Nanh, but the one-eyed Viet Cong, accused of leading the raid on the village outside Duc Co, remained silent. The interrogator, a captain assigned to the South Vietnamese Special Forces, repeated the demand for the forty-year-old guerrilla to confess, and when Nanh just grinned, keeping his opium-dazed eye glued to the far wall of the underground bunker, the captain slapped him on the cheek with a clip of his open hand. The prisoner was tied to a chair, his hands taped to the armrests, and when the interrogator suddenly stabbed a bayonet down into the wood between his outstretched fingers, Nanh flinched for the first time in thirty-one hours.

"Ah, some progress," the Green Beret sitting next to Sgt. Mark Stryker sighed. "Finally." The two Americans were seated behind a two-way mirror that ran the length of a makeshift wall, hastily erected to turn the ammo storage cache into a detention cell.

Stryker and Pvt. Alan Perkins, the soldier who had photographed the atrocity in the center of an unnamed village only a few miles from where they now sat, had been invited by the ARVN strike force coordinator to attend this interrogation. Word spread fast throughout Pleiku Province that the crazy Americans had offered a 500,000 piaster reward for the capture of the communist ringleader, and the Vietnamese were now anxious to demonstrate to the Green Berets how cooperative they could be in such matters.

The interrogator was now yelling again at Nanh, and just as it appeared he was going to plunge the bayonet down into one of the guerrilla's knuckles, he backed off and motioned for one of the ARVN guards to give the prisoner some water.

"One of Nanh's own cadre informed on him to collect the lousy grand," Perkins was telling Stryker, who had just reported back for duty after four days of mental health leave-of-absence. That was the slang term the soldiers attached to get-away-from-the-gore passes the commander handed out after particularly bad field incidents, and Stryker spent the entire time intoxicated and in the arms of Lai, who tried to understand why such a fuss was being made over a pile of arms. "The whole village was Viet Cong, anyway," she had told him, but she could not explain to the Green Beret why the communists would dismember their own future recruits.

"The strike force took it upon themselves to set up an ambush," Perkins continued. "Blasted ol' Quoc right outta his socks!"

"The VC don't wear socks." Stryker smiled for the first time that day.

"Quoc did."

"Quoc?"

"The strike force member who turned out to be the VC plant."

"Oh, right. Any more prisoners taken?"

"No. We neglected to post rewards on the entire squad. Only Nanh, the leader. Apparently the rest all died at the ambush site. No survivors. Funny how Nanh came out of it all without a scratch and the others all got blown to hell."

"Jungle justice," Stryker thought out loud.

"What's that?"

"Nothing."

Perkins pulled a cigar from his fatigue pocket and placed it against his lips, directly under his nose. He inhaled deeply, sighed with anticipation, and hunted around in another pocket for his lighter.

"You're not really going to light that thing, are you?" Stryker grimaced, feeling another headache coming on.

"Are you kidding, Sarge? These are Havana specials. My pop sends 'em all the way from Miami."

The small bunker was suddenly filled with a loud scream and both startled Americans looked up to see that the interrogator had rammed the bayonet down onto the Viet Cong's left thumb, severing the tip at the joint just below the fingernail. A thick stream of blood instantly appeared to ooze slowly from the brown stump, and Stryker was surprised to see that the injury did not result in a gushing fountain like he had expected.

"Aw, that crazy Nanh," Perkins muttered, shrugging his shoulders. "I didn't think he'd scream when they started in on chopping off fingers, joint by joint."

"What are you talking about?" Stryker looked over at the private, an eyebrow cocked in boredom, but he already knew the answer.

"Had a bet with the captain. I didn't think the bastard would break. Hell, he went through phase A already and barely flinched."

"A scream of pain doesn't mean he's been broken, but you're telling me they already hot-wired him?" Stryker was suddenly more interested.

"Yep. Ten hours ago. Juiced him for fifty minutes."

Stryker knew of few prisoners who had undergone the hot-wire questioning without breaking. The process called for the electrical wires from portable field phones to be connected to the prisoner's temples and testicles. An assistant then heartily cranked the generator lever on the telephone while the interrogator rattled off appropriate questions. If the wires connected to the prisoner's head didn't get results, the other set running between his legs usually did the trick.

153

The captain directed the ARVN guard to wrap a crude bandage around the bleeding thumb and then he slowly walked over to the prisoner's other side. He dramatically raised the bayonet above the VC's other thumb and held it poised to strike for several seconds, but Nanh still would not speak.

"Who issued the directive to cut off the children's arms?" the captain yelled at Nanh in Vietnamese, but the guerrilla, now blinking his one good eye rapidly to keep any tears from appearing, only stared straight ahead. "Who ordered the pregnant women disemboweled?" the interrogator screamed even louder. Stryker could feel another migraine coming on as Ngo Van Nanh remained totally silent.

The captain motioned for the guard to bring a small, battered briefcase from a locker against the doorway.

"Ah, what could our honorable interrogator have up his sleeve, now?" Perkins asked no one in particular, and both Americans watched as the man carefully opened the black leather case and pulled out a shimmering hacksaw.

"Uh oh," Perkins said, grinning. "The moment of truth." As if on cue, the captain turned to look at the mirror behind him and smiled back at the Green Berets. The captain winked his eye at the mirror and his expression said, Watch this!

Stryker slowly closed his eyes and began rubbing his temples with his forefingers. He was becoming disgusted with the interrogation and it bothered him that he could not rationalize the necessity for such sessions.

As the captain placed the hacksaw on top of the guerrilla's wrist and began to slowly saw the prisoner's right hand off, Stryker tried to visualize the children having their arms hacked away by the terrorist squad. After all, it was only an eye for an eye.

When Ngo Van Nanh began screaming at the top of his lungs, Stryker forced pictures of the pregnant women being disemboweled in the village square to flash before his mind's eye. And when the sergeant finally looked up and saw the guard pouring small amounts of salt into the gaping crevice already sliced halfway through the communist's wrist, he slowly got to his feet and started for the door.

"Wait, don't leave yet." Perkins sounded annoyed. "You're going to miss the water torture."

Jon Toi sat in the little backroom of his seventh-floor flat and stared at the eight-by-ten blow-up he had just tacked to the wall. The picture showed his own face in the foreground, eyes wide with terror, mouth agape. There was a straight razor at his throat and it was being held in the clenched fist of a fanatical murderess cowering behind him. The camera flashbulb had bounced a diamondlike sparkle back off the blade, but it was nothing compared to the haunting, evil gleam in the eyes of the fiend holding the Canh-Sat hostage, her lips curled back off her teeth in an animallike snarl.

Toi shivered when he spent more than a few seconds examining the photo, and when his wife walked up behind him and put her arms around his shoulders unnoticed, he flew across the room like a fleeing gibbon.

"Oh, I'm so sorry!" His fragile wife was sincere, twisting her hands awkwardly in front of her as though she were trying to wring tears from them. "I didn't mean to startle you, Toi. It must have been a terrible experience." She walked cautiously over to him and took the policeman stiffly in her arms, wiping the beads of sweat from his forehead with her palm. "I just thank the gods your American friends came to your rescue so bravely."

Toi backed away from her and brought his chin in with a smirk as he studied her from below heavy eyelids. "Hmph," he grumbled. If only she could have seen that crazy Bryant pop up out of nowhere and blow that hooker right out of her nylons. Never mind that poor Toi could have got his head cut off.

The exhausted Canh-Sat walked back over to the black-and-white glossy hanging on the wall and rested his chin in his hand for a couple seconds. A chuckle suddenly escaped him as he

155

remembered that goofy Bryant having the gall to take a goddamned picture—and even ask her permission to do it before smoking her into never-never-land.

"What are you giggling about, Toi?" His wife smiled, feeling suddenly playful and affectionate when she saw her husband's unexplained change of mood.

Yes, that had been comical, thought Toi, *quite a scene. That Bryant is one* dinky dau *character. Almost got me killed and here I am laughing about it all.*

Toi sat back down at the table and resumed cleaning his revolver, and when he noticed the one empty cartridge among the five magnum hot-loads, the vision of the dead American sailor's body swinging in that dark room from the hangman's noose found its way back into his tired mind. He slowly set the revolver down and snapped the cap off a bottle of beer.

He slid his chair over to the file cabinet against one wall and pulled the folder he had kept on the woman suspected of the soldier murders plaguing Saigon. He compared the m.o.s and evidence at the scene, but things were just not adding up. The signatures in the hotel registries were different and the names were different, although Toi would be the first to admit it did not take a brilliant criminal to utilize different aliases.

But there was something else wrong. Something he could not pinpoint. Something different about the manner of the woman he had followed for hours along the sidewalk cafes dotting Quach Thi Trang. Something missing in the eyes of the woman who had teased the taxi drivers and gone on to eat a banana in the most sensuous way he had ever seen food consumed.

The Vietnamese police officials who had swarmed over the Xin Loi bar after the shooting had thanked the American MPs repeatedly and congratulated Toi on cracking the case of the whore-turned-psycho. They assured him a promotion and medal for bravery were in it for Toi this time. But as the Canh-Sat stared uneasily at the piercing eyes of the now-dead woman staring back at him from the photograph he knew they were not the same eyes that had grabbed out at him from that taxi fleeing the Purple Dragon weeks earlier. Toi opened another beer and took a long swig before taking his eyes off the picture. But they eventually wandered back, and he knew down in his gut, the more he studied the woman's glare, that a second lunatic was still lurking the streets of the city, out there somewhere, roaming the dark.

Toi did not look forward to it, but he knew their paths would cross again before it was all over.

It was Stryker's third night watching the apartment house at 541 Thanh Mau. He was not even sure Jeff had continued to rent the place now that a new month had begun. *If the kid's got any smarts,* Stryker thought to himself, *he'd pack up and move to another part of Saigon.* There was too much chance the Provost Marshal's Office would have some men watching for him. It just didn't look good for the MPs to have one of their own on deserter status. The faster he was picked up off the street the better. But the young woman Stryker had questioned casually—Kim was her name—had maintained Rodgers still kept property in the third-floor apartment.

So Stryker would wait. And watch. He had a lot of time on his hands. Four days earlier, May first, he had signed out of the company on a thirty-day vacation leave. Well earned, the men told him. Yep, going to Bangkok for a month, he told the men.

Had to get away from Pleiku. From the slaughter taking place in the villages. Every day, a different village, a different tale of horror. Living nightmares, and Stryker had been a part of them. He understood what the nightmares really did to you. That's why he could not understand how Rodgers could stay in the apartment after the murder. *Maybe I'm just superstitious,* Stryker thought, but he pictured himself in Jeff's position often: sleeping in that dark room alone at night; tossing and turning with the pain and loneliness; rolling over to find her ghost lying next to you, or sitting silent and ashen in the corner of the room where they had killed her, waiting for the light of day to chase away her spirit.

Stryker found himself enjoying this little informal stakeout. Lying on the roof of the building across from Jeff's apartment house rekindled an old spark only police work could fan. Different in some ways from that danger he sought in the jungle, it still held an excitement found in few other professions. Up there, high above the unseeing, unsuspecting pedestrians. He felt in control of all who came and went, felt he held a power over all those simpletons repeating the daily routine of their dull, drab existence—although dull and drab were not words Stryker felt could be applied to *any*thing in Saigon.

It was times like this that he thought back to all the real stakeouts he had weathered with his partners. And how, inevitably, crouched on rooftops with high-powered scoped rifles at your disposal, you always joked with the other cops how it might be fun to change sides and sight in on some of those civilians for a brief sniping. The temptation was in everyone's blood, and Stryker shook his head over these thoughts, amazed at the fine line that separated good men from evil.

A taxi in the street below backfired as it coasted up to the apartment building and Stryker focused his binoculars on the back door just as Jeff Rodgers stepped out. He was wearing blue jeans and a gray windbreaker, and Stryker thought his old friend might be putting on weight. That would be unusual for a deserter on the run, as was the windbreaker on this cloudless, simmering day. It would mean he had a weapon underneath. Probably a .45 in a shoulder holster. Or one of the new pancake .jobs, pressed flat against the curve of the hip.

Stryker watched him pass through the security guard's station unchallenged, and after he disappeared in the courtyard and entered the foyer, Stryker trained his binoculars back on the guard shack. The elderly Vietnamese man inside had waved cheerfully to Jeff and made no attempt to

158

phone the police or MPs to report the American's return. That would mean either Rodgers had the police department's sympathies on his side, or the old man was just a space case who smiled at every passerby and wouldn't challenge an intruder if one walked right up and towed off his kiosk.

Stryker watched Jeff exit the exposed stairwell onto the third-floor veranda and walk over to his apartment at the end of the passageway. He watched him look about casually, including down at the street, then slowly unlock the padlock on the door and step inside. Even from this distance, Stryker could hear the deadbolt slide shut once Jeff was out of sight again. To his right, Stryker could see the twin spires of the cathedral rising above the treetops and for the next few minutes he busied himself focusing the binoculars on the sinuous Vietnamese maidens floating gracefully among the groups of people passing below, their bright blue, high-necked *ao-dais* slit from the waist down and covering white satin pantaloons that billowed gently against the breeze. Stryker scanned the statuesque faces of the girls crowding the street now. There were no hordes of noisy motor scooters racing up and down this dead end street, trying to beat the traffic lights, so the avenue overflowed with the women. Stryker noticed that only a few of them wore colors other than the striking turquoise, and he surmised they must be Catholics, parading toward the cathedral for classes or a meeting of some sort. As he focused on their elusive figures, hidden beneath the deceptive gowns, and listened to their delicate singsong voices drifting up to the rooftop, he found himself wishing one of them were next to him, if only to talk. He liked looking at beautiful women. And Vietnam had the most beautiful maidens he had ever seen. Legend had it the most beautiful women in the world were found in Thailand, but he would— and had—argued over that claim for hours.

Their delicate, amber bodies were almost like toys to him. At night, their firm legs, thighs tightened from years of squatting instead of sitting, fine-tuned the art of lovemaking to a degree

159

their Western counterparts could never master. Their enduring, ageless beauty stirred Mark's emotions like no other women in the world could. He spotted traditional gold bracelets draping the fragile wrists of almost every girl in the street below and as he watched them playfully brush the long, jet black, silky hair that fell to their waists when the wind was not teasing it, he wondered about the hypnotism such gentle ladies commanded.

Stryker briefly brought his binoculars back to fall on Rodgers' window and, satisfied the man was still in his apartment, resumed watching the crowds below.

It was something in their dark, mysterious, almond eyes, Stryker decided. You could be walking with an American girl on each arm, yet let one Asian beauty walking in the opposite direction lock those exotic, enticing eyes and her alluring smile on you and you would follow the Oriental without question, regardless of the hardships it might cause later. She was for now. And she was ageless.

Stryker felt himself growing hard as he lay on that hot, graveled roof. The heat made him think of Lai, waiting patiently up in Pleiku. And as he thought about the candles she'd place in the window tonight, and every night until he returned to her, he wondered what the hell he was doing two hundred miles from his woman, roughing it on a stakeout he wasn't even getting paid for.

"Check this out!" Private Broox held the newspaper out so the rest of the Decoy Squad could see the picture on page one. It depicted a scroungy mongrel mutt pulling at a severed arm that lay at the bottom of a huge pile of limbs.

"Christ, they were just children," Sergeant Richards shook his head in disgust, then went back to reading a pack of letters that had just arrived from the states.

"Goddamn VC," Bryant muttered and spat at the ground beside the jeep.

"Says here the ringleader of the guerrillas, a Ngo Van Nanh, was shot and killed trying to escape an interrogation session. At least that's the end of that, I guess."

"There's never an end to it, Mike." Bryant looked over at him seriously and Broox shuddered and moved around uneasily in his seat. He hated it when Bryant started talking weird.

"Hey, alright!" Sergeant Richards held up the contents of a care package he had received from home. "My old man sent me some more pocket flares and—check this out! A black Velcro watch band."

"What's that for?" Thomas leaned over and grabbed it out of his sergeant's hand.

"Covers up the luminous dial, burrito breath," Broox explained to him. "Jesus, do I have to clarify everything for you?"

Thomas stood up in the back of the jeep and drew his night stick. "I'll clarify your cranium!" he responded dryly. "Now am I gonna have to chase your young ass up and down Tu Do Street, or are you gonna apologize?"

"Hey, knock it off, you guys," Richards ordered. "Downer time. Got a letter here from the parents of Philip Anderson."

"Who the hell is Philip Anderson?" Thomas asked.

"That sailor who got offed at the Xin Loi bar last week," Richards explained.

"Jesus, we gotta spell everything out for you?" Broox began riding Thomas good-naturedly again. "How'd you make it through the academy anyway, butt brain?" Broox immediately bolted out of the jeep, Thomas hot on his heels.

"His parents want to know if I'll write to them," Richards told Bryant as he calmly watched Thomas chase Broox toward the Hotel Majestic, a look of detachment in his tired eyes. "They want me to tell them what happened. The details. The truth. Everything."

"You think you should—I mean, really level with them, including the hooker and the whorehouse and everything?"

161

"They say they got my name off the MP report. Hell, I didn't even know anyone from the 716th filled one out."

"Yeah, Thomas is to blame. Insisted we make some record of the shooting to go with the photo I took of Officer Toi. He claims the Vietnamese National Police tend to lose too many reports. So, you going to write to 'em?"

"I don't know yet, Tim."

"Well, I guess we better go and round those two up—before they kill each other." Bryant started up the jeep and pulled out from under the cool shade of the leaning palms. As they glided into the white heat of day, stretching down the wide boulevard to the river, Sergeant Richards looked at the once-majestic tamarind trees and decorative flower patches lining Tu Do with sad eyes. The belching blue exhaust fumes from the endless military convoys, and the pollution accumulating from hundreds of thousands of cyclos, Hondas and taxis were killing off the ancient trees. Richards wished he could see Saigon in the days of the French, when there were more rickshaws and pushcarts clogging the streets than sputtering motor scooters, and the trees were a vibrant blue-green instead of coated with ash and soot.

"Hey, I eat this shit up, Drill Sergeant!" Broox was laughing as he followed Thomas out of the Hotel Majestic. Two huge Chinese bouncers had the PFC in a headlock as they escorted him back out into the street down the steps to the waiting MP jeep.

"Let go of me, you overgrown—" Thomas started, but when he saw the impatient look on Richards' face he grew silent and the doormen set him free.

"Thanks, gentlemen." The sergeant gave the bouncers a semiformal salute and they returned a we-are-used-to-Thomas type smile and started back into the hotel.

"Goofus here knocked some old *papa-san* over when he was chasing me," Broox said, laughing, "and those two goons were on him like stink on—"

"Yeah, hey—when did the Majestic hire those apes,

162

anyway?" Thomas protested. "I mean, nobody gets away with—"

"Shut up, Anthony," Sergeant Richards said. "It's their country. Try and behave, okay? I know it's difficult, but try."

As the squad pulled away from the curb and started back down Tu Do, Bryant directed Broox to pull over in front of the Xin Loi bar.

A strikingly beautiful Chinese girl wearing black hot pants and a halter top was leaning against the red mailbox marked Ngoai Nuoc in front of the establishment, her smooth, dark legs crossed to accentuate her hips. As they approached, Broox found he couldn't keep his eyes off the girl's stunning legs. He was always amazed how soft and smooth Vietnamese women kept their legs. Nylons were almost unheard of. The heat and humidity made them uncomfortable, but the girls just didn't need them. Their legs, hairless and toned to near-perfection, needed nothing covering them.

The woman had spotted their jeep when it was still a block away, but she made no attempt to leave the curb or acknowledge their presence when Broox stopped the vehicle.

"Gentlemen," said Bryant, introducing the woman, "this is Co Hue Chean." Almost comically, the MPs all stood up on cue and bowed, causing Bryant to turn red. But he recovered quickly and held a hand, palm up, toward his sergeant. "This is honcho Richards, Chean. And this is Michael Broox—"

"And I'm Anthony," Private Thomas introduced himself, stepping down from the jeep gracefully and taking the girl's tiny hand in his own. As he bowed and raised her smooth knuckles to his lips, he couldn't miss the cleavage bulging forth from the halter top.

"Nice to meet you," she said softly in a high, heavily accented tonal voice. She pointed a finger at Bryant and rattled off a few words in Mandarin then turned gracefully on her heels and disappeared into the bar.

Thomas hopped back into the rear of the jeep and flipped his helmet a couple times in the air, and as Broox pulled away from

163

the curb he said, "Jesus, did you see those melons hanging out like a couple brown ten-cent water balloons! Holy Christ, who was that cunt, anyway?"

"That was Bryant's old lady," Sergeant Richards answered, and Thomas fell suddenly silent. He turned back to look at Bryant, an apology in his eyes but not sure how he was going to word it.

Broox stared at Bryant in disbelief. "*That* was the woman who stabbed your ass for going into a bar without her?"

"The one and only," Bryant answered proudly. "Don't ya just love her?"

"Oh wow, I just eat this shit up, Drill Sergeant!"

As soon as he saw the light go out in Rodgers' apartment, Stryker shimmied down the fire escape and waited in the alley's shadows, hoping his friend from the past was about to take to the streets and not turn in for the night.

Sirens grew, then faded in the distance, and the noise covered the sound of the door on the third floor closing. It was still a couple hours before curfew so Stryker knew he might be in for a lengthy wild goose chase, but Rodgers flagged down a cab and was dropped off only a mile away, in the two hundred block of Phan Dinh Phung. He entered a small cafe built into the front shell of a house, its living quarters hidden in the rear, and talked to several women in their late forties clustered around a small portable television set for a few minutes, then walked briskly another mile over to Bis Ky Dong where he entered unit sixteen from the rear. Stryker made note of the address and surveyed the roofline across the street in preparation for settling down for the night, but he was taken off guard when Rodgers came back out a few minutes later, a shoebox under his arm, and started back toward Phan Dinh Phung, the city's central north-south boulevard.

Stryker followed two blocks behind for several minutes, and as they approached Le Van Duyet, he crossed over to the other side of the busy street, ran a block ahead of Rodgers, then recrossed and started back to meet him head on.

"Hey, is that you, Jeff?" Stryker put on his best surprised smile as he stepped in front of Rodgers and held out a hand, acting like he was unaware of current events in the city and Jeff's involvement in any murders. "How's the old 716th treating you?"

At first Rodgers just stared at him as if in a daze, then he forced a smile of recognition and shook Stryker's hand. "Good to see you, Mark. Yes . . . uh, oh—yes, the 716th is doing just fine—I'm doing just fine, same as always. And what brings you down to Saigon?"

"R&R, old pal!" Stryker was all smiles now as he grabbed Rodgers by the arm and led him over to a cab. "Come on. Let me buy you a drink. Still drinking Singapore Slings?"

"Where we going, Mark?" Jeff recoiled, his eyes showing instant suspicion.

"Hey, why so edgy? You know that bar all the crazy Green Berets hang out in: Caprice's. And I take it back, brother. You owe *me* a beer."

"Okay, sure, Mark. Whatever you say." As Stryker watched the emotional wreck before him slip into the back seat of the Renault, he was amazed such a person could be suspected of terminating so many soldiers.

"I was sorry to hear about Mai," Stryker said softly after they had found a dark corner table away from the other patrons. Jeff insisted on extinguishing the candle on the wall beside them and Stryker raised no objection. "It must be pretty tough on you."

"I'll make it," Jeff said, suddenly cradling his face in his hands after several minutes of silence. Stryker strained to hear the sobs, but there were none, only a deep sigh that made him feel instantly sorry for his young friend.

"I'm sure the police will make an arrest, Jeff."

165

"I miss her so much," he replied, his voice cracking and breaking off toward the end. "She was all I lived for. I know that sounds corny, but . . . Well, you know how I wrote you about my love for police work and the street when I first came to Saigon?"

Stryker knew the rest by heart. He had heard it all many times before. Another twenty-year-old American suddenly found himself in exotic Asia, a stranger in a mysterious and hostile land. The adventure waiting down dark alleys was overpowering but could not compare with the tender arms of a devoted Vietnamese lover. Once you fell under her mystical spell it was all over. The glitter of patrolling beneath the flares of Saigon by night, of policing the toughest beat in the world, soon fell secondary to lying cuddled against the breast of a soft, warm Annamese maiden.

Even the ladies of the evening seemed to exude a magical power that kept the strongest of men returning to their lairs night after night. Stryker knew soldiers who swore by it: Saigon bargirls made the best possible wives once you took them out of the whorehouse. Then they became the most faithful, loving and hard-working of mates, dreading the thought of ever having to return to life on the street.

"At first I loved it on patrol," Jeff continued. "I lived only for the street. I hassled the hookers night and day. Then I found Mai, working in an orphanage. She had been sold to the nuns by her parents down in the delta. But she was happy—content among her little orphan children. She called them *Boo Dai:* the dust of life. I smuggled them my ration cards, Mark, so they could buy food for the kids. And when Mai told me the sisters were going to kick her out on the street because she was almost eighteen, I paid the nuns in cartons of Marlboro and Salem. Christ, I bought her from an orphanage, Mark! And I did it just to save face—next thing I know I own a seventeen-year-old cherry girl."

"So you fell in love under other than favorable circumstances." Stryker smiled like an older brother. "What's wrong with that?"

"She treated me like a king," he continued, slowing the words now as he calmed down a bit. "Cooked my meals, washed my clothes, massaged the soreness from my muscles every night, bathed me—things no American girl ever did for me, Mark. She was even teaching me Vietnamese."

"Because you wanted to stay here."

"Because I never wanted to leave Saigon. Or her."

"And your career?"

"You know, I loved the street. I looked forward to each new day and night on patrol. The shifts passed far too fast. And then I met Mai and I couldn't wait to get off the filthy street—yes, it went from the beautiful boulevards to the filthy street. Just like that. And I couldn't wait to get off the filthy street. And home to her. Each shift was suddenly dragging on endlessly. What kind of woman can affect a man this way, Mark?"

"A Vietnamese woman, Jeff. A Vietnamese woman."

They drank again in silence for several minutes while the band started to dismantle their equipment. The sign on the bass drum identified them as The Dreamers, and when it became apparent they were finished playing for the night, two Green Berets in uniform climbed up on stage and handed the guitarist a ten-dollar bill. As if on cue, the female drummer, a teenager wearing a black bikini, struck the cymbals, did a roll on the snare and began singing the Young Rascals hit, "How Can I Be Sure."

"Pretty good band," Stryker said, noticing Jeff was resting his face in his hands again, oblivious to what was going on in the real world.

The walls of the nightclub began vibrating slightly and a chandelier started to sway, and Stryker knew a squadron of fighter bombers had swooped past low overhead, but Rodgers did not even notice.

"I really miss her." Rodgers was speaking now not for Stryker's benefit but as if he hoped the words could be heard by Mai. "It's like a pain tearing at my chest from within. It hasn't

167

subsided all these weeks." He looked up at Stryker suddenly. "Would I be talking crazy if I said I think it's her spell over me . . . that I'm going to die over this, Mark. That maybe I want to die over this."

Stryker poured him another beer but Jeff brushed it aside. "And don't tell me there's a lotta fish in the sea, goddamn you," he continued. "Don't tell me that."

Stryker watched Jeff change his mind and grab the beer, pouring half the bottle down within a few seconds. He could see Jeff was not past the high stage. "I wouldn't tell you that, Jeff," he said, while he thought, *Sure, there's a lot of fish in the sea, but this is the South China Sea and in Saigon all you have are sharks and piranha!*

For the first time Rodgers smiled, as if he read Stryker's mind, and when he looked back up, the sergeant was holding a small notebook out to him. "For Mai"—he smiled back—"do what you have to do."

Rodgers' eyes lit up instantly, and he snatched the notebook from the Green Beret's hand. "Where did you get this?" he demanded, flipping through the yellowed and torn pages until he located the notes on the arrests of the six blacks several months before.

"Let's just say I took an interest in your case when I learned you were missing and about to be placed on deserter status."

"But how did you get into the barracks?"

"Hey, come on! Us Special Forces types are trained for just such behind-enemy-lines missions, right?"

"So you know?"

"Well, let's just say I suspect you're out to even the score a little bit. And I think you need that book to make sure the right guys catch hell. But tell me one thing: does revenge taste sweet?"

"I don't enjoy it, Mark. When I killed Webb he hadn't even confessed to being involved in Mai's death. I was acting solely on the word of a woman who lives in our apartment house— that she saw him leaving my room the morning of the killing.

She goes by the name of Kim. I showed her this snapshot." He handed the wallet photo of the three blacks posing arm in arm. "And she verified that the other two were also up there."

"This is Stubbs and Webb in this picture. But who is the third guy?"

"I don't know yet," he said, flipping the notebook pages. "Probably Chilton, but I won't know for sure until I track down Lance Jackson."

"How do you know they haven't all gone back to the states by now? How do you know you're not just killing the wrong people?"

"They can't go back home, Mark. They're deserters. Like me. Saigon is all they have left."

"So when will it stop?"

"When I've got the jade lady."

"What's inside the jade lady, Jeff?" Stryker asked softly, the apprehension betrayed in his voice.

Rodgers laughed for the first time that night. "After I killed Webb, I tore his room apart looking for it, Mark. This thing won't be finished until I have it back."

"Tell me what's in it." Stryker clamped a hand on Jeff's fists. "Tell me what's so important about a lousy statue."

The lights in the lounge were slowly coming on now, one by one, signaling closing time, and as he finished his beer, Stryker observed two MPs enter the bar. Jeff noticed them too and was on his feet and heading for the rear door casually. "It was a birthday gift, Mark. Just a birthday present. But it was the only thing she ever gave me."

"And you want it back."

"And I want it back."

Stryker watched him exit the bar just before the MPs started back toward the rear tables. He wasn't sure he believed Rodgers' story about the jade lady, but he decided it didn't matter and started finishing off another beer.

"Almost curfew, buddy." One of the MPs leaned over and grinned in Stryker's face. He held his night stick cupped in both hands, and although Stryker knew a dozen ways to take his stick away from him and turn it into an enema, the Green Beret just shrugged and started for the rear door.

As he merged in with the crowds racing along Duong Tu Do, Stryker peered above the sea of bobbing heads, searching for Rodgers. When he finally caught sight of him, several blocks ahead, he had to dart in and out of a swarm of cyclos and pedicabs to catch up. Several cabbies kept badgering him to take their taxis and he was grateful when Rodgers started down a narrow, deserted back alley where the taxis couldn't go.

Stryker could feel his defenses fall into phase yellow as the distant explosion seemed to rock the city. Somewhere a rocket had slammed into a fuel tank, and as the horizon lit up with a bright orange flash that seared the clouds and sent a low blanket of black smoke rolling across Saigon, Stryker could feel the rush of adrenalin that made it all worthwhile. Air-raid sirens began to scream mournfully all over the city, but no other rockets would fall that night. Just one solitary missile launched at a random target in the dark. Stryker wondered, as he followed Rodgers deeper into the slums of the city, how many couples had been killed by the rocket. And if they were prepared for such sudden, swift death from above.

XIII. ROOFTOP GUARDIAN

Jeff Rodgers was convinced an evil lurked in Vietnam. And that the demons haunting him were linked in some befouling way to that negative force. That the power made him do things he normally wouldn't do. Jeff had always been superstitious of that ominous tension constantly hugging the earth here, and knowing that Vietnam was a land restless with the ghosts of war dead whose bodies had often been blown to nothingness, leaving them nowhere to sleep, he felt sure he was destined to be dragged down into the same hell.

When Jeff emerged from the back alley behind Caprice's bar and saw the two black men walking down Cong Ly boulevard, he felt the evil overpowering him again.

Stryker saw Rodgers pull his commando knife from the sheath in his boot and start running for the two men. At first he wondered how Rodgers had identified them from the rear, and then his mind raced forward as his fear materialized: the man was going to murder two innocent people.

Stryker started running after Rodgers, but Jeff was already behind the man on the left and had jerked his head back, pulling the hair with his right hand. Rodgers then pressed the point of the knife against the man's stomach, under his rib cage, and jerked upward with all his might until the tip severed the liver and penetrated further upward, destroying, probing,

171

puncturing the bottom of the heart.

The man fell limp, dead even before his eyes had closed, and he fell to the ground in a trembling pile, one side of his face twitching violently.

The dead man's companion, a civilian contractor for Pacific Architects and Engineers, had started running wildly down Cong Ly at the first sign of the knife, fearing his time to be killed in a robbery had finally come, and when he saw a taxi slowly cruising in his direction he started for it, waving his arms desperately to attract attention.

The closer the cabbie got to the hysterical black man, the less he liked how the situation was developing, and he spun a wild U-turn and headed back down the street, the terrified civilian clinging to the doorlatch as he was dragged across the pavement.

Before the taxi could gather speed, Rodgers had grabbed onto the passenger side door and hauled himself in through the open widow. He slugged the small Vietnamese driver once and the sedan lurched to a halt.

The civilian, his knees and ankles badly scraped now, fell to the blacktop, breathing heavily. Rodgers pushed the driver down onto the floorboard and moved over behind the steering wheel, then slammed the door open against the civilian's incoherent face.

But the man was up and running again, this time off the street, over a chain barricade and into a parking lot illuminated by a single concrete lamppost. The civilian could see the door to a building a scant fifty yards off and he ran with all his might, his feet now heavy as cinder blocks, his chest ready to burst.

Stryker watched helplessly as Rodgers rammed the chain with the Renault. It snapped on the first hit, zinging back like a steel bullwhip and knocking the windshield out of a parked car ten feet away.

Rodgers then accelerated through the parking lot in a roar of grinding gears and spinning tires and easily caught up with the

172

civilian, ramming him into the wall of the warehouse and pinning his legs between the bumper and the crushed bricks.

Stryker started running for the crash scene, but Rodgers was already gone when he got there.

"You okay, buddy?" he asked the civilian, who was still pinned between the vehicle and the wall. Stryker bent over the hood of the car and examined the man's injuries.

Although he was conscious and appeared to be standing, Stryker could see that both his legs were crushed nearly flat. "You okay, mister?" he repeated.

"Yeah, I'm cool," the civilian replied with extreme effort, "but who *was* that dude, anyway?"

Stryker didn't answer, and while he surveyed the surrounding neighborhood, the little cabbie, who had been hiding on the floorboards, emerged from the taxi, his head darting about cautiously before he crawled out the driver's window. He immediately went over to the front of the car, inspecting the damage and ignoring Stryker.

The PAE contractor was beginning to lapse into shock now, and as he started moaning with pain, the cabbie jumped back in the Renault, fired it up and jammed the resisting gears loudly into reverse.

"Wait! Wait!" Stryker was yelling, grabbing at the Vietnamese through the window, but the little man let the clutch fly and the car jerked backwards. The taxi spun around, kicking up gravel, and disappeared from the parking lot in a cloud of dust. As pressure was released on the civilian's crushed legs, the blood held in place until then above the crude double amputation now gushed out in an uncontrolled flow, draining his body in mere seconds and killing the man even before his torso had flopped to the ground.

"Aw, Sarge, Thomas is faking it again!" Broox complained as they plotted the brightly colored pins on the sector map of Saigon. Blue for robberies, red for arsons and terrorist

173

bombings, green for burglaries and larcenies, orange for narcotics violations, yellow for auto thefts, and silver for sex crimes. The locations of homicides involving Americans were marked with white pins. Black pins denoted where victims of Jeff Rodgers were turning up dead.

"I'm not faking it, kimchi breath! There's nothing wrong with me putting a couple silver pins where my apartment is," Thomas said innocently, his eyes looking hurt.

"I'm not talking about that. You're plotting the other pins without even consulting the log."

"Not so. Not so."

"I'm warning you guys," said Sergeant Richards. "Quit placing pins more in one neighborhood than the others just cuz you wanna patrol the red light districts! I'll have you know I verify *every*thing after you leave here in the morning. If anything don't look right, I'll notice it. I'd hate to start dropping Article 15s in your personnel files," he said seriously, but they both knew Richards had never issued a letter of reprimand in his life.

"So what sector do we tackle tonight?" Bryant asked. He was getting bored with the antics of Broox and Thomas.

"Main Street," decided Richards as he searched for a pattern in the collage of colored pins. "Phan Dinh Phung."

"That's not main street," Thomas protested with a grin. "Tu Do is *main* street!"

That brought a smattering of applause and the men began donning their body armor.

"Why we been going out in uniform this week, Sarge?" Broox complained as he tightened the heavy bullet-proof vest. Thomas' night stick clattered to the floor as he struggled to fasten his web-belt. Bryant smacked him lightly in the stomach and said, "Tuck in that pot belly, soldier!"

"Because of the new provost marshal," Richards answered, referring to the recently reassigned commander of the 716th. "A full bird colonel, straight over from Germany. Doesn't like

174

his cops out of uniform. C.I.D.'s working on him. That's one of the reasons for this map: to show him how effective we've been in curbing violent crime where the victims have been Americans."

Just then a tall black soldier, his hair shaved short, wearing fatigue trousers and jungle boots but no shirt, entered the room. "Oh, excuse me, Sergeant. Didn't know anyone was in here. The captain sent me for the logbook."

"Sure, here, Davis." Richards smiled, handing the logbook to the private. "We're all done with it." Davis was in his early twenties and had large, drooping shoulders that made him strain to keep his head up straight. He was a big man, and was constantly jogging about the camp to keep in shape. A quiet man, just trying to be a good, low profile MP. Just trying to get through his Tour 365.

"By the way, my name is Craig Davis." He smiled broadly, offering a hand to the Decoy Squad. The mosquito-wing private stripes on his uniform immediately labeled him either a disciplinary problem or a newby in-country.

"You new in-country?" Thomas was sounding the same way he did when he was grilling suspected deserters downtown, but the smile remained on Davis' face.

"Yeah, just got in from Fort Polk, Louisiana."

"Hey, land of the Mardi Gras," decided Broox.

"Guess you could say that." Davis cringed noticeably, embarrassed.

"Well, you'll find a bit of Mardi Gras atmosphere here in Saigon, too." Broox smiled proudly, as if he were bragging about his home town. "Year round."

"Yeah, I noticed the fireworks are definitely not to be underestimated." Davis was frowning.

"Sounds like you got rocketed at Camp Alpha last week."

"My first day here. During in-processing."

"So where they got you working?" asked Bryant, genuinely interested.

175

"Well, I'm still in-processing. But I'll be assigned to Charlie Company. Static posts for a while. Guarding the gates and stuff."

"Well, welcome aboard." Richards patted him on the shoulder as they all started out of the room. "Now let's hit the street."

The Decoy Squad just happened to be sitting blacked out in a little cubbyhole down a back alley off Phan Dinh Phung, listening for the sounds of night crime, when a black soldier came racing around a corner down the street. The MPs all sat up straight in anticipation, expecting to see the man carrying a TV, or being chased by a jealous Vietnamese husband who had come home early.

For the last hour they had sat in that narrow driveway, listening for breaking glass, a muffled gunshot, perhaps a scream in the night. The proper stimuli to set them in action. But all had been quiet. Except for the dogs. Whenever a siren wailed in the distance or a rocket crashed into the heart of the city, the dogs howled and barked for several minutes afterwards. But that would signal their location, and restaurant cooks would set out to catch the wary animals, and soon all was quiet again.

When the Decoy Squad saw Jeff Rodgers race round the corner behind the black soldier, a .45 in his hand, they all tensed and burrowed back down in their seats, wishing they were somewhere else.

Except Sergeant Richards. "Okay," he whispered. "Get ready to start the engine when I tell you." Broox, behind the wheel as always, glanced back at Bryant. Their eyes met, but the specialist four only returned a sad nod. "Ready . . . ready . . ."

While Rodgers was still a good half block away, Broox hit the headlights and fired up the engine, halting the ex-MP in his tracks and according the black soldier an extra surge of

176

adrenalin as he raced past the squad and kept on going down the street.

Rodgers turned and ran back in the opposite direction, jumped a rickety fence and disappeared in the gloom.

"Broox!" Richards barked angrily. "Get out! After him! Take Bryant and get his ass! Me and Thomas will cut him off on the other side with the jeep!" The two MPs casually got out of the Beast and stood there in the street for a few seconds while Sergeant Richards slid across into the seat and sped off around the corner fenceline.

"Bummer," muttered Broox, as he drew his pistol. "Real fuckin' bummer."

"Come on, we better get going," said a frowning Bryant, and he started climbing the high fence.

Sergeant Richards spotted Rodgers as he came out on the other side of the yard. The deserter brought up his .45 and aimed directly at the windshield of the jeep, still fifty yards away, but dropped his sights just as suddenly without firing and started running down the alley again.

"I've got you this time, sucker!" Richards growled as Rodgers turned down into a dead end driveway that looked deceptively to be as wide as the other alleys.

Rodgers suddenly found himself trapped. High walls topped with barbed wire or broken glass embedded in the concrete rose up on three sides.

Like a desperate animal, Rodgers turned to face the MPs in the jeep as it skidded up sideways, thirty feet away. Sergeant Richards and Private First Class Thomas both jumped out on the left side and trained their pistols on him from behind the protection of the thick engine block. "Give it up, Rodgers!" Richards screamed. "Drop it, man, or I swear—I'll paste you where you stand!"

"You better do it, Jeff!" Thomas pleaded, although his weapon was also trained on the deserter. "He really means it."

Richards looked over at Thomas with a disapproving scowl, and just then a flare popped suddenly over them, illuminating the scene with a yellowish, flickering glow. Thomas looked back at Richards, but the sergeant had both hands cupping his .45, and Thomas wondered who could have fired it.

Rodgers was slowly going night blind from the drifting flare, and as he lifted his pistol to take aim on the MPs, a single shot rang out. But it was from the roof of the tenement leaning out over the eerie scene, and the round crashed down into the windshield of the MP jeep, sending shards of glass flying all over the block.

Rodgers, at first stunned, quickly recovered and dove to the ground as the MPs crawled under the jeep's chasis. He rolled down into the gutter and disappeared down one of the many sewer drainage vents that dotted the back alleys in this area.

A second and third rifle slug impacted with a sharp *ziiiiiing* on the street beside the jeep. One ricochet punctured the right front tire and, as the air spit forth in a noisy hiss, the MPs scrambled out to avoid being crushed.

"Who's doing all the shooting?" Broox wondered aloud, his voice cracking as they climbed the second fence to get back out of the apartment compound. They had spent several seconds checking behind bushes and under cars, but had come up empty handed.

"They must have him trapped," Bryant decided. "Come on. Give me a boost over this fence." But when Bryant reached the top, pistol still in hand, he became entangled in the coiled concertina wire, which was rigged to spring taut if an intruder attempted to breach it. Just as quickly, the whiplike recoil of the booby trap flung him to the ground. His fingers, tensing involuntarily as he fell the ten feet through space, jerked off a round when he landed on the other side, and the bullet drilled a hole clean through the calf in his left leg.

In the excitement and rush to avoid being hit by further accidental discharges, Broox jumped back over to the safe side of the fence, twisting his ankle as he landed down in the dark compound.

Up above them all, Green Beret Sgt. Mark Stryker, upset

178

that the episode had left two MPs injured, replaced the protective dust cover caps on the starlight scope attached to the M-14 rifle. He remained flat against the rooftop for several minutes then slowly rolled over toward the edge one last time to check the street below.

It was now crowded with curious Vietnamese, sleep still in their eyes, and Canh-Sat police jeeps were pulling up to the scene. From the rooftop he had an excellent view of the Decoy Squad as they carried the MP with the leg wound over to the medevac chopper just now setting down in the courtyard.

XIV. SWEET SUITE AT THE PALACE

Jeff gave the old woman behind the vendor's stand ten cents and she handed him a six-inch sliver of bamboo, piled high with small bits of twice-fried pork and balls of spicy, skewered beef. He dipped the satay in a bowl of red sauce and resumed wandering the little side streets snaking off from the Central Market. A vast castlelike formation of black clouds had rolled in over Saigon at dusk, but despite the rumblings low overhead, rain was slow in coming.

He stopped beside a newsstand, its Vietnamese-language women's magazines clipped with clothespins along vast lines of chicken wire. A bare lightbulb was strung overhead every ten feet or so, and the owner, a small, bent-over war veteran with one foot missing, was already hustling to cover his collection with tarps before the storm moved in.

Jeff pulled one of the small, laminated pocket magazines from its holder and examined the picture on the cover. It was Thanh Thuy, the Saigon musician—she had been Mai's favorite—and he flipped through the pages. The smell of the newspaper all around sent him back several months. To the first time he had tried to read *The Vietnam Guardian,* and Mai had laughed at the way he pronounced the words. He remarked that he couldn't smell ink on the paper—that everything in Vietnam had an aroma so different from its American counterpart.

"Including me?" she had asked, worry streaking her eyes.

"Especially you!" He had smiled back, taking her in his arms and falling down on the bed. "Your scent drives me wild."

Jeff walked over to the vendor and asked him what the magazine said about Thanh Thuy. "No speaky English," the old man responded irritably, never looking up at Jeff as he rushed about snipping strings off bundles of the *Saipan Post*. Jeff thought a minute then repeated the question in pidgin Vietnamese to the gnarled veteran, but the man only repeated, "No speaky English," and moved away from the American, busying himself with other chores on the far side of the stand.

Jeff stared at the picture on the cover for several minutes. The woman stood on a beach in front of several palm trees— probably Vung Tau, and held a straw conical hat in front of a purple and gold form-hugging *ao-dai*. The woman's long, silky hair, blue-black and shimmering like the sea at midnight, only enhanced the beauty of her high cheekbones and bottomless eyes. Her smile was secretive, the flare of her nostrils barely hiding a latent animalism that, in her posture, betrayed a threat to spring wildly from the cover at any time. The picture reminded Jeff of the nights he would come home from working the streets, just after curfew, and she would be waiting for him. They would sit on colorfully printed mats covering the hardwood floor and she would dish out bowls of long-grained rice mixed with boiled shrimp and then slices of heavily spiced beef and pork. Jeff would take his Tarot cards from the desk and make up the best possible future for them.

He had never learned how to use them, but it was easy to mark edges so that the Lovers and Good Fortune cards always appeared just at the right time. Mai would place one of the Thanh Thuy cassettes in the tape player, and although he could understand only some of the words, the music relaxed him instantly—soothing the soreness of twelve hours on patrol while she massaged his neck and shoulders.

Jeff could hear the soft, melodious words of the singer, and Mai humming in the background, their delicate singsong

182

voices reaching certain notes a split second before the chimes or violin, in the strange and haunting manner common to Vietnamese music.

"You buy or you no buy?" The vendor had returned. Jeff refrained from sarcastically complimenting the man on his sudden knowledge of broken English, replaced the magazine on a spotless rack and started off down the street.

He could remember the nights they had walked Saigon together. Hand in hand even though such public displays of affection were frowned on. It had taken several weeks for him to persuade her to even look him in the eye when they were outside the privacy of their tiny buffet. Then, he felt they were a part of the lively crowds overflowing from the sidewalks— the pedestrians mingling with the unending waves of motor scooters coasting down the wide, tree-lined boulevards and massing patiently at the intersections while the traffic cops funneled all the vehicles down into the narrower streets clogging the heart of the city.

Now he felt alone, totally isolated from the groups of Vietnamese filtering out from the restaurants and nightclubs into the balmy night air. As he passed the massive Rex cinema and saw the young couples paying photographers to snap pictures of them passing playfully before the illuminated water fountains, Jeff heard a young girl laughing at some joke the man with the camera had said just before pushing the flash button. The sound of her voice expressing such carefree joy in a land of so much misery made him stop.

Though he heard her laughing clearly, it was in an unreal, detached tone, the way one hears things when drunk and it sounds like voices are speaking through a hose or tin can.

Jeff moved closer to the girl sitting along the edges of the fountain wall. He wanted to tell her how beautiful she was in her rainbow-flowered *ao-dai*, how she so reminded him of someone special, but Jeff's feet moved sluggishly as if he were participating in a slow-motion home movie, and the girl was up and gone, strolling away with her friends before he could get

183

close to her.

Jeff stared down at the glittering dong coins at the bottom of the pool surrounding the fountain, and just as he was beginning to see Mai's face reflecting back at him in the water, a young couple beside him made their wish and tossed a coin into the pool, the sudden ripples destroying the image as it faded apart slowly.

"Hey, Joe! You want souvenir picture?" a harsh rasping voice came from behind him, and when he turned to see the old man in a black suit and bush hat who had taken the picture of him and Mai beside the fountains just before her death he suddenly saw her face flash before his eyes even clearer, more lifelike, and he rushed from the man and jumped into the nearest taxi.

"Where you go, mister? Maybe you want girl? Maybe you want dope? What you want, mister? You smoke pot, mister? Where you go?" But Jeff just told the man to take him on a tour of the city and they drove around in circles for almost an hour before the cabbie dropped him off in front of the imposing red-brick Notre Dame Basilica.

Jeff walked along Tu Do Street, passing beneath the shade trees hiding the main post office across from the cathedral, and though there was no sun to protect him from, the tamarinds seemed to lean out protectively over him, draping their drooping arms mere inches above his shoulders. As he headed downhill through the maze of postcard stalls reaching out from the pastel-shaded government buildings boasting the old French colonial architecture, he could smell the river almost a quarter mile away, to the southwest.

Jeff walked as if in a daze through the antique stands and coffee shops peddling croissants and exotic jams as he reached the halfway point between the docks, where the raunchy bars began sprouting up, crisscrossed Lam Son square and started down the much wider Le Loi boulevard, leaving the narrow Duong Tu Do, its banners boasting freedom and denouncing communism waving goodbye to him on the warm night breeze.

As Jeff started down Le Loi toward Dien Hong square and its Central Market, something in the air caused him to turn down Nguyen Hu, the avenue cluttered with thousands of flapping gold and red Vietnamese flags running parallel to Tu Do. Along the length of its center median was the flower market, its blinding colors assaulting the eyes even this late in the dark, moonless evening.

Jeff was drawn to the crimson roses Mai had loved so, but when he sat down at a table in the center of the open-air cafe surrounded by them and received his small cup of chrysanthemum tea, his eyes met those of the woman walking among the golden lotus petals and locked on.

She walked almost sideways toward him as she slowly went from flower to flower, pulling the petals gently up to her nose—her eyes always on his, a confidence and fearless smile attracting him even as it turned mildly seductive.

Like a weak magnet growing magically stronger, she eventually found her way over to his table and sat down across from him without a word being exchanged between them, his unwavering eyes the only invitation.

"The flowers are so beautiful this evening," she said to him after he poured her a cup of the tea, its aftertaste biting back at him. "Even with the rain this afternoon. Hardly any of the petals were damaged."

"Nature protecting her children"—he smiled—"that's why they call it a shower."

"But it was a downpour." She brought the tiny porcelain cup up closer to her eyes, casually inspecting its painted dragon design.

"Do I know you?" Jeff asked, his ingrown suspicions taking over, but he just as suddenly let down the walls, feeling her more to be just a streetwalker playing the field than any threat. It was getting close to curfew. She would have to latch onto a paying customer soon or go home for the night emptyhanded. No honey, no money. And that might mean no food till the next five-dollar joe.

"Must you know me?" she asked softly, her eyebrows wrinkling with the question's implications. "Can't we just talk and enjoy the flowers?" She changed the subject in midsentence, her thoughts wandering to the hum of the crowds flowing past on the street. "So many people," she concluded. "So many different kinds of people. White people, yellow people, black people, brown people. So many lonely people in the crowds." Her eyes turned back to his.

Her forehead fell several inches with the weight of the sadness, but her eyes remained locked on his, the pupils subtly pleading beneath the thin, almost invisible brows. "Do you have a name?" she asked, "or are you just one of the lonely, anonymous people passing through Saigon?"

Jeff smiled at her but still did not say anything to commit himself.

"My name is Vien," she told him as she reached across the table and placed her hands on his. Jeff noticed they were icy cold and wondered if that meant his were too warm, a sign of fever coming on.

Without any further conversation, her grip tightened slightly and she led him back out onto the street, wrapping both her arms around his left one in a protective I-don't-want-to-lose-you-in-the-crowd hug.

As they passed the Pan Am building, dark and chained up this late at night, his eyes searched out the large plastic model of a jumbo jet suspended over the slowly rotating globe behind the barred windows.

As they paused before the high plate glass window, she asked him, "What do you seek inside there, by the spinning world?" and Jeff could not answer, feeling an intense sadness in his heart at never being able to get on another plane bound for America, but then he caught himself smiling: hell, he didn't even have a passport, so what did it matter?

"What are you grinning at?" She put playful pressure on his arm as they entered the Palace Hotel. Jeff glanced at the reflecting tape identifying the building as number fifty-six when the doorman fluidly swept them through the entrance, and his mind flashed back to all the times management had called for the MPs here to escort a drunk GI back to his camp.

The guilt Jeff felt at being with another woman so soon after Mai's death seemed to fall from him like shattered glass as the girl from the flower market pulled him down on top of her in the dusty hotel room, its only light a candle flickering on the dresser.

Jeff felt the woman tightening her arms around him as she buried her face in his chest, and for a second he thought he heard a sob escape her lips, but all was silent except for music from the bar below vibrating the floorboards now and then.

He felt an uncontrollable sensation, an urge to completely cover this shivering waif and he slipped off her red blouse. As he began to move his hands down her smooth, soft-as-cotton skin along her sides and back, he found that the tightly fastened hinge closing her bra defied the clumsy efforts of his fingers. As he struggled for several seconds, he felt the urge to rip the fabric down the middle, but then her left arm came up and grabbed his, silencing their movement, her fingers worked on the hinge smoothly for a moment, until the clip slid free and the lacy top peeled from her skin and fell to the floor without a sound.

He watched the protected amber triangle below her chin spread out into a sumptuous expanse of flesh, her throat pulling tight as she laid her head back in subdued ecstasy when he kissed the swell of her breasts softly. The slightest scent of perfume was unable to compete with the arousing natural musk along the nape of her neck.

At first she clutched desperately to the elastic band along the edges of her hips, and he did not know if she was resisting or teasing, but then the tissue-thin garment was down around her narrow ankles and she kicked it off weakly, into the dark at the foot of the bed.

Her eyes were warning him off while at the same time her fingers encouraged him to hurry, and as he clasped his hands in the small of her back, slowly lowering himself between her thighs, her breathing grew shrill, more labored. It had a sense of urgency beneath the show of sadness and before his eyes she seemed to transform her fragrance, the curve of her body and the groan in her throat to resemble the woman he needed so much and thought he had lost forever.

Later, as she lay next to him, the side of her face snuggled up against his chest, he stared out the window at the flares drifting above the skyline. A sheet of monsoon rain was passing over the city, but its fury had yet to reach the outskirts of town where the flares floated among the silver clouds. As the torrential downpour rattled the tin of the roof overhead, he looked down at the long swirl of hair covering her face, merging with the dark. He smiled, the feeling of worry gone for once, and he held the woman tightly in his arms.

As she slept, the slightest rasping of a nightmare escaped on her breath, and in the dim glow filtering in from the flares he wondered what was going through her mind as her fingers subconsciously probed, again and again, at the hair on his arms. As he fell off into the abyss of sleep, there was no doubt in his mind the woman draped across his chest was Mai reborn.

XV. TANGLED IN A SPIDER'S WEB

As Dong filtered in among the servicemen crowding the dance floor of the Queen Bee nightclub at 106 Nguyen Hu, his eyes sparkled at the sight of so many dirty boots—all potential shoeshine customers. One GI wearing hush puppies and dancing up a storm with a Chinese waitress rated a grumbled insult from the boy as he brushed past several Americans hastily.

"Slow down, young man." The Canh-Sat reached out from the bar counter and grabbed Dong by the arm. "What's your hurry?"

"Let me go! Let me go!" The boy struggled to get loose, but Officer Jon Toi had a tight grip on his arm.

"Settle down, young man." The fire in Toi's eyes instantly silenced the shoeshine boy, and his shoulders stooped resignedly as his head bent toward the floor. "That's better. Now why don't you relax and give me a shine." And the Canh-Sat paid the price in advance.

Dong's attitude changed immediately, a smile creased his somber face, and he put down his box and set about buffing Toi's leather police boots.

"Don't I know you?" The Canh-Sat suddenly eyed Dong with mock suspicion. The boy could feel sweat break out everywhere under his T-shirt, but he calmly answered that he had never known any policemen or been in any trouble.

"You ever run a fruit stand, son?" Toi joked. Everyone in town knew the police and Army were looking for a young sidewalk vendor accused of poisoning the refreshments of ARVN QCs with glass splinters and razor blades, but Dong just shook his head vigorously in the negative and continued shining the cop's boots.

At that moment, a fight between Americans and some of the special combat troops recently dispatched to Vietnam by the Royal Kingdom of Thailand broke out on the far side of the dance floor, and Toi rose to assist the bouncer. At the same time, Dong scooped up his shoeshine box and disappeared out the swinging front doors between the legs of an American MP who had just climbed the steps up to the Queen Bee.

When the lone MP saw a Canh-Sat flying through the air inside the bar, he calmly executed an about-face and skipped back down to his jeep, where he reached for the radio microphone, then, after uttering a few coded numbers, leaned back casually on the vehicle's fender.

A couple minutes later, ten MPs entered the bar, and at the sight of the white letters glowing on the black helmets, the nightclub fell silent except for the two brawlers wrestling on the dance floor.

A skinny Vietnamese man with a scraggly mustache and a leather jacket studded with phony jewels ran up to the two combatants as soon as he saw the MPs flow in. The now-brave owner of the establishment began kicking at the two men and yelling in a mouselike voice, "Okay, MPs come! Now you go! MPs come! Out you go!" and he turned and bowed politely to the soldiers with the night sticks drawn, and commenced kicking the fighters a couple more times.

When Private First Class Thomas later located Jon Toi sprawled unconscious under a nearby table, he summoned several other MPs over and they carried the Canh-Sat across the dance floor to the bar, where they laid him out on the counter.

Sergeant Richards came over and tapped Toi on the cheek a couple times, and after getting no response, dumped a glass of melted ice in his eyes. That quickly brought him to, and as four MPs hustled the handcuffed prisoners out to a waiting patrol jeep, Richards propped Toi up and slapped him on the back like he was burping a big baby.

"Anything broken?" Thomas grinned at the dazed Oriental, and after Toi felt his jaw in several different places, opened and closed his mouth a couple times, then smiled and shook his head "no," the entire bar began clapping and whistling. A group of bargirls who had been clustered around the fallen policeman began pampering him like mother hens once it was determined he had sustained no serious injuries. Jon hopped off the bar though, and waved his American friends over to the closest table.

"Where's Bryant?" he asked anxiously about the MP who had now given him two cameras. "I wanted to tell him one of the major wire services paid me handsomely for some pictures I took of the Buddhist bonze torching himself on Nguyen Van Thoi Street last week."

"How much is 'handsomely'?" Richards asked.

"Twenty-five dollars, U.S." Toi beamed proudly.

"What a rip off," Thomas replied with disgust in his tone. "They'd've paid a Westerner four times as much, at least."

"Typical news media," Richards grumbled, ignoring the fact he knew twenty-five bucks was a month's salary to Toi. "Nothing but a bunch of bloodsucking bullshitters."

"Yeah, I go outta my way to razz those jerks always camping out at the Continental Palace—the clowns that cover the war from the terrace, sipping brandy in their spotless safari shirts," claimed Thomas.

"So where is Specialist Bryant?" Toi asked again, the smile still on his face though he now feared the MP might have rotated back stateside without saying goodbye. The Canh-Sat was not interested in their hatred of the press corps.

191

Richards exchanged tired looks with Thomas, and Toi began to fear the worst: that his American friend had become another statistic—a body count for the VC.

"Bryant was wounded two nights ago," Thomas finally answered him. "Took a round in the leg." The MP looked across the table and raised his shoulders slightly, avoiding Toi's eyes when he added, "As a result of hostile action."

"That was *you* guys in that incident over at Phan Dinh Phung?" Toi sat up in his chair, eager to hear a full accounting of the firefight.

"Yeah . . ." Richards began.

"Where there's danger and excitement, you'll always find the Decoy Squad," Thomas interrupted sarcastically.

"Fucking snipers," Toi almost spat the words out. The Canh-Sat rarely used English slang or profanity.

"Yeah, Broox screwed up his leg too. He's on light duty for a while—cleaning weapons at the Arms Room," Thomas explained. "Bryant is at Third Field Army Hospital. I'm sure he'll be back in a couple weeks. Until then, I'd like you to meet the two clowns we're stuck with as replacements," and Toi turned to see two men re-entering the Queen Bee after helping escort the prisoners out to the jeeps.

"Toi, I want you to meet Kip Mather," Richards motioned to a short, stocky buck sergeant in his midthirties with a brown bushy mustache the Asian sun had lightened many shades. Toi stood up to shake hands with the mellow-looking MP.

"Sit down! Sit down!" Mather laughed, pushing Toi gently back down onto his seat by the shoulders. "I thought you were supposed to be injured."

"Caught me with a lucky left hook," Toi explained good-naturedly.

"Gonna have to start calling him glass-jaw Jon," Thomas said, laughing.

"And this is Paul Kruger," Richards said.

Toi recalled both names as he inspected the downcast face of the slender private. He made no mention of the incident where

Kruger had panicked when his partner was ambushed by a VC sapper squad two months earlier—the same time Mather swooped in on the foot chase and captured the guerrillas, killing one in hand-to-hand combat. Instead, he kept the smile on his face and turned to Richards. "Who is in command if you have *two* sergeants on such a small squad?" he joked.

"Sergeant Richards is always in control," Mather said with a straight face. "I just make all the decisions."

Even Kruger smiled at that one, and Toi looked at the teenaged MP carefully, sorry that such a young man had to come to his country to witness—even participate in—such tragedies. But Toi also looked for the bright side of all such matters, and he felt deep in his gut that the Decoy Squad would be good for the kid.

"Some tea?" A tiny waitress in a gossamer-light *ao-dai* had glided up to their table, unnoticed, and when she bent over toward Kruger's cup the scent tingling his nostrils as their eyes met became a veiled invitation of better evenings to come.

Several blocks away, Jeff Rodgers was still in bed. He had awakened nearly twelve hours earlier, but the small tissue hanging a couple inches above his face, "Xin Loi, manoi" written across it in purple lipstick caused him to freeze apprehensively beneath the mosquito net.

Each time it snapped back in his direction, the electric fan in the corner of the dimly lit room would cause the sign to flutter back and forth, and when he noticed the wire running from the bed post above his head down to the room's distant doorknob, he began wishing one of Saigon's almost-daily power outages would strike. That would cut off the fan that threatened to set off the grenades wired to the bed.

Jeff could also feel a second wire looped around his left ear, running down around his throat, under the small of his back, up between his legs and tied around the big toe on his right foot. He could not see the grenade attached to this wire either, but he was positive there was one rigged to go off a few seconds after he got up an inch or two off the bed. He was amazed none of the bombs had detonated while he twisted and turned in his sleep. And the second *that* thought passed through his mind he realized last night had been the most relaxing, the soundest sleep he had had since losing Mai. Perhaps that explained it.

The thought also ricocheted through his mind that tripping one of the booby-trap wires would be the quickest way to join her again. But he knew he had too much to do in the coming weeks. Later, after the score was settled, he would have the luxury of planning how to leave Saigon and rejoin his Mai.

Rodgers knew that the hotel's pool lay below his window— he had always been careful to check for potential escape routes prior to sleeping in strange places, but he could not remember how close it was, and whether or not a leap from the second floor window would take him clear of the spired-umbrella-sheltered tables that dotted the courtyard below.

He moved his toe slightly and felt the wire running under his back tighten all the way to his ear. *God, she had been good! Why didn't I rouse while she was hooking me up?* he thought, and he yelled the words across his brain. *Because the damn hooker kept me aroused all night!* he rationalized. *Until sweet exhaustion set in.*

Rodgers tapped the headboard slightly, hoping to feel the grenade bounce a little bit back there, but there was no vibration. It must be securely taped instead of hanging from a supporting screw-eye device. That might make it easier to survive.

With three to six seconds after the pin was pulled before the grenade would detonate, he would have fallen below the second floor level on his dive out the window. The shrapnel would probably pass over his head. But if the grenade were allowed to fall to the ground and roll along the floor, the arcing chunks of hot metal could very well pepper his back and put him out of commission for a long time. And no telling what other little surprises that little vamp had rigged up as a bonus.

194

He began wondering what he had said over their cup of tea at the flower market that could possibly have angered her enough to want to torture him with such anxiety before his execution, and just as he came to the conclusion he had spoke of nothing except the rains there came a light knock on the door.

Jeff's body tensed and he considered yelling a warning, but he remained silent when the maid entered the room. The young Vietnamese woman, pretty despite the dull, white uniform and her pulled-back bun of hair, stared in shock at the white man lying nude on the bed, a network of wires crisscrossing his body.

When Jeff heard the pin behind the headboard clatter to the ground, he bolted for the window, snatching his pants off a chair as he ran, and crashed through the glass head-first.

His bare ass disappearing through the window in an awkward swan dive was the last thing the surprised maid saw before the deafening explosion tore off her arms and twisted her face into a bloody lump of torn and mangled flesh.

Officer Toi was in the first group of policemen that responded to the fire on the second floor of the Palace Hotel. When it became evident there was nothing anyone could do for the maid splattered across the walls of room 211, he walked over to the body lying beside the pool and clicked off a couple pictures before the investigators draped a blanket over it.

"Jon Toi! Jon Toi!" A young police private was running up to the Canh-Sat, excitement in his voice—he was dragging a frightened hotel chauffeur along beside him. "This hack driver says he transported a beautiful woman in a red dress downtown. He says she was cold as ice and had a set of piercing eyes that spoke a message no words could. He says she scared the hell into him."

"Where did you take her?" Toi demanded, shaking the unfortunate cabbie by the shoulders.

"The bus station. Central," he answered respectfully, and as

195

Toi ran for the nearest police motorcycle, he added, "but that was over twelve hours ago. She left in the middle of the night!" He raised his voice so it would carry to the running Canh-Sat, but Toi was gone.

It was not unusual for buses to be delayed a half day in Vietnam, especially at Central Station, where they often had to wait for incoming vehicles to arrive before a bus could be scheduled to leave the capital. Several times the entire system had even collapsed, and there was always the threat of bandits and terrorist roadblocks on lonely highways outside the metropolitan area, but with American aid Saigon was seeing a new transportation boom that might last longer than other government projects often doomed to failure from the start because of widespread graft and corruption.

Toi had stopped at a police call box and suggested men be deployed to set up roadblocks on the major highways leading north from the city—to Tay Ninh, Ben Cat and Bien Hoa. If his supervisors had asked, he couldn't explain why he felt Madam Pham V would head north. It was only that the results of all his footwork pointed to a diagonal pattern beginning southwest of Phan Dinh Phung, along the riverbank brothels, and ending to the northeast of Saigon's main north-south boulevard.

But the request for roadblocks had not been necessary. Even before he could arrive at the central bus station, Toi, who had been scanning the passengers aboard buses passing him in the opposite direction, spotted the sinister-looking woman in the crimson dress. On an orange bus heading north toward Gia Dinh. And, of course, as Toi noticed uneasily, her unblinking eyes had spotted and locked onto him long before he located her in the window seat.

Toi turned the motorcycle around and, despite the heavy traffic, swerved in and out of the awkward lorries and reckless cyclos until he was just behind the bus's rear bumper.

Most of the motorcycles utilized by the Vietnamese National Police were privately owned, and therefore not equipped with emergency lights or siren. Toi's was no exception, so he would have to follow the bus until it made its first stop. He could speed up and verbally order the driver over to the side of the road, but Toi was content to wait, hoping to rally any other Canh-Sats he might pass into joining the pursuit. He did not relish apprehending the cunning murderess alone.

Most buses in Saigon had extended bumpers and wide running boards that permitted extra passengers to ride along for half fare. The bus Toi was tailing had six or seven "undesirables" crowded onto the rear bumper, and when they spotted his uniform, they started in on him with a barrage of insults, mild threats and suggestive profanities.

Any other day, Toi would have enjoyed fighting the ex-cons and brave drunks, but this time he barely heard the catcalls, so anxious was he to arrest the phantom in the red dress and learn what power she possessed to so influence his sleepless nights with unsettling nightmares.

When the beer bottle glanced off Toi's cheek and another bottle shattered in front of the motorcycle, the last thing he saw before sliding across the pavement unconscious was her dark, haunting eyes narrowed in a mocking farewell.

Diana Ross and the Supremes were singing "Reflections" on the small wall radio Stryker had tuned to the American Forces Radio Network. He liked the way the song started out with special electronic effects, and after he turned up the volume he returned to the bed and kneeled back down over Lai's bare buttocks, his own legs spread apart as they pressed against her muscular thighs along the outside.

"What do you think about moving south?" he asked her as he resumed massaging her back.

"South?" she repeated the word, unsure what the question had been. Her mind always drifted off when he gently rubbed the soreness from between her shoulder blades then rapped the spaces between her vertebrae with the edges of his hands—like playful karate chops. She had never known of a man who

197

enjoyed massaging his woman like the Green Beret soldier did—it was just unheard of in most of the Orient, certainly in Pleiku!

Stryker moved her long, black hair off the nape of her neck and bent over to kiss the fragrant stretch of soft skin behind her ears. "Saigon. How would you like to move to Saigon?"

Lai had been resting her chin in the pillow, staring straight ahead out the window at the clouds racing past the eerie half moon. She moved her face onto its side and tried to look up at him out of the corner of her eye. "Leave Pleiku?"

"Don't think of it as leaving Pleiku," he whispered, running his tongue along the edge of her ear until she became annoyed and brushed him away. "Think of it as a new adventure—a chance to experience the big city."

"But leave Pleiku?" she repeated, astonished that he could consider such a thing.

"Why do you say it like that: 'but leave Pleiku?' You have nothing here but me anyway. You've said yourself no one would love you—would want you after you've been with me." Stryker regretted saying that before the entire sentence had even come out.

"But Pleiku is my home. Can you understand that? I do not like Saigon. All the people—they scare me. They are Vietnamese."

"You're Vietnamese, Lai."

"I'm Montagnard. I'm Hill people. They call us *moi*, in Saigon. That means—"

"I know what it means. They call you 'barbarians' only because you're savages in bed." He grinned, moving his knee to spread her thighs wide, but she resisted.

"I hate Saigon," she said. "There is more death in that city than in the jungles." The fear in her voice sent pangs of guilt through him that served to cool his desires. He rolled over on his side, bracing his head in the cup of his hand and watched her eyes as she spoke. "Saigon would destroy what we have," she said, pronouncing the bigger words slowly. "Saigon

198

eventually destroys all who have anything to do with her."

"The soldiers attacked Phu Son yesterday," he said. "They slaughtered forty-seven civilians."

"The soldiers? You mean the guerrillas—the VC."

"I mean the South Vietnamese soldiers. They dressed up in black pajamas and carried AK47s to imitate the Cong. They gunned down a generation of youngsters, purely for propaganda purposes."

Lai lowered her head and shuddered uncontrollably, realizing they could have chosen her housing project to make their point just as easily.

"I'm leaving the military, Lai," he told her, and her startled eyes flashed back at his.

"Leave the Green Berets?" she gasped, the whisper an accusation more than a question.

How could he think to do that? she wondered. In all her life she had never known any men who didn't soldier for their money.

"My enlistment runs up this month. I don't intend to stay in. I have a job offer in Saigon. The change could be good for both of us."

Lai sat up on the edge of the bed and turned away from him. As she watched the moonbeams sparkle in the tears rolling across her upturned breasts the fear that she had lost him now forever overpowered her and she ran from the bungalow and fled into the night.

"It's okay, Jon Toi." The elderly Canh-Sat official was standing beside his hospital bed, reassuring him. "We got her crossing the river into Cholon. That was a brilliant idea of yours to set up roadblocks around the city."

"Cholon? But she was headed— What color bus was she picked up on?"

"Well, green and white—one of the Chinese lines I suppose."

"And her clothing—what color dress was she wearing when arrested?"

"Colors of buses, colors of dresses," the supervisor sighed. "Poor Jon Toi. You need some rest. Let us handle it from this point. You did a fine job. It will be reflected in your personnel folder, should you ever put in for promotion," and the ancient dinosaur from the Vo Tanh police headquarters turned sharply on his heels and started for the door. "Get some sleep, Jon Toi."

Toi had hastily dressed and raced down the stairwell even before the supervisor's elevator reached the ground floor. Within fifteen minutes his taxi had arrived at number 252 Vo Tanh Street.

The Canh-Sats had the woman strapped down to a large table in a small, drafty cubicle deep in the building's second-level basement. She was stripped naked and spread-eagle on her back, her wrists and ankles tied to brass rings hanging from the corner edges of the polished table.

Toi rushed down the barren corridor leading to the last room set aside for interrogations, but he was stopped by a policeman who had been posted outside the steel door. Toi searched the pockets of the robe still draped over his trousers, felt the pain lancing the cracked ribs, and finally located his police ID.

When he was eventually allowed to pass, Toi discovered that the room he had once known to be entirely white, with an air-conditioner that cooled a guerrilla's resolve and took him out of the hot jungle environment where he felt safe and confident, was now painted over with zebralike stripes—offensive black bars, creating an illusion that one had entered a maze from which there was no escape, either physically or mentally.

A single light bulb hung a few feet over the woman and its harsh yellow glow cast grim shadows across her body, making her breasts appear much larger than they were and the soft mound below her flat stomach swell unnaturally.

A hunched over, mouselike Canh-Sat entered the room after Toi, smiling from ear to ear and carrying a collection of field

200

phones. Another, taller officer anxiously took the machines from him and set them up on the table beside the woman. Blood dripping from the tips of one hand indicated her fingernails had already been jerked off with pliers and her eyes darted about nervously as the policeman unrolled electrical wires from the field phones and attached copper spring battery clips to them.

Toi noticed that a red and green *ao-dai* was draped over a nearby chair. It was not the clothing his suspect usually wore. And Pham V would never permit such a look of terror to violate her confident features—he was sure of that.

The interrogator rubbed the backs of his rough fingers without emotion across her nipples until they sprang erect, and then he opened the tiny serrated jaws of one of the clips and let it clamp shut on one of them.

The woman, her long straight hair drenched with perspiration, bit her tongue and contained the scream trying to escape her lungs, but she was still moaning in agony when the officer let the second clamp close on the other nipple.

Without warning or compassion, he then spread her legs even wider with one hand while he inserted a third clip with the other into the folds of her vagina. His pudgy hand waved in the air without further ceremony and the bent-over assistant heavily cranked the field phones alive, sending a current of juice along the woman's tender chest that penetrated to her deepest insides. The screams escaped her this time, echoing through the room endlessly, and Toi closed his eyes and bowed his head.

The woman, spread out on the table for a growing number of policemen to see, had a history of involvement with radical causes, most notably the Buddhist student movement, but she was not a hardcore communist.

"All right!" she screamed again in Vietnamese. "I did it! I killed them! I did it!" she lied. "Please stop! I'm dying here! Can't you see? I'm dying here!"

Blood was beginning to drip steadily from between her legs

onto the smooth table, and when she could not tell the policemen who her cell leaders were or who ordered the murders, another bolt of electricity was shot into her loins.

The woman began crying uncontrollably, and when they tired of zapping her with the phone coils, the officer in charge removed the battery clips and attached clothespins to her nipples, then ordered his subordinates to lift her off the table as far as her bonds would permit, by pulling on the sharp, plastic pins. When her back cleared the tabletop a few inches, the Canh-Sat let go of the clothespins and she bounced back onto the hardwood roughly.

"Tell me the names of you intelligence people in this area," the officer in charge whispered into her ear as the cigarette between his fingers was slowly forced "accidentally" against the vaccination scar on her arm.

Between her screams, the woman rattled off several Vietnamese and Chinese names, and although Toi knew none of the people were active communists, the interrogator jotted down the names in a notebook anyway.

"I want the addresses where your cell meetings are held," the officer demanded, and when the woman hesitated because the only address she could think of in her delirium was her parents', the policeman waved another Canh-Sat into the room. He was carrying a small jar, and he handed it to his superior with outstretched hands, as if he found the contents repugnant.

The policeman held the jar next to her dazed eyes so she could inspect the huge army ants crawling about inside. "Do you know where I'm going to insert these if you don't supply us with some addresses?" He grinned down at her evilly, his lips an inch from her lips as he spoke.

Toi knew where the ants would burrow next. He had seen teenage girls have heart attacks enduring this form of torture. He watched as the interrogator, tired of listening to the woman's cries, stuffed a rag into her mouth. He then methodically placed a washcloth over the woman's nose and directed a corporal to slowly pour water onto the towel. The drowning sensation that followed was enough to drive people insane. Toi knew this was fact because in his earlier days on the force they had made him watch some of the interrogation sessions with North Vietnamese POWs to see if he had the stomach for police work.

As the corporal started in on his second jug of water the woman gagged for loss of air, her ankles straining against the ropes, her breasts quivering like jello as her chest heaved in jerking convulsions.

The woman's heart must have burst from the strain when the interrogator slid the lid off the jar, selected one of the vicious ants with a long pair of tweezers, and yelled, "Remove the wires from this whore's cunt!"

It made Toi sad and ashamed to see the woman's body suddenly still, because he had seen her eyes. He had seen her terrified eyes, straining to pop out just above the edge of towel covering her nose, and they were not the cruel, confident eyes of the woman haunting his dreams.

XVI. THE GUERRILLA WHO FLEW

Spec. 4 Bryant had voluntarily extended his tour of duty in Vietnam because he liked patrolling the big city. Especially a capital city in the Orient, crammed to overflowing with nearly four million potential troublemakers. Despite all his belly-aching, there was a special place in Bryant's heart for Saigon. He couldn't tell you why. But there were a lot of feelings he had about Southeast Asia that he couldn't explain.

Like why the round-eye top-heavy nurse shaking her rear back and forth as she walked by his hospital bed carrying bedpans failed to arouse him while the modest Vietnamese nun with the soft voice and the playful wink set his blood on fire every time she passed, distributing the free Bibles.

Bryant also wondered about the hookers standing on the street corners several floors below his window. Legs astride lamppost blocks and painted lips whispering provocative offers to passing soldiers, he couldn't remember the last time they'd set out to bust one. Hell, maybe they were legal, he decided. After all, they carried government-issued VD cards. But what about the Canh-Sats who launched raids on shack-up jobs where there weren't any papers making the couples legal? If that wasn't coming down hard on the whores he didn't know what was.

A low-flying Phantom jet screaming past drew his eyes back

205

out the window, and they eventually fell from the smoke trail hanging on the horizon to another girl staking out her territory at the other end of the block. A green and white Canh-Sat patrol cruised past, and the cops on board eyed them more as horny construction workers than professional peace officers. Nope, that was one job he didn't miss: collaring prostitutes.

One of his worst experiences had been at Fort Gordon, Georgia when his squad, recruited midway through the academy, participated in the arrest of three call girls whose pimp showed up firing his revolver, pumping off six rounds through the walls before they jumped up off the ground, rushed him as he was reloading, and wrestled the gun away.

Then there was the time when he was a private assigned to Fitzsimmons Army Medical Center in Denver. He and Sgt. Raul Schultz were loaned to the Metropolitan Enforcement Group (MEG) so some new faces could be used to entice the crafty escort services into sending more hookers out to the suburbs. They had spent two hours in the rain, waiting on a second-floor balcony for the officers inside to gain the trust of the prostitutes that finally arrived. Just as one of the girls proceeded to massage her undercover lover, the other hooker opened the sliding glass door and stepped out onto the balcony despite the downpour for a breath of fresh air. When she discovered the two dark forms crouching under the air-conditioner she began screaming and warning the people inside that burglars were climbing up the balcony.

Raul sprang after her as she ran topless through the suite and finally badged her at the front door. Bryant had started to spring from his crouched position also when he slammed his head into the bottom of the air-conditioner they had been hiding under.

By the time he shook off the daze he learned that the prostitutes were so relieved the apartment wasn't being robbed they were actually happy to be going to jail.

Bryant flinched at the memory. The bump on his head from the assault on the air-conditioner bothered him for several days. And now, here he was twelve thousand miles from home and he still couldn't keep from sustaining self-inflicted injuries. Boy, wouldn't that be a laugh if they paraded down the middle of his hospital wing for a Purple Heart award ceremony. After all, that crazy Sergeant Richards had wrote up the report to show that Bryant's gunshot wound was a result of hostile fire from the rooftop sniper so the incident wouldn't make the Decoy Squad look bad. But Bryant knew they never gave Purple Heart medals to MPs, and that was another thing he couldn't figure out about the 'Nam.

"Well, good afternoon, Monsieur Bryant," came a high pitched voice with a French accent from down the hall. He turned from the window to see the Vietnamese nun hovering at the foot of his bed. "And how are we doing on this pleasant Friday?" she said, beaming, handing him a letter from home.

"We are doing fine, Sister Hoa, and how are *you* doing?" He grinned and she erupted into laughter at his play on words.

She shook his healthy leg vigorously and said, "And how is the leg which stops bullets?" She asked the question with a nasty smirk, and Bryant gasped at her mistake and the realization she might treat the other leg—the injured one— even worse. His spasm made her laugh again, and she said, "Only kidding, Monsieur Bryant," and she tapped the injured limb ever so slightly.

"Oh, you little demon!" he growled good-naturedly and reached out to grab her, but she skipped off to the next bed and he forced his eyes out the window again, suddenly feeling guilty as he tried to picture the petite saint without her religious robes on.

Bryant almost fell out of his bed trying to get a better look at the figure darting across the street below. "Anyone got some binoculars?" he shouted, knowing there would be none on a recovery ward, and as the startled patients and Catholic sisters looked his way, he strained tired eyes against the afternoon sun but lost sight of the man.

Bryant stared at his bandaged leg for several seconds,

207

knowing the torn muscle would not yet support his weight. There was just no way he could dash down there and contact the sprinting American. Bryant had only seen his back and the top of his head, but the gray windbreaker, flapping in the wind, told him he had just spotted Jeff Rodgers.

"So here we are." Thomas had some of the MPs on the edge of their seats. The others either hustled to get their equipment ready for the guardmount inspection or didn't bother to listen, bored with hearing his war stories for the umpteenth time.

"Fort Carson is snowed in and our car's ice skating to a possible stick up. Some citizen complained that the store clerk was acting suspicious—hands shaking, counting out the wrong change, stuff like that. So we pull up, and sure enough this guy we've never seen before is behind the cash register. Well, my partner, this guy named Mick Boebick—yeah, really! That was his name. Anyway, Micky asks this guy for his ID and he says he ain't got none 'cuz he just lives in the apartment house behind the store. He don't drive, so he says. But the guy gives him a name and date of birth, okay? And we're low on pack sets, so Mick comes back out to the car to use the radio. Well, I been sitting in the car the whole time, 'cuz, hey—I'm nobody's dummy: I don't leave the unit 'less I have to. So Mick runs a warrants check and DMV and while we're waiting the clerk takes his mop and starts going at it real dedicatedlike, toward the back door."

Thomas laughed at this point and had to pause while he caught his breath. "Oh yeah—and when Mick was leaving the store with this guy walking right behind him—this is the funny part. Well, at first the clerk was real hostile, okay? Says he's tired of getting rousted by the cops all the time just 'cuz he's a longhair. Well, after Mick explains we're just trying to keep his young ass safe from the bad guys he has this change of heart and even pats old Mick on the back as he follows him to the door. Even says 'Thanks for checking up on me, buddy.'

"So here we are, waiting in the patrol car for a computer return, and as you know: them damn computers always go down when it snows. So we're sitting there waiting for ten . . . fifteen . . . twenty minutes. Midnight rolls around and the clerk comes back up to the front doors, waves, then locks the place up. Well, some broad pulls up—I guess she thought it was a twenty-four hour joint or something, so anyway she walks up to the doors just as we're rolling down a window to advise her the place is locked up and she jerks a door open—this clerk didn't lock 'em up so good after all, you know?

"Well, we dash into the store, true to form, and this jerk-off clerk is nowhere to be found. I mean, we check the cooler and the back office—everywhere. Then eagle-eye Mick notices the rear door is open and the clerk's smock is lying on the floor. Footsteps lead out through the snow to the fence in the rear parking lot.

"Well, we're frantic by now, right? Recheck the store upside-down, okay? And who do we find tied up in the restroom, bound and gagged with a cloth hand towel? The female clerk!

"I mean to tell you—we call in backup units, K-9 patrols, the whole gang. Even get back a computer check that says the guy gave us a correct name and DOB that checked out. Well, poor Micky is just ready to crawl under a rock and die. Seems this jerk-off hippie robbed the female clerk with a butcher knife.

"But he only got twelve lousy bucks outta the cash register, so after he ties up the clerk he takes it upon himself to play cashier himself for a while too—no, hey really! This is a true story!

"But the worst part, for Mick anyway, was having a robber with a ten-inch butcher knife under his smock walk your ass to the door with his fuckin' arm practically around your shoulder! I mean, the newspapers got ahold of the story somehow, and the guys wouldn't let him live it down. Razz, razz, razz. I mean, you'd've razzed him too, right?" Somebody

209

in the back of the room started snoring.

"So does this story have a moral?" a private in front of Thomas asked.

"Well, poor Mick spent three months showing artists' conception sketches to all the residents in the apartment complex behind the store that got robbed—did all that off-duty, no less. Sent teletypes everywhere. I mean, he wanted this scumbag *bad!*"

"And the lesson learned here?"

"Well, Mick stumbles upon this same guy breaking into a public phone coinbox just as he's about to give up on police work altogether. Fights with the guy and his old lady in the street until some sweetheart calls the cavalry and help arrives—and I mean it couldn't have come at a better time: this guy's old lady is trying to break a two-by-four over Mick's head while he's wrestling with the suspect!"

"The moral of the story, Thomas. The moral!" Some MPs were getting up and leaving the briefing room, but several rookies showed genuine interest.

"Well, they arrest this jerk, charge him with the full package: armed robbery, resisting arrest, assaulting a cop. 'Course, he only gets probation and a slap on the wrist, but that's another story.

"But you know what he's got in his wallet? One lousy dollar bill. But my friends, this just happens to be the same dollar bill the manager xeroxed, just in case of a hold up, so they'd have the serial number."

"Three months later, and all he's got left is the marked bill?" one of the rookies asked incredulously. "Now, that's justice!"

"Hey, do I stutter, baboon breath?"

One MP listening to the story turned with a puzzled look on his face to the man beside him. "Is that the moral of the story?" he asked seriously.

"The moral," Thomas interrupted, "and I must say that it applies quite well to our particular situation right here in the Republic of Vietnam, is that you don't turn your back on no

210

one! You just can't tell the good guys from the bad guys anymore."

The same man who had been dreading the possibility of a guardmount inspection now welcomed the appearance of two lieutenants as they burst into the room, their polished MP helmets balanced sharply on the edge of their foreheads.

"Attention!" someone called out dryly, but the lieutenant in the lead, a slender thirty year old, told everyone to remain at ease even before they could stand up.

"Gentlemen," one of the officers began as he laid a clipboard on the podium facing the MPs and glanced through it without looking up. "Let's start checking the oil on those patrol jeeps daily. Just like it says in the S.O.P. We blew two engines last month, and it wasn't because the men involved were travelling too fast."

A soft ripple of laughter could be heard through the room and someone motioned at Thomas.

"Weapons." The lieutenant placed a checkmark on his clipboard. "Had another M-16 turn up missing last month. Yes, I realize the MP involved had the weapon chained up to the machine gun support bar, but a lousy chain isn't going to stop a determined thief—especially when the prize is a new, American-made automatic rifle. So let's start slinging them babies *every*where you go! And I mean *every*where: the shitter, domestics, even coffee breaks—especially coffee breaks."

"The last one was stolen during a coffee break," one MP whispered across to another.

"The next man who loses his rifle better lose it because he died in the line of duty," warned the lieutenant, striking on a touchy subject. "Otherwise, I'm personally gonna send his ass home in an Army casket. Any questions?"

A private in the back of the room raised his hand, but the lieutenant ignored him, causing another round of mild laughter. "Haircuts. Now whatta you guys think this is, a combat zone or something?" Thomas slid down in his seat so he was somewhat hidden by the man sitting in front of him.

"You men are supposed to set an example for the other soldiers. You know the motto: 'Of the Troops and for the Troops.' For Christ's sake, there's a little old Vietnamese barber just down the street—charges a lousy fifty cents. Now that you know, there'll be no excuses."

"I heard he's a VC, Lieutenant," one of the rookies said seriously. "You ever seen his hooch, sir? Razor city!"

"Shit, that near-sighted *papa-san* is the president's grand-father," the officer exaggerated. "He's as patriotic as apple pie and nuoc mam."

No stray comments followed that revelation.

"Okay. Report writing. Gentlemen, you're sloughing off again." The lieutenant tipped his helmet back off his nose so the men could see his eyes for the first time. "I can't read half your scribble."

That's because you've always got your head up your ass, Thomas thought to himself.

"A lot of people see these reports: victims, lawyers, insurance companies, even the suspects. It's all public record, once I approve it and send it up to PMO. I don't know about you, but I like to make a good impression.

"All right, I wanna see a show of hands: how many of you lovelies shack up off post?" the lieutenant's tone was appealing to the men's masculinity. Almost every hand shot up. Including the men with white rings where their wedding bands had been. The second lieutenant in the room began handing out small index cards as the briefing officer continued. "Fill these out and turn them in before you leave tonight, gentlemen. Too many of you are impossible to get in contact with in the event of emergency alerts.

"From now on, when you hear the air raid sirens after a rocket attack, expect an MP jeep from Pershing to show up at your bungalow paradise to drag your ass back to camp so you can earn your overseas pay." A loud groan followed the new regulation.

"Item number six. How many of you Romeos have sex with

the nationals?" Less hands shot up this time, mainly out of suspicion. "Now I'm not talking about a short-time. I'm talking sexual intercourse on a regular basis."

A few more hands slowly rose.

"And how many of you gigolos with your hands up have never caught the clap?"

Several hands went back down, leaving only four or five in the air. The lieutenant stood up on his toes and began counting the hands and recording the names of the MPs they belonged to.

"Great, great. I'm proud to say you gentlemen will be part of a new research project the medics are conducting. They're trying to locate a new vaccine for this strain of penicillin-resistant VD making the rounds, and you guinea pigs are about to donate all kinds of blood!"

This brought a smattering of applause from the MPs who had "failed" the question. "I guess they figure anyone who can survive a week over here without contracting the black syph is worth a closer look at," said one.

"Okay, moving right along: Courtesy. There shall be no more contests to see who can arrest the most officers."

"Contests? What contests?" came a snickered whisper from the back of the room.

"As of this moment, that practice comes to a screeching halt," the lieutenant ignored the comedian. "Understood?" A few heads nodded.

"Special patrols. We need more spotlight checks of the sectors giving us problems with violent crime, and less bar runs on Tu Do. Sergeant Richards has been compiling statistics and has come up with the map you see behind me. Look it over, men. There's a pattern forming up there. I'm not sure what it is, yet"—he smiled down at Richards—"but check it out. And act accordingly. Concentrate your patrols where the bad guys congregate, and I might be handing out Arcoms come the end of your tours.

"Have a request here from General Westmoreland's office

that we spotlight the MACV headquarters building a little more often. Somebody's been running women's underwear up the flagpole and he wants a halt brought to it. And since we're on the subject of MACV: anyone know who's been shooting toy model rockets at the tower guards? These practical jokes are going to turn into a full-fledged firefight and somebody's going to get hurt.

"Okay, getting back to violent crime. The chaplain is having a mass for Pfc. Hill tomorrow. For you new troops, Patrick was gunned down in street fighting a few weeks ago. He paid the ultimate sacrifice to keep freedom alive here in Southeast Asia. So don't kid yourself: this ain't no vacation. Saigon's got its share of VC, too, just waiting for you to get careless. Now, I want to see you all at the mass tomorrow. I don't care if you're Baptist or not. We stick together in this brigade. That's what the MP brotherhood is all about." Thomas looked at the lieutenant suspiciously—it was the first time he ever heard anyone above the rank of sergeant talk about the existence of a brotherhood.

"Now let's hit the streets, gentlemen. Get out there and kick some ass!" And as a second thought, as the men were filing out of the room, he added, "But make sure you're in the right when you do."

"Awright! Hold it just a minute!" The other lieutenant grinned. "Every one of you swingin' dicks back in here. Why don't we have a little inspection?"

The men, their heads hanging sulkily, filed back into the room and began to line up shoulder to shoulder. The man on the far left put out his right arm, pushing the MP beside him away a couple feet per proper military procedure, and this continued with each successive soldier until they ran out of room and the far wall forced the line to spring back unevenly like a sprung accordion. They then came to the position of attention, drew their .45s, popped the clip into the left hand and held the automatic pointed skyward in the right hand, chamber locked open.

214

The lieutenant began with the MP on the left end of the formation. He started at the top, running his finger across the black helmet liner, checking the white MP letters for dust. Pivoting on his toes without moving a step in any direction, he visually checked the man's hairline, including the ears and collar length. He brought his eyes to within a couple inches of the stubble shadowing the man's chin to see if he shaved close enough. Then he checked the green fatigue shirt for the proper patches and made sure the laminated plastic MP armband had the Eighteenth MP Brigade combat patch sewn onto it. He tugged on the web-belt for proper fit and frowned at the laminated leather gear that didn't require polishing, but it was all there: first-aid pouch, dual ammo clip holders, holster, handcuffs case, night stick keeper, lanyard. He popped open the first-aid pouch and was surprised to find the regulation bandage inside. Most men usually carried cigarettes, rubbers or extra ammo there instead.

After making sure the inscription on the chrome belt buckle wasn't too radical—"I'm no fighter, just a lover" in this case—he checked the crease in the man's trousers, whether they were too baggy, and if his boots were spit-shined or scuffed. He then took the man's service weapon, inspected it for rust or powder residue, confirmed that it had a heavy layer of oil coating the insides, and checked the chrome magazine for hollow points or armor-piercing rounds.

"Get rid of those lousy hollow-points, Thomas," he sneered at the first man to be inspected, rules of the Geneva Convention never crossing his mind. "They'll jam up your .45 first shoot out you get in." But the private who had already been in three firefights in which his pistol had performed flawlessly, just nodded his head sarcastically as the officer turned right-face and went on to the next man.

The guardmount took thirty minutes and the lieutenant found all kinds of violations, mostly minor, which he marked down on his clipboard—these MPs hadn't been inspected in weeks. When he finished with the last man, he walked stiffly behind them, taking slow steps, and did a second inspection of their hair length. He was surprised to find only a few men needed a trim. "You gentlemen will remove all this 'home town' bullshit from the back of your helmets," he declared calmly, "before the next guardmount. Thomas—you will remove that profanity from the back of your helmet before you hit the streets tonight."

"But, Lieutenant," he protested. "It's not profanity. It's a good luck proverb written in Vietnamese, that's all."

"'Shove it up your rectum' is not a proverb, in any language," the lieutenant advised him amidst lingering snickers in the room, "and it offends the Vietnamese. Remove it."

"Yes, sir. How's 'bout if I stick an American flag back there?" But the officer ignored him and, after dismissing the platoon, he filed stiffly out of the building.

Thomas immediately slapped the ammo magazine back into his .45 and slammed a live round into the chamber as several men with only weeks left in Saigon scattered from his line of fire. He then flicked on the safety and smoothly tucked the automatic back into its holster, snapped the rain-cover flap shut, walked over to two rookies and put his arms around their shoulders. "Did I ever tell you about the time back at Carson when we raided the WACs barracks at four in the morning looking for drugs? Well, you can imagine the first place them K-9 doggies stuck their dope-sniffing snouts. . . ."

Private Broox eyed the helicopter suspiciously. He hadn't liked the crazy whirlybirds ever since he saw one get shot down and had to help scrape the mutilated corpses—some cut completely in half by the disintegrating rotors—into body bags.

Broox held his M-16 by the built-in handle over the chamber that also doubled as the sights and looked at the three Viet Cong prisoners marching in a single file in front of him toward the buzzing craft, its rotors already swishing lazily at the layer of steaming hot air blanketing the land. The prisoners were blindfolded and had their hands tied behind their backs with plastic flexicuffs.

In the lead was a grizzled old veteran, his nose defiantly in the air even with his eyes covered. His bare feet marched along in the dust with an exaggerated military bearing. Behind him followed a man in his midtwenties, the tire-tread tongs protecting his feet as he hustled along nervously. His brow was creased in fear of the coming unknown.

As Broox flinched when he put too much weight on the slowly healing sprained ankle, he noticed that the third prisoner had long hair pulled back and tied in a ponytail and, although her chest was pressed almost flat by the unflattering black tunic all three VC wore, the fluid movement of her narrow haunches as her tiny feet probed the ground clearly identified her as a female. Late teens.

Broox decided that maybe he didn't resent the light duty transfer to stockade security after all, so long as they kept giving him women to escort back and forth to Long Binh Jail. It didn't make sense to him to place an injured cop in an environment where his chances of wrestling around with unfriendlies were greater than on downtown street patrol.

When they reached the chopper, Broox watched the co-pilot grab the shoulders of the two men to help them climb up into the craft, and when it came time for the girl's turn, he placed a hand under the slight curve of her buttocks and helped lift her up, feeling the firm flesh beneath the thin black pajamas yield slightly under the weight.

As the chopper took off, its nose dipping almost to the ground before the straining rotors thrust it into the sky, Broox found himself in the rear of the passenger compartment with two of the stockade specialists. One of them was sitting beside the female, talking to her in whispered Vietnamese, but she sat sullen-faced, unmoving, showing no response, and the older prisoner kicked at him blindly a couple times before the second

MP slugged him back onto the floor. The first guard continued grinning as he spoke suggestive phrases to the woman and in his mind Broox could see the woman sitting there totally naked, still bound tightly, completely at the mercy of her captors.

Broox shook the vision from his mind and walked bent-over toward the front of the craft to watch the pilots at work, but he continued to see the female prisoner in his thoughts, and as he watched the pilot pitch the chopper side to side just above treetop level, he recalled all the times he had mused about running an interrogation center—oh, all the little devices he would build to make the question and answer sessions miserable for the little tight-assed communist ladies and such a thrill for himself. Yes, the lengths he'd go to get a confession!

Broox had been mildly surprised when he finally visited his first police dungeon in Vietnam. There, laid out on the table next to the prisoner, were all the tools of torture he had dreamed of—and even more devices than he had designed in his mind. What struck Broox was the extreme age of the items. Most of them had been around long before his birth.

The jungles spreading out before the cruising gunship appeared strangely quiet from this altitude, but Broox knew the ghostly silence was deceptive and could be shattered at any moment by a bullet crashing up through the floorboards and shearing off a testicle or two. Broox smiled when he noticed the pilots sitting on two flak jackets each. He placed his own steel pot on the floor of the craft and sat on it, trying not to think how painful such a wound might be.

The helicopter began to climb further from the earth, and as it reached a point just below the thick, misty clouds, he noticed they were arcing out over the South China Sea. He knew Long Binh to be in the other direction, but perhaps they were just diverting from above a hostile tract of land or a bad weather cell.

After Broox had asked a few technical questions about the helicopter, he noticed the co-pilot give the pilot an uneasy,

218

irritated glance, and thinking he was becoming a nuisance, Broox turned to start back to the cargo hold. But before he could rise from one knee, the chopper was suddenly banking sharply to the right. Broox grabbed hold of a wall harness and hung on tightly as the side door became the bottom of the craft. He could see a vast rice-paddy panorama spreading out before them—each level of dikes a different shade of lush, vibrant green. As his helmet clattered toward the opening and slid out into the vastness of space below, Broox heard the gunship's cannons burp off rounds for a few endless seconds.

A rocket, mounted on the craft's stabilizer fin popped slightly, fell from its pod, then ignited a few feet below the chopper and soared off toward the jungle below. The pilot muttered, "Damn snipers," under his breath as the craft tilted back slowly to a level course, then spiraled back down toward the coastline.

When he started back toward the cargo hold again his feet froze to the metal belly of the helicopter. One MP had resumed flirting with the unreceptive female, while his partner kept the barrel of his M-16 trained on the younger man, sitting frozen in a balanced squat, the blindfold keeping him silent.

Broox glanced about the passenger compartment nervously . . . feverishly. He checked behind some crates, nausea rising in his gut as he caught the eyes of the two Americans watching him closely.

When he failed to locate the oldest VC, the one who had kicked out at the MP earlier, he sat down on a flak jacket and stared at the misty jungle passing by below. Somehow he expected to see the old man falling, his legs kicking wildly as he plummeted toward the waves slapping at the sparkling beach.

One of the MPs was kneeling closer to the woman prisoner now, and as he brought his lips next to her ear and began to whisper something, she lunged out at him and clamped her teeth down on his nose, refusing to let go.

As the American screamed in agony, his partner bashed the stock of his M-16 repeatedly against the woman's head until

219

she released her grip and fell back against the floor of the chopper.

Broox lowered his head between his knees and fought to keep the tears in. He knew the woman had probably ambushed dozens of his countrymen before her capture. That she would not hesitate to send her child running out to enemy soldiers in the midst of a firefight, a grenade taped to its back. But this was not Broox's type of war and he shook his head miserably, wretching in disgust, longing for the familiar streets of Saigon.

XVII. LADY IN THE TIGER

Jeff Rodgers took a final sip from the tall glass of pineapple juice then set the frosty container on the giant spool table. He leaned back in the rattan easy chair and peeked over the rim of the sunglasses out at the Vietnamese girls frolicking on the beach, chasing crabs that raced about sideways on the white sand. He rubbed his shoulder briskly—it was sore and the pain often woke him at night. He could still remember with crystal clarity the fall from the second-floor window of the Palace Hotel.

He had crashed down on the edge of a huge umbrella, mounted on a poolside table, and knocked an elderly Frenchman into the ground. He didn't know if the old plantation owner died from a broken neck or a heart attack, but Rodgers shivered when his mind re-enacted the plunge toward the pool: he knew he didn't have enough momentum to make the water, and when his weight snapped the umbrella and he bounced off the concrete edge of the pool he felt sure the shock stunning his body would cause him to drown. But rolling into the pool off the dead and crumpled man had revitalized his senses, and after he surfaced, he pulled himself up from the waves, raced past startled diners and climbed the high courtyard fence back out into familiar territory: the alleys. Rodgers had not felt the pain until several hours later, after the adrenalin subsided, and he wondered now if he might have broken some bones.

Rodgers ordered a Singapore Sling from an arrogant waiter and settled back under the palm-frond umbrellas to concentrate on the young girls splashing about on the beach fifty yards away. They had cornered a bewildered stingray in the shallows of the coral seabed and one of the girls raised the flapping creature high above her head, ignoring its sharp scales. He watched the shades of beauty on her youthful face multiply as her smile and excitement grew, and Rodgers knew his first child would have to be a daughter. The other guys— his buddies from the 716th, the last friends he'd have—had always insisted they'd spawn a son, to carry on the family name. He laughed at this thought—he had accumulated a half dozen identities since deserting the U.S. Army. All he wanted now was a woman who could soothe the pains and perhaps later, when life resumed some sense of normalcy, a child. She would have long, silky, jet-black hair, just like her mother, narrow exotic eyes that would drive the schoolboys wild. And he would watch her grow through the years, becoming more beautiful with each waking dawn. Until she became a woman and some foreign adventurer came and stole her away to a distant land where it was high noon during Saigon's restless night.

"Hey, Mista!" The young girl clutching the stingray had run up to his table, followed by her shy friends. "You want you should buy souvenir me?" She smiled innocently, forgetting her English as she held out the dripping creature for his inspection. But Rodgers just stared at her dark, fathomless eyes, speechless, until she flushed with embarrassment and ran off giggling down the beach.

Lance Jackson kept telling himself he wasn't nervous. He snapped another set of chopsticks in two and rushed out of the coffeeshop into the street. He routinely glanced about for any

222

sign of cops, then started for the line of taxis parked in front of the Mississippi Soul Bar.

Who did this crazy white boy think he was, anyway? The black deserter was angry and he slammed the cab's door shut violently after he got in, provoking an irritated reaction on the face of the car's owner.

"Get out! Get out! Get out of my *see*dan!" the cabbie demanded, but Jackson reached over the seat and grabbed the skinny Vietnamese by the collar.

"Now listen up, dink!" he warned, his breath reeking of opium and ruou-de rice wine. "Get your ass in gear and take me to Cholon—number two Dong Khanh!"

"You pay me first!" the cabbie ordered, not intimidated by the tall black with the shaved head and monogrammed tooth sporting a clenched fist. "2500p! Pay, or get out! 2500p!"

"750p, you little runt! And you'll get it at the end of the ride!" But the cabbie was not one to be bullied. He sat rigid in the front seat, hands on the steering wheel, staring at the traffic passing by, totally uninterested in this loud, poorly mannered Westerner. When Jackson placed the snub-nosed revolver behind the driver's right ear, he threw the cab into gear and spun his tires for half a block down the street.

"Gonna have to go after this character," Jackson decided, talking out loud to himself, and the taxi driver glanced back in the rear-view mirror now and then, both curious and nervous about his strange behavior. "Gonna have to stalk his white ass like the panther I am and take him out of the scene. Before he gets any bright ideas about coming after old Lance-honey."

Jackson thought about how Stubbs and Webb had died. Slowly, violently, from what he had heard. Maybe this Rodgers character wasn't such a punk after all. Maybe he had to give him more credit. "But no amount of professional admiration will prevent me from tearing into this pile of white trash."

Jackson had spent the first few weeks in hiding when word hit the streets that Rodgers was out on a revenge spree, but it was against his nature to flee anybody and he decided to take the

223

offensive and go after this Rodgers dude. It was too bad he knew little about the ex-MP. It was so long since the black market arrests, and he had only caught a glimpse of him that morning of the killing. *Hell, I still can't understand why the cat is getting so riffed over losing a lousy chink broad,* he thought. *She hadn't even been a good lay.*

As the taxi swerved in and out of the slower moving traffic and started to cross the river into Cholon, he thought back to that morning several weeks ago.

They had just happened to come across Rodgers on his way home from working the street patrol and had carefully trailed him to his apartment. They were lucky the night shift made him so weary—he would surely have spotted the tail any other time.

And when he left again for work twelve hours later, they were waiting in the shadows. Him, Stubbs, Webb and Chilton. At first they had planned to jump his white ass and "reimburse" him for the time lost behind bars, but when they saw what a little cutie he had waving goodbye to him from the balcony, they came up with an even better plan.

After his cab left the area, the four of them silently climbed the stairs to the third floor and softly rapped on the door, speaking the Vietnamese phrase of greeting. To their surprise, she had opened the door without checking the window first, and it had been no problem pushing it back in on her.

They had taken turns with her and he could never remember a woman resisting so violently for such a long time. They could have had a real party if Jordan and King hadn't fled the city, bound for the black Muslim sects in Indonesia the week before. Chilton had finally tired of her attitude, though, flipping out berserk when she spit in his face.

Webb tried to pull him away, but Chilton began screaming as the spittle dripped down off his nose and lips. He pulled his switchblade from the pants piled on the floor and slashed her across the face, and in the frenzy of blood that flew about the room when she continued to fight back, he commenced

224

stabbing her over and over in the chest until Stubbs pulled him off and decided it was time to clear out.

Webb had written something on the mirror with a tube of graffitti lipstick he always carried—they found none in the apartment, the girl didn't seem to own any. On their way out, Jackson had taken a small jade statue from the dresser on a last-minute whim. It was an intricately carved Thai dancer, but didn't look at all that valuable. Perhaps a prostitute he knew would be pleased to receive it as a gift instead of the usual ten dollars. But she had not been impressed, and the next day he sold it to a pawn shop owner on Tu Do Street for a brick of hashish.

No, it was too much of a headache to have to always keep an eye out for this overzealous avenger. Best to finish his ass off now. Quickly. Before he got lucky and Jackson got hurt.

The taxi pulled up to a decrepit, ramshackle hotel, and Jackson hesitated climbing out when he noticed two white men walking toward his location from halfway down the block. But as they passed he discovered they were only two Aussie tourists, and the involuntary growl he felt rising in his throat persisted until they were out of sight around the corner.

He was not sure why he hated white folks so. As a kid in Atlanta he had never really been subjected to a lot of prejudice. But he had joined the racist gangs out of boredom, and their sick philosophies slowly infected his mental fabric until now he couldn't look at a policeman without picturing a rifle scope's cross hairs centered across his face.

Jackson turned down the narrow, filthy corridor to his left after entering the hotel and he walked slowly over to room nineteen, pausing for several minutes to listen outside the door before he knocked two short taps.

A strained male voice inside rasped his name out, barely audible even through the thin plywood door. "Lance?"

"Yeah, Marvin. It's me."

"Okay . . . it's cool, come on in."

Jackson took a rusted key from his pants pocket and slowly

225

turned the tumblers in the lock. When the door opened, he cautiously peeked into the room then entered when he saw the string on the shotgun poised at him was no longer tight on the trigger.

Marvin Chilton lay in the bed, a thick layer of perspiration coating his face and bare chest. A soiled bandage, coated with dried blood, was wrapped around his upper ribs.

"How you doin', bro?" Jackson walked slowly over to the other deserter. He was repulsed by the stench of old blood making contact with the stale, humid air in the room, but he sat down on the bed anyway.

"Not so good, Lance," he answered. Each breath took an intense effort because of the tight bandage now stuck to the partial scab infecting the hole in his chest. "But I'll make it."

"That's what you get for trying to hold up a jewelry store when they got one of them goofy turban-toting Calcuttans sitting out front with a musket." He forced a laugh as he pointed at the man's wound.

"Bullshit, Lance. You thought that museum relic was unloaded same as I did."

"Got something for you," Jackson sighed, making it known in his expression that it took quite a bit of self-sacrifice to obtain the bag he pulled from under his belt.

"What you got there?" Chilton asked, the hesitation in his voice betraying the distrust he felt for the other man.

"For the pain." And Jackson pulled a baggy of small heroin packets from the sack and set about lighting a candle to heat the spoons.

The tiger in the cage did not move, except for the huge green eyes that followed Rodgers quietly as he paced slowly back and forth before the jungle beast. Rodgers never let his own eyes falter, keeping them locked on the tiger's, as he wondered whether this cat had resisted capture or had been born right in that very cage.

He had been visiting the Saigon Zoo nearly every day now, since the vivid dream about the beast meeting him in an enchanted jungle had woke him one midnight. He walked the entire distance along Thong Nhut after passing the American embassy, and the tiger cages had quickly become his favorite places to sit and think. Sometimes he would toss some popcorn or satay into the cages, but the crafty animals never even rose to inspect the tidbits. Instead, they would lie in the corner shadows, back away from the heat and patiently watch his every movement—their great paws wrapped protectively around a slab of meat or juicy leg bone.

The big cats would humor him most of the time—taking a break from their restless naps to play the mind games that followed long hours of staring at each other. Rodgers was amazed at how long the tigers stayed interested in him—always watching his eyes, and he wondered what went through their savage minds, or if they really thought anything about him at all. Other than that he might make an excellent meal.

Rodgers was always disappointed when the zoo handlers made their daily rounds with the buckets of red meat. That was the only time the cats would rise to their feet and lose interest in him. They would now do all the pacing, anxiously licking their chops with long, drawn-out yawns that exposed deadly, gleaming fangs. All except one.

One especially cunning tigress would stare back at him unmoving, until he believed he could see her primitive thoughts dancing inside the recesses of the glowing eyes. She would sit crouched on her haunches, her smooth Bengal stripes rigid, until he was sure she was a stuffed display. He would lean toward the bars cautiously, watching the animal's eyes now moving ever so slightly as they followed his hands. And then, without the slightest warning, she lashed out at him, reaching outstretched claws with lightning speed to within mere inches of his chest. Then she unleashed a sorrowful, mourning cry that echoed through the building and set the other restless beasts into a frenzy of excitement and anticipation. She would keep her eyes on him the whole time she screamed her rage, but then she would take to pacing the cage rapidly, her agile shoulders brushing up against the bars as she turned back and forth. After several minutes she would casually extend a trembling paw out through the bars again, this time letting it hang in the air heavily a few seconds as though she was apologizing for frightening him and wanted only to make contact.

"How old is this enchantress?" he asked one of the zookeepers when they appeared to tell him it was closing time. Though it was obvious they did not understand the question totally, one who spoke pidgin English advised him the cat was only a few months old—had been chased down in the jungles of the delta, outside Mytho. As he looked at her one last time before leaving he remembered the nights they joked about reincarnation and how he wanted to come back as a wealthy playboy, searching the globe for romance. "And you wish to be a royal princess, perhaps?" he had asked her, but she surprised him by saying she would hope to come back as a deer—or better yet, a tiger. Roaming the jungle without the cares and worries that led to the death of men.

Jeff felt he could see Mai's eyes staring back sadly at him from behind the bars, and though the tiger made no move to strike out at him as he reached toward the cage, the zookeepers went into a panic at his behavior and quickly ushered him toward the exits.

The pain in his heart was unbearable as he listened to the lonely tigress now screaming long, drawn out, primeval cries at the darkness, mourning his departure. The sad wailing continued calling out to him desperately until he was several miles away and could no longer hear them.

XVIII. TENEMENT ROW

Kruger and Sergeant Mather were to saunter down the narrow alley in sector three and attempt to make contact with the cowboys rumored to be terrorizing the area. Thomas and Sergeant Richards would remain parked one block over, on a street parallel to the direction they walked. The stick-up artists were getting wary of groups containing four Americans—word of the Decoy Squad had swept through the Saigon underworld, and Richards' men hadn't made an arrest in several nights. They were hopeful that two off-duty soldiers, stumbling "drunk" along tenement row, would draw out one or two of the city's less respectable citizens.

"Take this flare," Richards had instructed the other sergeant. "If you get into something you can't handle then pop it over the roofline and we'll be there in a flash." Richards didn't like parting with the flares his father had sent him, but the PMO was running short on portable radios, and despite their successful arrest record, the Decoy Squad was mysteriously low on the list of the new commander's priorities. "On second thought, take two. They're a little tricky the first time you use them, but afterwards, no sweat. Just in case you send the first one through somebody's balcony window." Mather had laughed and gratefully accepted the flares although he didn't like mixing civilian gadgets with military work. Come to think of it, he wasn't at all pleased with being assigned to this new, innovative, anti-crime project. He felt much more comfortable supervising the privates operating the meat market or manning the static post towers that circled MACV annex.

Two nights earlier a nurse assigned to Third Field Army Hospital had been found dead in this alley by one of the Bravo Company units on routine patrol. Her shorts were hanging from one bruised and battered ankle, and her dress was hiked up around her hips. Vicious bite marks covered her neck and chest, and a syringe needle was sticking out of each eyeball when they found her.

Rape and murder were not all that uncommon in Saigon, but when the provost marshal saw the picture of the American woman's mutilated body—the whites of her eyes bulging grotesquely around the punctured and discolored pupils—he ordered the Decoy Squad to the neighborhood surrounding the tragedy and suggested they produce results immediately. As an incentive, they were authorized to work in civilian clothes again.

Richards doubted the victim's killers would ever be found. No one came forth to explain why she was wandering that dangerous alley after dark, and the m.o. suggested an argument over drugs. The rape didn't figure into it, but Richards didn't have the time to solve riddles involving drug deals gone bad— that was C.I.D.'s job, and you could never expect dopers to stick to the rules of narcotic rip-offs when an attractive round-eye, hard up for money, was involved.

Thomas had volunteered to dress up in drag, purse and all, the way the decoy units in New York City were currently operating, but Richards decided it would be too much hassle to shave his legs, and the idea was tabled by PMO anyway. They didn't want one of their MPs possibly showing up at the morgue in a dress.

Sergeant Mather watched Kruger closely as they walked the gutter, keeping out of the shadows lest the side street bandits, known as cowboys by both the Saigonese and Americans, might miss them. Mather realized it was pretty traumatic for a nineteen-year-old private to see another military policeman gunned down in the street even before you're of the legal age to drink real beer.

He could sympathize with the nightmares and guilt he knew the kid was suffering. But he didn't like the thought of PMO transferring the private to Decoy—probably the most dangerous squad to be on just then. It was supposed to be voluntary.

He would much rather have that new guy—Davis—to back him up if they got in a jam. True, Davis was black, and he didn't have a chemistry flow that allowed him to work smoothly with most blacks, but he had reviewed the private's 201 file and was impressed with the MP's apparent dedication to duty.

Kruger still approached each new day in a daze, Mather observed. He always had a faraway look in his eyes, and that sort of separation from reality could get you dead quick in this line of work. What young Kruger needed was a woman, Mather smiled to himself. A little Saigon schoolgirl to take his mind off Hill's death. Mather realized the shootout that left Hill sprawled out on his back in the middle of the street was an event that would remain with *any*one the rest of his life, but it was not something one had to dwell on every waking moment. Mather knew that's what the nights were for. Americans in Asia often had to do things they could not later be proud of, and that was where the nightmares came in. A woman warming Kruger's bed would chase the ghosts away and might just do the boy a world of good.

"Sergeant Mather!" Kruger whispered above the breeze rustling newspapers along the narrow alley. "Someone is moving up there—near those trash cans." *Good,* thought the sergeant, *patroling the way an MP should. Alert, noticing something I had not even spotted,* even though it just turned out to be some old *papa-san* scavenging through the piles of trash for food. As a flare popped several blocks over, its glowing orb

231

plummeting to Earth prematurely as the parachute snapped free, Mather hoped the other MPs one street away wouldn't see it also and mistake it for a call for help. But after the spinning light bounced off a rooftop and burst into a fountain of sparks, the night fell dark and quiet again, and they continued down deeper into the maze of tall, leaning tenements.

As they passed the old man digging in the garbage, a huge rat the size of a cat scampered out from the sewer drain beneath the dumpsters and raced forth into the open, on a direct collision course with the sergeant's polished boots. Kruger hopped up into the air even though the rodent was several feet away from him, but his sudden movement frightened the rat even more, accelerating its little paws until the creature bumped blindly into Mather's feet and ricocheted off. "Yuck!" the sergeant couldn't control the revulsion he felt, but the disgusting animal was gone even before the MP's hand had latched onto his gun. The incident left Mather queasy for several minutes afterwards, and he wondered how many different kinds of disease had been deposited on his shiny boots by the loathsome pest's festering snout.

Several blocks later they had still made no contact and Mather began thinking about Davis again. In the short time the private had spent at Fort Polk, Louisiana, he had participated in several felony arrests and had even disarmed a knife-wielding drifter who had wandered into the camp and was caught shoplifting lunchmeat from the commissary PX. The arrest had earned Davis an Army Commendation Medal, and the 201 file showed the award was made not because Davis had recovered the stolen merchandise, but because a civilian reporter witnessing the incident had written a long letter to the MP's commanding officer.

"Private Davis exhibited exemplary judgment," the letter read, "and refrained from shooting the berserk criminal because of all the innocent bystanders in the area, thereby undoubtedly saving several lives. The manner in which Private Davis expertly disarmed the suspect is a credit to his fine

232

military police unit and the professional training he obviously received prior to being charged with serving and protecting his fellow soldiers at Fort Polk."

The wording in the letter made Mather wonder briefly if the woman reporter was black also, and where she picked up the GI jargon that peppered the commendation and made the whole thing sound a little biased. He was sure Davis would have rather had the money that came with a promotion to Pfc. instead of the lousy Arcom, but the sergeant realized advancing up the ranks could be difficult for minorities completing their first tour of duty in the Armed Forces. Mather often felt the drawback to career development was especially prevalent in the Military Police Corps, which he sometimes wished they'd transfer outside the military hierarchy the way they structured C.I.D. Surely law enforcement would become more specialized and productive if only the Army's cops were not governed by Army officers who made decisions with their precious career goals foremost in their minds, who felt all MPs were better utilized performing a soldier's guard duties rather than street policework.

Mather thought he caught a glimpse of a figure jumping between rooftops high above them, but he kept walking in the slow, practiced stagger and avoided looking back up. Being too alert to his surroundings would signal the cowboys something was not right, so he ignored the warning bells clanging along the rising hairs of his neck and stumbled down the alley. He knew they didn't pay him enough to take such chances, but, after all, it *was* Vietnam, and he wasn't sleeping out in a rice paddy somewhere.

Two gunships, cruising side by side above the rooftops, appeared down the block suddenly as they passed low overhead, their twin rotors flapping at the warm, sticky air. He could see Vietnamese soldiers sitting in the open door hatches, their legs dangling out over the belly of the craft, into space. Their M-16 rifles were balanced in their laps and Mather wondered with a smile if the slightest turbulence might topple

233

them down to a messy death.

It was a sight you didn't see every day. It was something you never saw in the states, and the sergeant knew things like this were why he stayed in the military. He had received several recruiting brochures from the big civilian police departments when he was in Alaska, but the better pay could not compete with chasing the bad guys across the dark and dangerous capitals of exotic lands. Seoul, Bangkok, Saigon. Each had its own set of distinct memories and Mather was sure walking a beat in even Las Vegas or Brooklyn could not compare with cruising beneath the waving banners of Tu Do Street.

And of course there were the transfers. If you got tired of a certain town, or the women became a nuisance, you just requested reassignment to another state. Or another country. Now, that threw a cog into the court system when some punk you had to thump sued for damages and you had mysteriously skipped safely across state lines where civil claims could not follow. It was too bad that was how things were, and Mather was not proud of ditching some responsibilities, but he had seen too many bleeding heart civil judges award some radical half the arresting cop's next fifty paychecks just because resisting arrest usually resulted in several stitches at the emergency room.

Kruger could hear an engine growing louder in the distance, and just as he was about to bring it to the attention of the sergeant, a motor scooter swerved around the corner a couple blocks away and accelerated toward them at high speed.

Mather was surprised to see the two "Honda Honies" cruising down that back alley so late after curfew. Both dressed in black slacks and revealing halter tops, they zigzagged between the two Americans at the last second, so close that both men could smell the perfume on the night air and catch the daring challenge in their wide eyes as they flew past. *Damn*, thought Kruger. *So close I could smell the nuoc-mam on their breath!*

The MPs grinned at each other mischievously as the girls,

one sitting sidesaddle behind the other, disappeared down the street without saying a word. Their body language told it all.

"What's this?" Mather raised an eyebrow when the girl piloting the sputtering cycle made a U-turn and headed back toward them. The sergeant envisioned himself having to disappoint the private by refusing to accompany the girls to their apartments for a little late-night fun, so he was astonished when it became evident the hookers had something else in mind.

Kruger let out a startled yelp when the Honda passed between the two Americans again—this time the driver had reached out and latched onto the private's watch! But the thick leather band failed to snap and Mather watched helplessly as his partner was dragged several feet before the tiny woman with the iron-strong grip finally let go and the motor scooter disappeared in a cloud of dust.

Mather decided against signaling Richards with the flare, and as he resisted the temptation to place a carefully aimed .45 slug up the backside of a pair of pantaloons, he started down the road to Kruger. The girls just might be an appetizer to see if the Americans were undercover cops and Mather refused to take the bait, electing to wait for the big fish to come after them instead. Even if he was wrong, snatching GI wrist watches was a favorite pastime for the youth of Saigon and something he wouldn't get overly concerned about.

"You okay, Paul?" he ran over and went down on one knee to help the private up. The kid's knees were a little scraped, his nylon shirt was ripped down the middle, and his pride was tarnished, but he rose to his feet smiling with admiration at the wide, leather watchband that had defied the antics of the Honda Honies.

"Vo Dehb bought it for me"—he was beaming proudly— "She warned me the skinny flexband that came with the watch was no match for the watch-snatching cowboys, so she got me this band. I just laughed, Sarge. But she was right!"

"Vo Dehb?"

Kruger thought back to the gorgeous Chinese waitress who had poured him a cup of tea the night of the big bar fight at the Queen Bee. *It was definitely her own fault,* he laughed to himself. *If she hadn't drawn me under her spell with that mesmerizing smile, he wouldn't have returned the next five nights in a row just to drool over her as she glided from table to table.*

Kruger had been intensely fearful of the Asian women when he first arrived in Vietnam. All the instructors at the academy had told the recruits over and over, "Now you rookies destined for RVN and points East listen up! You mess with them misty-eyed Oriental maidens and you just might wake up minus some vitals! Take it from those of us who have already been there and back: they're nothing but heartache and trouble—you gentlemen just stick to the street and leave the pussy alone. More than one naive hotdog has been bedded down by an elusive lass who disappeared in the night to leave him lying above a half ton of dynamite."

Kruger had believed the stories in boot camp about the VC agents posing as prostitutes who would frequent the bars in Saigon with razor blades and bamboo slivers taped strategically between their legs. In fact, he had swallowed nearly all of the tall stories the well-meaning drill sergeants had fed him, bu Vo Dehb straightened him out on some points.

The first night she had barely paid him any notice, servicing his tea cup regularly enough and delivering fried rice paper *cha gio* rolls stuffed with noodles, crab meat and vegetables on time. But he was hoping for a friendly conversation and she denied him that.

On the third night she eventually smiled at him in bewilderment when he showed up shortly after dark again and ordered the same meal. "You're going to start looking like a *cha gio* roll," she had told him, more in a scolding tone than with any sign of kindness, and when he ordered a bowl of *pho* soup to go with the small cup of rice she ate on her break her mood changed to mild suspicion. "Are you trying to hustle a mother of twelve?" she had asked seriously, the giggle escaping her only after his jaw had nearly dropped to the table.

When the electricity went out the following night he had dashed across the street to a pharmacy and bought some candles to light up the Queen Bee's small restaurant. He sat surrounded by several inquisitive bargirls who took turns teasing him about his skinny body in between running back and forth to the windows to gaze at the lightning flashing and the rain pounding the city in a swirl of gale force winds.

"Yes, I think maybe you need fattening up," she had said when the restaurant closed and there was no one around to hear. She patted him on the stomach playfully and took him by the hand. Kruger had expected the usual horde of taxi cabs to swoop down on them when they left the restaurant, but the storm seemed to have driven everyone except the policemen off the streets. They had to purchase a newspaper to hold over their heads as they left the canopy protecting the sidewalk and crossed Nguyen Hu.

An old man, covered with Army poncho liners and torn plastic bags, rolled up beside them pedalling his clanking rickshaw and she had paid him fifty piasters to take them to a housing project off Nguyen Cong Tru. When she walked up to the long line of one-story corrugated wood shacks, Kruger began to feel a bit uneasy—he was sure he could see numerous pairs of dark, hostile eyes staring out at him from the even smaller dwellings on the other side of the alley, constructed of discarded ammo crates and splintered C-ration cartons. Here he had spent a whole week trying to go out with this beautiful woman, and now that she was finally taking him home he wished he was back in the relative safety of Pershing Field.

Good old Camp Pershing, where the biggest crisis was usually keeping the housegirls from peeking at you when you took a shower. He could still remember when he first arrived in Saigon and the company clerk told him, "Oh, don't pay any attention to the housegirls. You'll notice them squatting beside the shower stalls giggling. But ignore it. Here in 'Nam, they're not embarrassed by nudity. Hell, it's like in Japan,

237

where the men and women bathe together in public baths. So if you're in there soaping down and they start giggling, they're probably laughing about the laundry, weather, or colonel's secretary—not your little pecker." So Kruger spent the next three weeks ignoring all the women who lined up to watch him take a shower before Sergeant Schell had set him straight and the company clerk was ordered to quit bullshitting the newbies. The Vietnamese, for the most part, were as modest as anyone else.

Dehb had opened the warped door of the apartment building and dragged him past several bodies huddled beside the glowing coals of a cooking fire set up in the hallway. She held a finger to her lips, requesting he save the questions for later, and he followed her back through a rear door that opened up into another dingy corridor dividing several tiny stalls. He ducked his head down instinctively as a heavy rat scurried about on the tin roof a half foot above.

When she got to the end of the hall, Dehb produced a single key and unlocked a miniature padlock on the door of the last room. He followed her inside and found a cramped cubicle showing no signs of life except a green parakeet in a bamboo cage, its head turned back and resting in its ruffled shoulder feathers. As he closed the door behind him, the bird squawked irritably and sprang to the side of the cage closest to the girl, hanging upside-down with its talons squeezing the thin bars together as it eyed her anxiously. She took a jar from a corner of the floor and spread a pinch of seeds into the cage.

Kruger saw a thin straw mat covering a portion of the floor across from the parakeet, and except for a cardboard dresser there was no other furniture in the room. Against one wall were neatly stacked small boxes containing Chinese books and magazines, and atop the dresser was a hot plate and some bags containing rice and noodles. On the wall to his left was a tapestry depicting the temples of Bangkok, and below it a felt oil painting exaggerating the hips and bosom of a popular

Chinese singer, Frances Yip, her curves enhanced by a dazzling *chong-sam*.

Kruger took it upon himself to sit down on the straw mat, legs crossed, while she walked over to an altar mounted on the wall opposite the tapestries. She lit two candles on the altar that were placed on either side of a large likeness of Buddha and several smaller pictures of deceased relatives. He remained silent while she struck a match and lit long sticks of incense.

Vo Dehb knelt down before the modest altar and brought clasped hands to her forehead, the glowing sticks slipped in between the middle fingers. She bowed several times before the pictures, her eyes tightly closed as evasive swirls of smoke spiraled from the disturbed incense to the ceiling. Kruger felt a sadness, even desperation in her actions, and though he felt honored she would allow him to worship with her, the episode left him feeling empty-headed and ignorant.

Sergeant Richards leaned over and nudged Thomas. "You awake?" he whispered and the private sprang upright in his seat.

"Of course," he answered irritably. "It's just these double shifts you gotta work to get on this squad. They're starting to wear me down a little, that's all."

"Yeah, I can sympathize with that. Sometimes I wonder if the glory is worth it," he shot back, grinning.

Richards had backed the jeep down into the loading dock of an abandoned warehouse, and as the minutes dragged on, he worried that Mather and Kruger might have advanced so far down the block he'd be unable to see their signal flare.

A police jeep charged past them, its blue roof beacon rotating slowly as it rushed to some disturbance in the direction opposite where Mather and Kruger had set out. "Probably going to the bathroom," Richards joked about the Canh-Sat patrol as their vehicle skidded around a distant corner and disappeared down a side street.

"Or to pick up a pizza for headquarters," mumbled Thomas, and he recalled the time they stopped a speeding ambulance back in Carson only to have the driver hand them a slice of pepperoni with extra-thick crust.

Richards decided he would wait ten more minutes before leaving their cubbyhole to search for the other members of the squad.

Ten blocks away, Mather was beginning to wonder if the night was going to be an entire waste of time and manpower. The only nibble they had after the Honda Honies failed to return was when someone up on a rooftop tossed a garbage can full of rotten food down on them, but it had landed several feet away and the laughter accompanying the fleeing footsteps told them only children were involved.

"Ten more minutes and we call it a night," he told Kruger, but the private merely nodded absent-mindedly and the sergeant was afraid he was reliving the killing of Patrick Hill again.

But Kruger was thinking about that first night Vo Dehb had taken him home with her. He remembered how the fire flashed in her eyes when he leaned over to kiss her as she stirred the warming rice. She had pushed him back away and proceeded to chop up some celery and bean sprouts which she would add to the soup. "You can come stay with me whenever you like," she had told him coldly. "You can read my magazines over there and I'll cook for you if you like, but I'm not a whore!"

Then she took a stalk of celery and handed it over to him, an innocent smile suddenly replacing the frown. "You like?"

He had taken the celery, thinking, *Yes, I like what I see,* and wondering why she had taken him home with her if she didn't plan to sleep with him. Kruger was intrigued with her behavior, and as he slept on the uncomfortable straw mat, separated from her by a stuffed dragon, he watched the cockroaches fall from the walls and realized, sadly, that this must be how the other half lived.

240

"Kruger!" Sergeant Mather repeated, and the love-struck private looked up the street in time to see the fleeting shadow dart across the alley and disappear between two buildings.

"What do you think, Sarge?" Kruger asked. He did not really want contact tonight, and he was beginning to resent being the only member of the Decoy Squad who was not a volunteer. He'd much rather be back in Dehb's tiny apartment, feeling the warmth of her body radiating through the sleeping dragon.

"Pay dirt," Mather confirmed, and seconds later three figures appeared in the alley behind them. "Okay, we run," the sergeant whispered, "but not too fast," and as they trotted away from the cowboys, two more shadows materialized before them, blocking their path and cutting off their escape. The MPs froze midway between the two groups and allowed the Vietnamese to cautiously close in on them.

As Mather reached slowly for the flare in his front jeans pocket, Kruger called out, "We're not afraid of VC," in a drunken slur, and he stumbled against a trash can for their benefit.

"We no Veeyet Cong," one of the cowboys answered. "We just want money. All you money."

As soon as they were close enough to see that several of them carried machetes, Mather stooped down to one knee, scraped the flare against the pavement, and pointed it at the closest figure.

The fireball exploded out at the man in the center, bounced off his forehead and shot skyward. It arced out over the tops of the buildings to their left, settling down to float along on the warm night breeze for several seconds before disappearing beyond the roofline.

Kruger and his sergeant drew their pistols at the same time, but before they could yell a warning, two of the cowboys charged, waving their machetes menacingly above their heads.

Kruger emptied his clip at the men, and all five rounds missed, bouncing off down the alley amid deafening concussions. But Mather smoothly shot first the cowboy on the left through the shoulder and then knocked down the other man with three blasts in quick succession, reducing his face to a crimson mush and catapulting his body backwards several feet. The man in the middle had been knocked flat on his back by the flare impacting on his forehead, and as Mather tossed Kruger a fresh ammo clip the sergeant went down on one knee and jammed the barrel of his .45 into the man's rib cage. He intended to use the stunned cowboy as a shield, but when he turned around he saw that the other two Vietnamese were running away down the alley.

Mather reached for the second flare and was just about to run it across the blacktop when an MP jeep, its red hood lights blinking back and forth just below the windshield, skidded around the corner on two wheels and cut the cowboys off.

As Richards and Thomas hopped from the jeep, pistols drawn, the cowboys split up and raced down opposite lanes that ran off the main alley behind the tenements.

"Go help 'em out!" Mather instructed Kruger. "I'll be okay here." As the private took the side street which Thomas had run down, he set about handcuffing all three prisoners, including the dead men, to each other.

Sergeant Richards loved this part of police work. It was especially challenging to pursue suspects on foot under cover of darkness; the only thing that could have made it more exciting was for a light blanket of drizzle to sweep through the city. Rain always made the chase more demanding. Richards slowed to a virtual stop when the echo of the man's footfalls through the narrow alley ceased to reach his ears. He raised his .45 so that it pointed skyward as he crept forward, his back sliding along the wall in anticipation of the fool trying to ambush him.

Private First Class Thomas was running with all his might, using the weight of the automatic pistol to help propel him forward even faster as his arms merged into fluid movement with his sprinting legs. Up ahead, he could hear the suspect gasping for air as he knocked over trash cans and stumbled into potholes in his haste to get away. When he came to a dead end and found the cowboy trying to scale a high, chain-link fence, Thomas holstered his .45 and jumped up to grab the man by the legs.

The hood kept kicking at him though, and after he took his .45 back out and yelled *"Dung lai!,"* the Vietnamese for halt!, the cowboy shrugged his shoulders, smiled innocently, and leaped back down to the ground, his hands already clasped over his head in submission as he landed on the cement.

At that moment, Kruger raced around from behind a building, firing blindly, and both Thomas and the cowboy dove to the ground as the rounds sliced through the thick, muggy air where their chests had just been.

"Christ, Paul!" Thomas yelled, his trembling hands holding his helmet down over his eyes. "It's me! I'm on your side, remember?" and as an afterthought, he reached over blindly and grabbed the terrified Vietnamese by the collar to make sure he didn't crawl away in all the commotion.

Sergeant Richards knew he was better at this than the hood he was chasing. He didn't care if the guy had been born in this neighborhood. Or was even a combat-hardened guerrilla. Richards felt confident he would come out on top in a street fight with the man because this was what Richards did best. No punk who ran at the first sound of gunplay was worth a pinch of ginseng in his book, and he was confident he would have a prisoner in custody within the hour.

"Chieu hoi!" The man broke the silence several yards away, and Richards watched him emerge from a recessed doorway, in the exact spot he thought he'd be, his hands above his head. "I surrender!" he repeated, loud enough to bring several rudely awakened apartment dwellers out onto their balconies. *"Chieu hoi!* No more shoot!"

A young woman, who had perhaps loved an MP years before, clapped when she saw the black-and-white, laminated armband Richards had hastily snapped onto his jacket when the chase began. A crazy thought about the girl raced through his mind as his arm automatically came up and the .45 pointed at the cowboy's chest.

Richards was thinking, *I'll bet that dame hands me an envelope and tries to tell me her old MP boyfriend is back home stateside, did I know him? and could I please send him this letter through the cheaper Army postal system?* (which was free to soldiers serving in Vietnam) when he pulled the trigger and blew the cowboy practically out of his Ho Chi Minh sandals. The man doubled over as the round flattened out his stomach and tore through his lower back, knocking him off his feet onto his face. The grenade he had been clutching in one hand exploded beneath his body with a muffled report that intensified to a deafening roar as the corpse was flipped end over end off the unyielding blacktop.

Thomas was asking Sergeant Mather how he wanted a certain part of the report to read when a black sedan pulled up. C.I.D. agent William Sickles popped his head from the air-conditioned interior out the tinted window into the humid night air shifting uneasily about the Decoy Squad. Dozens of Canh-Sats were milling about, tagging evidence or putting down chalk around the outlines of the dead Vietnamese.

The Decoy Squad sat in their jeep, and each man had a clipboard balanced on his knee as they completed their supplementals.

"How many bought it tonight, Gary?" the warrant officer asked Richards, but the sergeant just grinned and held up three fingers.

"Wish Broox and Bryant could have been here," Thomas was telling Mather. He had put behind him the incident with Kruger, labeling it harmless overenthusiasm. As he began erasing an incorrect code on the form thirty-two, a screaming girl rounded the corner down the block and raced for the safety of the policemen. A stocky Vietnamese man was chasing the

244

thirteen year old, and he caught up to her while they were still fifty yards from Richards' jeep. The man grabbed the barefoot girl, clad only in a thin sarong, by the arm and roughly dragged her back down the alley.

Mather and Thomas stared at the commotion for several seconds then resumed writing their reports without showing any further interest, but Richards and Kruger climbed out of the jeep and started after the couple, dragging a Canh-Sat along with them.

"She admits he is her father," the Canh-Sat translated when they finally caught up to the two. "Claims he was trying to sell her into prostitution. There are some men at the house now who are willing to trade drugs and a large quantity of American cigarettes for the use of the child for five years."

"Why you low mother—" Kruger started to reach out for the father's throat, but the man calmly backed off as Richards and the closest Canh-Sat restrained him.

"It is his right." The policeman tried to calm Kruger. "It is his right to do with his daughter as he sees fit. Perhaps she would have a more comfortable life living in a brothel anyway."

"Yes, it would probably be better to have her screw GIs for a few years than beg in the back alleys the rest of her life," another Canh-Sat agreed.

"At least she'll have learned a skill when she returns home," the first Canh-Sat added.

"I'm sure her father will want to keep her *then*." His partner nodded his head with a wide smile and both Vietnamese started laughing.

"You condone what he's trying to do?" Richards asked the policemen even as he continued to try and hold Kruger back, but the Canh-Sats didn't answer. They kept on their faces the smiles Vietnamese exhibit even under the worst of circumstances. Richards glanced down at the flat chested, malnourished girl and wondered what kind of man would seek such a child out in a whorehouse.

245

"Well, anyway we shall investigate the claim about narcotics," the policeman told the MPs and after escorting the father back to a jeep where he was detained, they followed the girl back to her fifth-floor apartment.

They gave Kruger five minutes to position himself on the rear fire escape, then Richards and the Canh-Sat kicked in the locked door and rushed inside. There was a brief scuffle as two men tried to dump some packets of heroin down the toilet, but the American succeeded in recovering the drugs and the elderly dope merchants were subdued without any further trouble.

Richards checked the one backroom to the apartment and found a middle-aged woman with needle tracks running the length of her arm propped up in a sitting position in one corner. The sergeant failed to find a pulse, and deducted from the way she was leaning against a windowsill that the men had been planning to drop her body out the rear window into the alley below when the daughter had suddenly bolted from the apartment and fled.

Along one wall Richards noticed cartons of Salem cigarettes stacked to the ceiling. Against the opposite wall, shiny new American-made M-16s lay heavily oiled in thick protective wrappers. A shoebox was filled with stolen GI ration cards, and several pillowcases full of loose marijuana were piled atop a desk. Richards rifled the drawers and found a notebook containing the names of several Americans who had been involved in transactions with the black marketeers. He slipped it into his pocket while the Canh-Sat was preparing to escort the arrested drug runners down to the street.

As the prisoners filed from the tenement and out to a waiting police jeep, Richards started back to show Sergeant Mather the notebook when a woman's ghastly scream froze him in his tracks. The long, drawn-out cry had been one of intense agony, the unearthly kind of groan Richards had only heard before in the interrogation cells at Long Binh Jail. It was not the kind of scream you heard when a woman was petrified with fear. It was

246

the kind created by excruciating, unbearable pain. Richards could immediately tell from which building across the street the sound had come, but so horrifying was the noise his body refused to move even a step in that direction.

Among the three Vietnamese policemen who rushed past Richards, the blue-gray mist swirling at their feet in the gloom, was Jon Toi. He had been dispatched to assist with the prisoner transport and took it upon himself, as the senior Canh-Sat at the scene, to find out why a woman in his sector of Saigon was screaming.

Toi directed one of his men to circle around back of the apartment house, then he and the other policemen rushed in through the front door. Several tenants were already mingling out in the hallway of the ground floor, the women in silk robes or casual sarongs, the men mostly in pajama bottoms or baggy GI shorts.

They all whispered in hushed tones among themselves, and when Toi questioned the closest person—a woman wrapped in a satin nightgown with sweat of the hot night beading along her throat and chest—she made the slightest gesture to a room halfway down the corridor. Toi could see in her eyes that she was fearful of cooperating, afraid talk between neighbors might later reveal her involvement. And such gossip could eventually leak to the person making the woman in room fourteen scream, and didn't they all have enough problems already?

Toi rushed to the edge of the door and motioned for the tenants to back off down the hall. Then he listened briefly, his ear along the edge of the seal, and when he heard no movement inside the apartment he drew his revolver and lifted three fingers toward his partner. The younger Canh-Sat nodded that he understood, and Toi responded by slowly raising one finger at a time until the count of three had been reached. They both planted heavy boots against the thick door and kicked it in.

The one-room apartment was thick with cigarette smoke, now sent swirling with the flying wood panels, but Toi had no difficulty spotting the woman's body in the center of the living room floor. The dismembered torso, its arms and legs hacked off and missing, lay in a pool of blood. The head was grotesquely twisted to one side, the neck snapped. There was no one else in the apartment.

Toi briefly searched the buffet, then he hurried back out into the corridor when he saw the MPs from the Decoy Squad enter the building. The Canh-Sat stopped them several feet from room fourteen and requested that they leave the crime scene area. "Thank you, gentlemen," Toi smiled. "But this is not a matter for the U.S. Military Police. The victim is Vietnamese. We'll take it from here."

What Toi did not tell Sergeant Richards as he smiled through his teeth was that he found a set of American dog tags lying at the edge of the pool of blood.

XIX. HOT POTATO HERO

Stryker brought the telephoto lens into sharp focus and snapped the picture of the wealthy Chinese businessman kissing the expensive call girl on the cheek. He shifted his weight on the swaying fire escape so as to get a better shot through the window of the seventh-floor suite across the alley, and Stryker clicked off several more photos as the man unbuttoned the woman's blouse and led her over to the bed.

Later he would follow the woman back to her apartment, jot down the address and anything else his employer's client might find interesting, then pass the file on to his new boss, Gean Servonnat. It was turning into a simple job and Stryker was becoming accustomed to the nights spent chasing unfaithful husbands and the days spent following up missing persons cases—and there were a lot of persons missing in Vietnam just then. Gathering evidence of possible industrial espionage and locating runaway daughters was a far cry from jumping out of helicopters, and Stryker was beginning to enjoy the easy life.

Lai had refused to join him in Saigon, but she would eventually come around, and since accepting an honorable discharge from the Special Forces last week he was even beginning to let his hair grow a little. Stryker still worked out every morning though, completing a complicated routine of aerobics, t'ai chi ch'uan shadow boxing and bio-feedback exercises. You just never knew when the life of a private investigator might turn down a dangerous alley, and when that time came he planned to be ready.

Sometimes he would keep copies of the more risque photos he took and the idea entered his mind that he might start keeping files on the characters he met in this new line of work. Just in case he ever split from Monsieur Servonnat and struck out on his own. That thought didn't strike him very often, though. The devious Frenchman was paying him good money to run his errands and do his dirty work. Stryker was aware the man was probably charging clients five times the amount he paid his detectives per case, but the wages were still more than enough to live comfortably on.

As he started down the fire escape, Stryker noticed two Special Forces soldiers walking up the street below him. After carefully replacing the camera in its watertight case, he subconsciously reached up to straighten his own beret and felt a sharp pang of disappointment when he remembered it was no longer there.

"My Dear Mr. and Mrs. Anderson," Richards began the letter. He leaned back in the jeep, trying to think of the right words to say. The other members of the Decoy Squad had entered a coffee shop for their break, but he had decided to remain outside and take in the first cool breezes that followed dusk. He had been waiting much too long to write the letter.

Across the street, dozens of young women waited in line while a scholarly looking schoolboy with thick, black glasses casually slipped another piece of damp paper into his typewriter. The kid had set up a little table under one of the tamarind trees and was charging the girls ten cents a page to put together love letters in English for their boyfriends back in America. Most of the girls were poorly educated and had gone back to the bars after their soldier boys had rotated out of the country.

The men often wrote an unexpected letter or two when they arrived home and discovered they could not cope or adjust easily to life with an American fiancée. Richards knew the loneliness that the men often fell into usually led them to send money back to Saigon along with promises that they would soon return to Vietnam and marry the girls. It was just too difficult to say goodbye to their Saigon experience.

Although they continued to work in the whorehouses out of necessity, Richards knew the women faithfully sent anxious letters swearing their loyalty to their boyfriends and claiming they now had a respectable job as a seamstress in one of the factories. The girls would make a point of it to dispatch several letters a week—often to more than one man—almost as insurance against their old lovers forgetting about them, and Richards had even seen some of the women bring their current boyfriends with them to wait in the long lines at Le Loi park. There were many girls who flocked to the little boy with the typewriter day after day, continuing to send letters long after the soldiers who had left their hearts in Saigon quit writing back.

"Your son was the unfortunate victim of a communist ambush," Richards started to write, but then he remembered the sailor's parents had obtained a copy of the military police report somehow and it would probably make some mention of the fact that their son had been stabbed to death in a whorehouse. Richards crumpled up the letter and took out a new sheet. The stationery showed two grunts huddled behind an M-60 machine gun in a rice paddy taking hostile fire, and had FROM VIETNAM: FUN CAPITAL OF THE WORLD emblazoned across the top.

"Your son served honorably in the U.S. Navy until . . ." Richards wadded up that one, too, and began counting the number of women lining up at the typewriter across the street. The schoolboy had produced a battery-powered lamp and seemed prepared to work late into the night.

"Seaman Anderson was walking along Tu Do Street when a

251

pickpocket stole his wallet and ran into the Xin Loi bar—your son chased the subject into the establishment but was unfortunately ambushed by the thief's accomplices, waiting in a dark hallway." Richards reread the letter several times then tore it in half and tossed it into the gutter under the jeep.

"Hey, you could get two-to-five in Chi Hoa jail for littering in this town," Sergeant Mather laughed as he came out of the coffee shop carrying two ice cream cones. "Just love this Vietnamese ice cream," he said, handing one to Richards. "Never tasted anything like it! No matter what flavor you buy, it always tastes like creme de caramel."

"Where's the dynamic duo?" Richards asked without smiling. He was still upset that Thomas had turned the jeep's headlights on prematurely, warning Rodgers the Decoy Squad was about to nab him. The sergeant could understand that the men felt an obligation to protect and look out for each other. Hell, no one else was going to think twice about what dangers the MPs faced out on the streets. Everyone knew that police work led to early deaths instead of retirement, and that cops had one of the highest rates of suicide in any job category. But that was old news and the people didn't care anymore. Only the families and sometimes the girlfriends. Richards could remember finding out that his fiancée back in the states had taken out a hefty insurance policy on him without telling him, and that had led to their breaking up. So he could understand why the MPs stuck up for each other. Especially the younger men, who saw a romanticism or warped sense of duty in aiding the escape of a fugitive friend. Even some of the higher-ups were saying, off the record, that they hoped this Rodgers maniac would dispose of a few more undesirables before he finally got caught.

But damn, Richards thought. *Murder was murder. Rodgers was turning into a cold-blooded lunatic. He had to be stopped before more innocent people got killed.* Accounts of his escapades had already leaked out to the newspapers, and it just wouldn't do to have a deserter smearing the good name of the

252

military police corps worldwide. And besides, once they caught him—if they didn't blow him away—they could turn him over to the shrinks and get him the help he needed! *No, Rodgers wouldn't spend any real time in the stockade. He was too wacko and belonged in the psycho ward.*

"What's the long line across the street all about?" Mather asked as he struggled to keep the rapidly melting ice cream cone from dripping all over his chin and uniform.

"Broken hearts club," he answered with no humor in his tone. "Writing home to Papa. Bucking for a ticket stateside." His eyes saw things a thousand miles away as he watched the girls lining up. Some laughed and joked as they met other girlfriends in the line, while others stared at the ground in a daze, cigarettes balanced between expertly polished fingernails, burning away unsmoked.

"More power to 'em," Mather said, surprising the other sergeant. "We come over here and Americanize an Asian country, and turn all their women into whores. Hell, I hope every last one of 'em gets some sucker to take her home to Ma and Pa."

"There were prostitutes here long before the U.S. entered the war," Richards said, feeling suddenly energetic and primed for a debate. "You can't blame all of this on us."

"I guess you're right," the stocky buck sergeant decided as he pulled an o.d. green handkerchief from his pocket and began polishing his belt buckle. "It's just that these poor girls must be awful tired of having to go out and find a new boyfriend every twelve or thirteen months. I mean, they give their all to these foreigners, expecting nothing in return except quasi-loyalty and a bag of groceries once a month."

"Well, there's always suckers like you and me," Richards interrupted, "who keep re-enlisting for Vietnam because we don't have enough brains to do something worthwhile with our lives," and both men began a light, uneasy laugh as they realized the truth was too painful to face.

Richards noticed a souvenir shop a few feet down from the

cafe they were parked in front of, and he got out of the jeep without another word to Mather. He walked over to a postcard rack set up on the sidewalk and chose a scene showing naked children riding a monstrous water buffalo that was shoulder deep in a flooded rice paddy. The MP sergeant took a black pen from his shirt pocket and began to write, "Dear Mr. and Mrs. Anderson, Your son's tragic death was a shock to us all. Am not at liberty to discuss the case with you right at this time, but will write a lengthy letter later. If it helps, rest easy: Philip died instantaneously and did not suffer. Best wishes to you and your family. Signed, Sgt. Gary Richards, #407048225, 716th Military Police Bn. Saigon. APO SF 96309."

He purchased some under-the-counter Vietnamese stamps from the shopkeeper, insisting on picturesque jungle scenes instead of soldiers, combat, or anything relating to the war. He pasted on the colorful stamps and started to deposit the card in a mailbox on the corner when he hesitated, then returned to the shop. He bought a blue international airmail envelope depicting a jumbo jet flying over a map of Indochina, and slipped the card inside, added more stamps, then headed back toward the mailbox.

"So here we are." Thomas slapped Kruger on the back as they sat at the restaurant counter. He had all but forgotten the man had nearly drilled him full of hot lead only a couple nights earlier. "And I mean to tell you—here we are just cruising the streets on routine patrol, okay? Now it's snowing like unreal amounts of white, okay? But nice, big, soft flakes coming down real slow. No wind—just real quiet, pleasant conditions for patrolling. And I'm out there on the outskirts of Fort Carson, trying to spot Pike's Peak with my telescope."

"Your what?" Kruger asked incredulously.

"Hey, do I stutter, gutter breath? Telescope! I always carried a telescope for surveillance activity. You know—you have to stay one step ahead of the dirtbags who make their living stealing from decent folks like us. Well, I could go on and on about that. . . ."

"So here you are . . ."

"So here we are, me and my telescope eyeballin' ol' Pike's Peak. . . ."

"One-man patrol?" Kruger was feeling ornery.

"One-man patrol. Definitely. Hey—who could put up with me for twelve hours, right?" and Thomas began laughing at his own joke. "So I'm scopin' ol' Pike's Peak and what zips by me but this dude on a snowmobile. I mean, hey—right there on the street. It's not like I'm out in the boonies or something— I'm right there on Fort Carson's main drag and this son of a bitch runs circles around my patrol car then splits."

"Big deal."

"Big deal? Big deal, you say? Hey Krug—this guy is bare ass naked! I mean, here he is running circles around a military police cruiser on Main Street, U.S.A., flipping me the bird, and all he's wearing are combat boots and a gas mask! That's right, a gas mask so I can't identify that scumbag."

"You gotta be shittin' me."

"Hey, Krug—I wouldn't shit you. You're my favorite turd. So anyway, here I am, tossing my telescope in the back seat . . ."

"I just can't believe you actually patrolled with a telescope," Kruger interrupted the story again.

"Hey, barf breath, would I make something like that up? Other guys carried a lot weirder stuff than that, but hey! You gonna let me tell my story, or not?"

"Well, we probably should get out to the jeep. Those two sarges out there are probably thinking—"

"Hey, sit tight! What's more important, anyway? So I crank up my unit and try to chase the snowmobile, but I'm spinning circles on a patch of ice and ain't going nowhere! So I call for backup, right? And they send the chase car my way, okay? I mean, we're talkin' real souped-up Plymouth Fury, 440 under the hood, dual carbs—hey, a real chopper's dream!

"And my hero is driving—none other than the duty officer, Lieutenant Slipka! I mean, this is a cool dude we're talkin' about. Went through basic just a couple years before me. Made sergeant, no sweat, but remained one of the guys, you know? Could crack night sticks with the best of 'em. Went to college on his own time off and freaked out everyone by becoming a butter bar—all this before his enlistment was up, too! I mean, hey—we got the same first names, right? So the guy can't be all bad, even if he *is* a second louie.

"So this snowmobile phantom sees another patrol car comin' up the road real fast—I mean, we're talkin' a hot run, code three, lights and siren. Well, he boogies off into the blizzard before ol' Tony Slipka can arrive on scene."

"And I bet the lieutenant didn't believe your story. Did he wanna know what you were doing out in a snowstorm with a goddamn telescope? Sounds kinda kinky to me."

"You hit the nail on the head, Kruger dear. I'm huffin' and puffin' tryin' to push the patrol car off the ice, telling Slipka my story and he's just standing there with his shit-eatin' grin and accusing eyes. I mean, this guy has a way of smiling at you and making you feel about this tall," and Thomas bent over on the stool and held his hand a half foot off the floor.

"So what happened then?" Kruger showed more interest in the story when the MP beside him ordered them both a slice of pie.

"Salvation, ol' Krug! Now, don't get me wrong—I love this Slipka. I mean the guy was a number one cop—could kick ass and take names with the best of us."

"But . . ."

"But his one weakness was he was such a skeptic about certain things."

"Skeptics make good cops."

"Well, yeah, maybe."

"Hey, Thomas, I'd be a little leery of a guy reporting a streaker on a snowmobile myself—especially if he always dragged a telescope around in his patrol car."

256

Thomas ignored the remark and continued, "So Lieutenant Slipka is standing there wiping the snow off his blue-tinted glasses—yeah, he had these neat, blue-tinted glasses everyone feared he'd quit wearing when he made lou. And he's standing there like a statue of Clint Eastwood—indestructible, okay? Combing snowflakes out of his blond hair with his fingers—giving me the evil eye and that skeptical stare as I'm getting back into my unit.

"And the goddamn streaker races by again! Bare ass and all! Perfect timing! Carving up circles in the ice around us again, only this time he moons the lieutenant! Right there on Main Street! Sticks his frosty red rectum right up not five feet from Slipka's face!

"Well, I didn't know if I should fall back in the snowbank laughing or commence to pursue, you know? But Slipka hops in his patrol car and practically calls out the whole battalion! Hey, can you blame him? He's not gonna let some jerk-off get away with that!

"So we chase this guy all over camp—twenty-some cars crossing Fort Carson code three in a fuckin' blizzard, sliding off the road at every curve and intersection. And this guy is just running circles around *every*one. Set up a roadblock and he'd just take to the hills and come up right behind you, ready for more. Hey, have you ever seen a snowmobile in action? Every damn MP company should have one!

"Anyway, ol' Slipka gets crafty and rigs up a cable between two trees and just somersaults this dude out of his snowmobile on the third pass. Funny as hell—I can remember it still: that damn thing cruising down the road minus its driver.

"So this bare-assed clown wearing combat boots and gas mask hightails it out across the snowbanks hoping to get away despite having the wind knocked out of him."

"And?"

"And Lieutenant Slipka swoops down on him like stink on shit. I mean, I'm expecting the fight of the century but the guy holds up his hands to surrender, knowing full well he's about this close to getting a night stick shoved up his bare ass," and Thomas held up two fingers to indicate a couple inches.

"You gentlemen working tonight or not?" came a stern voice behind the two privates. Thomas turned to see the lieutenant who had held the briefing earlier that week and told Thomas to get a haircut.

"Uh, yes, sir." Kruger was already off his stool and heading for the door. Thomas began combing down the hair that stuck out behind his ears and started to follow.

"Where's your M-16, Private Thomas?" the lieutenant glared, taking a notebook from his pocket as he sat down on the stool Kruger had just vacated.

"I left it in the jeep, sir. With the sergeants. I'm sure it's safe," he said, adding more respect to his tone than he'd used in months.

"See to it that you keep that hummer in your possession at all times from now on. I mean what I say at those briefings." Thomas nodded his head and left without saying anything else, but the lieutenant stopped him. "I don't mean to come across as a hardass, Thomas, but one of these days you're going to get sniped at or something and you're going to wish you had that extra firepower."

"Yes, sir," he answered, whipping an informal salute on the officer even though they were indoors.

Kruger was waiting for him outside and as they walked down the steps to the jeep, he whispered to Thomas, "Boy, that Faldwin is a real pain, isn't he?" When Thomas didn't make any comment Kruger added, "Someday somebody's gonna frag his chickenshit ass!"

"Why didn't you warn us, Sarge?" Thomas quipped as they hopped into the jeep.

"Warn you about what?" Richards answered. "If you got your shit together, you got nothing to worry about."

Sergeant Mather leaned back in his seat and sighed, his smile revealing perfect, gleaming teeth. "Ah, Lieutenant Jack Faldwin," he said, "the stories I could tell you about that candy ass." But he was not quick to elaborate.

"So what ever happened with that nude snowmobiler?" Kruger asked Thomas.

"That *what?*" Richards turned in his seat, then looked quickly down both stretches of road in case he had missed something whizzing by.

"Well, ol' Slipka tore the dude's gas mask off and lo and behold—if it ain't Sergeant Raul Schultz!"

"The MP sergeant Bryant was on that prostitution bust with? Where he assaulted the air-conditioner?"

"The one and only! Came down from Fitz to kick around old times—hey, it was the best entrance a guy coulda made!"

"That's the kind of guys they usually send to 'Nam," laughed Mathers.

"Is he still a sergeant?" asked Richards.

Just then an old man on a bicycle—its handlebars piled high with miniature loaves of buttered bread—teetered out into the middle of a nearby intersection without seeing a taxi that came speeding down the street. The car skidded for several feet at the last second but still struck the bicyclist, and loaves of bread were scattered for half a block as the old man bounced off the windshield. Within seconds, traffic all around the accident had screeched to a halt and small groups of curious spectators filtering in off the sidewalks gradually turned into a noisy crowd.

"Why don't you go see if you can give 'em a hand with traffic control," Richards told Kruger and Thomas, "till I can get some Canh-Sats over there." The two privates jumped out of the jeep, stuck their night sticks in their webgear, threw M-16s over shoulders and started running toward the accident. Richards picked up the jeep's radio microphone and made several attempts to contact headquarters, without success. "Must be a goddamn dead zone," he told Mather, referring to those low spots in the terrain radio waves notoriously bypassed.

"Here"—Mather tossed him a dong coin—"there's a phone

259

back in the coffee shop. The number is 24822."

I know the damn number, Richards thought to himself, but he just smiled and stepped from the jeep. *Two sergeants on one patrol is beginning to become a real pain in the ass,* he decided, wishing Broox and Bryant would hurry and return to the squad.

Just as Richards started up the stairs to the coffee shop, a Honda motor scooter flew past the MP jeep parked thirty feet away. Sergeant Mather had barely made eye contact with the beautiful woman driving when the girl sitting behind her, the breeze tugging at her halter top and black pantaloons as they sputtered by, tossed a live grenade in his lap.

It bounced off his belt buckle and clattered to the floorboard of the jeep and just then Mather decided he had never been so scared in his life and he'd rather die on Tu Do Street, gun blazing.

The sergeant awkwardly lifted his steel-soled jungle boots as high away from the floorboard as he possibly could and concentrated on pulling his body out of the seat with suddenly sluggish forearms when the grenade detonated, blowing the jeep onto its side. Mather could feel himself blacking out even before the jeep stopped rocking, and he welcomed quick death, hoping it would sweep over him instantly, without pain, without him ever learning how many arms or legs had been torn from their sockets and scattered sliding across the filthy street.

Kruger and Thomas whirled around at the sound of the magnificent explosion even before the blast rolled out across the street and knocked them to the pavement. Richards hadn't even been looking at the jeep when he started up the steps into the coffee shop, and he decided later that the terrific flash of light singing his eyebrows was seen as a reflection in the cafe's front picture windows. The sergeant flew around as the jeep was upended and stared in shock as small pieces of hot, smoking shrapnel seemed to whiz past in slow motion on both sides of him.

It was an unwritten rule in Saigon that when a bomb went off, nobody moved. Not for several seconds—perhaps a full minute, just to play it safe: anyone running, either to or from the scene, was fair game for a police bullet. That's why people always froze when there was an explosion close by. It didn't matter if they were jogging, sweeping the sidewalk, or just moving a set of chopsticks from a pile of rice to an open mouth. All movement ceased.

When Kruger saw the motor scooter bearing the two Honda Honies materialize from the billowing cloud of smoke he sprang to his feet and dove for the girl controlling the handlebars. The scooter crashed over onto its side in a shower of sparks and both girls tumbled heavily across the blacktop and slid to a stop with their arms and legs badly bruised and scraped.

Kruger managed to keep the driver pinned to the ground as she slowly struggled to escape, and Thomas drew his pistol and tackled the other girl as she rose to one knee in a daze. Without seeing any weapons—only the sight of Sergeant Mather's severed foot spinning from the rolling ball of smoke and bouncing with a dull thump along the blacktop—Thomas placed the .45 against the woman's left temple and pulled the trigger as she struck at him with a tiny, clenched fist. Thomas felt suddenly dizzy as her skull completely fell apart in a spray of blood, and he jumped back as the hot, empty cartridge bounced back from the ejector and seared his cheek. He didn't notice just then that the sound of brass clanking across the pavement was not the .45 shell but a bayonet the girl had hoped to plunge into his heart.

Bryant wasn't sure how to respond to the cable from his parents. He clearly remembered signing one of those forms prohibiting the Army from notifying his family of any wounds received, short of death itself. But, of course, Uncle Sam had lost the paperwork and dispatched the telegram.

Bryant sighed as he wadded up another letter, unable to complete even the first paragraph. "Dear Folks, War is hell! Ha ha, just kidding! Guess you heard about my accident," and he promptly tossed that one into the trash can beside his hospital cot.

"Dear Mom and Dad, A funny thing happened to me on the way to the stake out last week. . . ." Another one wadded up.

"Dear Dad, Tell Mom not to worry. I'm okay, just a flesh wound. I guess I'll tell you how it happened and you decide which parts to tell Mom, okay? And, really—it doesn't hurt much at all." Bryant folded that one and tucked it under the notebook when he saw Sister Hoa enter the wing and start in his direction with someone else—a woman in tow behind her.

When he recognized Hue Chean following the nun, an uncomfortable look on her face, he wanted to pull the pillow over his head and hide under the covers.

"Good morning, Specialist Bryant," Sister Hoa emphasized his rank. "You have a visitor," and she turned and started back toward the stairs before he could acknowledge. The nun had forced a slight smile, and the way she bit her lip as she walked off only served to accent the disapproval in her voice.

"What's *her* problem?" Chean asked as she sat on the edge of the bed, dropped her heavy purse on his injured leg, and flicked her nose at the nun. "She don't like the way I look maybe?"

Bryant flinched as he brushed the bag aside, but recovered quickly and kept the grin on his face despite the shock waves of pain shooting up from the tender bullet hole. He stared at her tight-fitting halter top and revealing hot pants and wished for the first time that he wasn't on injury leave but was back in the top physical condition he so prided himself on. Even though Chean hadn't let him into those pants in months it was nice to know he could outlast her if the time ever came again.

"You're the last person I expected to see at a hospital," Bryant said. "I thought you didn't like to look at sick people."

"This place gives me creeps," she admitted with distaste, looking about the room with darting eyes as if she half expected mutant laboratory bugs to hop out at her from the corners. Then after that little performance she opened her eyes wide and threw her arms around him. "But I miss you *so* much, Timmy! I worry so much when I hear goddamn VC shoot you!" And Bryant instantly wondered who in the Decoy Squad had tried to bed her down after going to the trouble of delivering the bad news.

"Funny you become so concerned after all these weeks," and he hugged her back, taking in the scent of her tangy perfume and the bulge of her chest against his. "Or could it be that you just came to make sure I still got you down as beneficiary on my GI life insurance."

Hue Chean recoiled as she pulled away from him slowly. "You still have *me* on policy?" she winced at the rebuff but gave him a wink that said, I know you're only kidding about all this.

She ran her fingers along the bandage around his calf lightly and stopped just short of the red stain in the middle that grew slowly every few hours. "Does it hurt too much, Timmy?"

"I'll live," he muttered. "So what's new down on the street? Your father make you a full partner in his restaurant yet?" Bryant referred to the cafe tucked away at the back of the cavernous Xin Loi bar.

"I suppose you think I would marry you and support you rest of our life if that the case?" She laughed. "What does a private in American Army have that Hue Chean could want?" she asked playfully, raising her nose in mock conceit.

"I'm a Specialist Fourth Class," he corrected her. "E-4. That's three promotions above buck private, okay? Ten times the amount a Saigon policeman makes, and—" But Hue Chean was not listening.

She ran her fingers back up along his thigh. "You want to play chicken?" She grinned. "Just tell me when to stop, brave boy," her fingers continuing to tiptoe up his leg toward his crotch.

"Uh hmmmm," came a female voice behind her, and Hue

Chean straightened her back rigid, startled at the sight of Sister Hoa. "Excuse me, Specialist Bryant," the nun said, "but you have a phone call. Will you take it now—at your bed?" But an American nurse was already wheeling a portable telephone down the corridor. Bryant noticed the overweight WAC give both Sister Hoa and Hue Chean a wry look at the sight of them clustered around him, but he ignored her disapproval and picked up the receiver.

"Joe's Mortuary," he said dryly. "How tall are you?"

"Tim?" came the hesitant whisper at the other end. Bryant immediately perked up in the bed and his ear tensed as he strained to hear past the bad connection.

"Rodgers? Is that you, Jeff?" Bryant's mind flashed back to the night Thomas took him into his confidence and told him Jeff had somehow gotten into his footlocker and "borrowed" some ammunition. Thomas had left the trunk unlocked after that and had piled it full of clips, C-rations, and what money he could spare.

"Yes, Tim. It's me. I'm sorry to bother you, but . . ."

"Where are you?" Bryant cut in excitedly, but he checked his enthusiasm when he saw Sister Hoa and Chean staring at him curiously.

"I need to talk to you, Tim. It's gone too far." Bryant could hear the shaking in Rodgers' voice above the traffic noises in the background. "I'm ready to give it up, at least I think I am. There's so much I need to do still, but this isn't the way to go about it. I think I'm ready to surrender, but I want it to be to you."

Bryant listened intently, his lips unable to move as Rodgers continued, "The other guys are so psyched up about this thing—so trigger-happy, I wouldn't stand a chance. It's open season on Jeff Rodgers right now. And I don't want to have to kill a cop. I wouldn't be able to handle that, Tim."

Bryant heard excited shouts in the background and Rodgers appeared to have dropped the phone—was running away. Bryant stuck a finger in his other ear to block out the sound in the hospital wing as he pressed the phone receiver in tighter.

"Jeff! Jeff, are you still there?" But he knew Rodgers was running for his life. As fast as he could, away from the phone booth.

Two sets of boots rushed past the dangling phone as it swayed back and forth above the sidewalk. Bryant could hear muffled shouts in Vietnamese and English—probably one of the Combined Police Patrols. And then someone was running back toward the phone booth.

"Hello—who is on the other end of this line?" someone who had picked up the receiver was speaking in a strained, authoritative tone. But Spec. 4 Timothy Bryant kept his mouth shut, reached over and broke the connection.

XX. RED CROSSES MAKE THE BEST TARGETS

Toi studied the new photos he had tacked to the wall of his private back room and began jotting more notes on his clipboard, trying to bring it all together. But try as he might, the Canh-Sat could just not connect the murder of the secretary in room fourteen to any of the other unsolved murder cases plaguing the Vietnamese National Police in May, 1967. Toi kicked his boots off and propped his tired feet up on the table as he flipped the cap off a bottle of "33" beer.

Perhaps he should have told Sergeant Richards that he located Rodgers' dog tags at the scene of the gruesome murder—the beaded metal necklace was snapped in two as if it had been broken during a scuffle. He had tried to talk with Bryant about the matter, but when he visited Third Field Army Hospital he was told the Specialist Fourth Class was in physical therapy that morning and wouldn't be taking visitors for the rest of the day. No matter—there would have been nothing Bryant could do anyway.

Toi smiled as he noticed the walls no longer had any space clear of his macabre photo collection, but the grin quickly faded as his eyes surveyed the pictures of the crime scene in room fourteen. She had been a twenty-four-year-old secretary working at one of the travel agencies in Cholon. It was still not clear if the intruder had forced his way into her home or she had known her attacker and allowed the madman to enter.

Toi had not noticed any signs of forcible entry on the door before they kicked it in, but a window in the bedroom showed recent jimmy indentations around the latch. Investigations Bureau was trying to determine how old the pry marks were.

Toi's bloodshot eyes surveyed the eight-by-ten glossies for the hundredth time in the last two days, left to right. The first was a view from the hallway and showed the splintered door and the dark interior of the apartment. Something resembling a bloodied sack of grain was in the background, centered by the doorframe.

For the other photos Toi had turned on the lights in the apartment, and they only served to illuminate the savagery of the murder. Four photos from different angles depicted the mangled torso of the naked victim. Her arms and legs had been viciously chopped off and carted away by the assailant. Red impressions on the woman's cheeks showed where the killer's strong fingers had grabbed hold and snapped her head back to abruptly silence the last scream. The secretary had once been very beautiful, her long hair falling to the waist of her slim body, but all that remained now was a mass of abrasions and discolored bruises. Her once silky, jet-black hair had been torn out in spots and the delicate features of her face beaten to a pulp.

The next five photos circled the body in a grid pattern, taking in the splotches of blood coating the walls, the overturned furniture, the shattered and empty aquarium that had crashed to the floor during the scuffle. He wondered how anyone could have ripped away four limbs in the short time between the woman's last scream and Toi's arrival outside her door—unless the killer had started mutilating the victim while she was still alive!

Toi had not used any of his private film on the other parts of the house, but the detectives who showed up to conduct the crime scene investigation later told him they had found nothing unusual in the victim's clothing, closets or dresser drawers.

Of course, they had meticulously photographed everything, just in case. Toi could remember his brief stint with the Investigations Bureau. Photograph this, photograph that. It was those crazy American police advisors that insisted they take pictures of everything, no matter how insignificant it seemed at the time. And damned if they hadn't located a vital clue or two upon reviewing those same photographs later.

Toi examined the dog tags again carefully as he opened another bottle of beer. He liked to place the cans from the fridge in the ice box for half an hour before consuming them when he got home from work—it seemed to have a quicker effect on his body that way, especially on the hotter days when the humidity made even a pleasant ninety degrees a cooker and he had spent all afternoon out on his TCP box.

They'd have his head at headquarters if they knew he'd pocketed the tags, but Toi was convinced Jeff had nothing to do with this murder, regardless of what other activities he was accused of participating in.

Toi could feel the beer finally taking hold of the pain at the base of his skull and massaging it away into a numbing dizziness as he stared at the photo depicting the woman's broken neck. The brutal disfigurement—the obscene contortions of the woman's tortured face, frozen in its final agonizing death throes, jumped out at Toi, reminding him of the murdered nurse found in that deserted back alley. Her killers had left hypodermic needles swaying in her eyeballs and he knew Rodgers wasn't involved in that homicide either.

Toi wondered where Rodgers was just then. He pictured him wandering exhausted down some filthy side street, wet and hungry, scavenging for food and shelter, and he thought back to when he first met the American.

The combined downtown Police Patrols placing two U.S. MPs with two Canh-Sats had seen nothing but friction those first few months. The English-speaking policemen originally assigned to the Canh Luc Hon Hop usually ended up sitting out their tour of duty at headquarters, where interpreters were in great demand and short supply. That meant the Vietnamese who ended up on the patrols spoke little English and most Americans hadn't bothered to learn the language of the country they were serving. So the entire shift saw the Canh-Sats talking only to each other and the MPs ignoring their counterparts. Toi smiled as he recalled that even he had remained cool toward the Americans at first—rumors of their arrogant ways and disrespect toward Vietnamese custom and culture had preceded them.

The first call Toi had responded to with Rodgers was a routine bar fight at the Olympio on Le Loi Street. But the brawlers inside were far from routine. One was a Navy boxer from San Diego, who stood a full foot taller than even Rodgers, and after he politely moved the MP aside, the barrel-chested sailor hoisted Toi's partner above his head and whirled around in circles as though he couldn't decide which mirror to toss the tiny Vietnamese through.

Rodgers had rushed up behind the giant, jabbed a night stick in his kidneys then grabbed him around the chest in a bear hug after he dropped the Canh-Sat on the counter. The sailor had lifted Rodgers off his feet and twirled him around a couple times also, claiming his fight was with the "damned Orientals" only, but Jeff had slapped his palms against the ape's ears, knocking him to his knees. Toi had been all prepared to charge, but the American quickly took control of the brute, and the Canh-Sat stood back out of the way to watch Rodgers grab the man's thumb and twist him down flat on the floor until he could be frisked and handcuffed.

After additional units arrived to mop up, Rodgers had made a point of taking Officer Toi aside and apologizing for the way the American had insulted the people of Vietnam.

Toi knew drunks often made remarks they weren't sincere about, and few things heard on duty were taken personally by the Canh-Sat. But he appreciated what Rodgers had tried to say that evening, and never quite forgot the man's act of compassion. And that admiration included subduing the sailor without breaking two night sticks over his skull—Rodgers had taken him down with the minimum amount of force necessary to effect the arrest.

"Another beer, Toi?" Lan had walked into the room and draped her arms around his shoulders from behind. Toi clasped the loyal woman's hands in his own along his chest and prayed she wouldn't make any remarks about the new set of photos that now covered her bamboo-design wallpaper.

"We've got enough here to jerk your commission, Lieutenant," C.I.D. agent Sickles advised the officer from First Signal Brigade. The man sat in a chair in the middle of an empty room with the warrant officer and Sergeant Richards leaning over him.

"You don't have shit on me, mister," Clifford Jacobson replied, his eyes glued to the floor. Richards watched the man's fists clutch at the armrests of the chair and he hoped the soldier would lose his cool and come up swinging. Despite his size—almost six-foot-five—most of it was undisciplined flab, and Richards hadn't cold-cocked an officer in months.

"Distribution of drugs, procurement of illegal firearms for hell-knows-what purpose, involvement in a child prostitution ring," Sickles read off the notes on his clipboard.

"My name on a lousy list found in some illegal search don't amount to a hill of beans," the lieutenant snapped back.

"We're talking murder scene." Richards grinned as Sickles added, "Plus we've got you drunk in uniform on April first—being hustled into a taxi on Nguyen Hu Street by a prostitute."

"Big deal."

"Did you know that hooker, Lee Thi Diep, alias Lisa Lee, murdered a sailor a couple weeks later, and was killed by our boys after she took a Vietnamese policeman hostage?" Sickles felt a wave of satisfaction sweep through his tired bones—he had been waiting a long time to see Jacobson's face when he unleashed that little tidbit of secret information on the man.

Jacobson swallowed hard, but refused to look up at the two interrogators. "If you bozos got charges on me, fine. Otherwise, I'm leaving. Walking out right now," and the lieutenant started to rise from his chair. Richards slammed him back down roughly, using two hands on his shoulders.

"This contraption," Sickles explained as an MP wheeled in a green box then hastily departed, "is a voice analysis machine. It will tell me if your answers to our questions are accurate, or if you're trying to deceive us."

"I'm not talking anymore without counsel present," the lieutenant sneered. "Do you understand what that means? I am requesting—demanding—to be represented by a—"

"Shut the fuck up and listen to the man!" Richards brought his nose down to the officer's face, daring him to interrupt again.

"Yesterday a Miss Nim Thi Sang was murdered downtown. Butchered. Raped. Dismembered."

"I've got an alibi!" Jacobson cut in. Sweat was breaking out on his forehead and the sight of it made Richards feel good inside for a change.

"I'm sure you do. I'm sure you do, Lieutenant." Sickles grinned. "But how are you going to explain the woman's arms and legs turning up in the trunk of your rented Toyota this morning?"

"What?" Jacobson flew to his feet and Richards slammed him back down.

"Don't worry, Lieutenant. We got a proper search warrant from a military judge after we brought you in for questioning. Even had the Vietnamese police present during the search— just to ensure no procedural regulations were violated as far as jurisdiction goes," Sickles advised him.

"We wouldn't want *this* one thrown out of court on a technicality," added Richards.

"Bet you're gonna tell us you didn't even know you've been driving around the last eighteen hours with a twenty-four-year-old virgin's dismembered limbs in the trunk of your sports car, eh, Jacobson?" It was Sickles who sneered this time.

"You ever seen what it's like in a Saigon prison?" Richards loved to see officers squirm under fire.

But the lieutenant now stared ashen-faced at the wall and his eyes began to glaze over with rage. "Why that goddamned Jacks—" he started to say, but he cut himself short and jammed a knuckle nervously between his teeth.

"Spit it out, Jacobson!" Richards now leaned nose to nose with the signal officer. "Who is it you think set you up?"

"We know you're involved with Stubbs and Jackson in this blackmail bullshit," Sickles said. "And you made the mistake of getting involved with Vietnamese hoods who keep detailed records of their buyers and sellers."

"But now we're talking murder, Jacobson." Richards grinned again. "You got the time for such a crime, sir?" and he slurred the sir, showing little respect.

Sickles had not yet figured out how the bloody arms and legs had gotten into Jacobson's Toyota, and he wasn't sure who had killed Nim Thi Sang, but he didn't think Jacobson was involved.

"Right now, Lieutenant, we want to know two things. Just two things, then we'll let you go back to your hootch for the night. Of course, you'll have to walk 'cuz we're keeping your auto on the blocks, but you'll remain a free man for the time being."

"Just two things," repeated Richards.

Jacobson looked up at them but didn't nod his head one way or the other.

"Number one: Jeff Rodgers. Military policeman. How does he fit into your operation?" Sickles asked. "And number two: We're looking for a little statue. A statue of a jade lady—a Thai dancer. We think you or one of your boys got it stashed

273

somewhere. We think that's why Jeff Rodgers is knocking off blacks. Simply because he wants the damn statue back. Looks like you just might be the first white boy he cuts in half."

Jacobson stared at the two men for a long time before he finally said, "I got nothing to say. Go ahead and lock me up, but I got nothing more to say!"

"No such luck." Richards walked over to the door and opened it for the lieutenant. "I've just decided you're a free man—for now. Course, if that crazy Jeff Rodgers is lurking out there in the dark waiting for you, well—hey, what can I say?"

Jacobson started for the door and, despite the grave look of apprehension masking his face, rushed out into the street and disappeared.

Private Kruger broke the leg of chicken from the bird's body and handed it across the mat to Dehb. She sat cross-legged before a candle by which she was reading a magazine that catered to Chinese movie star fans.

"No," she said, "you eat, Paul. Too sticky. I no want it all over my books."

Kruger shrugged and took a chunk of white meat from the bone even before she had finished her sentence. Vo Dehb had her hair pushed up off her shoulders and clasped in back with a plastic bow because of the heat in the stuffy, little cubicle. Kruger was especially attracted to her when she put her hair up like that, but he knew she'd refuse any advances he made, so he concentrated on devouring the chicken instead.

"It's too bad about your honcho," she said, furrowing her eyebrows in hopes it would make her look more sincere. "I'm glad he live, but sorry he lose foot." And then a bright smile flashed across her face. "Tell me again how you kicked that VC bitch's ass!"

Kruger just stared at Dehb as he munched on the chicken slowly, but his mind's eye was already recreating the scene rapidly: The jeep was flipping over and Mather's leg was

274

tumbling through the air. The Honda was barreling toward them out of the cloud of smoke and before he knew how or why, he had leaped onto the speeding motorcycle and grabbed the woman driver around the throat as the bike crashed and slid along the pavement in a shower of sparks. Even as he struggled to pin down the driver Kruger had seen Thomas place his service weapon against the passenger's head and pull the trigger. He saw her face splatter all over the street and a bayonet fall from her raised hand. He had thought the sound of the .45 discharging would cause the woman he wrestled with to stop resisting, but she fought on even as Kruger applied a police choke hold—his right arm around her throat, his right fist cupped inside his left elbow, while he forced her head forward with his left forearm. For over a minute the girl had kicked her muscular legs wildly and flayed her arms at his head the best she could, but she finally passed out for lack of oxygen just as he was ready to crush her windpipe. It wasn't until then that Kruger noticed pieces of blacktop and bone marrow were still raining down around him from the grenade explosion fifty feet away.

Paul wanted to tell Dehb about how intense the desire had been to snap the woman's neck in two, and how difficult it had been to control the power over life and death once you had it in your grasp, but he just kept chewing on the chicken bone, wondering when Dehb was going to remove the stuffed dragon that kept them separated at night.

Mark Stryker had spent the last five hours questioning the employees at the Palace Hotel, and every one of them had come up with a different description of the American who jumped from the second-floor window just before the grenades exploded. Some described the man who had crashed down into the sun umbrella as a twenty-year-old athletic type, while others swore he was an overweight redhead. One man even claimed that the person who dove from room 211 was the elderly Frenchman himself, the guy who ended up dead under the poolside table. But that was normal. Stryker had never investigated a case where the witnesses could agree on anything, let alone a description.

And now Gean Servonnat had assigned him to put together a report on the Palace Hotel incident. "The old Frenchman owned a big rubber plantation outside of Saigon," Servonnat had told him. "Carried a substantial life insurance policy which the company is now refusing to honor. They claim the policy does not include acts of war, which they consider all acts of God in Saigon. Need you to prove it was just an accident. Or even criminal. Should be open and shut. So don't take too long on it," his new employer had told him. "I've got other cases to close up north."

"Anything near Pleiku?" he had asked, thinking of Lai, and how he missed her more with each night's passing.

"We'll see what we can come up with for you, my friend," Servonnat had answered. "I've always got something going on somewhere in our beloved Vietnam."

When Stryker found Jeff's name in the Palace Hotel registry next to a Pham V. he was astounded that he would still be using his real name. But then again perhaps it was the man's way of seeking help. He had been leaving clues all over Saigon, yet only Stryker knew his safe house was on Bis Ky Dong Street. And the ex-Green Beret wasn't ready to take Jeff off the streets just yet. First, he had Mark's blessing in his attempts to terminate Jackson and Chilton.

The C.I.D., Vietnamese police, and even Stryker were unable to track the two deserters down. But Rodgers had an extra edge on his side: vengeance. And Stryker knew that could well be the most powerful incentive there was.

"And this hotel maid, Ngoc Y-von. You say you've got no problems with her background whatsoever?" Stryker was asking the manager of the Palace Hotel for the third time. He just couldn't shake the nagging suspicion the woman accidentally blew herself up with the same bombs she was

276

planting. It had happened to better VC than her before, but Stryker had no hard evidence to tie down any of the employees at the Palace Hotel as suspects and it was obvious he was just grasping at straws. For now, who tried to blow Jeff out of a second floor window would have to remain a mystery. Stryker walked down to the pool and examined the area where the Frenchman's head had slammed against the concrete. As he completed a report that would say the old plantation owner slipped on the wet cement and split his skull, Stryker noticed the large, steel spikes protruding from all the umbrellas around him. He saw Jeff diving from the second-floor window toward the water. And he saw the ten-foot bamboo stakes outside of Pleiku where the VC hung the heads of three new government officials every month.

"Holy Christ, is that *you*, Sarge?" Bryant propped himself up in his bed as they wheeled Sgt. Kip Mather down the corridor on a guerney. The sheet covering the MP dropped off abruptly where his right leg was missing, and the realization half the man had been blown away made Bryant swallow hard.

The sergeant didn't look over at Bryant as they wheeled him past, he just stared straight out into space. "Jesus, he's lost his left hand, too," said Broox, who was sitting on the edge of Bryant's bed. "What a way to get a ticket home."

"So finish your story." Bryant turned away from the sergeant's direction as two orderlies started to transfer the sergeant's broken body onto a cot. He hoped he could keep the tears back until his story-telling friend could get his mind on something else.

"Well, it's really spooky, Tim. I mean, here we were one minute cruising above the rice paddies and next minute we're upside-down taking hostile fire and one of the prisoners 'falls out' the open hatch on the side."

"You're puttin' me on!" Bryant's eyes lit up.

"No, man! And here I am ready to freak out and they're all

277

looking at *me* like, 'If you talk, pinhead, we're gonna toss your ass out too!' "

"So did you turn them in? I mean, obviously, you're alive and well."

"What could I do? They filled out a goddamn casualty report. Swore sideways the dink fell out during evasive maneuvers while we were under fire."

"You'll never disprove that one!"

"I'm not out to disprove anything, Tim. It's just that I felt guilty as hell."

"Guilty? Why the hell would you feel guilty? You were just along for the ride, dummy!"

"It's just that I feel shitty as hell that I even participated in something like that. I mean, Jesus—I'm a cop! We were *all* cops on that damn chopper, outside the pilots. Damn."

"So whatta ya plan to do? Just forget it, I hope."

Bryant's bed slid a few inches across the floor as a thunderous explosion rolled in across the compound and rocked the hospital walls. Another mortar impacted in the middle of the street that ran below Bryant's window and Thomas crawled under his cot as the third sixty-round blew a parked jeep upside-down only five feet from the hospital's main doors.

"Them snake-belly VC are walking their mortars right down the street toward us," whispered Bryant in awe, as he watched the explosions kick plumes of gray smoke and dust dozens of feet in the air before the sound and shock wave rolled up and rattled the building's walls. "They're trying to mortar a goddamn hospital!" and Bryant envisioned the giant red cross that was painted on the building's roof and walls being used to sight in the mortar tubes.

"You nut!" yelled Broox from under the bed as he watched Bryant limp over to, then lean out the window, trying to get a better view of the incoming.

As another jeep and then an ambulance was upended by the walking mortars and flipped onto their tops in a puff of blue

278

smoke, Bryant leaned further out the window as if he were trying to get a better look at a float in some parade below. "Yes, siree!" he looked back and winked at Broox. "I eat this shit up, Drill Sergeant!"

"Hurry up, kid!" Private Davis urged the shoeshine boy to hustle the spitshine. The VC were walking the mortars closer and closer to Dong's sidewalk banana wagon and the MP didn't feel lucky that morning.

Dong continued buffing the tall, black cop's jump boots, painfully aware he wouldn't get his quarter until Davis could see his own smile in the boot's mirrorlike toe.

Davis lived off post in the network of one-story tin shacks clustered behind Third Field Hospital and he often stopped the first shoeshine boy he saw each morning. It was so much easier to pass the guardmount inspections when kids like Dong, with their magic brushes and secret methods, produced a spitshine it would have taken Davis an hour to equal. Except for the head-to-toe inspections, Davis loved being an MP, and he saw the little hustlers lugging shoeshine boxes at every corner as just another necessity in life.

Davis had been watching the mortars come in, listening intently to their overhead flutter and the sometimes-whistle that could detonate on a thick rain cloud. He perked his ears for the distant *whumphhh* that signaled the location of the launch tubes, and he decided the squad of sappers was positioned somewhere in the vicinity of his own housing project!

Davis took the unauthorized Smith & Wesson model 28 .357 magnum from his belt and started running back down Nguyen Hoa Street until the string of tenements came into view and the *whumphhh* of mortars shooting skyward in their gentle arc toward the hospital grew louder. The MP was positive the squad would shut down and move out long before he could get near them, but what Davis did not expect was that their hasty

279

retreat would take them right across his path.

When he saw the four men trotting around the corner of a home constructed almost entirely of empty beer bottles and C-ration cans, Davis went down on one knee and sighted the four-inch Highway Patrolman revolver on the man bent over with the mortar tube on his back. He had planned to instruct them to halt and capture as many as possible, but things just never worked out the way he planned them to.

The second their eyes met, Davis knew none of the VC would stick around to chat with him, and before he realized it, he was firing one, two, then three quick rounds off in rapid succession without calling out any warning.

All four guerrillas slid like baseball players stealing home in their haste to avoid the .38 specials Davis had loaded in the magnum, but the rounds tore into the corner of the glass house, smashing out its main corner supports and sending one side of the structure caving in amidst breaking glass and folding aluminum.

Davis cursed under his breath and aimed several feet to his right this time as he popped off another round. He struck the guerrilla beside the one he was aiming at and when the bullet tore out the man's ankle the last thing he expected was for the other three VC to produce rifles swung over backs and return his fire.

The MP flattened out on the ground as the rounds zinged in around his head. He lifted his revolver up and fired off the last two bullets without aiming, hoping he'd get lucky again and the Cong would just decide he wasn't worth it and filter off into the trees at the edge of the compound. When the sounds of the guerrilla's rifles discharging no longer cracked in his ears, Davis looked up and was horrified to see the three VC charging toward him, their weapons thrust forward and hate blazing forth from their eyes.

The MP frantically searched his pockets for the speed strips of extra ammunition, but they were gone. He definitely remembered placing three of the six round strips in his thigh pocket as he left his shack and headed for the nearest shoeshine boy. Of course! That was it! And Davis was amazed he could smile at the realization the Vietnamese kid with the quick eyes also had quick hands that had picked his pockets while he read his *Stars & Stripes* newspaper, waiting for his scuffed boots to magically take on a mirrorlike spitshine.

If I ever get my hands on him—if I ever get my ass out of this one, I'm gonna kill *that little jerk,* Davis thought, and he decided right then and there that little Dong was home free because the charging guerrillas were now only a few feet away from cutting him to shreds with their bayonets.

XXI. BRIEFING ROOM BLUES

"Sounds like the end is here," former U.S. Army Private Chilton whispered as he strained to sit up in his bed. The bandage wrapping the chest wound was now stiff and dry, and every move was made only with the most painful effort.

"Naw, just some Charlie out there lobbing mortars into downtown," decided Lance Jackson confidently. He had raced over to the window at the first sound of explosions, knocking over a coffee table in his excitement and revealing the anxiety both men felt.

"How much longer we gotta camp out in this hole?" Chilton asked his friend. "I thought you was gonna get me a medic for this here hole in my gut!"

The grinning Jackson did not answer, but turned back toward the window so that Chilton could not see the expression on his face. *I did my best, Marvin old pal*, he thought to himself as he remembered leaving a substantial deposit with a Chinese pharmacist, who agreed to arrange for an Indian doctor to treat his friend. After three days went by and the physician still had not shown up at the Dong Khanh hotel, Jackson returned to the pharmacy on Nguyen Hu demanding his money back. The Chinese owner, a plump man in his sixties, had just laughed at Jackson's antics, claiming the deserter had been foolish for trusting the rug peddler from New Delhi.

The pharmacist claimed he had no control over the behavior of "outcast Indians," so long as he had set up the deal in good faith. When Jackson had reached over the counter, the wary pharmacist produced a derringer which he pressed flat against the deserter's flaring nostrils until the American slowly backed out of the store.

"Hey, I'm cool, brother," Jackson had promised, grinning all the way out into the gutter, his hands cautiously raised above his head. But he knew the pharmacist had a lovely daughter who visited him each evening after performing her secretarial duties. When the naive, vivacious bachelorette flagged down the taxi that evening, Jackson had followed her home to a tiny, isolated apartment.

"Yes, I just don't know how much longer till them damn VC overrun this lousy town, Lance," Chilton was saying, and he had started singing, "When you hear the pitter patter of little feet, it's the Arvin Army in full retreat."

But Jackson didn't respond. He was thinking back to the night he had jimmied the bedroom window of the girl's apartment and walked in on her as she was lying in the bathtub. He still felt a thrill rush through his veins as he remembered the startled, terrified look on her helpless face as he appeared in the doorway of the bathroom. Jackson reviewed each delicious detail in his mind as he recalled dragging the screaming woman from the water, perfumed bubbles still sliding down her smooth, firm body. He had thrown her roughly onto the living room carpet and held her face down as he slowly unfastened his belt.

And then a knock had come at the door—several neighbors were responding to her cries for help. But after he snapped her slippery, fragile neck, the concerned whispers outside the door had gradually lessened, then stopped altogether, and Jackson smiled as he remembered how that night had been a first for him.

Yes, I'm a one-hundred-percent jungle mentality, he proudly thought to himself as he recalled how he had then balanced her firm, still-warm haunches in his shaking hands and defiled the dead woman from behind.

Jackson looked out the window at the firetrucks racing past the congested traffic in front of the hotel. The mortars had suddenly stopped, but their distant concussions slapping at the skyline had been followed by an intense exchange of machine gun fire, and he wondered how many people would die in the firefight, and if the rain would sweep in that afternoon like always, to wash the blood down the sidewalks to the gutter.

"I don't know how much longer I can make it in here, Lance," Chilton was saying. "I can't even feel my legs sometimes. It's like they've gone to sleep, but without the tingling sensation." But Jackson was not listening. He was thinking back to the tingling that had excited his entire body when he came up with the brilliant idea to "accidentally" drop the set of dog tags next to the woman's body. The same set of tags he had taken from the bedpost of the MP living on Thanh Mau Street—after he and his boys killed the uncooperative Vietnamese woman there and walked off with the jade dancer. He had snatched up the dog tags as an afterthought, but now they would come in handy, and that crazy Rodgers had never even noticed he wasn't wearing them anymore. Few soldiers in Saigon wore them anyway, preferring to attach the tags instead to key chains, or drape them over a whore's bedpost. Jackson laughed out loud as he suddenly remembered the time he had skipped out on a prostitute without paying, only to have to return later to reclaim the dog tags he had left on her bedpost.

"What's so funny, Lance baby?" Chilton strained against mucous clogging his throat.

"Oh, I was just thinking how that pig Rodgers will now have the whole Vietnamese National Police force on his ass, not just the MPs. Now that he's gone and killed and brutally raped one of their own dinks."

"What're you talkin' about, bro?" Chilton was leaning forward in the bed now as though it were important he be consulted on all murders going down that week.

285

"Don't sweat it, Marvin," he answered, deciding it was better Chilton didn't know how he started to leave the dead pharmacist's daughter then returned and took the butcher knife from the kitchen. Hacked off both her arms and legs and wrapped them in a sheet before leaving. Sliced them off with such speed and precision it had surprised even himself.

Jackson's mind involuntarily flashed back to the dead woman's mangled face staring up at him from the bloodied, dismembered torso. He recalled how he rushed from her dark, creepy apartment, and he thought instead about the shock Jacobson was going to get when he found the severed limbs stuffed into the trunk of his sports car. *Or maybe I'll tip the cops off to this,* he had thought at the time, still incensed at how the signal brigade lieutenant had abandoned his loyal black marketeers, cutting off their money flow when things started to get a little hot.

"I asked you, Lance, how you know about some dink murder and you ain't told ol' Chilton?"

Jackson whirled around on his heels and lashed out at the man in the bed. "Put a cork in it, Marvin! Or I'm gonna pull the plug in that chest hole and shut you up permanently!"

Military Police Pvt. Craig Davis had decided then and there he was going to stand up and die like a man. He hastily got to his feet as the three VC guerrillas charged forth, threw his empty revolver at the closest soldier—who merely ducked under the wildly tossed weapon—and raised his fists in preparation for some final, honorable hand-to-hand combat.

At the sight of this challenge, the guerrilla leading the charge let out an ear-splitting war cry and extended his bayonet with locked arms.

And just as Davis accepted his doom, a Cobra gunship suddenly descended from the skies, hanging suspended between the imposing brick tenements rising up all around. A co-pilot was leaning out the side hatch, motioning for Davis to hit the ground, and as the craft slowly swung around to face the MP over the backs of the guerrillas—its rotors flapping noisily like a monstrous enraged dragonfly—Davis dove back to earth. The gunship's insectlike nose dropped a few feet before its cannons burped off two expertly placed rounds—the three VC were tossed into the air like rag dolls by the impact, and they somersaulted over the prone MP and crashed down behind him in a fury of flame and showering rocks.

Davis, stunned himself by the dual high-explosive projectiles, crawled over to the nearest enemy soldier and picked up his rifle. The AK47s stock crumbled apart in his hands so he stumbled over to the next guerrilla, looking for his weapon. It was nowhere to be found—probably thrown several feet clear by the explosions, and the MP felt a terrible fear take hold of him: an intense belief the guerrillas were going to rise up at any second to finish him off.

As the gunship crew, hovering above the smoke-lined scene, watched on with silent indifference, Davis went from man to man and slowly strangled the wounded Viet Cong to death.

A paper airplane drifted lazily from the back of the squad room, striking the desk sergeant on the bridge of the nose as he strained tired eyes against the duty roster on his clipboard. Muffled laughter broke out among the two dozen MPs crowding into the briefing room but abruptly subsided as the water cooler burped loudly with the release of some bubbles.

A small cloud of mosquitos buzzed dully around a yellow fluorescent light that periodically went out for a few seconds, and now and then a daring mouse would venture out to within a few inches of the briefing sergeant's podium before one of the privates in the room tossed a paper airplane at it too. "Awright, knock it off!" growled the forty-year-old staff sergeant as he scratched his balding crown and refused to look up at the teenaged cops—he elected instead to feel about the top of the podium for his black helmet liner as he kept his eyes studiously glued to the clipboard.

Several MPs instinctively bent down in their chairs as a Phantom jet swooped low over the compound, its sonic boom soon following to shatter several windows in the orderly room across from the barracks. The living quarters themselves were safe from such antics; their windows were mere screens intended to keep the bugs and the bombs out. Glass was prohibited.

The desk sergeant looked up at the ceiling briefly as though his steel blue eyes had locked onto the thrusters of the fighter plane. "Someday I'm gonna position a gun jeep out in the middle of Pershing Field and pluck them fly boys right out of the sky—rock their socks off with mad Molly," he muttered, referring to the M-60s mounted in the rear of most MP units. "They're gonna wish they were safely up in the Hanoi Hilton before I get through with 'em!"

He propped the helmet atop his head, routinely tilted it down to the bridge of his nose, and lit another cigar as he resumed reviewing the hot sheets.

"What the fuck . . ." The NCO jumped a foot into the air and flipped off his helmet. As the white MP letters slid to a halt across the floor upside-down, a giant salamander flopped out and scampered into a corner. The briefing room erupted into applause as even the few middle-aged veterans present showed toothy grins.

"Awright, which one of you cherries—" he began, trying to stomp on the slimy amphibian, but he had to give up as the creature slithered out of sight under the bullet-riddled TV set that hadn't worked in years. The sergeant brushed the ashes off his flak jacket and slowly surveyed the troops in front of him, eyeing the congregation suspiciously from one side of the room to the other. But he resigned himself to the fact that the prankster would probably remain anonymous and switched his concentration to the stool that had mysteriously appeared behind the podium.

"Well, blow me over," he mused sarcastically. "No tacks to

puncture this sergeant's delicate posterior?" He feigned intense surprise when the stool failed to collapse under his weight, and as he twirled around in circles before the restless MPs, he wondered aloud, "Any more booby traps?" as he coasted to a stop and rechecked the podium.

"Okay, back to business." He smiled, despite the grumblings of discontent that rose across the room. "Got us a newbie in the battalion today. A Private Rocco Statterhouse."

"Rocco?" Several of the veterans repeated the name loudly as if it sounded just a bit hard to swallow.

"Hey, Rocco-baby!" Someone in the room had already pegged the private a playboy. "Why don't you stand up and take a bow?"

The desk sergeant leaned both elbows across the podium and dropped his head between his arms in mock despair. He didn't have time tonight to put up with the men roasting a cherry straight out of the academy.

"Yeah, front and center, Rocco!" another veteran yelled.

A stocky Italian with a thick, black mustache and a I-ain't-afraid-of-you-guys smile slowly rose to his feet, clasped his fists above his head and turned a little circle where he stood, stiffly bowing to the men on all sides of the room before sitting back down.

"What kind of Italian name is Statterhouse?" the desk sergeant asked curiously with no disrespect.

But before the private could answer, another MP had interrupted, "Hey, cherry, I got twenty-four days left in this sewer! How many *you* got left?"

"Twenty-four?" someone else called out, preventing Rocco from replying. "Now here's one short duck!" A tall, lanky buck sergeant stood up. "Only six and a wakeup!"

The room erupted into applause, and someone else concluded, "A single digit midget!"

When Statterhouse stood back up to respond to the original challenge, the desk sergeant could only shake his head slowly—aware the new soldier was walking straight into a virtual tornado if he stood up to the hardened street veterans of the 716th.

"Well, actually, I volunteered for Vietnam." Statterhouse beamed proudly. His claim was immediately met with several skeptical catcalls and a flying night stick that missed by several feet and bounced off the blackboard, clattering to rest at the desk sergeant's feet.

He slowly picked it up and began patting the palm of his hand, signaling silence in his briefing room, as Rocco continued. "No, really, guys!" he said, still smiling enthusiastically as he watched the sergeant massage the night stick. "This is where the action is! Real big city police work. Especially for someone like me who's not old enough yet to get into a real police department." Rocco caught himself too late, quickly detecting the hostility in the room in response to his remark.

"Whatta ya mean 'real police department'?" the desk sergeant interrupted this time.

"Well, what I meant, Sarge, is that—"

"I'll have you know, young man, that we lost three men in street fighting last year. Two more already this year, and it's not even June yet. We've made four thousand felony arrests on town patrol alone, and been involved in"—the sergeant consulted his clipboard briefly—"thirty-seven police shootings. . . ."

"But, Sarge . . ."

"I assure you, Private, after you complete your tour with the 716th and return to L.A. or the Big Apple or wherever you're from . . ."

"Boston, Sergeant." And Statterhouse slowly took his seat.

"Boston. Well, when you return to Boston and put in ten years fighting the scumbags of Massachusetts, I wager you'll still look back on your year in Saigon as the hairiest, most rewarding of your life."

"Oh, I don't know if I'd go *that* far," a veteran in the back of the room whispered loud enough for the sergeant to hear, and several MPs broke out laughing.

"Believe me, Rocco," another sergeant in the middle of the soldiers stood up and spoke. A dead serious look in his eyes traveled across the room to the private. "We don't even really consider ourselves soldiers here. We're cops. We have a brotherhood here second to none. I don't care if these guys are constantly complaining about 'Nam in general and Saigon in particular—and the conditions under which we work. When it comes right down to it, I'd place my life in the hands of any man in this room. *That's* how dedicated to the MP corps they are, and *that's* how much trust I have in their abilities and competence."

"You better not trust your life to *me*, Sergeant, sir," one of the privates behind him called out and several men laughed again, knowing the two had argued about haircuts the week before.

"I don't want you to get me wrong," Rocco stood up again. "I hope to stay in Saigon as a career MP—"

"What'd he say?"

"I hope to get me a bunch of VC just like you guys. I hope they send me where the bullets are flying and the punji sticks are the thickest!" But the veterans had resumed their unruly behavior, and the desk sergeant motioned for Statterhouse to sit down.

"Now can we get on with the bullshit?" the briefing NCO asked his men although he never looked up from his clipboard. He received no verbal permission, only a few grinning headshakes. The man rifled through his notes, dropped some MI Wanted posters depicting U.S. deserters on the floor, and continued without pausing to retrieve the bulletins. "Anyway, as I said earlier," but he stopped in midsentence, and his eyes scanned the distant horizon intently through the screened windows. More than a few of the men slowly lowered their faces into their laps and covered their heads with folded arms, expecting to feel an incoming rocket slam into the compound, but the night remained silent. "Have a request here from

Ambassador Lodge for special patrol," he began again without warning and those MPs who had sheltered their heads raised them again, just as slowly. They showed no embarrassment, and the men around them hadn't seemed to notice. It was just that some of the soldiers had accepted their fate in Vietnam, and others subconsciously refused to. "Seems some of the ARVN soldiers are littering his yard with beer bottles again. You guys on town patrol see what you can come up with."

"Shit, too," someone muttered from the back of the briefing room, but the whisper carried to the front of the group and the desk sergeant looked up. He blinked a couple times as if only mildly annoyed by his disrespectful patrolmen, then continued.

"All men will start signing for the shotgun ammunition, effective yesterday. The arsenal is coming up short and has decided you clowns are either selling it on the black market, or celebrating Tet nine months early."

"Shootouts, Sarge . . ." Someone volunteered an explanation, but the man just continued to read from his clipboard.

"Have *another* 'request' here from General Westmoreland's office."

"Who?" another anonymous hero spoke out sarcastically.

"He's getting tired of showing up for work each morning," the desk sergeant continued, "and having his secretaries complain about the women's underwear fluttering from the MACV Headquarters flagpole. Now I'm sure none of you gentlemen—and I use that term loosely—are behind this, but let's see what you can come up with.

"Okay, practical jokes. Which one of you clowns has been launching toy model rockets at the guard towers over at the annex?" The room remained silent except for the burping water cooler, and no hands went up. "Well, another rocket flew into Horowitz's tower last night—you gentlemen remember Horowitz: the forty-year-old Spec. 4 due to retire next month? The man they stuck in the towers so he could complete his tour 365 safely? Well the poor guy nearly had a heart attack when the cherry bomb glued to the nose of the rocket blew up in his nice, little, safe tower. Now, why don't you guys have a little compassion.

"All right, what else is on the agenda. . . . The hookers at the Mississippi Club are alleged to be tricking without valid VD cards again. Check 'em out if you get a chance."

"You got it, boss!" several voices chimed in unison.

"I mean—" But it was no use. The desk sergeant was fighting a losing battle. "Hit the streets," he sighed, cutting short the briefing. His hands went up slowly in mock despair, as the troopers filed out to their MP jeeps.

"Rocco, you'll ride with Lieutenant Faldwin tonight," one of the younger buck sergeants advised the new man. "But he'll probably assign you to one of the MACV patrols before the night's over. He's out making gate checks right now, but he'll pick you up in a few minutes and show you the rounds, so stick around."

As he stepped out into the balmy evening air, Statterhouse overheard two men talking about this Lieutenant Faldwin.

"Yeah, Sergeant Schell's briefings are so much more laid back and informal than that hardcore Faldwin's," the man complained. "I wish they'd transfer his ass north to the DMZ where he might mellow out a little."

But Rocco ignored the unpleasant talk and breathed in the slick, humid air, expanding his chest as he did so and stretching out his arms to show his contentment with events in his life just then.

Pvt. Rocco Statterhouse had finally stepped foot in Saigon, South Vietnam. And damned if the VC better not watch out now!

XXII. CHASING BY STARLIGHT

The first punch took Stryker by surprise, but he remained on his feet and grinned as his chest bent toward the ground and his left foot kicked out like a baseball bat, catching the huge Oriental in the jaw. The ARVN major was knocked off his feet and crashed down heavily into the dirt.

"There's no reason for all of this," the ex-Green Beret began, but the soldier rolled over and produced a revolver from inside his belt. As he struggled to lift himself to his knees, Stryker backed up a couple feet and raised his hands out from his sides to show he was unarmed.

"Turn around," the Vietnamese instructed as he finally made it to his feet, legs swaying heavily. And as Stryker clasped his fingers and cupped his hands across the top of his head, he wondered how he got into these situations.

It had been an interesting case, and should have been easy enough to close. Someone at the South Vietnamese Army Training Center, behind Pershing Field, was intercepting good-will packages of food and medicine at the Saigon docks and selling them on the black market.

Originally sent by volunteer organizations in the U.S., the manifests were seized by the ARVN officer for "customs inspection" then mysteriously disappeared in the custody of heavily armed soldiers and their two-and-a-half ton trucks. The civilian do-gooders had hired Gean Servonnat's agency to determine who was behind the hijackings so that an official protest could be lodged with the Vietnamese government, hopefully curtailing the illegal activity. No one was so naive as to think the smuggling could be halted entirely. Misappropriation of property by the Saigon government went all the way to the third-floor throne in the Doc Lap palace on Cong Ly Boulevard.

"Just don't get excited, Major," Stryker warned the officer as he felt the cool barrel of the revolver placed against his skull, behind the right ear. The major then coiled his pudgy fingers around Stryker's belt in the back, neatly lifting the American off his feet as he directed him toward the empty sedan.

Stryker had uncovered a great deal more than his original assignment required: an Army officer who had hundreds of phony names on his payroll roster. That meant the fat major pocketed the paychecks of those phantom warriors. But that was old news. It went on everywhere, and Stryker wasn't impressed until he discovered the officer was using military aircraft to smuggle huge amounts of marijuana from distant fields northeast of Saigon to the processing factories in Cholon. But even that wasn't shocking. Nor was the gun-running operation out at the apartment on Nguyen Hoa Street, where children were sold into prostitution and junkies were dumped out of fifth-floor windows.

It was the illicit affair Stryker had uncovered that took him by surprise and could mean big bucks if the American ever fell on hard times and resorted to blackmailing ARVN majors.

It had taken Stryker only three nights to snap a photo of the major with his lover—a part-time male model who also ran a clothing store on Le Loi. No, it just wouldn't do to let the men know their major found his pleasure in limp-wristed boys instead of the talented tenants of the bordellos on Tu Do. It would be devastating to morale, not to mention the security of the officer's career.

"Too bad you snoop where you no belong, Sergeant

Stryker," the major grinned as they approached the dike overlooking the Saigon River. "Now it time for you to take little swim." But when Stryker heard the hammer on the revolver click back into single action, his old military police training took over instinctively—before he even realized it.

Talk. Distract the suspect, his mind was ordering him, and Stryker was speaking even before a plan of action could form in his head.

"I left the negatives with a friend," he said. "You kill me now and they go to the *Vietnam Guardian, Saipan Post* and *Stars & Stripes.*"

When he completed the threat and could feel he had the major's thoughts distracted from pulling the trigger to recovering the embarrassing negatives, Stryker made his move.

True to his police training so many years ago, only improved upon recently by the rigors of the Special Forces camps, the ex-sergeant reached up with his right hand as he pivoted on his left foot. He also ducked to his left and bent forward as he grabbed the ARVN's gun hand and twisted it back around and into his stomach.

The procedure had to be done in a split second, and it had to be done when the suspect's concentration was somewhere other than on his trigger finger or you could kiss your skull goodbye.

As soon as the revolver was twisted around and snugly rammed into the folds of the officer's belly, Stryker kicked the man's feet out from under him, then twisted the major's thumb so far from the other fingers it sounded like it would break off.

"Drop it!" Stryker warned, and when he gathered the desired leverage, he flipped the more easily controllable soldier onto his back and jerked the weapon free. "I oughta cancel your ticket, fatso," he whispered as he brought the gun down heavily against the officer's nose, "but all I want is information."

A large chunk of skin ripped free from under the unyielding

metal and the ARVN began moaning as blood squirted out farther with each accelerating heartbeat.

The major grunted as though he didn't intend to talk, so Stryker brought a knee down hard on the man's groin and rammed the revolver up against his shredded nose again. "I'm assuming a lowlife like you would be carrying hotload hollow-points, and *we know* what hotloads'll do to your nasal canals, now don't we, Major Phuong?"

"What is it you want, Sergeant Stryker?" the officer sighed.

"I'm no longer a soldier, Phuong. I'm a civilian now, so your military influence means little to me anymore and I doubt you could get my permanent residency status cancelled in your wonderful Vietnam."

"You will always be a soldier, Sergeant Stryker. Whether it's as a mercenary or in some nation's legitimate army. Just like now. Who do you soldier for now, Stryker?" the ARVN gasped for air as the American leaned harder on his knee against the major's chest.

"It's *me* who's asking the questions here, Phuong. Now listen close. You had some dealings with some black Americans recently. Deserters. Real scum-of-the-earth types. Sold you some medical supplies for hash. You recognize the names? Jackson, Chilton, Stubbs, Webb . . ."

"I recognize the names," Phuong nodded irritably.

"Do you recognize the name Rodgers?"

"Should I, Stryker?"

"Don't get cute, asshole lover," and Stryker raised the revolver into the air again.

"Okay, okay, Stryker. No, the name does not bang a gong."

"Ring a bell."

"Whatever. I have never heard the name."

"So you're telling me, as far as you know, a white man who goes by the name of Jeff Rodgers is not involved in your operations in this town?" Stryker pulled the hammer back again on the pistol and the tone of his voice told Phuong, *I know you're lying and I'm gonna smoke you if you don't level with me,* but Phuong maintained he knew no Jeff Rodgers and Stryker breathed an unnoticeable sigh of relief.

He started to let Phuong up off the wet ground, then hesitated. "Oh, one other thing, my dear major. You know anything about a jade statue? A little Thai lady—a Thai dancer. You know anything about that?"

"This country is full of statues, Stryker. Thousands of fucking statues in Saigon."

"Well, this is a little Thai dancer," Stryker repeated calmly, patiently. "And I want you to keep an eye out for it. I want you to contact me the minute you hear *any*thing about a little jade lady. You understand me clearly, Major Phuong? You cooperate with me and just maybe the negatives that could so harm your corrupt career might not fall into the wrong hands after all."

"What about this other information you have gathered?" Phuong eyed the American suspiciously. "The guns and dope. The little girls."

Stryker led Phuong over closer toward the edge of the dike. "Oh, I'm still gonna burn you on that, Phuong. I mean, it's only fair you don't get out of this one scot free. You want me to do my job, don't you?" and Stryker shoved Phuong over the edge of the dike and down into the dark, murky river below.

"Welcome to the Decoy Squad," Sergeant Richards extended a hand and Pvt. Rocco Statterhouse shook it heartily.

"I'm really honored to have been accepted, Sarge." Rocco smiled a bit too much for Richards' taste. "I know you usually don't take newbies into the squad."

"Well, we're suddenly short a man." Richards returned the smile. "And most of the men on the waiting list for Decoy duty have passed—they're all kinda burned-out this month."

Thomas tried not to show his amusement at how smoothly

Richards avoided telling Statterhouse he was replacing a sergeant who had his arm and leg blown off only a few days earlier while on his coffee break.

"But I'm sure you'll work out okay," Richards concluded.

Kruger emerged from the Orderly Room with a couple letters and paused beside the new MP jeep the squad had been given to replace the mangled Beast. "Sure don't match the paint job the Beast had on her," he complained half heartedly as he ran his fingers across the pitted o.d. green surface. "Oh well, here, Sarge, a letter for you . . . and three for you, big Tony—must be nice to have so many cherry girls back in the world praying for your safe return."

Thomas just grinned as he smelled the different perfumes scenting each pink or red envelope, then stuffed them up into his helmet liner unopened.

"Aw, shit," Richards moaned as he opened the long, white envelope with the red-and-blue airmail stripes crisscrossing the edges.

"Anderson's folks again?" Thomas asked wearily, referring to the parents of the sailor stabbed to death in the Xin Loi bar months before.

"Yeah," he advised, "I sent 'em a postcard a little while back, but I just don't know how to—"

"You sent 'em a *post*card?" Thomas straightened up in his seat. "A lousy *postcard?*"

"Well, I was gonna write 'em a—"

"Jesus, Sarge," Thomas continued good-naturedly as Rocco looked on uneasily. "You gonna send *my* folks a goddamn postcard when some hooker slices into me?"

"Aw, get off my—"

"*All units* . . . All units vicinity the yacht club, number sixteen Nguyen Du." The dull, unemotional voice of the dispatcher followed three emergency sirenlike tones over the radio net. "Have a reported burglary-in-progress . . . VNP has no units available to respond . . . they request we assist . . .

300

units to handle."

Richards picked up the microphone as soon as three MP patrols acknowledged the call. "Do you have a description of the suspects? Over," he asked as he waved Statterhouse into the jeep.

"Negative, at this time. Will advise as we get further, over."

"Cloud Dragon, this is Delta Sierra Two. Roger and out," Richards answered.

And as the dispatcher in the fortified bunker at Pershing Field cleared the net with a simple, "Cloud Dragon out, at 2340 hours," the Decoy Squad roared through the main gate to cover the other units responding to the Cercle Hippique. Statterhouse smiled with mild excitement: he loved it as their jeep bounced past the startled gate MP and slid sideways into Saigon. He thrived on the collage of expressions streaked across the beautiful women's faces crowding the meat market: fear, admiration, confusion, excitement, even arousal.

Especially arousal, Rocco decided, as they watched these brave men race from their secure camp into the dangerous neon world beyond the concertina. *Yes I'll have to return some night and have a talk with that one girl pressed up against the bomb wire—the one whose high cheekbones and propped-up chest cast such sensuous shadows as the flashing red lights raced past her.*

"Did you see that?" Thomas reached over and grabbed Richards' arm to draw his attention, and the sergeant almost swerved off the road.

"Jesus, Anthony! You're gonna get us killed! What is it?"

"That chick! That chick back at the meat market! Did you see what she did? Did you see what she did when we zipped by?" Thomas doubled over in his seat laughing.

Rocco had seen what the girl did: she pulled down her halter top when the MP jeep roared by and squeezed her breasts together to make her chest look like a smiling face with two huge, brown eyes. Rocco just knew he was gonna *love* this town!

301

The private patted the .45 on his hip as the MP jeep raced in and out of traffic—its single emergency strobe on the hood doing little to move the hordes of taxis and motor scooters out of the way. Those oncoming vehicles that did see the cruiser pulled over to the side of the road and doused their headlights as a courtesy to the cops. Rocco had never seen anything like that before.

This is it, he thought, as the adrenalin started rushing through his veins. *This is what I been training for the last sixteen weeks! Now it's time to go out and burn me a scuzzball!*

"All units responding to number sixteen Nguyen Du. Suspects are described as two Negro males, twenties . . . nothing further, over."

"Cloud Dragon, this is car thirty-five," came a static-edged voice. "Anything on weapons? Over."

"Nothing further, car thirty-five."

Statterhouse leaned out from the back seat of the jeep a couple times as it skidded around the traffic circle on Le Loi. He felt the hot air and exhaust fumes and the gnats slapping at his face, and he knew he had never enjoyed anything so much in his life. The blaring siren parted the masses of jaywalking pedestrians blocks ahead of them, many turning startled Oriental faces their way as they dashed up on the sidewalk at the last second.

Richards soon cut the siren off, though, and Rocco remembered his academy training: Burglary in progress, silent response, code two.

As the Decoy Squad entered the block housing the yacht club, Statterhouse noticed a blackened tenement that had been rocketed recently. He had to admire these people: war all around them, yet they still found the time to play around on yachts, of all things!

An MP jeep sat blacked-out nearly a hundred yards north of the yacht club, and as its two patrolmen rushed down the tree-lined avenue on foot, weapons drawn, Thomas reached over and cut the lights for Richards too. The sergeant killed the engine and let the jeep coast up next to the first unit. The four MPs then spread out along the side of the road, in among the thick tamarinds and protruding palms, and silently waited for any suspects the first men might flush out.

A third unit soon arrived on scene and it cruised by so silently and swiftly that Statterhouse almost missed it. *Boy, those dudes are real pros,* he thought, in awe of the vets swooping in all around him, *maybe I'll be that good someday.*

For ten endless minutes nothing moved on Nguyen Du Street, as the MPs began their slow, cautious search of the clubhouse. The clouds overhead moved, and the half moon shone down curiously now and then, but mostly it was as dark as a tunnel—the blackness pressing in on them, thick enough to part with their arms.

Statterhouse squatted between two leaning palms and waited patiently for something to happen. He recalled they had told him in the academy that the majority of these burglary-in-progress calls resulted in the suspects fleeing the scene long before the police arrived, and he was just about to chalk this one up to experience when the shot inside the yacht clubhouse sliced through the night stillness. The report echoed back off the wall of a huge tenement crowding the opposite side of the street and Statterhouse rested his hand on the butt of his .45 in anticipation as a half dozen more rounds went off.

"*Dung lai!*" came a shout from the rear of the building. "Halt, you mother—I said, halt! Military Police!" Several more shots followed the first few.

"Jesus Christ!" a different voice was yelling now. "Somebody out there get to a radio! We've got an MP down!"

"Stay in Thomas' shadow!" Richards instructed Rocco as he and Kruger ran across the street, heads low, sprinting toward the exchange of gunfire.

"Stay right here!" Thomas in turn ordered him. "Don't move, while I get back to a jeep and call in a chopper. You got

303

that, Rocco? Make sure no one comes out this way!"

Christ, I'm no dummy, he was thinking as he nodded his head at the departing Thomas. *What's so hard about watching the front entrance, anyway? No self-respecting crook would try to escape this way, that's for sure! They'd go out the back!*

When the tall, skinny black wearing dark clothing and gloves emerged from a clump of bushes along the side windows of the clubhouse's ground level, Rocco felt his heart start to pound. At first he prayed the man was just another MP, but when he crawled a few feet across the grass then bolted for the street, Rocco knew the man was one of the burglars.

He drew his .45 and aimed it at the suspect, then glanced back anxiously to see if Thomas was on his way back from the jeep yet. The burglar was racing right toward Rocco, but he knew he couldn't fire without a warning and he couldn't get his mouth to open.

As the man got close enough for Rocco to see the whites of his eyes darting back and forth wildly, the MP felt a surge of confidence and daring pulse through his body. He stepped out in front of the suspect and yelled, "Hold it, buddy! Right there!" but the fleeing burglar ignored Rocco's command and sprinted past as if the MP had never been there.

"Why, you son of a—" Rocco turned red with anger and embarrassment as he spun to pursue, but first he stole another glance up toward the jeeps to make sure Thomas hadn't seen what transpired.

The black was soon growing smaller as he merged against the dark, and Rocco yelled, "Thomas! Into the tenements! I gotta foot chase!" before he fell in pursuit of the man.

Thomas had just finished requesting more help on the radio when he heard his rookie partner call out that he was chasing one of the burglars across the street and into the maze of buildings stacked along the west edge of Nguyen Du. He grabbed the M-16 chained to the radio brace and took out after them.

Rocco Statterhouse had been running nearly a minute now, but he was not yet out of breath. He had practiced daily for just such an exercise. "You really need your wind in the foot chases and barroom brawls," they had drilled into his head back at Gordon, "that's why we're running you two miles before breakfast every morning."

So long as Rocco could hear the suspect panting ahead in the dark as they raced deeper into the maze of alleys, the MP was confident he was conducting the chase properly. If the suspect stopped running and remained silent, then Rocco would go about catching him in a more cautious manner, but for now he was content to make almost as much noise as the burglar as they both crashed through clotheslines and over wash buckets.

Rocco had seen the man's back one time as they raced down the winding alley that snaked back and forth across both sides of Nguyen Du. He knew that they might frown on him shooting a fleeing burglar, but the man had left the scene of gunshots where an MP was down and that meant the guy was a free fire zone all unto himself.

When they entered a long, straight stretch of alley, Rocco brought his .45 up, chambered a round and jerked off two bullets on the run. He had been unable to aim properly because of the speed of the foot chase and the rounds bounced harmlessly past the burglar, ricocheting off down the alley.

Rocco pulled himself up to a shaky stop, raised the automatic again and popped off three more rounds, but the suspect was now a good fifty yards away and the slugs fell short.

This guy must be a fuckin' track star, Rocco decided as he resumed the pursuit. *I hope ol' Thomas is homing in on the sound of my shots.*

The thought of losing his first suspect—and in a cop-shooting no less—spurred Rocco onto high speed he did not know he possessed, and as the alley veered sharply to his left, the MP caught sight of the exhausted suspect, only a half block away now, leaning against a wall, holding his side.

Rocco brought up the .45 and fired once more until the slide locked back on an empty chamber. *Ain't this asshole going to shoot back?* he wondered as he hit the ejector button and the empty magazine clattered to the pavement. The suspect darted down the nearest corridor running between apartment houses. *Gonna have to start carrying seven rounds like everyone else,* he decided as he rammed a fresh clip into the butt of the .45 and continued running. He would have been surprised to know that most of the MPs in Vietnam carried eight rounds in their pistols—seven in the clip and one locked and loaded in the chamber, ready to go. It just didn't make sense to them to waste precious seconds cocking the awkward slide manually before having the capacity to fire. With a cartridge in the chamber, all one had to do was jerk off the safety tab with the thumb and squeeze off a round. The exploding gases then cocked the slide back automatically and rammed a fresh bullet back into the smoking chamber, anxious for more action. The cop didn't have to do anything but aim and hold his breath, squeezing the trigger gently for the best accuracy.

Rocco raced around the corner his suspect had disappeared behind, and although caution told him to slow down and take it step by step, the suspect was not hiding in wait for him.

"Aw, shit," Rocco muttered under his breath as he came to a fork in the alley at which point the corridor between buildings ended. He was too far behind the burglar to have seen which route the man took, and just as he was about to yell for Thomas, there came a noisy racket to his right as a trash can lid clattered to the blacktop.

Rocco was immediately disappointed when he rushed down the side alley and was met by a large cat pouncing in the opposite direction, chasing a mouse-sized cockroach. The disappointment vanished however when he looked up and saw the edge of a shadow flash past a building corner. Rocco took the .45 off safety again with his thumb, strangely feeling the

306

cold steel rub against his skin like a favorite mistress, and he cautiously peered around the crumbling brick wall.

When he saw the suspect darting around to the back of the building, he ran as fast as he could until the distance quickly closed between them and the man found himself at a dead end.

When the suspect discovered there was no way out of the sealed-off driveway—there was a tall barbed-wire gate directly in front of him and even higher walls on either side—he came to a halt, his back to Rocco.

I've got your black ass now, Rocco thought, grinning. "You're under arrest!" he shouted, even though they repeatedly drilled into your head back at the academy that MPs used the word "apprehension" instead of "arrest." But the civilian term sounded so much better to Rocco, just like it did on all the cop shows on TV and in the movies. They were the greatest, and here was Rocco Statterhouse, making probably a homicide arrest on his first night out, just like Batman and Robin! Yes, he had spent endless hours at the outdoor theater during his week of in-processing watching all the police flicks, and here the real thing was just as exciting as Hollywood!

"I want you spread-eagled on the ground!" he instructed the burglar.

Rocco held the .45 out with both hands as he locked his arms and repeated the directive, but the man just slowly raised his hands in the air and turned around to face him. When their eyes met and the black burglar realized he was at least ten years older than the green MP, a broad smiled flashed across his face, and he started coming toward the smaller MP, one cautious step at a time.

"Okay, hold it right there!" Rocco said. "I told you to spread-eagle on the ground. Now do it!"

"Or what? What you gonna do to *me*, little piglet? I is unarmed, can't you *see* that honky? I is as clean as—"

"On the ground, you're under arrest. On the ground," Rocco repeated more softly, but there was none of the fear in

307

his voice that the burglar was hoping for.

"You gonna shoot me, white boy?" The suspect was laughing as he grew closer to Rocco. "No, I don't think you have the *balls* to shoot me, pig," and he spat the word out on the ground with rage on his curled lips. "'Cuz you *know* you can't shoot an unarmed man, white boy. Well, you better make up your mind what you gonna do, 'cuz in a second I'm gonna be on top of your white ass. I'm gonna be all over you! I'm gonna walk outta here with your gun, sucker! And then I'm gonna . . ."

"Kiss off!" Rocco grinned as he pulled the trigger and watched the round cave in the suspect's chest and throw him backwards, off his feet. The man was dead before his body crumpled to the ground.

Pvt. Rocco Statterhouse walked over to the burglar and kicked him over onto his back. He briefly patted him down and went through his pockets then checked his wallet. The cracked and faded Army ID read: "MERLYN JORDAN, PVT E-1. 1st SIGNAL BRIGADE, RVN."

Rocco put the ID back in the burglar's pocket then took a switchblade from his jacket and placed it in the suspect's hand. He squeezed the fist shut tight and rolled the body back over onto its stomach so that the weapon would be clenched good and firm by the time the investigators arrived and rigor mortis stepped in to stiffen the fingers solid.

The military police private stepped back, put his hands on his hips, and stared down at the dead burglar. He tried to feel upset, troubled, even remorseful, but he found himself unable to keep the grin from stretching his face muscles taut, and he concluded right then and there he had never experienced more of a feeling of job satisfaction in his entire life.

Rocco looked up with a start as a sliding glass door on a balcony overhead slammed shut. His eyes suddenly met the defiant, accusing stare of a hauntingly beautiful woman in a crimson red dress as she looked down at him from the third floor.

308

Rocco grinned up at the unsmiling woman, and curled the fingers on his right hand in the shape of a pistol. He then raised and pointed it at the woman's head, pulled the make-believe trigger and silently moved his lips as he said, "Pow!"

It wasn't until then that an unearthly smile slowly crept across the woman's face, sending an eerie, unexpected chill down the MP's spine.

XXIII. STEALING THE FAMILY JEWELS

Sirens wailing against the night raced across Saigon and converged on Rocco's location. Within minutes, a sea of flashing red and blue lights cast elusive beams against the walls of tenements rising up all around as dozens of military police jeeps squeezed into the narrow alley and sealed it off.

"You okay, Statterhouse? You sure you're okay?" Thomas was patting the private on the shoulder and escorting him everywhere he walked—keeping the other MPs at arm's length, especially the admirers who had almost completed their tour 365 without killing any "bad guys"—until C.I.D. Agent Sickles pulled up in his black sedan and ordered that Rocco be isolated until the warrant officer could question him.

"Any witnesses to the shooting?" was the first question out of Sickles' mouth, but when Rocco nervously gazed up at the balcony above the dead deserter, the woman in the sexy red dress was gone.

"No, none that I know of," Statterhouse answered, his voice cracking.

"You okay, MP?" the C.I.D. agent stared him straight in the eye for a few endless seconds, and when Rocco finally nodded his head that he was, Sickles patted him on the back and pointed over to his car. "Have a seat in back," he said. "I'll be with you shortly."

Sickles walked back over to Private First Class Thomas and motioned him away from the other MPs. "What's the situation at the clubhouse?"

"One MP dead. Delaney. Took a hollow-point between the eyes." Sickles took a deep breath at hearing this news, then slowly, painfully exhaled as he looked down at the ground. "Two suspects involved. Both black. One ended up here," and Richards pointed down at the dead suspect, lying on his stomach with one leg twisted under the other. Sickles went down on one knee and examined the man's face but didn't recognize him right off.

"Still has that look of intense surprise on his face." The C.I.D. agent grinned, and then he pulled the suspect's wallet from his pocket and opened it up to the expired ID card. "Merlyn Jordan."

"Ring a bell?"

"Merlyn Jordan . . . Jordan . . ."

An extra jeepload of MPs had pulled up to the scene and Sickles motioned for them to form a crime scene perimeter extending fifty yards down both sides of the alley. He pulled the gold C.I.D. badge from his own wallet and snapped it onto his belt then advised Sergeant Richards to leave one other squad of MPs at the scene in case they encountered any problems with the Vietnamese on the block.

"You should be okay," Richards replied. "Curfew should keep 'em on their balconies for the next few hours."

"I know, but just in case. And you can have the other units return to the street and resume patrol. Give the rookies enough joy time to wander over and get an eyeful, then get them the fuck outta here. You guys are screwing up my crime scene."

"Why do you call it a crime scene?" Richards asked. "Looks like just a righteous shooting of a scumbag cop-killer, that's all."

"Habit, Gary. Just habit. Okay: shooting scene. Happy?"

"Whatta you think about Rocco?"

"Statterhouse? Well, I don't like the way the dead man is

312

still holding onto the knife—you'd think a .45 slug would have jarred it right out of his hands."

"Shit, I've seen a bunch of suicides, murders, you name it, where the victim was found clutching the weapon!"

"Okay, simmer down! Other than that, it does look like a pretty righteous shooting. As long as your MP comes across with the right answers and I don't locate any hostile witnesses, I'm sure you can have him back in a couple days."

"Hostile witnesses?" Richards frowned.

"Anybody I question around here who says Statterhouse planted that blade on the dirtball there."

"Aw, come on, Harry!" Richards feigned astonishment. "Whose side you on anyway? My men don't carry no throw-down weapons. I prohibit it—you know that."

"Yeah, Gary. Whatever."

Sickles patted the dead man's body down lightly, careful not to stick himself with any hidden syringes, or razor blades tucked in the man's afro—now that was a favorite lately. He checked the forearms for needle marks and found what he was looking for.

"Tracks," Richards observed.

"Yeah, real dirtball, Gary, real dirtball." Sickles began walking slow, counterclockwise circles that extended farther out from the body with each revolution. The C.I.D. agent kept his flashlight trained on the ground. "So tell me what you saw over at the clubhouse," he requested and they continued walking cautious circles until they were thirty feet out from the corpse.

"Apparently, Delaney was going through the ground floor of the clubhouse. Taking it real slow. Had his partner only a few feet back. Was opening cabinets and one of the suspects was hiding behind the last door. Popped a cap right in Delaney's face. Instantaneous."

"And his partner?"

"Emptied a full clip into the cabinet, but the damned storage bins run all the way through the center of the building. Left a

313

good blood trail, but the suspect escaped out the other side."

"Blood trail?"

"Yeah. Unfortunately, it ended down at the docks."

"Heavy blood trail, or just drops?" Sickles asked. He had paused in his search of the alley to examine Richards' face more carefully.

"Looked like a good shooting, Harry. Two or three hits. The asshole will turn up somewhere. Either floatin' down the river or—"

"Get an MP patrol at each of the major hospitals," Sickles told him. "And have dispatch phone as many clinics as possible. Tell 'em we'll double any bribe the suspect pays the clinic to keep quiet."

"Okay, Harry. Okay."

Sickles frowned at the nickname then resumed looking for evidence.

"What we looking for anyway, Sickles?"

The agent's frown deepened and he said, "We won't know till we find it, Sergeant."

A few minutes of silence followed, then the C.I.D. man asked, "Delaney have a family?"

"A wife and daughter . . . three months old. He hadn't seen her yet. Was born six months after he got here."

Sickles slowly shook his head again. "Can his partner identify the suspect?"

"Only that he's black."

"Wonderful," Sickles said sarcastically. "Any age?"

"That's it, Harry. Actually, I think the guy did pretty damn good, under the conditions."

"So we got one wounded suspect and one dead one, correct?"

"That's it. Just two."

"You call that pretty good under the conditions?"

"Hey, get off my case, Harry. What can I tell you?"

Another jeep had pulled up and three specialists from MPI dismounted with camera equipment. Sickles walked over to

314

them and briefed the team leader on what he knew.

"And I want photos of the alley, starting at that intersection"—he pointed fifty yards away—"and continuing up to the body, with a photo every five feet. I want photos of—"

A man's scream, strained to such high pitch it almost sounded feminine, broke forth from one of the tenements that rose up menacingly behind the crime scene. After the initial long, drawn-out cry, there came several more agonized gasps that could be heard all the way down in the street, and then terrible moaning.

"Oh, you bitch! You lousy, lousy bitch! Look what you've dooooone to me!" and the middle-aged voice screamed again hysterically. "My God! What have you done?"

Sickles and Richards both looked up over their shoulders and followed the gaze of several apartment dwellers to the third-floor balcony where the screams had come from—were still coming from.

"Somebody's screaming in English up there," Sickles looked over at Richards irritably. "That makes it an MP affair. Maybe you better check into it."

"Ahhhhhhh! You lousy bitch! Oh my God!" came yet another agonizing wail, then a door slamming shut and light footsteps fading away in the night. Richards motioned for Thomas to check it out and the private took another MP and started looking for a way over the high barbed walls to get into the apartment-house courtyard.

"Now, I want pictures of the body from this angle, and . . ." Sickles was instructing the MPI squad as Thomas and his new partner raced up the stairwell to the third floor.

"Military Police!" he called out in English as they waited outside the door of the apartment Sickles had pointed them to, but only loud, unrestrained sobs from inside reached their ears and Thomas began kicking at the door. It withstood his best efforts, however, and he and the other MP had to lock arms and hit it together with their shoulders before the latch

315

finally snapped and it caved in.

Thomas directed his flashlight at the figure sitting naked in a chair against the far wall. The man's neck was held back in agony as his head stared at the ceiling in shock. His feet were braced apart on the floor and his legs were spread slightly open as he clutched at his groin with both hands.

"General Lindquist!" the MP beside Thomas gasped, but the American sitting before them did not respond to his name being called.

"Look what that slut did to me!" he cried deliriously as he removed his hands from the deep gash where his testicles had been neatly sliced off. A stream of blood began to ooze out when the general removed his hands, its smooth flow trickling, then suddenly gushing with each heartbeat, trickling then gushing.

"My God," Thomas whispered as he reached for the compress in his first-aid pouch.

"That slut cut off my balls!" the intoxicated general screamed incredulously. Thomas turned when he heard the giggles of some curious apartment dwellers crowding into the doorway, and he fought to keep a straight face.

Officer Jon Toi took the news calmly, for he had suspected all along that the woman Specialist Four Bryant had shot in the mouth as she held a straight razor to the Canh-Sat's throat was not the woman responsible for the crime wave sweeping Saigon just then.

"We have identified the woman as Lee Thi Diep."

Toi ran the name through his notebook but he had no file on her at home.

As they walked down the brightly lit corridors of police headquarters, Sickles' eyes wandered to the slender figure of a female officer who approached them with her attention buried in a pile of reports she carried. Toi and the C.I.D. agent split apart just in time as she rushed between them and continued

316

on down the corridor. Sickles' head turned as his eyes now followed her shapely, bouncing behind until it had disappeared into an office. "She's one of you?" he joked with admiration in his tone. The admiration was for the body that radiated intense beauty despite the unflattering uniform, and that admiration would last so long as the policewoman remained in the office and not out on the street. But before Toi could comment, Sickles continued, "Yes, Lee Thi Diep. Goes by the alias of Lisa Lee. Definitely a head case—I grant you that, but a check with VNP records section shows she was incarcerated during the murder at the Purple Dragon and the knife attacks on soldiers at the Bong Lai and La Pagode nightclubs."

"So we still have a crazy lady on our hands," Toi concluded for the C.I.D. agent's benefit, although he knew long ago the murderess he had seen fleeing the Purple Dragon and riding a bus to Gia Dinh was still on the loose. He had known the communist sympathizer the police had tortured to death in the basement of the building they now walked through was not the woman they sought. And he knew Sickles was going to tell him the woman suspected of stealing an important U.S. Army general's scrotum wore a crimson red, low-cut dress.

"I'm sorry you had to hear it this way, Officer Jon." Sickles frowned especially for the Canh-Sat's benefit. "But we can't afford to let our guard down as this killer is out on the streets."

"No explanation is necessary." Toi smiled sadly as he thought back to the evening the woman inside the Xin Loi bar had held the blade tightly against his throat. He could still see, clear as crystal, his friend Bryant pop out of nowhere, jam his huge .45 past Toi's terrified face and squeeze off an explosive round past his ear and into Lisa Lee's smile. "And how is my good friend Timothy Bryant?" The smile remained in place.

Sickles returned the smile this time. He liked to talk about live heroes instead of dead ones. "Oh, Bryant is doing fine. I hear he goes back on duty tomorrow, in fact."

"And this new man, Statter—" Toi paused over the difficult name.

317

"Statterhouse. Yes, good man. Came through my investigation clean as a whistle. Put him up for a medal. They're going to give him an Arcom at the guardmount tomorrow. Why don't you make a showing? I'm sure you'll have a good time. Some donut dollies from the USO will be serving coffee. Sounds like they're gonna make a big show of it."

"And will you be there, Mr. Sickles?" Toi inquired politely.

"No, my daughter's class at the elementary school is giving a play tomorrow evening. She's going to be an Annamese princess who gets rescued from a dragon by—"

"Oh, yes!" Toi's face lit up. "You have a Vietnamese wife."

"Actually, she's from Thailand. I met her in Sattahip, on the southern coast. But our three girls speak only Vietnamese and English."

"Perhaps someday you will take them to visit Siam." Toi shook his head as if there was no doubt such a trip would come to pass.

"Yes, an assignment to Bangkok would be nice," he mused, "but those Thai drivers are *bookoo dinky dau!*" and both men laughed. "They drive on the left side of the road over there, you know."

"Yes, so I've heard. I've always wondered why Vietnam is the only country in Southeast Asia where we drive on the correct side of the road."

"And do you have any information for me?" Sickles changed the subject and Toi flushed noticeably red as he recalled snatching up the dog tags from the pool of blood before anyone spotted him.

"No, I have received no tips on the jade lady statue. But I continue to pump my informants and have even checked several pawn shops myself."

"Hhmmmmm," Sickles took out a handkerchief and began wiping sweat from his brow. Already his safari shirt was soaked from the midday heat and humidity.

"If I may say so, Mr. Sickles, I really believe you're concentrating on the wrong subject. I don't feel the tiny Thai

318

dancer holds any clues to cracking this black market activity you're working on."

"If I locate the jade lady, Jeff Rodgers will be right around the corner. I'm sure of that."

"And the other Army deserters? Are you close to nailing them yet?"

"Well, Toi, my friend," and the C.I.D. agent put a heavy arm around the policeman's shoulder even though he knew it was against Vietnamese custom. "I'll tell you something in confidence, because I know you can keep a tight lip." Sickles examined the Canh-Sat's eyes briefly, then continued as he walked him over toward a long table in the National Police Headquarters cafeteria. "The suspect Rocco Statterhouse dusted in that little back alley off Nguyen Du was none other than Merlyn Jordan."

"Merlyn Jordan?" Toi winked an eyebrow as he shuffled through his memory banks.

"Merlyn Jordan. Private. U.S. Army deserter. Was one of Lance Jackson's gang." Toi looked up at Sickles with mild surprise. "Yes, one of the six dirtballs Rodgers arrested when he first arrived in 'Nam."

"But I thought—"

"Yes, we also thought he skipped out to Indonesia. Intelligence had information he was hiding in one of those mosques the Muslims were building in Djakarta."

"Military Intelligence can be a contradiction in terms." Toi smiled. "Are you sure your information is accurate?"

Sickles ignored the overused joke and pulled a cigarette lighter from his pocket. He placed a Vietnamese Blue Ruby cigarette in his mouth and flipped the lighter open. An inscription on the side read: "KOREA, LAND OF THE MORNING CALM. BATTLE OF INCHON, 1950." Sickles tried repeatedly but could not get the flint to ignite the wick.

Toi frowned in disgust at the sight of the Vietnamese cigarette and handed Sickles a Winston. He lit it for the C.I.D. agent, using a stick match, and sat down at the table.

319

"We believe the other suspect, wounded at the yacht club, was Stephen King, one of Jordan's associates. Hopefully, he's carrying three or four slugs in his gut and will turn up shortly—on your morgue table, if we're lucky."

"And this King . . ."

"Is the other deserter we thought had fled south to Djakarta."

"That now accounts for all six."

"More or less. We don't believe King and Jordan were involved in the murder of Rodgers' girlfriend."

"But that doesn't mean Jeff won't go after them."

"Exactly. Anything's possible. Rodgers' hootchmates claim he kept a little pocket notebook detailing all his police activities—arrests, court-martial dates, crime scene notes: everything. But we didn't find it when we searched his locker."

"Maybe he kept it at his apartment down on Thanh Mau."

"Well, you Canh-Sats told me you searched the place top to bottom and no mention was made of the notebook in any of the reports."

Toi thought back to all the photographs he had taken in Jeff's apartment, and how he had never been able to mount them on the walls of his private little back room, out of respect for the American's feelings and the loss he mourned.

"I hear you now have two new Decoy Squads." Toi changed the subject as they left the cafeteria and walked along some narrow corridors that eventually led to a side exit and the parking lot.

"Not really. It's just that General Lindquist—you've heard about the General Keith Lindquist affair?"

"Yes, of course. It's all over Saigon. The American officer assigned to the Inspector General's office who lost his loins to one of our ladies of the evening."

Sickles didn't mention that C.I.D. suspected the notorious Pham V. was also involved in this assault. "Well, General Lindquist is on a rampage to bring this woman to justice. He put pressure on the provost marshal to increase patrols downtown until an arrest is made."

"And the PMO buckled under pressure?"

"Hell no! They just laughed. With our current manpower shortages it was a nice change to have MACV authorize eight more MPs for town patrol. They're to concentrate only on this assault on the general, and they've been put on loan to C.I.D. and MPI, but right now they're just out there cruising the back alleys and augmenting our regular graveyard shift."

"Do you think the general will ever get his balls back?" Toi couldn't resist that one.

"Are you kidding?" Sickles laughed so loud that several pretty policewomen shuffling papers up and down the halls paused to watch him curiously. "That son of a bitch never had any balls in the first place!"

XXIV. DEATH FROM BELOW

"All units in the vicinity . . . number twenty-three Lam Son Square . . . next door to that location . . . at the liquor store . . . robbery in progress . . . involving U.S. soldier . . . code zero . . . handle with caution," came the bored voice of the dispatcher over the radio net, clear despite the background static.

"Car thirty-five responding . . . from the Hotel Majestic."

"Car ten responding . . . from Phan Dinh Phung and Le Van Duyet."

Kruger cocked his ear at the radio. *Hhmmm. Number twenty-three Lam Son Square: the Caravelle Hotel.* He calculated how long it would take him to get there. *That's only a few blocks out of my patrol assignment.*

"Car ten Alpha responding," the radio droned on, "from the MACV annex PX."

"Car Zulu Two responding . . . from the Eden Roc Hotel."

Kruger was not with the Decoy Squad just then. He was still completing his primary tour of duty: twelve hours on a "roving patrol" that took him back and forth the length of Tu Do Street and prohibited him from roaming more than a block over on either side. It was the "bar run," high-visibility patrol, and usually required two MPs, but Kruger's partner had called in sick that night so he was working a solo unit, 11 a.m.

to 11 p.m.

"Cloud Dragon, this is car thirty-five . . . request a description ASAP."

"All units, Cloud Dragon"—the dispatcher identified the command post with its dramatic code name—"Stand by." The dispatch center's designation usually changed every two months, but the cars themselves, actually jeeps equipped with dual red lights and several different types of sirens, remained the same to avoid confusion.

"Cloud Dragon, this is car ten . . . we have just stacked it up at Checkpoint Six Alpha . . . request an ambulance and a sergeant, this location."

Kruger waited a few seconds then flipped on the jeep's red lights. When no other units advised dispatch they would replace car ten, he started in the direction of the liquor store next to the Caravelle, leaving his patrol sector and activating his siren when traffic funneling onto Tu Do Street became too congested.

"All units, this is Cloud Dragon." Kruger turned up the radio mounted in the back seat so he could hear the dispatcher above the rush of hot night air swirling in around the jeep's windshield. "One Caucasian male . . . described as five-foot-ten, 190 pounds . . . wearing striped shirt . . . armed with an automatic pistol."

Kruger cut the siren as he left the main thoroughfare and skidded down into the maze of alleys he knew could cut his travel time by several minutes. He leaned heavily into each turn as the jeep slid around corners—several times on only two wheels. And when he coasted up to the rear of the Caravelle he found he was the first unit on scene.

Kruger had only just dismounted when an American wearing a blue and green striped shirt came flying around the corner—a brown paper sack in one hand and a .45 in the other. He froze at the sight of the MP, giving Kruger enough time to draw his own weapon, and as soon as the suspect saw the cop's gun leveled at his chest and heard the sound of sirens in the

324

distance growing stronger, he threw down his own pistol and raised the bag of money up over his head.

As the MP slowly approached the robbery suspect, his mind raced back to an incident in his youth he had completely blocked out until then. "Down on the blacktop," he instructed the suspect. "Nice and slow, hands out at your sides, spread-eagle."

The suspect complied immediately but Kruger was seeing something totally different in his mind's eye.

It had been two years before he was drafted into the Army when it happened. He was only in high school, working in a liquor store as a stocker. The place had been robbed, and Kruger was now seeing himself spread-eagled on the floor, some punk's gun at his head while two accomplices rifled the cash register.

"Kruger! Hey, Krug buddy! Back off, man!"

Several MPs were suddenly pulling him back away from the suspect on the ground, and Kruger was startled to see he was kicking the man viciously in the head.

"Jesus, Krug!" Thomas was now between the MP and the prisoner, smiling broadly. "Settle down! You got the guy! Good bust! Eh, but just calm down, okay? He ain't going anywhere." Thomas was patting Kruger on the back now and telling the other MPs what a good job his friend had done, but they had just stared his way with icy eyes and the expression on their faces told Kruger they didn't condone brutality, especially from an MP who had jumped the call and left his patrol area.

One of the squad sergeants—an expert at looking the other way when his men accidentally dropped a prisoner—was now frisking the suspect and handcuffing him behind the back.

"Well, he looks okay to me," he told no one in particular as he examined the man's bruised and battered face. "No fractures . . . no stitches needed."

The suspect was carried by two MPs over to Kruger's jeep and deposited roughly in the back seat. His handcuffs were then tied with flexi-cuffs to a bar running along the vehicle's floorboard, and an improvised seat belt further fastened him tightly into the vehicle.

"Okay, Kruger." The squad sergeant walked over and handed him the automatic the suspect had used in the robbery. The slide was locked back and the sergeant had a clip in the other hand. "Six rounds." He grinned. "Hollow points. You guys coulda had a hellacious firefight!" He handed the two items over to Kruger and told him, "Be sure and book that stuff before you go off duty." He allowed himself a rare grin. "So we don't mess up the chain of evidence." Kruger merely nodded and stuck the automatic under his belt.

"Hey, check this out!" Thomas had picked up the brown paper sack and was inspecting its contents. "There must be a hundred thousand p in here!"

"That's only about two hundred bucks," Kruger muttered as he sat down in the jeep and braced his clipboard on the steering wheel. It was the same amount they had gotten in Salem, three years earlier.

More and more of the MPs who had responded to the robbery-in-progress call were now returning to the streets, leaving all the paperwork and book-in to Kruger. "Let's stick around and help him out," one of the men told his partner. But the reply was, "Screw him! If he wants to jump our calls, he can handle all the reports, too."

Thomas was the last MP to remain at the scene while Kruger completed the top half of the form thirty-two. "You'd think the Vietnamese police would have found it in their hearts to drop by and chat," he said dryly, and when Kruger didn't answer, he walked back over to his jeep, got in and left.

"Why'd you have to go and kick me around like that?" The prisoner looked over defiantly and spoke his first words since being handcuffed. "Shit, if you didn't have that gun and—"

Kruger slammed his clipboard into the prisoner's face and punched the man in the stomach with a single, wide-arcing swing. He then turned sideways in his seat and kicked the prisoner with such force that the flexi-cuffs snapped and the man flew out of the jeep onto the ground.

Kruger calmly got out of his side of the jeep, took the custom-made rosewood night stick from its brace beside the seat and started walking over to the prisoner groaning on the ground. He didn't see the young girl standing on the dark balcony across the street, but she was watching his every move.

The provost marshal was a colonel who enjoyed discipline, pomp and circumstance, and sharp uniforms. So it was difficult for him to keep the proud smile on his face after he pinned the Army Commendation Medal on Rocco Statterhouse's chest and the private returned only a sloppy salute, refusing to make any acceptance statements to the men following the snappy guardmount inspection the colonel had conducted himself.

"For conduct above and beyond the call of duty," the citation read, "where in his capacity as a military policeman responding to a reported burglary-in-progress, Private Rocco Statterhouse pursued one of two armed and dangerous suspects who had just murdered a fellow MP. After a lengthy foot chase, Private Statterhouse captured the suspect, who resisted apprehension and was killed."

The donut dollies from the USO swooped in on cue after the awards ceremony and began handing out cups of coffee and tiny bags of potato chips.

"Yes, I think it would be nice if you described the entire incident for your fellow MPs." The tall colonel had smiled down on Rocco. "Critique it for them, step by step. Not many of us get into bona fide shoot-outs during our careers and I think the other men could benefit from your experience." But Rocco had curtly nodded and walked over toward the latrines, then disappeared out a side door.

When he got back to the barracks, he tossed his uniform and the green medal into his locker and slipped on jeans and a

"FEEL SAFE TONIGHT: SLEEP WITH A COP" T-shirt. Then he walked through the uneasy layers of mist creeping in over the camp and exited the main gate without checking out.

"Tu Do Street," he told the first cabbie to pull over for him.

"Where on Tu Do, Joe?" the smiling Vietnamese asked, but Rocco just stared out at the evening traffic clogging the side streets.

"Just Tu Do," he said. "I'll show you where to drop me off."

Rocco rolled the back window of the cab down and breathed in the thick, hot air that rushed in, chased out the cool atmosphere, and was already sticking to his forehead. The cabbie gave him an irritated look and reached over and shut off the air conditioner.

As they passed the Continental Palace, Rocco noticed a black soldier browsing among the postcard racks set out along the sidewalks, and the MP's mind suddenly flashed back to the look on Jordan's face when he pulled the trigger and sent a round crashing into the man's chest. But the vision disappeared just as quickly and Rocco head himself say, "Here. Right here. Number one Tu Do."

"Ah, Hotel Majestic"—the cabbie grinned his approval—"300p."

"100p," Rocco corrected him coldly as he pulled some folded piasters from a pocket.

"200p." The cabbie bargained down a little.

"100p." Rocco remained firm, and then he looked the cabbie in the eye. "You shoulda started this bullshit when I flagged you down."

"150p." The cabbie kept the smile on his face. "It is *you* who should agree on price before you get in. If no do that, then you must pay whatever I say later."

"100p, asshole."

"Maybe I call MP, huh? Maybe I call MP, 'cause you bookoo trouble, they take you go monkey house!"

Rocco pulled the .45 from his belt and slammed it down on the headrest of the cabbie's seat. "Who do you know carries these?" he yelled into the man's ear, straight faced.

"100p," the man answered calmly, not one to argue with such firepower, and Rocco handed him the money and got out.

As the taxi sped away from the curb, Rocco could hear the driver singing, "One, two, three, motherfuck MP."

The American started at the Majestic and walked through as many bars on Tu Do Street as he could get to before curfew, but he was unable to locate the woman in the red dress who had mocked him from the third-floor balcony before slashing off General Lindquist's nuts. It was important to Rocco that he locate the woman before C.I.D. did. It just wouldn't do to have her confess to all the murders in Saigon then add her little bonus about the MP she saw kill an unarmed man and place a switchblade on the body. And it was almost as important to Rocco that he meet this ghoul face to face and see if he could wipe that mocking smirk off her lips.

"You look for boom boom?" A young girl had appeared in front of Statterhouse, and she lightly smacked her tiny clenched fist in an open palm twice when she said boom boom.

"You look a little young for me, honey." He stared down at the eleven-year-old with boredom in his eyes and irritation in his voice.

"Not me, Joe," and the girl pointed up the sidewalk to a woman standing beside the doors to the La Pagode. She wore a silver miniskirt and a tight, see-through halter top that pressed her breasts out flat and wide like two swollen pancakes. "Her. Only 2,000p. All-nighter. Clean snatch, Joe. Make you feel good all over."

"Snatch? Somebody oughta wash your mouth out with soap." Rocco just shook his head. "Get lost, runt," he snarled as he started off in the opposite direction. The woman who had been leaning in the doorway rushed up behind him as he began walking away and she slipped her arms in through his.

"You no like what you see, mister?" she said softly with a throaty voice. "I make you feel just like home, Joe. What you like call me?"

329

"I'm looking for my old lady," Rocco answered, "otherwise, I'd love to go home with you, honey." He changed the tone of his voice and she tilted her head curiously.

"What your old lady name?"

"You'd probably know her by the red dress she wears"—Rocco grinned, and he moved his finger along the top of her halter, pulling it down a couple inches—"real low cut, just like yours."

"But what her name?" the woman demanded, stamping her foot on the sidewalk in a mild tantrum.

"Well, let's play a little game, sweetheart. I'll tell you the first letter of her name. And you see if you can guess it, okay?"

The prostitute gave Statterhouse an impatient frown but didn't argue. When he told her the letter V, her face lit up and she grabbed Rocco's hand with a child's excitement.

"Oh, yes, I know that one." She grinned as she dragged him back down the sidewalk. "Wears a different dress every night—but same color. Yes, always red. Very nice." She nodded her head. "Very fancy."

They walked several blocks along Tu Do until the American was beginning to think the girl was just trying to get him so tired that he'd give up and go home with her. They passed two Canh-Sats, standing beside a telephone booth, their narrow eyes intently watching all who moved past them in the street while their rigid bodies, nearly dwarfed by the huge American-made revolvers, remained frozen in place. Beggars sat along the curbs, some with limbs missing or horribly deformed with leprosy and syphilis. Some had babies, covered with scabs and parasites, clinging to their shriveled bosom. All had cups or plates clutched in their outstretched hands for catching the coins passers-by threw at them from a safe distance.

Statterhouse watched the lorries, taxis and private sedans jam up under the banners of Tu Do Street, while motor scooters with pretty girls riding sidesaddle on the back darted in and out of the stalled vehicles. Blue clouds of exhaust fumes seemed to settle over the prostitutes and peddlers lining the

330

sidewalk's edge and he wondered what just one napalm canister dropped right down the center of the boulevard would do to the lively crowds overflowing the curbs.

"She in there!" The woman stopped in front of a bar that only had signs in Vietnamese and French. "She always in there. Now you pay me!"

"*Xin Loi, manoi!*" he muttered at her as he started into the bar. The sign over the door read, "Le Brodard Givral."

"You no *bic?*" The woman had grabbed his arm. "I want 500p."

But he pulled away and walked into the bar, the woman right behind him until a Canh-Sat saw her fist in the air and moved to restrain her. The policeman dragged her down the nearest alley for "a little talk."

Rocco waited a few minutes just inside the doorway to survey the small crowd inside, and he immediately spotted her sitting at a table along the far wall, alone.

It unnerved Rocco when he noticed that she had spotted him first—had her eyes on him the whole time, ever since he entered the nightclub.

"Is this seat taken?" He smiled down at her, and she brushed aside strands of jet-black hair from above suspicious eyes and motioned for him to sit down.

"I remember you from the shooting," she said matter-of-factly, holding his eyes and making her tone accusing.

"I'm flattered you remember anything at all," he said.

"What is it like to kill a man?" she asked quietly.

"What is it like to steal a general's family jewels?" He grinned, and she smiled for the first time.

"Oh, you heard about that, did you? Such an unfortunate incident. Sometimes these blind dates just get all out of control, don't you know?"

The woman had her bosom propped upon the table top, and Rocco couldn't help but notice the outlines of her nipples pressing against the fabric. "Do you have a room here?" he asked.

331

"Oh, but of course." She smiled even more as they touched upon neutral territory. "Would you like to see it?"

"Don't you want me to buy you a drink first?" Rocco asked seriously.

"Do not mistake me for a harlot," she snapped, but a refreshing innocence returned to her face as she rose to her feet. Rocco watched her breasts sag slightly under the weight of rising then spring back to their original firmness as she reached over and gently took his hand. "I'll show you my collection of dresses!" She grinned evilly now, and when he felt her fingers tighten unnaturally across his he had to fight the urge to recoil from the woman's clutch.

He could feel the hairs rising on the back of his neck as she led him through the clouds of cigarette smoke and the clutter of bar patrons jabbering rapidly to complete their stories of gossip and intrigue before the curfew clamped silence down on the capital.

A few curious heads turned their way to watch them climb the corner stairwell to the rooms above, but their departure from the bar was quickly forgotten. She released his hand as she pulled a tiny key from her purse and inserted it in the door. She entered first, turning her back to him, and he followed behind a couple feet, fighting off the arousal as she brought one slender arm back and smoothly pulled down the zipper on her dress even before he had closed the door.

As he pulled the .45 from his belt and started to rush toward her back she seemed to sense the attack and whirled around with an animallike growl rising in her throat and a straight razor in one hand. He watched her smooth, ripe breasts sway slightly as she rushed to face him and brought the blade around in a blinding flash that caught him above one eye and sprayed blood all about the room as he dropped the pistol and leaped on her.

She continued lashing out at him as he clamped his powerful hands down on her throat and choked with all his might. They spun around in circles across the room, upending furniture as he tried vainly to snap her neck and she repeatedly sliced deep gashes into his forearms and head.

Officer Jon Toi was standing on the sidewalk outside the Brodard Givral, purchasing a Vietnamese newspaper from a street vendor when their two thrashing forms crashed through the sliding glass door and out onto the second-floor balcony. Toi dropped the newspaper and drew his revolver as the woman screamed in Vietnamese, "Help! He's trying to rape me!"

The man's back was to him, but Toi could see he had the woman's throat gripped tightly in his fists as he smashed her back and forth against the wall. Toi brought his sights down between the man's shoulder blades but just as he squeezed down slowly on the trigger, they whirled around again and the discharging round smacked into the woman's back with a dull *whumph!* that tore a scream from her chest and threw her to the ground.

All that was left in Toi's gun barrel sights now was Rocco Statterhouse's shocked eyes, and as the American raised a cinder block above the woman's head, Toi jerked the trigger two more times in rapid succession and virtually blew the man's face off his skull, back into the bedroom.

Jeff Rodgers had spent the last few days knocking on doors in the Tung Chou area, showing the cautious apartment dwellers composite drawings he had made of the likeness of Lance Jackson. But most of the Vietnamese who studied the charcoal sketches of the black man with the shaved head and evil smile would only go so far as to point and giggle curiously at his unique tooth ornament, then politely slam their doors shut in Jeff's face.

Stryker patiently followed his old friend from neighborhood to neighborhood, cautiously remaining back in the shadows whenever Jeff doubled back or executed cunning half circles to check for tails.

He was unsure what the younger American was up to, and had made the decision to approach Jeff when they came to one of the busy, major intersections, but a black soldier in civilian clothes had emerged from an after-hours club and was sneaking home down the back alleys when Jeff spotted him.

Stryker had focused his folding binoculars briefly on the big Negro and he didn't think the man's face matched those of any of the six deserters whose mug shots "Harry" Sickles had shown him months before, but Rodgers was staying right on top of the man. When they came to a stretch of alley with little cover, the man spotted the "white ghost" following him and darted down a driveway into the dark courtyard of a sprawling French villa. The man laid low beside a stretch of bushes for several minutes, then when he saw no activity, pulled himself up the compound's glass-tipped wall and flopped down on the other side.

When he landed beside Rodgers' boots, his feet spread apart menacingly, the black soldier flew to his feet and bounded down this new alley blindly. Rodgers stayed a block behind the man, and made no immediate attempt to narrow the distance.

Though he could have fired a round into the fleeing soldier's back at any time, the hunt had become a game to Rodgers and he was beginning to enjoy making his prey sweat a little before he closed in for the kill.

The black soldier was becoming more frantic each time he entered a new block and saw none of the familiar landmarks that told him he was not lost—only the grinning face of that white fool leaning out from each corner as he wandered deeper into the city. Twice he had pulled the cheap revolver his landlord had sold him for ten U.S. dollars, but each time he pulled the trigger the cartridges were struck by a weak hammer that needed a stronger spring, and the weapon failed to fire. He couldn't understand why a white American was pursuing him through the side streets of Saigon at three in the morning, but he had been warned there were cowboys lurking in the strangest places after curfew, and damn if there still wasn't that maniac deserter loose out there in the night killing off the brothers, but he had been so sure all that was just talk.

When Rodgers finally tired of the game, the black soldier had sprinted nearly two miles and was leaning against more and more lightpoles as he paused to check behind him, holding his side tightly. The man threw his useless revolver at Jeff when Rodgers jumped from a low rooftop and raced screaming toward the black.

The two Americans sprinted in and out of a dozen more housing projects before the black soldier darted out from between two parked lorries and was squashed into the pavement by the lead APC in a rumbling tank convoy.

When the huge armored monsters finally clanked to a stop and the dust began to settle, Rodgers emerged from the narrow corridor between two tenements and walked out under the dim streetlight that illuminated the crushed soldier. He reached down and took hold of the man's shredded uniform and, with the help of members from the tank crew, pulled the horribly dripping slab of meat free from the impressions in the soft blacktop and rolled it over.

Stryker watched as the deserter pulled a sheaf of stained military orders from the dead man's wallet. Rodgers read the paperwork quickly then viciously kicked the corpse once in the side in front of the startled Vietnamese. He then dropped the orders down into the stench of blood collecting at his feet and slowly walked off down the nearest alley.

After he had disappeared, Stryker emerged from the shadows amidst the ARVNs still jabbering rapidly as they looked down at the flattened American. Stryker reached down and plucked the papers from the sticky goo, already thick with buzzing flies, and read the dates on the military orders assigning the dead man to his unit in Saigon. Stryker felt the nausea rise in his gut as he discovered the man had only arrived in Vietnam two weeks earlier and couldn't have been involved in the murder of Jeff Rodgers' girlfriend.

XXV. THE WAR MAGICIAN

There were tears in Vo Dehb's eyes as she prayed before the towering gold Buddha. Though she held them tightly closed, the tears still rolled forth, and soon light sobs could be heard inside the dark, cavernous Xa Loi temple. Two monks, cloaked in orange-hooded robes, scurried past the woman and disappeared in the gloom of incense drifting along the holy shrine's walls. Vo Dehb remained bowed on her knees for several more minutes, her hands clasped to her forehead in intense prayer.

Kruger found it odd that there were no other people in Saigon's largest temple at that hour of morning, but as he watched Vo Dehb from the doorway of the chantry, the overwhelming silence and the hundreds of flickering candles in the otherwise dark pagoda fanned the fires of his memory as he thought back to the events that brought both of them here.

When he was beating the prisoner at the scene of the liquor store robbery, Kruger did not see an American soldier at his feet each time the night stick came down, crushing the man's skull further. Instead, he was reliving the holdup several years earlier in which he had been the victim.

For such a long time he had blocked the experience out of his mind but now it all flashed back with crystal clarity, as if it had happened just the day before. Kruger had been working several

337

jobs at the time, and the one at his uncle's Salem, Massachusetts liquor store entailed stocking the recently delivered crates of liquor between the hours of midnight and three.

It had been just after closing, while he was making a fresh pot of coffee, when the three Hispanic men walked in. Run down from working three jobs to save up money for college, he had not even heard them enter, and the next thing he knew, a large man with a Pancho Villa mustache had jumped on his back from behind and pistol-whipped him to the floor with an automatic. Kruger's mind was still not reacting properly, even then, and as he asked, bewildered, "What did I do to you? Who are you guys?" the man on his back kept Kruger's face pushed against the floor and yelled, "This is a robbery, stupid! Gimme your watch, your ring, your wallet!"

Kruger lay stunned for several seconds as the gunmen held his face down by the hair, so they couldn't be identified. Several strands of the hair were jerked out as the men continued to beat at the back of his head and shoulders, yelling, "Your watch, your ring, your wallet! Your watch, your ring, your wallet!" over and over.

He strangely felt no fear just then, only rage at having his personal property taken—*It is not fair to steal from the underpaid clerks and laborers. Just take the cash register receipts and leave,* he was thinking—but two of the men had begun kicking him in the side when he didn't act fast enough and all he could think of was how much he didn't want to die on the floor of a liquor store. How many things there were that he still wanted to do in life. How many more noble and honorable ways there were to die than at the hands of a hood on a concrete floor in Massachusetts.

"I've just escaped from Utah State Prison, you son of a bitch, and I won't think twice about killing you! Now hand it all over! All of it!" They were dragging him across the floor, still with his face smashed against the concrete, up to the safe. Kruger had told them he didn't have the combination, but they only pressed their guns against the back of his head and said, "Well, then goodbye, sucker!" and the thought of dying in that situation was so—not revolting to Kruger, but disgusting. He didn't want the papers to read "Paul Kruger dies in liquor store robbery." He either wanted to live a long life as a renowned geologist, or die in an honorable fashion: a war perhaps, or a televised gunfight on the streets of Boston. Something spectacular, lasting. Not like butchered cattle with a bullet behind the ear.

Kruger had no doubts in his mind right then that they wouldn't hesitate to kill him just for the thrill of it, and though the fear was still mysteriously missing, he complied with their demands and located the combination to the safe on a slip of paper under the coin tray in the cash register. His eye caught the paper sack beside the safe containing the revolver his uncle kept in the store, but he knew the minute he went for it they'd splatter his face all across the floor. He couldn't imagine where his uncle was—probably passed out in the cooler again, sampling the wine, but he remembered hoping the police cars that so often cruised by, their spotlights checking the rear of the store, would drive by just then. "Come on! Come on! Come on—let's go!" one of them, acting as a lookout, was yelling to the others.

After he got the safe open, two of the men rapidly swept the bills into a sack—choosing one right next to the revolver, and after kicking him a few more times in the side for good measure, they raced through the store, knocking over displays of liquor and heaving a keg of beer through the front plate glass window. "Don't call the cops, or you're dead!" they had warned as they retreated out the front door. "Stay on the floor and count to one thousand!"

But Kruger was on his feet the second the door slammed shut. He grabbed the .357 from the sack, jumped over the counter, and ran out of the building just as a car was pulling up. The man in the car saw his huge revolver, pointed to the boy's right, and Kruger dashed around the corner and saw the three

339

men running for the alley. He raised the revolver on single action and sighted on the center man's back, but the hammer fell on either a dud or empty chamber and the cylinder refused to rotate, frozen in place by years of non-use and poor maintenance.

At the sound of the hammer falling loudly, two of the men turned around and fired several shots at him just as he got the cylinder open, slammed it back down on a different round and popped off a slug. The hoods dove into a truck moving slowly across the parking lot and fled in a fury of burning tires without fighting back.

As they came toward Kruger at high speed, he aimed at the truck's windshield and jerked off two more rounds, striking the driver's door with loud cracks that bounced back at his ears.

The anger of losing his wallet, with all its precious photos and mementos, the high school graduation ring, and the watch he had bought with his first paycheck was only fueled by the escape of the suspects, and the inability of the police to make an arrest later. When the stolen truck was recovered the next day and the owner threatened to sue him for the bullet holes and blood stains, Kruger was further aggravated by his inability to identify the suspects who had kept his face pressed against the floor.

Kruger was smart enough to realize his survival had been a matter of luck—four convenience-store clerks were later robbed that night by the same suspects and one was shot to death—and now that he was "safely" in Vietnam he didn't have to worry so much about the circumstances that might surround his death. It would surely be honorable if it happened in the Orient.

As he watched Vo Dehb slowly lighting more incense sticks and candles he recalled what the drill sergeant had told the men of his platoon when they learned they were being shipped to Vietnam. "If you're going to the 'Nam you should be proud!" he declared as they struggled to do push-ups in the fog—their rifles cradled across their knuckles as they strained against the

340

added weight. "A soldier is allowed to choose when and where he wishes to die."

Kruger left the shadows beside the sealed doorway when Dehb rose from before the shrine and walked down the steps toward him. The smile and happiness he had hoped to see were gone and the sadness in her eyes reminded him of the tinge of remorse he felt when he came-to at the robbery scene and realized he had beaten his prisoner to death.

At first, panic had seized him, then mild acceptance as he noticed the young Vietnamese girl watching him from a balcony—her horrified eyes also filling with tears at what he had done.

"The gods tell me it will not work," Dehb advised him. "They say only trouble comes with a man who has fled his army," and she took his hands in hers. "But the gods have been wrong before, Paul, and I know you are a good man. You will stay with me. I will never let them take you away."

Stephen King was sure he would drown as the current swept him out into the middle of the Saigon River. The undertow grabbed at his ankles and pulled him under several times like some demon from the deep.

When the MPs had swept down on him and Jordan at the yacht club, they had been taken totally by surprise and forced to hide in the storage cabinets running the length of the first floor warehouse bay. They were earlier told the scuba gear at the building was easy pickings—security was lax if not non-existent—and that the gear would bring a high price from the Viet Cong, who were trying to sink more and more ships anchored at Saigon's docks.

He had been sitting with his knees squeezed up to his face and his pistol propped out in front of him when the door flew open and the white MP letters were suddenly glowing in the hazy opening. He had jerked off one excited round, saw the man's helmet fly off backwards, but couldn't even tell where the bullet had struck before several thunderous discharges behind the fallen cop flashed toward him in the dark. He felt three hot chunks of metal tear into his right leg and smash him back into the storage cabinet. He was twisting and crawling rapidly away even as the lead skewered him like sizzling pokers, and it wasn't until he had dragged himself out the opposite end of the storage bin and rolled from the open window that he realized he was losing large amounts of blood.

King wrapped his T-shirt tightly around the wound—all three holes were mere inches from each other on his thigh—and was careful not to tie the makeshift bandage too tight. He was in extreme pain but wasn't in fear of dying and didn't want to lose the leg later because of a hastily applied tourniquet.

He woke up the next morning, washed up on the banks of the river among a small forest of piled driftwood. He managed to drag himself up to the treeline beyond the banks where he lay suffering in agony till well past dusk—passing out several times from the loss of blood and infection that sent mild waves of shock across his body.

A taxi returning to the city from Nha Be took him to a doctor who King knew from the physician's post-retirement, drug-running activities, and the deserter kept the Vietnamese away from the phone until the wounds were cleaned out and patched up. Though the doctor insisted he remain still for a mandatory recovery period—at least two weeks—King left the man's home as soon as he summoned the strength to limp out to the street and flag down another taxi. "If you don't rest, you will have a noticeable limp the rest of your life!" the doctor called down to him, but King ignored him and got stiffly into the cab.

"The Montana BOQ," he whispered to the driver, careful not to display the waves of pain wracking his body up the nerveline from his legs. There was heavy traffic along the outskirts of Saigon, and as he waited for the taxi to maneuver down along the main highway into downtown, King tried to picture what Lt. Clifford Jacobson's face would look like when he answered the knock on his door and came face to face with

342

the man he had set up.

It could have only been the Signal Brigade officer, King reasoned. He had been the one to originally pass on the tip about the non-existent scuba gear at the Cercle Hippique, and hadn't Jackson told him the lieutenant was acting weird lately and hadn't come through with their latest payoff for the shipment of medicine they had delivered?

When he arrived at the Bachelor Officers Quarters, King spent several minutes in the lobby, sunk down behind a newspaper in one of the plush easy chairs. No one had even noticed his shabby appearance and torn pants. When he determined there would probably be little activity in the corridor branching off to his left, King casually walked down to Lieutenant Jacobson's room and knocked lightly in their pre-arranged, simple code. After no answer came, he pulled the survival knife from his boot, easily slipped the lock, and entered the room.

King quickly checked the bathroom and window, but there was no one in the hooch, and the window hadn't been opened in months. He pulled the trunk from under the cot where he knew the officer kept his log, money and some unauthorized souvenirs.

He took the roll of bills stuffed inside the white, ceramic "buffy" elephant and reviewed the last entries in the journal. "Motherfucker is writing everything down in some kind of code," he muttered under his breath, failing to recognize the smooth curves of Thai script.

King tore the notebook up into several pieces, then placed them into the bathroom sink and set the pile on fire. He went back to the trunk and pulled the shoebox of M-26 grenades out from under the photo albums. The same grenades he had jokingly tossed into King's lap several weeks ago after he yelled "hot potato!" King examined the explosives and decided they were probably live. He set one beside the door frame, another behind the door itself, and a third beneath the heavy shoebox. King ran a line of fishing-pole wire from all three grenade pins, around the hanger rod in the closet, and back over to the door knob, then slowly opened the bedroom window and climbed out into the night.

King smiled as he counted the roll of bills he had taken from the lieutenant's footlocker. Almost eight thousand dollars. That would surely be enough to get him out of the country and onto a barge destined for Indonesia and the holy mosque of his Black Muslim brothers.

Toi rushed into the Brodard Givral nightclub and several customers and waitresses calmly took cover behind the stage or under tables at the sight of his gun out of its holster.

"The stairs to second floor! The stairs!" he yelled at the nearest bargirl, and though she kept her face hidden and flinched her eyes like she expected to be struck at any moment, she swung one arm back around and pointed in the general direction of the staircase.

Toi was up them in four strides and as he paused to orient his sense of direction, he heard the ground-floor rear door of the nightclub slam shut.

"Damn." The word escaped him as he smashed into the only room overlooking the street and spotted the edge of Rocco Statterhouse's deformed head partially visible through the opening to the balcony. At his feet, Toi saw the trail of blood leaving the room, and he frantically followed it back down to the ground floor only to find it ended abruptly in the alley behind the bar.

Two blocks away, hidden back in the dim recesses of a hotel linen room, Pham Thi Vien lay across a pile of soiled sheets, sobbing as she examined the bloody hole in her red dress—torn above her right breast where the bullet had exited, carrying splinters of shoulder bone and bits of crimson silk with it.

Vien pulled her fingers from the sticky mess that was slowly coating her chest and raised them in front of her eyes to see why she felt so numb and wet. She stared for several seconds at

344

the blood dripping down along the contours of her hand and shuddered as the lifelines crisscrossing her palm were slowly covered.

Though extremely weak, she struggled to rip small strips from the sheets stacked high all around her and as she stuffed the white fabric into the gaping hole above her lung Vien tried to think about the canal that ran through her old village north of Gia Dinh. She wanted her last thoughts at death to be of the deer barking inside the forest and the magpies whistling at her from up in the leaning palms.

Countless sirens converging on the neighborhood bounced in at her from all directions, driving Vien deeper into herself as she clamped bloodied hands over her ears and lowered her head between her legs, but the only thing she found when she closed her eyes were the faces of all the men she had killed, staring back at her with haunting, defiant snarls.

Officer Toi ran down the alley until it curved back around to Tu Do Street, and after he was unable to locate any further signs of the blood trail, he started crisscrossing the housing projects behind the avenue of bars, searching for any clues to the whereabouts of the woman he had wounded. Several other Canh-Sats eventually caught up to him, but he ignored their warnings that the MPs arriving back at the scene of the shooting were getting quite unruly at the news their fellow cop had been gunned down by a Canh-Sat.

When he returned to the bar, Toi saw that the street in front of the Brodard Givral was sealed off with dozens of U.S. Army MP jeeps, and the sight of so many flashing red lights sent a shiver of uncertainty through him. The barrel of his revolver was still warm against his thigh when he re-entered the nightclub through the rear door and walked back up to the shooting scene.

Several American MPs turned as he entered and they directed accusing glares his way, but no one made any statement until Lieutenant Faldwin said, "What happened in here tonight, Officer Toi? The bartender says you rushed in

345

here like a crazy man with your gun drawn. What can you tell us?"

Toi ignored the men and walked over onto the balcony. He looked down at the dead military policeman for a few seconds, then abruptly turned away. He didn't want the Americans to see the tears welling up in his eyes. He could not remember having cried since he was a child, and as he leaned on the balcony railing and looked down across the fluttering banners over Tu Do Street, he wondered how he could make the tears stop and what had possessed him to kill the American in the first place.

Kim hadn't been so excited in years. When Jeff Rodgers showed up at her door with flowers and asked her to go on a picnic with him, she was overjoyed. And now here they were on a grassy hilltop overlooking the Saigon River and he was cutting a deck of fortune-telling cards and telling her to pick seven at random.

"Lay them face down," he told her as he concentrated on the brown cards and avoided her eyes.

"Now tell me where you learn Tarot." She giggled as she neatly lined the cards up in the grass, anticipating only the brightest of futures.

Kim wore her long hair tied casually up off her shoulders. The loose bangs hiding her forehead were as sensuous to him as the picture on the first card he turned over. "The Empress." She smiled. "What does that mean?"

Jeff pretended to study the card intently as he counted the stars on the woman's crown of leaves: twelve. She wore a long, gold robe that hid her feet and was closed tight at the throat. In her right hand was a crystal wand, and at her feet, growing stalks of corn. "What does it mean? What does it mean?" Kim demanded, bouncing up and down impatiently as she knelt back on her haunches.

Jeff looked up at her face, but his eyes soon fell to the soft

346

amber of her throat and the form-hugging blouse made of white silk which he could see right through. She wore black shorts, trimmed up to the bottoms of the pockets, and as he watched the ripe swell of skin along the edges he began to wonder what motives had brought him to seek her out again.

"I must first examine several cards to accurately tell your future," he said as he turned the second card over: four of swords. Kim tilted her head curiously as she inspected the frame showing a man lying on a table with his eyes closed and hands clasped. Beneath the table was a sword pointing to his feet, and all along the wall behind him appeared a large plaque with three swords mounted on it—all pointing down menacingly at the man.

When Jeff turned over the third and fourth cards, Kim frowned at the sight of a woman sitting in her bed, her face in her hands as she cried: the nine of swords. The other card showed the back of a woman, sitting in a boat with six swords stuck into the craft's bow. A man with a long pole was pushing her out to sea.

"Doesn't look too good," she whispered at the sight of so many swords. "Can you tell what it means yet?" Jeff hoped the deception didn't show on his face: the cards were marked. He had picked them up in an Indian curio shop on Nguyen Hu but had never learned how to read them properly. Out of boredom one night he had bent the corners on the most sought-after cards then proceeded to "read" the futures of the housegirls in their apartment building. The forecasts always turned up favorable in this manner, and after some, through a fluke of coincidence, even came true, word soon spread across the neighborhood that Jeff's talents rivaled those of the area *mjao* until even the most skeptical *mama-sans* sometimes came to him to have their fortunes told. But now, due to his recent irregular travels, most all of the cards were bent or torn and he could no longer control which ones were chosen. No matter— he would interpret even the bad cards in the most favorable light, making things up as he went along. Like he always had.

347

The fifth card was the three of swords, and when Kim saw the huge red heart pierced by the swords she shook her head sadly and said, "Yes, of course. My life. Three GIs steal my heart, then leave me for America. Yes, very true, very accurate. But what do they all mean together, Jeff?"

He turned over the next card and the sight of a naked woman gathering water at a stream made Kim blush despite her salty background. When he saw the woman's overly endowed bosom on the card, Jeff's eyes shifted up to the breasts held back but not hidden by Kim's blouse. She caught his eyes wandering and she reached over and put her hand on his as he started to turn over the last card. "The Star?" she read the sixth card. "What does it mean?"

Jeff's lips did not move to answer as he turned the final card over. Kim's eyes lit up mischievously at the sight of the Lovers. A naked couple stood reaching for each other before a purple mountain and blue-green stream, her hair blowing in the wind, held her hands out protectively over the lovers.

Kim brushed the cards away carefully, then leaned over and put her lips on Jeff's. He did not resist, yet he did not respond physically, and she rose to her knees and fell over into his arms, arcing her slender back to make sure he felt her breasts pressed against his chest.

Jeff suddenly realized that this was not why he had sought Kim out, and the rush of guilt that swept over him radiated across to the woman. "Too soon?" She smiled down at him sadly as she felt his body remain unresponsive. He could barely nod his head up at her and she could see his eyes glazing over with torment and mournful emotions.

Kim rolled over into the grass beside him and propped her head up on one arm a few inches from his ear. "Maybe you feel better if I tell *your* fortune, okay?" She livened up again at the thought, but Jeff did not answer.

She sat up and shuffled the cards quickly then held the deck out to him. "Cut," she said authoritatively, and he reached over and split the deck. "Now, pick seven," she said, copying his actions.

Kim watched the first card fall into the grass. It was the Tower, a card that depicted a burning castle and a husband and wife leaping to their deaths. Kim frowned again as she decided this card could represent so many of the terrible things that had already happened to Jeff.

The next card he picked showed a maiden walking across the air with the symbols of different creatures in each corner. "Hhmmm, the World," Kim read the card, and Jeff looked over at it and wondered why the things he sought were always on the far side of the Earth.

The third card was the ten of swords, and Kim recoiled at the sight of a man face down on the ground with ten swords in his back. She hastily tossed the card over her shoulder as if Jeff had not already spotted the bad omen.

"The hanged man," Jeff whispered lightheartedly as she took the next card from him. It showed a man suspended upside-down from a tree—his ankle tied to a branch and the sun shining brightly behind his head.

"The hanged man?" Kim brought the card up to her eyes as if she expected the man to speak back to her. "What the hell does this mean, Jeff? The hanged man? It's not fair for you! You are a nice man, a good man!"

Kim hesitated as she reached for the next card. "This game is too cruel—I no like it!" Then she flipped the fifth card over and saw the skeleton in black armor riding a white stallion through a field of corpses. Kim threw the card down and ran down the hillside to the riverbank, crying softly, and Jeff knew she had turned over the death card.

The thought of dying just then caused Jeff to sit up in the grass and he toyed with the vision of joining Mai for several minutes before he turned over the next card.

A beautiful woman sat on a modest throne with scales in her left hand and an upraised sword in the other. Beneath her feet was the word, Justice, and the Roman numerals, VIII. The card reminded him he still had much to do in this life, and he started to get up to leave then paused to examine the last card.

Jeff smiled again as he looked down at the Strength card. An Oriental woman wearing a purple robe with flowers in her hair—golden flowers—was clutching a jungle cat in her arms and petting the wild animal's throat. It in turn was licking her hand and Jeff could hear the tigress roaring in the night as if the card were alive.

All four men in the MP jeep turned their heads as a taxi skidded around a corner down the block and ran the red light in front of them. Several other cars nearly crashed into the Renault but the Americans just resumed reading their mail and listening to Broox digest the newspaper.

"Hhmmm . . ." He decided he had found something unusual enough to share with the others. "Officials of the Saigon Zoo report the escape of a Bengal tiger. The Vietnamese Police have been called into the investigation because it appears someone unlocked the cage from the outside, allowing the beast to walk out sometime after closing yesterday."

"What some people won't do for a good time," said Thomas.

"Says here the tiger was an unusually stubborn creature that had been well behaved until recently."

"Probably got pregnant," offered Richards, and his eyes were viewing scenes from his past again.

"Officials were candidly glad to see the animal gone," Broox continued, "this claim from one source who requested to remain unidentified. He said the big cat had been keeping residents near the zoo awake all night with her endless screaming. The cause of the tantrums had never been determined."

"So how's your leg holding out?" Richards asked Spec. 4 Tim Bryant and the MP just shrugged.

"No complaints, boss. I've been running on it lately, so I should be able to hold my own if we get into anything tonight."

"That's not why I brought it up." Richards sucked in his

350

cheeks as he turned to look away from the MP. The sergeant was becoming uneasy at the change in his men. They were turning more defensive and irritable at the drop of a hat, and he suspected it all centered around the shooting where one of their own was killed by a Saigon policeman.

"Delta Seven Two . . . Delta Seven Two, this is Cloud Dragon, over," came the transmission over the jeep's radio. Broox picked up the microphone and answered, "Delta Sierra Two, go."

"Advise Sergeant Richards he's got an urgent phone call from a Mister . . . well, I'll spell it phonetically." The dispatcher's voice suddenly lost its professional tone, but he resumed his military bearing just as quickly. "Papa, Hotel, Uniform, Charlie. Wants you to call him ASAP, over."

"Delta Sierra Two, roger, out."

"Cloud Dragon out at 1845 hours."

Richards grinned as he decided that was the closest he had ever gotten Staff Sergeant Schell to say "fuck" over the radio. One of Richards' informants used the code anme, Phuc, and he had the man call in a couple times a week using that name in hopes the desk sergeant, who sometimes dispatched out of boredom, would slip up over the air. Phuc was just about as common in Vietnam as Jones was in America.

"I'll be right back," he told Broox as he stepped out of the jeep and walked over to a phone booth. "I better make that call . . . just in case."

"I just can't believe Toi dusted Rocco." Bryant forced the sentence out, as if each word burned his lips.

"He definitely did it," Thomas replied. "The question is: Why?"

"The way I hear it, Toi thought he was saving a rape victim from her assailant. They're saying he got so upset when he recognized Rocco afterwards that he accidentally shot the girl, too!" said Broox. "But that's bullshit. Toi is a better cop than that."

"Well, if you listen to rumor control, you're fucked anyway

351

because they've always got everything ass-backwards."

"Beats me why the woman ran anyway," added Thomas.

"And how Toi could *let* her get away," said Broox.

"Toi didn't do much talking from what I hear," Bryant told them. "He won't talk to no Americans except Sickles."

"C.I.D.?"

"Yeah."

"Bet he'd talk to you, Tim," Broox said, but Bryant just shrugged his shoulders again.

"Gives a guy a sick feeling in his gut, somethin' like this does." Thomas looked at the other two MPs as if he was trying to convince himself they felt the same way.

"It's almost as crazy as this Kruger thing," Bryant said. "The dude goes out of his way to capture a robbery suspect then sticks the scumbag to death. *Then* he goes AWOL on us. Just don't make sense."

"That's the only thing that *does* make sense." Thomas turned to face him. "Would *you* stick around if they were gonna come and jack your ass up on murder charges?"

"Well, maybe he could claim self-defense, or resisting, or even attempted escape."

"Christ, the guy still had handcuffs on when they found him beside Paul's abandoned jeep."

"Hey, I've had plenty of handcuffed barfbags fight me with their boots kicking all the way to the slammer!" Bryant replied.

The argument got more heated until Richards could hear them all the way in the coffee shop across the street. He slipped the coin in the phone and dialed his contact's number. After a few seconds he said, "This is Gary. Let me speak to Mister P."

Richards was kept waiting for several minutes until a harsh voice came on the line and said simply, "Your jade dancer statue is at number 159 Tu Do, at the . . ."

"The Than Le souvenir shop," Richards said automatically. It was his job to know all the addresses on Tu Do, and the Than Le could be a real hot spot when Americans misunderstood the pricing procedure and tried to tear the place down rather than bargain for what they wanted.

The line went dead and Richards trotted back out to the MP jeep and instructed Broox to start for 159 Tu Do Street.

"Hit the red lights and beat feet," he said, "but don't call it in. This one's for Rodgers."

Bryant flinched noticeably at the mention of still another MP in trouble, but Thomas was off on another subject as they passed the La Pagode nightclub, its fancy, spired roof searching for the ominous, low-hanging clouds. "Hey, you guys ever hear Petula Clark sing 'Don't Sleep in the Subway' with an Asian accent?" But before they could interpret that question and come up with an answer, he continued, "Well, let me tell you," and he pointed at the La Pagode, "they got this chick in there, she sings with that band Hammer and she sounds just like Pet Clark except she's Vietnamese. And what a looker!"

Bryant leaned over and nudged Broox on the arm as he shifted into second gear. He motioned over to Thomas, placing a hand next to Broox's ear as if he were about to tell a secret, then spoke just loud enough for all to hear, "Did Thomas ever tell you 'bout his little telescope?"

Richards smiled at the joking MPs. Perhaps his men would survive what Saigon was doing to them after all. But the smile would leave Richards' face as soon as he arrived at the souvenir shop and found the jade lady to be long gone.

Stryker pulled the pillow down tighter across his ears as he rolled over in the huge bed on the third floor of the Miramar Hotel, but the ringing phone easily penetrated the bag of feathers. He had been out on the rooftops all night, watching a homely secretary sneak from hotel to hotel in her attempts to make a drug buy. Her employer suspected the thirty-five year old of embezzling a substantial amount of company funds and Gean Servonnat had assigned Stryker to see what the woman intended to do with the money.

Then he was to retrieve the money from her before she could lose any of it. As far as he was concerned, the whole night had been a complete waste of time. No one in the drug trade would have anything to do with the woman. Her face was unknown to them and, he reasoned, she looked too much like a policewoman.

Stryker reached over and fumbled with the phone receiver, dropped it twice, and spoke a groggy, "hello" into the mouthpiece.

"Sergeant Stryker, this is Major Phuong." Stryker immediately sat up in the bed. "Your jade lady. Do you still want it?"

Stryker tried not to appear excited when he answered, "Yes, of course. What have you found out, Phuong?"

"It is in the display window. The Than Le shop, number 159 Tu Do."

Stryker hung up the phone and pulled himself out of bed. He slipped on some jeans, thongs, a "FLY THE FRIENDLY SKIES OF LAOS" T-shirt that showed a helicopter gunship taking on a surface-to-air missile, and rushed toward the door. The phone began ringing again, but he ignored it and started out of the room. The bombs falling from the B-52 above the chopper on his T-shirt appeared to dance in the sky as he flew down the stairs.

The light of day was so bright, even with the heavy cloud cover, that Stryker had to shield his eyes with a hand as he stumbled along curbside, still half asleep, looking for a taxi.

"Where you go, Joe?" A cabbie had appeared out of nowhere. When Stryker gave him the address, the Vietnamese shrugged irritably then drove off without giving the ex-Green Beret a chance to get in.

Then Stryker remembered he was already in the one hundred block of Tu Do Street and he turned back toward the shade of the buildings and began looking for the Than Le souvenir shop.

"Ah, yes, the Thai dancer." A jovial, ever-smiling shopkeeper motioned him through the dusty entrance of the Than

Le emporium.

"Then you have it?" Stryker's excitement rubbed off on the old man and his smile grew even wider to reveal several gold and silver teeth.

"Yes . . . yes . . . come in! Come in!" and the man led the American past a shy, refreshing counter girl who hid her eyes behind a feather duster that was too bright and beautiful to be used for cleaning off store shelves.

The shopkeeper led him over toward the display case at the front window. "Black GI sell it to me several weeks ago. Actually I steal it!" The shopkeeper laughed uproariously and Stryker and the counter girl joined in just to keep the man in a good mood. "Boy, did I skin him! But I give you good deal," and he ushered Stryker over to the corner of the shop and pointed at the middle shelf of the case.

The shopkeeper immediately fell into a long uninterrupted stream of Vietnamese profanity when he saw that the statue was gone.

"May I borrow your phone?" Stryker asked, but the man just continued cursing unintelligibly, and the only word he recognized was cowboys.

Stryker walked back over to his hotel room and dialed the number he had for Major Phuong, but there was no answer. A siren down in the street outside brought him to his window, and he watched with detached interest as an American MP jeep skidded up to the Than Le souvenir shop. Four cops jumped out and went inside for a few minutes, but by the time Stryker got back down to the store they had left in a swirl of dust.

He remained in his room the rest of the day, in case Phuong called again, and that evening Stryker tuned into the American Forces Radio Network and tried to write a letter home to his sister. She had written recently to tell him the marriage hadn't worked out, just like he implied but was kind enough never to say out loud. The jerk had left her with child then abandoned them both, alone and broke in the big city. The letter was postmarked six months earlier.

As he crumpled up the third attempt at writing a brotherly response, Stryker's ear perked up when he caught the familiar introduction to a favorite song on the radio. Janis Ian was strumming her "Society's Child" all the way from the world and he marvelled at how certain songs brought a rush of precious memories or confused emotions from different stages and periods in his life.

He had been thinking of Lai, alone up in Pleiku without him, but this song sent a flood of pictures before his eyes, and they were mostly of Belinda, the girl he had gone steady with all through high school—almost married her until he got drunk one night and, after a lengthy discussion with several members of the VFW lodge, decided to enlist.

As the song wound down to a close he realized he was seeing her house and the street she lived on—even her "I'll never STOP loving you" necklace that was made of silver and fashioned in the form of a stop sign. It was designed as both a play on words and a warning charm to be dangled between the breasts—a hint he was forbidden to explore any farther down her dress until she saw a ring. But her face was a blank now, and he knew as he ran one of Lai's scarfs over his face, her scent taking him instantly back to that dark, primitive little hut in Pleiku, that he would never love another American woman again.

C.I.D. agent William Sickles couldn't be sure how it started. He knew it began over a year ago, when his wife was in the hospital, giving birth to their third child. But he couldn't tell you how the affair with the college girl actually started. Only that it had grown to a point where somebody was going to get hurt. Sickles knew he didn't want to suffer any hurt himself. And that he'd gladly die before bringing any kind of pain or grief down upon his beautiful Thai wife.

Swon had borne him three wonderful daughters and had never once complained when he dragged her off to Vietnam or

356

the countless times since when he was called out in the middle of the night to investigate shootings involving the MPs. No, it would have to be the mistress who took the fall.

Sickles had been attending a lecture on terrorism at Saigon University when the guest speaker recognized him in the audience and asked him to step up and tell some war stories. So the C.I.D. agent told the mostly college-age students about the times he had dismantled bombs hidden beneath MP jeeps and captured the leader of a VC suicide squad that had been planning to assassinate Ambassador Frederick Nolting, and when the chubby, nearly bald American sat back down in the fifth row he noticed that the gorgeous student seated on his right refused to take her eyes off him.

At first Sickles couldn't believe that a slender Vietnamese teenager with night-black hair down to her ass and a cheerleader figure could have the slightest interest in an overweight, cigar-chomping cop. And now that he thought back on it, perhaps that was why he had been foolish enough to follow the girl home to her tiny bungalow. No one had flirted with Sickles in over ten years, and even he needed to feel attractive to protect his self-respect, despite the way his appearance had deteriorated in the last decade—since Korea.

When she never asked for money or threatened his job or family, Sickles took the plunge—feeling a little something fresh and extra on the side might actually be good for a man his age, in such a stressful occupation. After all, he wasn't getting any younger.

When the girl told Sickles—almost two years after they started seeing each other—that she would go to his wife if he didn't supply her with certain classified documents, Sickles knew he had to make a decision about who was going to get hurt.

It wasn't going to be the U.S. Military Police or MI Information Branch, and it certainly wasn't going to be him. But Sickles still hadn't decided what to do and he realized time was getting short. When he met Sergeant Richards and

357

General Lindquist at the S-3 office across the assembly field from the 716th MP Headquarters he knew his head was not going to be in this discussion.

General Lindquist still walked with a terrible limp as a result of the injury he received after hours, off post, during martial law curfew.

"Gentlemen," the general began with an unnatural strain on his ashen face, "I want to be brought up to date on your efforts to capture the woman who . . . who . . ."

Who sliced off half your pecker, thought Richards as he fought off the smile.

"Who so savagely attacked me and the other soldiers . . ."

"Well, actually, General," began Sickles, "we have reason to believe she was critically wounded by a Saigon policeman two days ago on Tu Do Street."

"You can rest assured, our men are pulling out all the stops trying to nab this woman," Richards added. "One of our own MPs was killed trying to arrest her last week."

"Yes, so I've heard. Have you gotten back the lab results on the blood she lost at the scene? Maybe we can match up her blood type with those of the suspects compiled from the VD-care violation roster."

Sure, Sickles was thinking, *everyone wants to play police officer these days. Why don't you just keep out of this and let us handle our own investigations? We're doing our best to get your balls back*. But he said, "Well, I'm frustrated, to say the least, about the delays in getting samples to and analysis back from the labs in Tokyo."

"What kind of delays?" the general asked, and he took out a small notebook. The look in his eye said heads were going to roll over this.

"Well, I'm confident we'll crack this case a lot sooner than most people think, General. It's just that the Tokyo lab handles criminal evidence from all over the Orient, and they're pretty swamped with this Iron Triangle narcotics bullshit going on right now."

The general stood up and, with a serious expression on his face, pointed at his groin and asked, "You're telling me dope is more important than my ding dong?"

Sickles couldn't believe the man had said that. It was apparent he was dealing with a real space cadet. *Lose your balls, you lose your brains.* "Well, sir, a lot of our boys in Southeast Asia are dying of drug overdoses and—"

"What can you tell me about her?" the general interrupted. "Where's she's from—what's her name? Is she VC or just some jilted South Vietnamese maiden-turned-psycho? I'd like some answers, gentlemen."

"Well, sir," replied Richards. "You probably know more about her than anyone. You're one of the few to survive her attacks so far. Perhaps if you could cooperate a little more with our composite sketch artist—"

Sickles broke in abruptly, "We think she lives north of Saigon, in the Gia Dinh area. Or at least that's where she's from. According to the Canh-Sats, her name is probably Pham V. We don't know what the V stands for yet."

"And what are you—we, the Americans—doing out on the street to bring in this woman?" the general sat down on his desktop stiffly.

Sickles surveyed the general's tall, lanky frame and gray flattop haircut a few seconds before answering. He still couldn't believe they had given the man his own temporary office at Pershing Field, so he could be closer to the investigation.

"We've assigned eight MPs to scour the red light district in an attempt to come up with fresh clues and information," Sickles said, even though he knew the general was already aware of the additional men combing the streets.

"And, of course, the Decoy Squad is concentrating every extra minute on drawing this woman out into the open," added Richards.

"That sounds to me like your men are out there bedding down the whores in hopes one of them might turn out to be our girl," the general said.

Richards would have told him that statement made the general look pretty bad himself if Sickles hadn't stepped in and said, "But hopefully she's crawled under a rock somewhere and died. Like I said, we believe she's badly wounded with a .357 round in her back."

"Hmmmphhh," the general snorted as he reached for his brief case. "Probably wishful thinking." He pushed the thick, wire-rimmed glasses back up on the bridge of his nose and started out of the room. "Just keep me posted."

After he had left, Richards walked the C.I.D. agent over to a coffee machine. "Something bothering you, Harry?" he asked with genuine concern. "You don't seem to be yourself today."

Sickles looked up with a surprised expression. He hadn't thought anyone could tell. "No," he lied. "I was just thinking about Rocco Statterhouse."

"Yeah, terrible tragedy. Think they'll give him a medal?"

"We would arrest him, Gary. If he had lived. Seems he kept a journal, of all things."

"A diary?"

"Yeah. We got a hold of it after the PMO went through his locker to pack up his stuff and send it home to the next of kin."

"So what's the big revelation?" Richards laughed.

"In it he wrote of the remorse he was starting to feel over having killed an unarmed Merlyn Jordan, then placing a throw-down knife on him."

"You gotta be shittin' me!"

"And we got some young Vietnamese girl in the office yesterday with her parents. Seems she witnessed Private Kruger beat the liquor store robber to death. Wanted to file an official complaint. We didn't tell them Kruger went AWOL on us."

"Do we have any intel on his whereabouts?"

"Are you kidding? We got three thousand deserters living underground in Saigon as it is. Believe me, I'm least worried about an AWOL MP right now. He'll turn up eventually. They

360

all do."

"So what else is buggin' you, Harry?"

"Were you with the 716th when Mark Stryker was an MP here?"

"Oh, sure. I remember Mark went into Special Forces or some spooky-tunes outfit. Wasn't content with our occasional sniper and slash-happy hookers. Wanted to jump out of perfectly good airplanes and have 'em pin silver jump wings on his son's chest and all that macho stuff."

"Well, he's a private investigator living in Saigon now. Over at the Miramar. Major Phuong has filed a complaint against him."

"Phuong?"

"Yeah. Says Stryker has been putting pressure on the ARVNs to help him solve some missing persons cases."

"Phuong's full of shit."

"Perhaps, but I want your Decoy Squad to roust Stryker every chance you get."

"What?" Richards' jaw dropped as he stared at the C.I.D. agent.

"You heard me. Put the squeeze on Stryker. I want his ass out of Saigon."

XXVI. NEVER PLAY GAMES OF CHANCE
IN A HOLY PAGODA

"So here we are at four in the morning, and it's freezing outside—cold as a witch's—yeah, and we're climbing the fence into the motor pool."

"Thomas reminiscing about Fort Carson again?" Richards took a seat at the bar beside Bryant.

"Yeah, sounds like his condom story again."

"So we're crawling up to all the provost marshal's sedans—I mean, he's just washed and polished 'em all up for the Independence Day parade, so he's got 'em secured behind lock and key so none of the MPs will get 'em dirtied up."

"Sounds like every post I've ever been," whispered Richards.

"I mean to tell ya, it's okay that cops are out there chasin' down the bad guys in open-air jeeps that already have three hundred thousand miles on them—I mean them babies saw hookers in the back seat during the Korean War, okay? But you think they'd give us a couple warm sedans? Hell no!"

"Hell no!" agreed Richards good-naturedly.

Thomas looked over at his sergeant with a frown of disapproval but continued the story, assuming Richards must be getting drunk already. "So we're all low crawlin' up to a whole fleet of shiny new Plymouths—"

"Plymouths?" interrupted Bryant.

"Hey, they get the best stateside."

"I'd take a Chevy Malibu over a Plymouth anyday," muttered Richards as he started in on another bottle of "33" beer.

"So we're crawlin' up to these *Plymouths*." Thomas leaned over closer to his sergeant as he said this. "And, hey, they got these gung-ho airborne guards trotting around looking for infiltrators and all this dramatic stuff, but yours truly makes it 'behind enemy lines' and we attach these rubbers to the exhaust pipes of two dozen sedans."

"That musta been quite a sight." Richards joined in with the mild laughter.

"Hell, Sarge, we had silver balloons exploding everywhere. Popping right off the exhaust pipes and showering the crowd with—"

"Yeah, I can picture it, Anthony. I can picture it."

"I mean these hummers were shooting into the crowd quite indiscriminately! Didn't matter if you were man, woman or child. Get in the way: you got zapped with the lubricated model!"

Two Vietnamese girls had appeared on the extra-wide counter behind the bar and were dancing to the music of the CBC band. The lead singer, a tired-looking woman in her early thirties with long hair and a sparkling *ao-dai* that clung to her knees and ankles, was singing her version of "Morning Dew."

"What'd I tell you?" Thomas and Broox both exclaimed at the same time. "She sounds just like Petula with a Vietnamese accent!"

"Yep," said Bryant, "this sure beats Fort Carson," even though he had never been to Colorado.

After she finished her first song, the weary singer spread her feet apart on the stage as wide as the tight dress would permit and arched her spine back like a cat stretching. She held her arms out wide, the microphone cord dangling from one slender hand.

The woman leaned her head back until it appeared she might tip over backwards, and just as the edge of her waist-length hair touched the teakwood floor, the drummer began a loud, steady snare beat. The woman's right knee rose to her chin slowly until the MPs sitting at the counter would swear she'd have to fall over onto her back at any second, but her foot came down harshly several times, stamping on the floor to the beat of the drum, and as the guitars charged in she began screaming "Some Velvet Morning" to the immediate and thunderous applause of the soldiers crowding the bar.

"See! This place is great!" Broox declared. "She sounds even better than my Vanilla Fudge album!"

"Vanilla Fudge?" Richards tilted his head over at Broox, a question mark in his eyes. "I must be getting old."

"You're just now noticing?" the private nudged him in the side.

The go-go girls on the counter were trying to outdance the leader of the band but there was no contest. Hoang Thi Thao had been around too long. The only thing they had going for them were their tight-fitting white bikinis, but Thao had a following all her own, and that evening it seemed to be the entire nightclub.

After five more songs imitating American hits, she sang one very slow, terribly sad song about the war, but it was entirely in Vietnamese. Although the song was about a Saigon bargirl who had lost her American boyfriend to a VC bullet, the soldiers all gave her a standing ovation and began shouting requests.

"Time for a break, fellas," she said in a deep, throaty voice, and she walked off with a cold wave despite the loud protests. Sgt. Gary Richards watched the woman's face closely, wondering if the sad song about the Vietnamese girl losing her boyfriend to a VC bullet was a true, personal experience of hers, set to music, but he saw no tears running down her cheeks, only that tensing of facial muscles when one is trying hard not to cry.

The men soon began singing, "We Gotta Get Out of This

Place" in a drunken, accelerating slur, over and over until somebody finally dropped a few coins into the juke box and the huge speakers in every corner of the building came alive again.

"Ain't this place a riot!" Broox leaned over so Richards could hear him, and the sergeant forced a smile as he looked around nervously at the boisterous crowd. They were slowly turning into an unruly mob and Richards was thankful the Decoy Squad was off duty and out of uniform.

"What was that lead singer's name?" Bryant yelled toward Broox above the roar of the patrons.

"Hoang Thi Thao."

"I wanna tell her I love her!" Bryant was pouring the ba-mui-ba down by the pitcher and several times he almost teetered off his stool. "I wanna tell her she's the most beeeeyoutiful piece of leg in this land! Hell, I wanna take her home to Mother!"

"So go back stage and tell her!" Thomas egged him on.

"What was her name again?"

"Hoang Thi Thao."

"Hell, I can't remember all that," Bryant complained.

"Just think of her standing in your bedroom." Broox set the scene, slowly moving his hands out in a circle to represent a dream fantasy taking shape. "Standing in your room, naked. Ready to go another round. Just stepped out of the shower. Nothing but that flimsy towel wrapped around her voluptuous, golden body."

"Jugs jutting out so firm and full she can barely wrap the towel all the way around her body!" Broox joined in on the fantasy.

"But how's all that gonna help me remember her name?" asked Tim.

"Yeah?" agreed Broox, also confused as he wiped spilled beer from his chin.

"Hey, just remember the towel. Can you remember 'towel'?"

"Yeah, sure. Towel."

"Okay, so remember 'towel' minus the 'l.'"

"Towel, minus the l. That's towe."

"Correct, sewer breath. That's her first name! Now just go back there and call her towel-minus-the-l: Thao, and tell her you're in love with her and want her body."

"Then we'll come visit you in the monkey house," said a grinning Richards.

"Towel . . . want her body . . . towel . . . want her body." Bryant swung around on his stool and started to step down when Hue Chean appeared in front of him and buried her fist in his gut.

"Sit down!" she commanded, and Bryant fell back obediently in his seat. "You not go nowhere!"

Thomas leaned over toward Sergeant Richards. "That's Hue Chean," he whispered. "She's the one who stabbed him when—"

"Yeah, yeah, I know." Richards motioned for silence. "Don't get her pissed off," and both men sunk their heads between their shoulders and snickered.

Chean folded her arms and took a stance in front of Bryant, and he meekly turned around to face the go-go girls again. They both stared down at him with amused looks on their faces as they gyrated wildly to the juke box music. Bryant frowned and lowered his lips to his glass, muttering, "Women: can't live with 'em, can't live without 'em."

As CBC stepped back up to the stage after their break, Thomas motioned at Broox to take a look at some people entering the bar. "Now that's interesting," observed Sergeant Richards as he watched Lieutenant Jacobson follow General Lindquist over to a corner table against the far wall.

"Yeah, that Jacobson is a bad apple," decided Thomas. "I wonder what the general is doing with him."

"Aw, give old one-star a break," requested Bryant, slurring his speech till it was almost unintelligible. "How would *you* like to go around the rest of your life without any balls to bounce around?" He fell silent a couple seconds and then, as he realized how crazy his own question had been, started laughing hysterically.

"What's so funny, soldier boy?" came a seductive voice over the loud-speakers, and the off-duty MPs all looked up to see the strangely energized Hoang Thi Thao pulling the microphone off its stand and walking slowly over toward Bryant, her firm, sensuous legs now exposed to above the thighs in an orange-pink hot pants outfit. "I said what's so funny, honey?" Thao repeated, her eyes downcast threateningly at Bryant despite the evil grin on her face. "You laughing at *me*, soldier boy?"

Bryant's eyes grew wide with anxiety as he watched the sexpot approach, and he began shaking his head, "no" from side to side to the delight of the cheering drunks around him.

"Step your young, innocent body up here!" she commanded, pronouncing each syllable to the slow clash of a cymbal on the drums behind her. The crowd in the bar went wild, urging Bryant to climb up on stage, then climb up on her. The drummer began thumping the bass drum to the beat of a strip tease and Thao moved her body in inviting circles as she held her arms out to the American.

Bryant glanced back at Chean briefly, then started up onto the stage despite the glare she trained on him.

Thao grasped Bryant's hand and began singing in Chinese to him, using lewd, provocative tones, and although the soldiers in the bar smiled in anticipation and bewilderment, the Vietnamese women in the nightclub began giggling and blushing at the words of the song.

After a few minutes, those same words changed magically to English and the music's speed increased as the lead singer began dancing awkwardly with the drunk GI.

"Looks like ol' Bryant's in second heaven!" Broox declared and he bit his tongue and glanced behind him, ducking at the same time, but Hue Chean was gone. "Well, look who just walked in the door." Broox grinned and he saw Craig Davis walking toward them. He was wearing his uniform and webgear.

"Well, if it ain't the Black Buddha!" Thomas declared, referring to the way the MP had recently shaved his head completely bald. Thomas reached out for a handshake, and although Broox flinched at the title, Davis kept the broad smile on his face and put his arms around the men of the Decoy Squad.

"Looks like that soldier up on the bar should be carted off to the detox ward," Davis joked as he noticed Bryant doing a combination twist and foxtrot with the Vietnamese beauty.

"Yeah, ol' Bryant's havin' a great time. But there's gonna be hell to pay when he goes home tonight," predicted Broox.

"So they got you on town patrol, now?" Sergeant Richards asked as he brushed ashes off the vacant stool beside him. The seat had been occupied up until the uniformed MP entered the bar.

"Why do you think he's gone and shaved his fuckin' crown?" asked Thomas, all smiles. "So now all the girls in soul alley can give him a *real* head job!"

"Just don't let them *rub you* the wrong way!" joked Richards, and all four men cracked up.

Davis nodded nervously when he saw Richards brushing the ashes off the seat. "Oh, no—thanks, Sarge, but I can't sit down in here. It's against the rules, you know that. They finally give me a downtown beat, you know? I don't want to mess that up."

At that moment one of the patrol lieutenants entered the bar and started over toward the sight of Davis' helmet bobbing over the top of the crowd.

"Oh oh," muttered Thomas. "Don't look now, but a real alpha-hotel has just walked in."

Richards turned and frowned when he saw the MP lieutenant. "Well, if it ain't Jack Faldwin. Wonder what he's doing in our little pagoda?"

Davis immediately snapped to semi-attention as Faldwin reached the bar. "You're supposed to be out on the street, Private Davis," he growled at the MP. "Watching your beat, not the go-go girls."

"Yes, sir," Davis answered and he turned to leave.

"Aw, lay off the man," Richards defended him. The sergeant was also beginning to feel the effects of the alcohol, but he still knew how far he could go with the officers of the 716th—even Faldwin.

"Put a cork in it, Richards," he replied, not bothering to look the sergeant in the eye. "You're drunk."

"Sure I'm drunk, Lou, but our man Craig here isn't doing anyone any harm. He's just completing his bar check. We had a fight here and Craig cleared 'em out, that's all. He's a fuckin' hero, Lou. Didn't even call for backup!"

"*We* were his fucking backup!" declared Broox, and he fell over his stool onto the floor, scuffing up Faldwin's spitshine.

"That correct, Thomas?" The lieutenant turned to the man on his left as Richards stooped down to pick Broox up. "Did Davis just break up a bar fight?"

Thomas hesitated, then thought of the argument Bryant and Hue Chean had had. "Yes sir. Things looked pretty bad here for a while. But everyone split when they saw Davis come in."

The lieutenant gave a skeptical grunt and surprised both men by sitting down at the bar. "Is that Specialist Bryant up there?" His mouth tightened as he watched the drunk American throwing his clothes off, piece by piece.

"I never seen that duck before in my life, sir," Thomas answered.

Thao was now moving away from Bryant to sing a slower, softer song, and Thomas and the revived Broox took this as their cue to climb up on stage and retrieve their friend.

Richards swiveled over in his chair slightly when he noticed ARVN Major Phuong enter the nightclub wearing civilian clothes. He looked more like a wire service reporter than a soldier in his olive-colored safari suit. The huge Vietnamese didn't appear to notice the off-duty MPs causing the slight disturbance on stage as he brushed through the crowd over to General Lindquist's table.

The MP sergeant watched a heated conversation turn into a loud argument, but the harsh words were drowned out by the music from the amplifiers. Phuong stormed out of the nightclub before the song ended and more applause filled the building.

"How many short-timers do I have in the audience?" Hoang Thi Thao smiled broadly as she completed another tune. Several hands shot up into the air.

"Thirty days!" someone in the back of the room yelled.

"Nine and a wake up!" another man called out.

"Nine days left in Vietnam." She kept the smile on her face although it hurt her to think these men were so desperate to leave her country—so that younger boys could take their place and die here. "Is there anyone with less time in Saigon than nine nights?" she asked.

"I leave on my freedom flight tomorrow, honey!" a master sergeant among the first few tables replied, and he raised clasped hands above his head like a victorious gladiator in response to the cheers from the men around him.

"One night left in Saigon," she sighed. "I would think you'd be hiding in an underground bunker at Camp Alpha," and her reference to the out-processing installation at Tan Son Nhut airport brought another round of laughter and applause.

"You leave Vietnamese girlfriend behind, Sergeant?" She switched to pidgin English and shook her finger at him in mock reprimand, but the soldier jumped to his feet as if he feared all this silly talk just might get back to the states.

"No ma'am!" he said. "I haven't had any girlfriends since I been here. I'm a grandfather!"

This revelation brought a drum roll and cymbal crash from the band and after Thao laughed with the audience she held her hand out to the American and said, "Come right up here, Sergeant!"

As the fifty-year-old NCO pulled himself up onto the stage, Thao brought the microphone closer to her lips and said sincerely, "I just want all you wonderful men out there to

371

know the noble sacrifice of allied soldiers will never be forgotten," and when the master sergeant finally made it onto the stage she made herself take him in a bear hug and forced a long, passionate kiss on the career soldier's lips.

After the clamor of applause, cheering and vulgar suggestions died down, the sergeant staggered off toward the edge of the stage feigning surprise, honor and satisfaction, all in one shit-eating grin.

Thao rocked back on her heels, enjoying the reaction of the audience, and she called out to the sergeant as he leaped off the stage into the arms of the men at his table, "Now take *that* memory home with you! Hide it in your treasure chest of Saigon souvenirs, and never, *never* tell your wife about it."

The lights inside the La Pagode nightclub were slowly coming on, one by one, as curfew approached. Richards watched as the arrogant Lieutenant Jacobson got up from the general's table and walked out of the building. The look on Lindquist's face was "I'm gonna stay in here till they carry my ass out," and he sat staring off into space, his bulging, bloodshot eyes unblinking.

"I think it's time we got Mr. Life-of-the-party out of this dive and home to Mama," suggested Thomas, and he pointed at the unconscious Bryant, passed-out face down in a bowl of canh rau hot and sour soup.

"I think you got a point there, Anthony," agreed Broox, as he rose from his seat and started to lift one of Bryant's arms up over his shoulder.

None of the men at Richards' table saw the little Vietnamese *papa-san*, clothed in beggar's garb, walk up toward the far end of the nightclub and skillfully roll a grenade off several tabletops into the lap of Gen. Keith Lindquist.

The general glanced down at the bomb, but made no attempt to reach for it. His bulging, unblinking eyes resumed staring at the far wall and became even more bloodshot when the

372

explosion tore his body nearly in half and flung his thick, wire-rimmed glasses across the floor to the other side of the room.

As the shrapnel whizzed toward them, Richards had jumped on top of his men and sent all three crashing under the table. Broox was flattened protectively atop Thomas. Bryant was somewhere at the bottom of the heap, still passed out. They remained frozen for several seconds after the grenade detonated, expecting additional blasts to rock the building. The lights flickered briefly, then the power went out altogether, but there was little panic—only total silence except for the hustle of nervous survivors crawling toward the exits. A few bargirls screamed out of habit, but that was to be expected.

"What the hell happened?" Broox whispered over to Richards.

"It looks like the good general was involved in some illicit activities with Phuong and Jacobson," the sergeant speculated. "I think he was gambling on making some big money before his retirement next year."

Broox sat up on the floor and began waving the smoke away with both hands before he added, "And someone just dealt him out of the game."

"Definitely a losing hand," said Thomas with a giggle, as his eyes locked on the twitching fingers of the severed hand that had landed only a few feet from his face, and the troubled tone in his voice set Sergeant Richards to worrying about his men again.

XXVII. CANDLES IN THE RAIN

There was no candle in the window.

Layers of heavy, shifting blue smoke were drifting on the night air, swirling mostly along the ground as Stryker entered the housing project on the edge of Pleiku. A sense of mild curiosity fell over him as he noticed a section of the compound near the entrance had been burned to the ground. Ten bungalows that had once housed large, noisy families now lay in a pile of charred bamboo and palm ash.

Seeing the damage and destruction did not really strike home to the man until he climbed the steps to his old house-on-stilts and found that his key no longer fit the lock. Then it all came rushing in at him: the destroyed stretch of homes had probably been wiped out by the VC and not just a fire. Stryker grew as tense as a jungle animal—phase red—as the anxiety settled over him.

When he kicked in the door, the first thing that struck him was the lack of wall tapestries he had grown to miss. Instead, a single warped lacquerwood sketch depicting a child on a water buffalo hung unevenly along the far wall. And the teakwood floor did not flash back at him like a mirror—the way it always had before, especially at night, after Lai had spent hours scrubbing it. Now it was dull, lifeless.

Stryker rushed into the bedroom and found a Vietnamese

couple sitting up in bed, terrified at the midnight intrusion—the woman clutching the sheets up around her chest.

"Muan Lai!" Stryker spoke in pidgin Yarde. "Where is she?" But the man and woman just stared back at him dumbfounded. Stryker noticed a carbine lying in a corner next to the bed, but the man didn't seem to be contemplating its use. The ex-Green Beret switched to another Hill dialect. "This was my home!" he yelled, pointing an extended index finger at his own chest. "Where is Muan Lai, my woman?" But the couple just continued to exchange bewildered looks and there soon came a pounding at the front door.

Stryker rested his hand on the .45 in his belt and backed out of the bedroom.

"Stryker! Is that you?" came a voice from the dark, outside. It was Alan Perkins, one of the Green Berets assigned to the hamlet. He was surrounded by a squad of strike-force members, armed to the teeth. "Is that you causing all this commotion? Come out here, bud! And leave those people alone! It's the middle of the night!"

Perkins did not feel confident confronting the ex-Special Forces sergeant, especially in the dark—most especially after Stryker had just discovered his shack-up job was not home, waiting for him.

"Where is Lai?" Stryker emerged onto the porch, and the moonbeams sifting down through the rolling clouds showed his hands at his sides were unarmed. "That you, Alan?"

"Hey, Mark, ol' buddy. Good to see you back. How's Saigon and civilian life been treating you?" Stryker walked down the steps to the red clay but didn't answer, and Perkins put his arm around the man's shoulder and casually escorted him toward the village chieftain's residence.

"What happened at the main gate?" Stryker asked as he observed the Montagnardes lower their rifles upon recognizing him.

"Sapper attack," he muttered. "Hit us with mortars last week at three in the morning—came over the fence, killed two

376

militiamen and carried off a bunch of the women before we could get the main force platoons out here—calm down, Lai wasn't one of the kidnapped girls." Stryker could feel the guilt fighting to burst from his chest as he thought of how terrified she must have been during the attack. So alone, so vulnerable. "Tossed a whole bunch of satchel charges on their way out," Perkins continued. "Just blew the shit out of this ville."

"That doesn't speak very well of your defenses, Private." Stryker slipped and fell back into military thinking, but he caught himself before Perkins could answer and asked, "Where is Lai?"

"We don't know, Mark." Perkins' eyes kept to the ground. "One morning there was a duffel bag with all your stuff in it sitting on the porch of the Orderly Room. Lai was gone—your hooch mostly vacant."

"We sent two letters to your Saigon address, but received no reply."

"Well, I move around a lot."

"No, your post office box." Stryker had to admit he hadn't checked it in weeks. "We took up a collection and paid your rent for May, but you never showed, Mark. There's a critical housing shortage now, due to that enemy attack. A lot of people got burned out of their homes. We rented yours out." Perkins started searching for explanations. "Hell, we thought maybe you gave up on Vietnam and went back stateside. Or you could have been terminated in Saigon for all we knew—Jesus, the way things are going down there . . ."

"When can I get to my stuff?" Stryker asked calmly, not wanting to hear reasons. Nobody in Pleiku owed him any excuses. Or compassion.

"It's still at the Headquarters Hooch. In the captain's storage locker. I don't think anybody's even opened it. There was a combo-lock on the bag. Come on, I'll let you in right now." Perkins' disposition cheered up now that he again had a mission in life.

As they walked through the silent compound, Stryker could

hear gunfire several miles west of the village. A helicopter was hovering over a distant battlefield, its red tracers showering the ground from four separate machine guns. The effect was one of seeing four solid shafts of bright, glowing light holding the craft in the air. Now and then one or two green tracers would arc up at the chopper from the ground, disappearing into the night sky as they missed the "Jolly Green Giant" and burned up in the low-hanging clouds.

"Puff?" Stryker asked the Green Beret, without pointing to the fascinating spectacle.

"No. Just something the boys at MACV rigged up for us. Nice effect, wouldn't you say?"

"So what's the latest atrocity in these parts, Alan?" and Stryker flinched at his choice of words.

"You really want to know?" the private asked. He gave Stryker about three seconds to change his mind, then started in on the gory details. "Found three of the women yesterday," he said, "stripped to the waist and buried up to their chests in the clay out by those giant ant hills a couple miles west of the ville."

"The ant hills?" Stryker shuddered as his mind set to work recreating the scene.

"Yeah, handcuffed 'em behind their backs and buried 'em three feet from the mounds. Hell, Mark, them damn ant colonies extend for a dozen yards underground out from each hill. You know that."

"Yeah, you can't dig foxholes out there without cutting into their little tunnels."

"So these guys are real artists, I guess. They bury these girls with their tits propped up above ground, right at the dirt line. I mean, it must have looked fairly arousing when they left 'em there—"

"Jesus, Perkins."

"But by the time *we* found 'em, they were all chewed up to hell. Dead, of course. The search party told me their breasts had swollen to twice their natural size and some had burst. All

378

of their faces were a mass of bite marks. Looked like somebody napalmed them. Needless to say, I got stuck with the burial detail. The story of my life!" he said sarcastically. "All fun and no glory."

Stryker was left alone once they got to the Orderly Room. He couldn't remember if Lai had known the combination, or even if the bag had been locked. Then he smiled as he decided she had probably picked it the first night he had left her by herself.

He opened the duffel bag to find a note inside, on top, and he was pleased but not surprised. He had known she could not leave without some kind of goodbye. But the letter was not dated and simply read:

> My Mark,
>
> Why you no come back? Now I so lonely and the candles make me more sad. I go back to my people. I take all the pictures so you forget. Forget me and find a nice Saigon girl. The bottoms of their feet are softer.
>
> Chao ong,
Lai

Stryker carefully placed the note in his pocket and checked the bag. On top was a scrapbook. He opened it slowly, disappointed to find she had not exaggerated. All the snapshots of her or the two of them together were missing.

She had also taken the wallet-sized photo of him posing in his Green Beret uniform after graduation from the Special Forces training camps. She had left the photo, taken in Saigon "after he had lost his innocence," where the innovative cameraman had superimposed three negatives to merge profile and frontal views of the handsome Green Beret into one final picture. Lai had never been impressed with tricks done in Saigon.

Stryker set the album aside and pulled out some clothing.

Two sets of tiger-stripe fatigues, one set of civilian clothes, his shoulder holsters and web-belt. A boonie hat with a "VIETNAM 1967: I'M SURE TO GO TO HEAVEN BECAUSE I'VE SERVED MY TIME IN HELL" patch on it. And one of the safari hats with snaps up one side that an Australian had traded him for a VC battle flag. Lai had often worn it when they were in their playful moods. She had even refused to take it off when they were making love one night and Stryker had been unable to get very far. He smiled now when he thought about it. He had rolled off her and complained that he felt like he was humping an Australian grunt, and she had thrown the hat at him and chased him naked around the room and out between the huts under the midnight moon. He was surprised, now, that she hadn't taken it with her.

Stryker noticed the plastic envelope, in which his address book had been sealed, was partially open. He examined the contents briefly, wondering which address, if any, she had copied down.

At the bottom of the bag was an unfamiliar box. It had a citation wrapped around it with a rubber band. He set the piece of paper aside without examining it and opened the small, flat container. Inside was a Purple Heart medal and a hand-written note from his captain:

Sorry we couldn't present this to you before you left the Service, Mark. But you know how Washington can get tied down in red tape. We both know you don't really deserve it (har har) just for catching a slug through your ear, but what the hell! Signed, Cap.

Stryker snapped the box shut and tossed it gently onto the tiger-stripe fatigues. *They probably presented it to Lai when they couldn't reach me,* he decided. *I'll bet she was the proud little wife,* and then pangs of guilt shot through him as he thought of all those nights she had spent alone, watching for him by the window, lighting her little candles.

He opened another plastic bag and set his few other medals out on the fatigues in color-coded order: red ones first. National Defense, Good Conduct, Bronze Star. Beside his country's third highest award he placed the gold and red Vietnam Service Medal and the green Vietnam campaign star. On the end he laid the multicolored Expeditionary Medal, for his three years in Korea. Stryker stared at the medals for several minutes, thinking about what his life had amounted to: six, no seven lousy pieces of tin. A lot of memories, a lot of experience, a string of broken hearts left behind at each port, but Christ—he didn't even have a savings account.

Remembering something suddenly, Stryker shot his hand down and felt around on the bottom, past the familiar Vietnamese music cassette cases, until he located the ankle bag. His heart slowed and he felt embarrassed that he would think she'd have taken the gold coins and silver dollars he had saved since his aunt gave them to him decades before.

"Forget me and find a nice Saigon girl," she had written. *Poor Lai*, he thought, *those nice Saigon girls would all have taken my gold from me*.

He picked up the Vietnam Service Medal again and examined it closely. He could spend hours looking at the dragon walking through the bamboo jungle. And the gold flag with its red stripes above the disc was something that would always catch his eye. Such a simple design: three red, horizontal stripes on a saffron field.

"The saffron field," Lai had told him one night as she patiently sewed small flaglike patches on his uniforms above the heart, "means the earth. Sacred earth—precious as gold, the earth of our ancestors. The red stripes are the three regions of Vietnam and stand for the happiness we seek, no matter what the war brings."

Stryker lifted the bag upside-down and dumped the rest of the contents on the floor: only some rolled-up socks and a rain jacket.

"Everything there?" Perkins had been silently watching

him from the doorway for several minutes.

"Looks okay," he said softly, still thinking about all the nights Lai had spent patiently teaching him things about Vietnam he had never learned in his two tours in Saigon five years earlier. He hoped she didn't view it now as months wasted or precious time lost from her life forever. He knew an American woman would, but not Lai. Instead, he wished she saw what they had as something special, as he had. A phase in their lives they would both look back on fondly, whenever the memories returned. Stryker knew that, for him, the memories would rush back whenever the rain storms passed over his empty bed, pushing the heat aside as they pounded on the tin roof, creating an Oriental music all their own.

Perkins walked back into the room just then.

"You got a place I can bunk tonight?" Stryker asked the private, aware there might not be any rooms in the village after the sapper attack.

"Sure, Mark," and he pulled a small key chain from around his neck. "I'll be out on night patrols for the next ten hours. You can stay in my hooch. Just don't wake the housegirl. I keep her pretty busy in the daytime—she needs her beauty sleep."

Stryker paused as they started back out into the sticky night air. "You got a chick in there tonight?"

"Yeah, but she sleeps on the floor on a mat," and Perkins suddenly eyed Mark suspiciously. "She's jail bait, Stryker. No touch!"

Both men laughed as they started over to the line of huts set aside for the Americans. They weren't much different from the other bungalows except that they were strategically placed away from the perimeter for easier defense.

Stryker perked his ear at the sound of deer barking beyond the treeline. "You don't hear that much anymore." Perkins had heard it too. A projectile suddenly shot skyward from a corner guard tower with a sparkling *swiiiiiish!* and in a few seconds a flare popped above the treeline and the animal sounds stopped.

Stryker smiled: you just couldn't be too careful. The VC made animal sounds in the night that even fooled the barking deer sometimes.

Stryker sat up in his bunk, propped against the pillow, reading Lai's note over and over.

Now and then the girl lying on the mat across the room would shift restlessly in her sleep, rolling onto her back with one knee leaning sensuously against the wall. Stryker reached over to the small fan on the empty crate beside the bed and moved it so that the cool breeze would flow across the room and settle over the girl.

In the flickering candlelight she definitely did not look like jail bait. She had brushed the covers off, and though she wore GI shorts pulled tight with strings at the bottoms, nothing covered her chest. Stryker spent several minutes watching her lips move silently in some far-off dream, but his eyes were always drawn back upon the healthy breasts beckoning to him like smooth, golden pyramids in the night, their tips jutting skyward, pulsing slightly with each breath and heartbeat, softly illuminated in the moonlight that was his candle.

Stryker forced his gaze to shift back up to the girl's tender face. Her hair was so black he could barely distinguish it in the growing darkness. He lit another candle and watched the surge of light dance across her high cheekbones. He doubted the girl had ever worn any makeup in her life—would ever have to. And the innocence he detected in the trusting curve of her closed eyes made him change his mind and accept what Perkins had told him about her age.

Stryker took the black leather wallet from his pocket, opened it to the metallic green map of Vietnam molded onto the plastic inside and ran his fingers along the jagged line where highway fourteen would run south the two hundred miles from Pleiku to Saigon. He wondered briefly what Lai had meant in her note about "I go back to my people now." He had thought her people were all from Pleiku. After all, who was that old man he had traded all the farm animals to for her?

He opened the wallet to the cracked and yellowing photo section and flipped past the IDs and medical alerts until he found her picture. It was black and white, showing her with a bewildered look on her face—back when she was just learning what a camera was. He would never forget the look on her face when he snapped her first Polaroid and she watched her likeness appear in seconds. Mystification was replaced with a quiet astonishment and innocence that would come back to Stryker every time he looked at the wallet photo.

The girl at his feet stirred again, coughing softly against the muggy air filtering in through the open window. As she slowly rolled onto her side and then her stomach, Stryker could see in the smooth lines defining the gentle swell of blurred amber cupped between her arms something of all the women he had known and loved in Asia.

Her long hair, now draped across her shoulders and hiding her face, reminded Stryker of the time he had walked up to a girl in Pleiku from behind, mistaking her for Lai. The way the women of Vietnam all wore their hair long had deceived him, and the lady he had hugged almost broke his arm when he tried to kiss her ear. Stryker instantly remembered the distinctive gold and coral earrings the stranger had been wearing—the minute he saw them he knew he had embraced the wrong princess. Lai wore no jewelry.

When he later told Lai about the incident she had become very upset, accusing an evil enchantress of trying to seduce him and steal her man away.

"You've got to be kidding," he had replied, laughing. "It was *me* who walked up to *her!*"

"She drew you to her with her breath of magic," Lai claimed and it was the first time he learned how superstitious the hill women were. "Can you describe her face?" she demanded.

"Well, no—not really. It happened so fast, I just—"

"Of course," she had interrupted him. "It was Le-hong."

"What?"

"Le-hong, trying to steal you away from me."

"Le-hong?"

"Yes. Long, black hair. She always turns her back to men before she traps them. Because if they saw she has no face, they would know she is a ghost. But you must be careful, because once she catches you, you will find she has many faces."

"Lai, now you're talking crazy. This woman was flesh and blood. I touched her skin, smelled her perfume, tasted the edge of her ear."

A bolt of jealousy flashed through Lai's eyes and she raised her voice at him. "But you saw her face?" she demanded.

"Well, no . . . but . . ." And she sat him down at the table, lit an extra candle to ward off the spirits trying to listen, and told him about the legend of Le-hong.

"There was a soldier, Mark—an American, much like yourself. He had just witnessed much death and killing in the jungle, like you. He was sitting alone, in a bar in Saigon, drowning the pain of what he had seen with whiskey. Sitting in a room with dozens of other people, but all alone. Raining outside, raining terrible bad. And when he looked up from his glass, there stood a woman outside the window, soaking wet in the rain, staring at him sadly, with no smile.

"The American rose from his chair and rushed outside, but there was no one there. He ran down the back alley behind the bar: nobody there too. So what can he do? He returns to the bar.

"And the next time he looks up from his glass, she is sitting beside him, at his table. They talk, but it is only with their eyes and their minds. He buys her Saigon tea then they roam the flower stalls of Le Loi and Nguyen Hu, sometimes even hand in hand.

"But the curfew sirens mourn the hour of midnight, and suddenly she is running away, through the rain again, his jacket draped over her slender shoulders.

"He chases her, thinking it all a game he must play before she will sleep with him. But she seems to be getting farther and farther away from him down the side streets, no matter how fast he runs, until he tires of the charade and only wants his jacket back.

"He wonders why the sidewalk militiamen she races past do not even seem to see her, yet they rise to their feet startled as he runs by.

"And then she rushes into a tenement, blackened by years of war and arson, and slams the door shut in his face. He only wants his jacket, he yells at the door, the rain beating down on him harder now. Is that her face pressed against the window above the door?

"He returns the next day, hoping only to retrieve his jacket, but an old *mama-san* answers his knock, and when he tells her the girl's name, the woman flies into a rage, cursing him in Vietnamese, points to a distant hill beyond the jungle, then also slams the door in his face.

"A young boy, who overheard their conversation, tells the American old *mama-san* claims the girl he sought died in rocket attack ten years earlier. Is buried in the graveyard over that hill, beyond the restless treeline.

"Dark rain clouds were now slowly covering the sun, but he began walking toward the cemetery.

"The graveyard was not small, but as he reached the top of the hill and looked down on it, it was easy to locate the grave of Le-hong: the flowers he had bought for her the night before were scattered across it. And his jacket, fluttering in the breeze, lay draped over her tombstone."

XXVIII. TOUGHEST BEAT IN THE WORLD

Davis was taking the corners on two wheels. He kept the siren toggle switch pressed forward with his knee while he struggled with the steering wheel to keep the jeep from rolling. The two girls on the Honda he was chasing had snatched his watch right off his wrist, and they had the gall to do it while he was sitting in Le Loi park, in his MP jeep, munching on a bamboo sliver of satay, watching the sun set over Saigon.

"This is car eleven!" he called into the microphone as they left the maze of alleys in lower downtown and took a straight stretch of road into heavy traffic. "I'm now eastbound on Le Van Duyet, approaching . . . approaching . . ." Davis strained his eyes at the street names but they were all going by in a blur and many corners didn't even have signs.

"Gimme a cross street, car eleven." The unemotional drone of the dispatcher at Pershing Field was quite a contrast to that of the excited private. After several seconds of silence, other units began acknowledging the pursuit.

"Car ten responding to cover from the Xin Loi bar."

"Car Niner-Alpha, from Knox Street static post, MACV."

"All units, clear the net," interrupted the dispatcher. "Code One. Clear the net. Cloud Dragon to car eleven, gimme a cross street, Davis."

There were several more seconds of tense silence until Davis finally called in, his siren rising in pitch in the background. "We're now northbound on Phan Dinh Phung!" He was concentrating on sounding calm, more professional, but the excitement remained in his voice, and several MPs across the city, who elected not to join in on the chase for one reason or another, turned down the volume on their radios.

"Gimme your speed, car eleven and gimme a description of the suspects."

"This is car eleven. Speed approximately sixty klicks, chasing two Victor-November Foxtrots on a white Honda fifty." The dispatcher wrote down, "Two Vietnamese National Females" on his notepad and reached for the transmitter pedal.

"What's your p.c., car eleven? What are you chasing for? Over."

"Larceny of a watch," Davis replied. "Mine!"

The four men sitting in the Decoy Squad car all broke out laughing at the same time. "Did he say 'mine'?" asked Thomas incredulously.

"That Davis is a laugh a minute," added Bryant. "Sitting in a marked MP unit somewhere, in complete Military Police uniform, and he *still* manages to let some Honda Honey snatch his Seiko!"

"You should talk," said Broox between laughs. "At least Davis' old lady don't follow him around to bars, and kick ass when he steps outta line."

"That's 'cuz his old lady's stateside, water-buffalo breath! Davis don't even know what *it* looks like here."

"Did you ever get a date with that singer at the Pagode bar?" Richards leaned back and gave him a now-don't-bullshit-me stare.

"Well, actually . . ."

"Yes?" Broox also turned around in his seat. "This has gotta be good."

"Hey, sounds like he's getting close," Thomas interrupted, referring to sirens growing nearer several blocks over.

"We stay put," Richards told Broox. The four of them were

388

staked out a block down from Jeff Rodgers' safe house apartment on Bis Ky Dong. "I'm not jeopardizing this stake out for a couple lousy Honda Honies."

"Maybe they're friends of the two who blew up Sergeant Mather," Broox said, trying to make his boss feel guilty, but Richards' mind was wandering back a few nights to when he was contacted by Mark Stryker.

He had heard the note get slipped under the door of his hooch, but when Richards ran to look out into the hallway there was no one to be seen. He ran down the dark corridor of the barracks' top floor and looked out the windows to the ground below. A young girl on a bicycle was rapidly pedaling away. *Wonder what she's doing on post—how she got in*, he thought, making a mental note to check back with the main-gate MPs later to see if she had signed in.

Richards walked back to his room and picked up the small sealed envelope lying in the doorway. He sat back down on the bed, shoved aside the pile of crumpled letters he had been trying to write to Seaman Philip Anderson's parents. He took the commando knife from his boot and neatly sliced the envelope open. Richards was surprised to see the note inside was from Stryker, but it contained only two sentences: "Heard you have been trying to contact me. I'll meet you at the Nam Do Restaurant, 199 Nguyen Thai Hoc, Friday, 1900 hours. M.S."

Their rendezvous had been strained initially. There's always a bit of uneasiness at first whenever ex-cops meet with men still working the street.

"The desk clerk at the Miramar says your goon platoon has been by several times looking for me, Gary. What's up?" he had asked.

"Needed to talk to you about this Phuong character."

"Phuong? Did he put me on the black list?"

"Something like that. You know Lindquist?"

"That jerk who got his pecker liberated by a VC housegirl?"

"Something like that," Richards had repeated without

smiling. He wasn't enthusiastic about telling a former Green Beret that he had been given the task of booting Stryker out of Saigon. "Well, I think Phuong and Lindquist got something going. Phuong asked Lindquist to have us run you out of town. Now, it's not my business why Phuong has a hard-on for you, but I just thought I'd warn you."

"I'm not worried about the ARVN," Stryker had answered. "In my circles we call him Phuong the Fag. You're right—him and Lindquist probably *do* have something 'going on.'"

"Well, I just wanted you to know. He keeps asking for progress reports, but we just tell him you're out of town, lying low, and that keeps him happy."

"You'd think they'd send that moron stateside, what with the way that chick carved him all up."

"Who knows what goes on at Puzzle Palace," he had said, referring to MACV headquarters.

"Yeah, Disneyland East. Well, I'll tell you what, Gary. You did me a favor, now I'm gonna do you a favor. How bad do you want Jeff Rodgers?"

"Rodgers?" He had almost shot up out of his seat. "I want that man bad."

"That's what I figured." Stryker handed the sergeant a slip of paper with the Bis Ky Dong address on it. "I've thought about this for a long time. Jeff needs to be taken off the street. He needs help. But I just can't bring myself to bring him down—my involvement is too personal. I was following him around for several weeks, hoping to make some sense out of this whole mess, hoping there was some justice in what he was doing, but—"

"But too many innocent people are getting in the way."

"Not just getting in the way. Jeff's going *out* of his way to ice anyone who even remotely resembles Lance Jackson or Marvin Chilton."

"The guy's flipped out, that's all. We all lose a part of our minds in Saigon, Mark. Somehow, someway. Nobody ever leaves here totally intact—that's why guys like you and me

390

keep coming back. The states just can't hack it after you've lived in 'Nam. God forbid we ever pull out. Men like you and me will have nothing left—nowhere to go."

"Just don't kill him," Stryker had said, ignoring Richards' little speech. "Take him off by the rules."

"Or we'll be having another meeting," Richards anticipated the warning.

"Or we'll be having another meeting."

Richards recalled how Stryker had gone on to ask if the Military Police or C.I.D. had anything on the jade lady. He told him about the wild goose chase at the souvenir shop and that none of his informants had turned up anything since then. He then requested that Richards keep him informed about any developments in the case, and the MP sergeant told the private investigator that to do so would only be professional courtesy and therefore required.

Broox's excited voice broke into his thoughts. "Hey, Sarge, I think they're headed right for us!"

"Now eastbound on Bis Ky Dong!" Davis' voice came over the portable radio, scratchy, suddenly weaker the closer he got.

"I told you guys to sit tight," Richards mumbled, and he thought back to all the trouble he had gone through to get the Volkswagen convertible they were using for the stake out. Stryker had managed to sneak it out of his employer's "fleet" and though it was definitely out of the ordinary, even Bryant agreed that an alert Rodgers would never be fooled.

"Here they come!" Thomas sat up in his seat at the sight of the MP jeep now chasing the motor scooter toward them.

They were only a half block away when Broox said, "Watch this, Tim," and he leaned out of the VW and rolled a night stick into the path of the Honda.

"Oooo-weeee!" Bryant began clapping as the front tire glided over the billy club without incident, but the stick then bounced into the spokes of the rear wheel and locked it, causing the bike to skid sideways. The girl riding sidesaddle on the back flew off the Honda at high speed but was stopped dead when she landed against the front of a parked lorrie.

"Holy shit," Thomas gasped as the woman's entire body appeared to splatter like a tomato against the truck, then slowly slide off into the gutter in a broken heap.

The motor scooter slid around in a semicircle until the frozen rear wheel forced the rest of the bike to flip end over end.

The driver, a woman in her early twenties wearing only shorts and a halter top, flew from the Honda and slid bouncing across the blacktop. The MPs watched in disbelief as her body—its broken arms and legs already flopping about like a rag doll—finally came to rest in the middle of the street, only to be run over by an overloaded bus that couldn't stop in time.

The three MP jeeps skidded up to the scene, their sirens dying to a slow wail, and Davis jumped out, gun in hand, and rushed over to the body caught under the chasis of the bus.

"What the hell's that crazy sonofabitch doing?" Thomas asked Richards, but the sergeant could only skake his head, painfully aware that all the commotion would probably scare Rodgers away for sure.

Davis was dragging the woman's body out from under the bus—the halter top had been torn off by the impact, and her breasts now flopped back and forth loosely, lifeless.

Before a growing crowd of curious spectators, Davis plucked his watch off the dead girl's wrist and walked back over to the other MP jeeps. "Damn thing's broken!" he complained, holding the cracked crystal to his ear, then up for their inspection.

"No shit, Sherlock," the MP closest to him responded.

"You shoulda bought a Timex," the other commented dryly.

The four MPs wearing civilian clothes in the Volkswagen convertible scooted down in their seats so Davis wouldn't see them and attract additional attention to the stake out. The men of the 716th had not been warned at briefing to stay away from the stake-out area for fear a sympathetic "brother" might attempt to tip off Rodgers. "You better hope he doesn't find your night stick out there anywhere," Richards told Broox, and he was thinking, *Anywhere but Saigon and you'd be up on manslaughter charges for pulling a stunt like that!*

"He's bound to find it," said Thomas. "It's all mashed up in the spokes of that Honda." Two Vietnamese police jeeps rolled up without their emergency equipment on, and Thomas voiced the hope they might handle the accident investigation so the Americans could clear out of the area.

"Who you guys?" A shoeshine boy was leaning into the Volkswagen off the gutter.

"Beat it, kid," Bryant said.

"You guys cops? MPs?" the kid asked matter-of-factly.

"No, we're AWOL," Bryant answered sarcastically.

"You guys *are* cops," the boy decided and he reached over and lifted up Richards' jean jacket, exposing his submachine gun, a MP40 Schmeisser nine-mm, salvaged from a German armory.

"Get outta here, you little brat!" Thomas shooed the boy off down the sidewalk, but he just walked over to the corner and sat down on his shoeshine box.

"Is that that kid Dong?" Richards asked Broox, and the private told him there was no way they were even remotely related.

"Dong's got more manners," Thomas agreed, "and more class."

"None of 'em knows how to make a decent cup of coffee," complained Bryant. He was still remembering the day he couldn't hustle a refill for his baggy of ice coffee.

"Any of you clowns noticed any movement up in Rodgers' window?" Richards asked.

"Nope, it's still dark," Bryant said, lowering his binoculars.

"I didn't ask if it was dark," Richards said irritably. "I asked if there was any movement inside."

"The world of a deserter is always dark," Thomas explained to Bryant what the sarge meant. Rodgers would be used to living with the lights off or the drapes closed.

"Oh oh, looks like trouble." Broox had noticed two women walking toward the VW, eyeing the men. "Ladies of questionable virtue, if you know what I mean."

"Niiiiice car." One of the girls leaned into the convertible, propping her breasts atop the car's door to exaggerate their size. "You boys civilians?"

Richards could see the dollar signs in her eyes. The second girl had put an arm on his shoulder and was running her fingers through the hair on his right arm. He could smell the heavy layer of perfume mingling with the alcohol on her breath and the smog in the air.

"You like to buy me Saigon tea?" she asked softly. That was the code name for a night in the sack. But before he could answer, the shoeshine boy had walked past and said, "Canh-Sat," warning the girls the four men were cops.

They were off and on their way without any further conversation and the three enlisted men gave the shoeshine boy a dirty look while Richards just smiled and kept his eye on Rodgers' window.

"Little jerk-off," Bryant muttered in the boy's direction, but he was out of hearing range, having returned to the street corner where he continued to monitor their every move with suspicious, hostile eyes.

"Maybe you should go over and dust that punk," Thomas joked with Bryant, but there was no humor in his voice.

"Definitely better keep an eye on him," Richards observed. "He looks like the kind of squirt that's just mean enough to lob a grenade in your lap."

An hour later, Richards noticed an American woman standing across the street, watching them closely from the shadows of a basement stairwell. As soon as they made eye contact, she came out and started walking toward him, and he could see in her the woman he had left behind in Tampa so many years ago.

Richards was not particularly pleased with still being a buck

394

sergeant at the age of thirty. But he could be doing a lot, lot worse, and over the years he had come to accept his place in life. There had been the dreams, of course. He had left Florida to attend West Point, and she had been so very proud of him, writing a letter every day. They agreed to marry after he became a lieutenant. Maybe he could even get a duty assignment to Hawaii—what a honeymoon that would make! And of course he'd major in law or medicine.

But Richards had never made it past the first year at the Point. Fed up with the unrealistic discipline, hypocritical honor code and arrogance of his instructors, he finally decked a pompous rich kid whose father knew a dozen congressmen— which was even more reason to punch out the brat—and they decided to leave him a private and make him an MP, where he could put his fists to better use. She hadn't written much after that, and when they sent him to Germany in 1960 he lost track of her.

"Are you gentlemen in the military?" the woman asked Richards after she made it across the busy street over to the Volkswagen. The MPs eyed her suspiciously and none of them answered immediately, choosing instead to look toward Richards for guidance. The sergeant took his time examining the woman and made no secret of the fact his eyes were searching out everything.

She stood taller than all the Vietnamese who flocked past the VW to watch the Canh-Sats scrape the Honda Honies up off the pavement. Richards guessed her age at about twenty-five. Her slender figure was in no way complemented by the straight shift and dull T-shirt she wore. The skirt was thick red, black and green nylon, and the shirt had a large green marijuana leaf stenciled across the front and the words, "QUESTION AUTHORITY" below it. Her hair was piled up on top of her head, blond with dark roots showing and held in place by a multicolored sweat band. Richards inspected her legs and was repulsed to see the calves were thicker than his own, and hadn't been shaved in months.

"The reason I ask is that I've been told an American deserter is living in this block somewhere. I'm with the Lonely Globe Press, out of D.C. and I want to do a story on him."

"Ain't no deserter living in this neighborhood, honey," said Broox without looking at her—he sounded very bored with journalists.

"And how can you be so sure of that?"

"Look, why don't you take a taxi over to Third Field Army Hospital," said Thomas, "and interview the real heroes. The guys with the broken bodies and missing limbs."

"The baby killers?" She smiled, hoping the insult would touch a raw nerve, act as a catalyst that might get an award-winning interview under way. It did. Richards turned and glared at her until she dropped her eyes to her notepad and began examining empty, blank pages, very studiously, one after another.

"Actually," she said, taking a deep breath and pressing on into hostile territory, "our readership is more interested in the men who choose not to fight this war than the ones who've taken to burning down villages and raping Vietnamese women."

"We only rape VC women." Thomas flashed icy eyes at her that locked on hers as he spoke coldly, slowly, until she looked away.

"Look, lady," Broox said, frowning as heavily as he could, "why don't you go get—"

"I'm afraid we don't know anything about any deserters," interrupted Richards. "We're just here to meet some people." He wanted to tell her about the four *heroic* deserters who raped and murdered the Vietnamese woman at 541 Thanh Mau Street.

"But I would really like to know what you think of the American presence here in South Vietnam," and she produced a pencil. "You know, down to earth, grass roots interview with some honest to goodness GI types," she said sarcastically.

"They are cops." The shoeshine boy was walking past again,

396

and he started running as Bryant reached out for him.

"What does he mean, cops?" she asked, mildly shocked, and then she started laughing. "In this?" she pointed at the funny looking Volkswagen convertible.

"We're off duty," said Bryant. "It's a rental." When Broox started laughing at this, the journalist drooped her shoulders and tilted her head at them.

"Come on, boys—level with me. What's the gig?"

Richards ignored the question and asked one of his own. "If you're so against the war, why are you here, instead of marching on the White House?"

"I shoot pictures, not people, honey."

"You gonna let her get away with that crap, Sarge?" Bryant sat up in his seat, looking like he wanted to slug a woman for the first time in years.

"Look, Miss . . ." He paused for her to give her name.

"Whatever," she said smartly.

"Miss Whatever. Look, we're just MPs here to enforce military laws, okay? We haven't burned any villages down in a coupla weeks."

Bryant started laughing and Broox and Thomas had to look away from their sergeant to keep from joining in. "We go out on patrol every day," he continued, "arrest looters and robbers and thieves. Make sure some of the dirty hookers don't get mixed in with the clean tricks and start a VD epidemic, break up bar fights and family disturbances. But mostly it's just a lot of boring, routine patrol. Unless you love Saigon. That's about the extent of it. We're in the military, but we consider ourselves cops first, soldiers last. We put in a twelve-hour day then we go home to Mama or the barracks. In twelve months we go back to the world. Unless you love Saigon. If you love Saigon, then you keep coming back until you start looking, feeling and thinking like a Vietnamese."

"Speak for yourself, Sarge." Broox grinned good-naturedly.

"Unless you love Saigon?" she sounded astounded. "How could you love Saigon? This place is a cesspool."

397

"If you did your homework, you'd know the Orient affects American men and women differently." Bryant had suddenly gotten serious. "The women, when they make the trip here, usually do it out of curiosity. Or because—such as in your case—their job brings them here. They find only hard work and harsh conditions. Little romance. And when they find it—it's usually with other Westerners. They quickly tire of the heat and stress of war—even here in Saigon, where a rocket can fall on anyone, any place, any night.

"The men, on the other hand, find Asia much different. There is an adventure here that runs much deeper than those first few visits to the temples and the ruins. There is the mystery of the women here—something the American men can seldom overcome.

"The heat is endured—it blends with the scent of lovemaking under a slow-turning Casablanca ceiling fan until every wave of heat reminds the man of the woman waiting downtown for him. They draw you under their spell, if you will. Every slender maiden, floating past on the Saigon breeze, in her form-hugging *ao-dai* and long, sleek hair, is a potential enchantress. And when you mix that with the excitement or threat of war, there results a chemistry that changes American men forever. It is something that permanently bonds their soul to the Orient. I don't care if they return to America and are not drawn back for ten or twenty years—the memories are with them day and night. The sight of an Oriental woman draws them from whatever they were doing.

"After dark, they are beside their American wives, but their thoughts are twelve thousand miles away, and when they make love, the woman beneath them has long, black hair and the firm, magic thighs of a Vietnamese.

"Don't fault them for this or try to place blame. It is something they have no control over. It is just that they have been mentally branded by the hot fires of the exotic, and there is no cure for that."

The woman reporter stared at him in silence for several

398

seconds then touched the tip of her pencil to her tongue and grinned evilly. "How about if you repeat all that crap for me and I'll write a feature story on you and your Oriental hangups and we'll send a free complimentary copy to your wife in the states?"

Bryant laughed out loud at the woman. "I'll tell *you* what: how about if you give me your address and I'll send you a wedding invitation."

"What?" Broox choked on the swallow of lime canteen Kool-Aid he had just taken.

"Gentlemen"—Bryant turned to face the Decoy Squad as he stood up in the convertible—"Hue Chean and I are getting married next week, and you're all invited!"

"Why you *dinky dau* MP!" Richards stood up to shake Bryant's hand. "To think you've been keeping such a secret all this time."

"He probably *has* to get married," joked Thomas. "Did you get in trouble, Timmy?"

All four men began clapping each other on the back and shaking hands. Thomas reached out and shook the reporter's hand. Broox and Richards shook each other's hands, and then laughed some more, trying to decide why. "Don't we get some cigars or something?" asked Thomas seriously.

"That comes later, lizard breath," said Broox. "When they make a dozen little *baby-sans*."

"Is Timmy-san Jr. going to be an MP?" asked the woman standing beside the VW, but the men were now ignoring her, and she eventually walked off unnoticed.

A few minutes later, as the congratulations and merriment continued, Richards noticeably slinked down in his seat and lost the smile on his face. "Oh oh," he muttered, "here comes Number Ten honcho," and when the others turned to see Lieutenant Faldwin responding to Davis' traffic accident they also lowered themselves from sight.

"This is turning into a real farce, Sarge," said Thomas. "If Rodgers really *is* anywhere in a ten-mile radius, he's not going to make himself seen with all these MP armbands standing out in the middle of Bis Ky Dong, no way!" Just then small arms fire erupted sporadically several miles away and the different possible causes for it raced through Richards' mind as he spoke.

"Just sit tight." The sergeant remained unemotional about the prospects of the stake out. "Looks like the Canh-Sats are gonna handle all the paperwork except the larceny. I'm sure they'll clear out within the hour."

Static began to come over the portable radio between Broox's knees, and he lifted it up to the dashboard, flicked off the squelch for more power, and turned the radio over until he got the clearest reception.

"Attention all town patrols," the dispatcher's voice came over the net weakly.

"Damn battery," muttered Broox, "isn't worth a shit."

"Attention all units, vicinity Phan Dinh Phung and Bis Ky Dong. Canh-Sats report an intense firefight between unidentified forces. Traffic being re-routed eastbound on Bis Ky Dong. They are requesting ten patrols for traffic control only at this time. Units to respond acknowledge."

"Aw, fuck," grumbled Thomas. "Now half of Saigon will be cruising down this street. This is just unreal, simply unreal."

Richards watched with admiration and envy as Lieutenant Faldwin excitedly directed the three patrols at the fatal accident scene to respond to the area of the firefight. It was times like this he wished he was back in uniform.

Officer Jon Toi watched with keen interest as ARVN Maj. Phuong Van Minh's black sedan cruised past his traffic control point in the intersection of Phan Dinh Phung and Bis Ky Dong. It was preceded by two carloads of his personal bodyguards—members of the elite Vietnamese Special Airborne Forces—and followed by four gun jeeps loaded down with heavily armed infantrymen. Out of courtesy to the soldiers—Toi still fondly recalled his years with the ARVN Rangers—he had stopped all traffic on Bis Ky Dong and smartly waved the troopers through with his left hand while he saluted sharply with his right.

The gleam of pride and precious memories sparkling in Toi's eyes just then turned to shock and disbelief as machine guns, positioned on four different rooftops overlooking the busy intersection, opened up on the convoy with a ferocity that sent Toi scrambling under cover of the nearest parked car.

He watched the countless tracers flash down like Hollywood space lasers from four distinct points high above and come together on the roof of Major Phuong's sedan. He took the pair of folding binoculars the MP Bryant had bought for him from a sweat-soaked pocket and trained them on the dark rooftops.

Red and green tracers flowed down in a steady stream, many bouncing off the street to ricochet back up into the night sky. But despite the thunderous salvo Toi was able to identify several of the shadowy forms darting about on the rooftops above—and they wore South Vietnamese military uniforms!

Toi could hear wounded civilians, caught in the crossfire, screaming in agony all around him, but he was powerless to respond. There was just too much hot lead bouncing around and he didn't even have a first-aid kit. As he speculated on the cause of the battle—it could be any number of things: A fight over black market territory or shop control, or perhaps a feud between commanders—the Canh-Sat rested his hand on the butt of his revolver. And as he shifted around beneath the chassis of the Renault taxi, scraping thin tears into his white police shirt, he wondered how many ARVNs he was going to have to kill to survive another night in Saigon.

Several miles away, Lt. Clifford Jacobson of the First Signal Brigade, paused briefly as he listened to the sound of gunfire erupting in the distance. When he heard no incoming rockets or artillery, he shrugged his shoulders and handed his ID card to the MP at the security gate.

"Evening, Lieutenant." The MP saluted sharply, but Jacobson just snatched his card back without returning the salute and turned to enter the main entrance of the Montana BOQ.

The MP frowned for a couple seconds at the officer's behavior, watched the man get safely into the BOQ building, then resumed reading the tattered Doc Savage adventure novel.

Lieutenant Jacobson rustled his fingers around in his pocket, past the bundles of narcotics money stuffed to overflowing, and located his keys. He smiled as he thought about the look on General Lindquist's face when the grenade rolled into his lap at the La Pagode nightclub, and then he slipped his key into the lock.

When he opened the door and heard three pieces of metal bounce atop the stained and warping tile inside the dark room, he was still too engrossed with the successful assassination of the meddling general to attach any significance to the slight noise: just another mouse scurrying away from the door, his mind told him.

The officer ignored the light switch and began loosening the gold belt bucklet that kept his hundred-dollar slacks up as he headed toward the bathroom. He was still thinking about the stupid general when the three blinding explosions tore his consciousness out the back of his head and disintegrated his earthly body into just so much dust on the hot, sticky night breeze.

The MP at the security gate dropped the book he was reading and threw himself flat on the floor when he caught sight of the roof erupting into flames and splinters out of the corner of his eye. He held his arms tightly across the top of his helmet as the blast rolled over the back of his flak jacket, taking the guard shack with it. The concussion knocked out his hearing temporarily.

After the last of the broken boards and smoking debris

rained down on him and the only sound was fire crackling on the BOQ roof, the MP slowly peeked out from under his helmet to survey the damage.

As he rose to his knees and began brushing the dust off his uniform, the private grinned, slowly shook his head from side to side and whispered beneath his breath, "Maybe now you'll salute next time, asshole."

Sergeant Richards bit on his lip as the firefight several blocks away slowly grew in intensity.

It was an unwritten rule that all cops in the city responded to an officer's call for help, and this was the first time in his career that he hadn't raced at breakneck speed in the midst of a dozen other wailing, roaring units to the assistance of a brother losing the odds game.

He could see the same anxiety growing in the eyes of his men. They all had nervous hands busy as their ears caught every distinct barrage of automatic weapons fire over on Phan Dinh Phung. Thomas was curling his cement-filled "barbell" cans like there was no tomorrow. Broox had his night stick out and was flexing his wrists against each other with it. Bryant drummed his fingers rapidly against the car's dashboard, his eyes glued to the dark window across the street, but his mind seeing policemen crouched behind parked cars returning fire at a dozen rooftop snipers.

"Listen, guys." Richards broke the uneasy silence. "They don't want us over there. They've got enough help. It's a Vietnamese affair."

The heavy traffic being funneled down Bis Ky Dong away from the street battle was now creeping along bumper-to-bumper past the Decoy Squad, and Richards' heart sank as still another MP patrol zoomed past code three, siren screaming and lights flashing as it recklessly swerved in and out of the hopeless jam of cars, bound for the shoot-out.

"Look, we're out of uniform," Richards rationalized, "and

those guys are just going over to detour civilian traffic anyway. You're not going to miss out on any action." But the attempt at persuasive psychology did not fool anyone sitting in the car. They knew none of the MPs racing toward the arousing clamor of gunfire would stop short of the action to just direct traffic. Even if the probable traffic jam on the outskirts of the battle forced them to abandon their jeeps, every man would be running the last few blocks, M-16 in hand, eager for hostile contact and the surge of adrenalin that made the job worth it.

"I don't believe it." Broox had straightened up in the front seat and had his eyes glued on the crowds flowing past the apartment house across the street. Traffic was now at a halt, moving only a few feet every minute, and an American had stepped from a taxi and was darting in and out between the bumpers, making his way toward the sidewalk. "Is that Jeff Rodgers?"

All four MPs slowly climbed out of their undercover sedan and spread out along the block before starting through the river of automobiles clogging the street.

The American paused in midstride as he surveyed the endless line of motionless headlights strung out in front of him. He glanced down the street in both directions as if unable to come to some kind of decision, then turned abruptly and slipped down the alley that ran off Bis Ky Dong to the rear of several apartment buildings.

"He's running!" Richards called out to his men above the din of a thousand idling engines, and all four MPs drew their weapons and closed in on the dark entrance to the side-street their sergeant had pointed out.

Richards was suddenly at ease when he felt the heft and power of cold steel in his hands. He chambered a round into the submachine gun and felt the adrenalin start to flow: his forearms were shaking now ever so slightly despite the heat and humidity in the oppressive air. There was no doubt in his mind Jeff Rodgers would resist arrest. And there was no doubt in Richards' mind that he would cut the American in half

404

before he'd let any of his men risk injury. Yes, he'd let loose the entire thirty-two-round clip at Rodgers before the maniac could even contemplate drawing any weapons. And he would feel no guilt at taking out the former MP in a hail of hot lead— the man had forsaken his membership in the sacred brotherhood when he deserted the United States Army.

Broox watched his sergeant shift into high gear at the sight of the shadow sprinting away from them down the opposite end of the alley. Broox had his .45 out, and there was no doubt in his mind that he would use it if cornered and forced to defend himself. But he had no desire to participate in gunning down Jeff Rodgers. Once a cop, always a cop, he decided. It was perfectly fine with him if Sergeant Richards was so intent on killing a brother—then *he* could be the one to live with the guilt afterwards.

Thomas hastily struggled to snap shut the flak jacket as he hustled to keep up with the other men. His fingers were numb with the excitement of impending death and as they repeatedly failed to button the bulletproof vest, the thought occurred to him they might also fail to pull the trigger of his automatic at the right time. As he finally got the body armor in place, he shrugged his shoulders at the worries: he hadn't qualified at the firing range in three months anyway and knew he was even worse in a nighttime shoot situation.

Bryant was thinking about Hue Chean as the cold steel left his shoulder holster and almost slipped from his sweaty palms. No matter how hot it was, he could always run his fingers along the icy slide on his .45, and that would serve to refresh him like a day on the beach at Vung Tau or a foot beat in the air-conditioned corridors of MACV. But the cold steel also served to remind him of how cool Hue Chean had been to his advances since he had met her. As they neared what he knew to be a dead end around the dark corner ahead, Bryant was wondering if he would live to see his wedding night and the look on Chean's face when the months of restraining his lust finally exploded between her smooth, tight thighs.

"Hold it right there, Rodgers!" all three men heard Sergeant Richards yell as they trapped the elusive shadow at the barbed fenceline closing off the side street.

"Get your hands in the air—*now!*" Richards ordered, "or you're one dead motherfucker!"

The slender form before them froze in the middle of the alley then slowly rose his hands above his head until Richards could see the empty fingers spread out between twinkling stars riding high above the roofline.

All four weapons were trained on the American's back, ready to release their fury, when Richards directed him to slowly lie spread-eagle on the pavement.

"Don't shoot!" The young, unfamiliar voice hit the MPs like a bomb blast. "I don't have no guns! I didn't do nothin'!"

Richards rushed up and grabbed the American by an elbow, twirling him around before he could go to his knees as instructed.

The terrified face of a seventeen-year-old stared back at the gun barrels and his fingers reached even higher for the sky when his bulging eyes focused on all the weapons.

"Who the fuck are you?" Thomas yelled, but before the kid could answer, Sergeant Richards had whirled him back around and shoved him up against the barbed wire.

"Search him!" he ordered Broox, and the private holstered his .45 and began the pat-down.

Thomas stood to one side with his automatic in the kid's left ear and he took the wallet Broox handed him and tossed it over to Richards.

The sergeant shook his head slowly and glanced back at the dark window up in the apartment house before sifting through the American's ID cards. "I asked who the fuck are you?" Richards repeated, and when the teenager started to turn his head to answer, Thomas slammed it back up against the fence.

"Don't move until we're done searching you," Broox whispered, slightly embarrassed at his partners' high-handed tactics.

406

"I'm an American civilian," the kid answered carefully, drawing each word out slowly as his voice struggled to remain calm. It cracked anyway, when he explained, "My father is an embassy consular official. I go to New Asia High School on Tran Hung Dao. That's between Cholon and Saigon—"

"We know where it's at!" snarled Thomas. Broox let out a tortured sigh, popped the clip out of his .45 and ejected the live round. Then he holstered the weapon, unbuttoned the flak jacket and sat down heavily on a trash can at the edge of the road.

"I am an exchange student," the kid continued. "I've already been grounded for running my sister's bra up General Westmoreland's flagpole. I don't want no more trouble."

"You don't build toy model rockets as a hobby, do you?" Thomas asked sarcastically, not expecting an answer.

The youth's innocence softened Richards' temper and a laugh finally escaped him as he released the long, stress-filled breath he had been holding in his chest. He looked at the kid's form pressed flat against the barbed wire then back down at the government dependent's red ID card.

"Nick Uhernik," he read the name off. "What kind of name is that?"

"Sounds Russian to me," Bryant muttered suspiciously, but the kid could not see the smile on the MP's face.

"It's Hungarian," the teenager explained. "Means the soldier from Czechoslovakia."

"Hungarian?" asked Bryant. "Ain't they communist?"

"He's clean," Broox told the sergeant after completing the frisk.

"You can turn around now," Richards advised.

"I'm as American as you!" he said to Bryant defensively. "I was born in Pueblo, Colorado!"

"So what's the soldier from Czechoslovakia doing running around after dark through the back alleys of Saigon?"

"And without a weapon," Broox added accusingly.

"Kinda past your bed time, ain't it?" Bryant grumbled.

"Well, I was just sneakin' over to see my girlfriend. She lives on Nguyen Gong Tru. That traffic's so bad I thought I'd take a short cut down the side streets on foot. Last time I was in the area, this alley went through."

Richards now had his notebook out and was copying some information from the ID card. "I think we're gonna arrange for an MP jeep to escort you safely home," Richards decided. He expected the kid to kick the ground in protest, but he just smiled and his eyes lit up with excitement.

"Me? Ride in an MP jeep?" he asked. "Shit, that'll be more fun than hunting frogs down behind the Hotel Majestic!"

Broox and Thomas just turned and stared at each other.

"I'll never figure out the younger generation," mumbled Bryant. "Always out on the street at all hours of the night. And this is Saigon!"

Jeff Rodgers watched the four MPs walk the teenager out of the black alley and back into the stream of headlights cruising slowly along Bis Ky Dong. He moved back away from the windows as they crossed below his apartment, then returned to his chair and sat back down in the dark. From this vantage point he could survey all that went on beneath his silent world, but no one could see in unless they splashed a spotlight or flare across the window. He dared not close the drapes, for any activity in his room would be followed by the door crashing down and several people having to die.

Rodgers was doing more and more thinking about dying recently. His attempts at tracking down Jackson and Chilton had met with nothing but dead ends and false leads. It appeared Jackson had abandoned his apartment on Tung Chou and his notebook showed no address for Chilton except the signal brigade barracks, which he wouldn't go to after deserting the Army.

As he watched more and more beautiful Vietnamese women

408

leaving their stalled taxis down on the street, their sparkling eyes darting back and forth anxiously while their flowing hair mingled with the dark of night as they nervously hurried home on foot, Rodgers thought back to the picnic he and Kim had taken on the banks of the Saigon River. He asked her what she thought of all the Buddhist monks taking their lives in fiery suicides as a political protest, and she had answered she could not understand how anyone could drench themself with gasoline, then strike a match.

"I could not bear the pain," she told him. "I am not a strong person and I do not think I could find the courage to take my own life—not for any reason. No matter what we must suffer, bad times pass. Things eventually get better. When you kill yourself, then what is there? There is nothing. *Fini.*"

"But you don't believe in heaven or—" he had asked.

"If you are Catholic, then you believe there is only hell after suicide. That means fire. The burning monk dies by flame only to spend an eternity in fire."

"But the monks are Buddhist. They would believe in a better life after death. Don't you believe in reincarnation, Kim?"

"There is nothing after death, Jeff." She sounded like she believed what she said. "There is only now, today. When you die: all is *fini.*"

"I have been reading about *seppuku,*" he told her then.

"*Seppuku?*"

"Japanese ritual suicide. With a special, sacred dagger," and he had brought an imaginary sword to his stomach and plunged it up into his heart.

"No talk *dinky dau,* okay, Jeff? You scare me sometimes."

"There has to be a better world beyond the rising sun," Jeff had told her, and she was taken aback by the sincerity in his voice.

"Jeff, you must face life, not death. Saigon is all you have left now. Mai is gone forever. You will never be able to meet her beyond any rising sun. The Japanese and all their stupid rituals and beliefs are—I just have no time for them. Their arrogant businessmen come to Vietnam and expect us working girls to walk on their backs all night. Forget Japan. All things Japanese are plastic . . . phony.

"All you have left now is Saigon." Her eyes moistened and grew to look very sad. "And me."

Jeff remembered how he had moved away when she reached out to touch him. He rushed down to the river and walked along the banks for a long time, Kim following silently, protectively behind him. Until they had tired of discussing the flowers and the birds, and they raced like carefree children back up the hill to the picnic basket.

Another MP patrol raced by on the street below, its red lights piercing the fog and mist with bright, slowly revolving beams. He listened to the mournful wail fade off into the night and the sight of so many lawmen cruising past reminded him of the wanted poster he had spotted nailed to a light pole on Phan Dinh Phung. It had a crude photocopy of his likeness below a brief physical description and name. Beneath the picture was the eye catcher: "REWARD: 5,000,000 PIASTERS FOR DESERTION AND MURDER." He had torn down the bulletin and ripped it apart. Then he started laughing: to think they only put a ten thousand dollar price on his head!

Jeff listened to the battle raging over on Phan Dinh Phung and the sound of so much relentless gunfire reminded him of the talk he had had in the bar with Mark Stryker. The former Green Beret had tried to get him to turn himself in—to seek help, but Jeff had just laughed and told him "Jeff Rodgers hysteria" was so bad on the street that he'd be shot on sight.

"Perhaps a priest," Stryker had actually suggested. "You could take a priest into your confidence and he would have to grant you sanctuary until something could be worked out."

Jeff had simply laughed in Mark's face at this proposal, and when the deserter told Stryker about the time he had attended on outdoor Sunday mass at Pershing Field only to witness the chaplain catch a sniper's bullet between the eyes, Stryker just

410

got up and left the bar, shaking his head in submission.

During the initial series of shots beginning the ambush, Toi had watched Major Phuong's car skid over to the side of the road. He had seen the tracer rounds bounce harmlessly off the sedan's armor-plated roof. He was taken by surprise when the other cars, loaded down with bodyguards, protectively surrounded the officer's besieged vehicle like true professionals only to have the major bolt out a rear door in a state of confused panic. His huge frame had made an ideal target, and Toi squeezed his eyes tightly shut after two solid lines of glowing tracer merged to zero in on the man's broad back. He was only twenty feet from Toi, running straight toward the Canh-Sat, when the bullets slammed into him from behind and exited his chest, still glowing as they bounced off the pavement and ricocheted into several fleeing pedestrians.

Major Phuong had taken a dozen rifle slugs, and there was no doubt in Toi's mind that the ARVN officer was dead. He hoped the soldiers high above on the rooftops would also see this and break off the attack, but the firefight continued and even increased in intensity as American MPs, armed with M-16 rifles and M-60 machine guns, began arriving on scene.

Toi could not condone placing so many innocent civilians in the crossfire, but he understood why the rooftop snipers continued their fusillade. The memories of his days with the South Vietnamese Rangers were fresh in his mind as he hugged the blacktop beneath that parked taxi.

He knew the frenzy that possessed soldiers setting up an ambush—the latent desire to shoot down on so many helpless, unsuspecting targets had finally been authorized and unleashed. It was the power to mete out death that changed good men into evil, ruthless monsters and it was one of the reasons he had left the Army.

When the MPs all showed up with weapons blazing, Toi crawled out from beneath the peppered, blue-and-yellow

411

Renault and got down on one knee beside the thick engine block. He took aim at the muzzle flashes erupting on the roof and slowly fired a round on single action every few seconds just to make it look good. Within the hour, MACV finally authorized some gunships to enter into the hostilities, but on hearing the helicopters approach, their rotors beating dully at the thick, balmy air, the snipers melted away into the night. By the time the choppers were hovering above the rooftops, their huge searchlights playing back and forth across the tenements, the feuding soldiers had disappeared.

Toi searched the anxious faces of the MPs, now slowly leaving cover as the gunship pilot signaled the all-clear, but he failed to spot any of his friends from the Decoy Squad. He badly wanted to tell them about the diary they had found in Rocco Statterhouse's locker. The journal where he confessed to killing the unarmed Jordan during the foot chase following the cop killing at the yacht club. The dirty looks he had received for so many days following Rocco's death were most painful to Toi—he valued the Americans' friendship even above that of his fellow Canh-Sats.

When the MPs on the nearest gun jeep walked up to Toi and slapped him on the back after the shoot-out—the exhilaration of the city street fighting still racing through their blood—Toi smiled for the first time in almost a week. The brief stint of combat had made him a brother again.

"Why are you doing this?" William Sickles wiped the sweat off his brow and stared at the woman across the table from him. "We had such a wonderful relationship going. Why ruin it?"

"Money," she answered coldly. "The information you hand over to me will set me up for life. Never again will I have to sell love to survive. Never again will I have to spend my nights beside a fat American slob like you. Never again . . ."

Sickles couldn't hear the Vietnamese woman's words anymore. His eyes watched her sensuous lips moving silently as she unleashed bitter accusations against him, but he did not hear anything. As his eyes fell to the rich bosom in the low-cut evening dress, breasts pressed against the table in all their splendor, he was remembering all the nights she had made him believe she enjoyed their lovemaking.

"I cannot give you any documents from MP Headquarters," he told her. "It would mean my head. They are very careful in guarding against espionage. You've got to sign in and pass by half a dozen cameras just to take a shit. There's no way . . ."

"Saigon is full of spies. Perhaps you should take lessons from one."

"There's no way," he repeated. "They shoot spies in Saigon."

"Then I go to your wife." Her eyes burned into his with obvious hate. "I tell her everything."

"Then you wouldn't get any top secret information at all."

"But it would almost be worth it, don't you think? Me walking up to the mother of your children—me in my sexiest halter top and see-through hot pants. It would kill her, Bill. To hear how you've been screwing a girl half her age for two years now. To hear what I can do with my mouth—what I have been doing with it—she'd die! It would make her heart black to hear all that, and she would die. Right before your eyes: the pain would be unbearable to such a loyal wife as yours. The hurt would murder her!"

Sickles swallowed hard when it came time for him to respond. "I could kill you. I could take you out in the alley back there and put a bullet in your head. Nobody would care about just another whore found floating in the Saigon River." He felt terrible about saying such horrible things to a woman he still strangely cared about, but he loved his family too, and he knew he was trapped—backed into a corner.

"You won't do a damn thing to me," she said defiantly. "I have it all on tape—all of it, Bill. I kept a tape recorder under my bed! You fool. You stupid fool! Reading poetry to your Vietnamese mistress, then making the springs bounce half the

413

night—and all on tape!

"And if anything happens to me, my girlfriend hand-carries the cassettes to your wife, first class, special delivery!"

Sickles watched in silence as the beautiful woman rose to her feet.

"You better decide soon—by tomorrow night," she announced. "Now I am going to walk out of this Cheap Charlie restaurant and you're not going to do a thing about it."

The girl concentrated on making her sexy bottom bounce with each step as she marched from the room, and Sickles was not surprised when the sight of her tight, sensuous figure, now tensed in anger, aroused him just as it had the first night he saw her.

Sgt. Kip Mather stared from the window of his third-floor hospital room out across Saigon, at the tracers ricocheting off the rooftops of tenements crowding Phan Dinh Phung Boulevard. He watched the two gunships cruise low past his window in response to the call for assistance. And he watched them hover above the buildings without firing a shot, their powerful searchlights sweeping back and forth through the thick clouds of rising gun smoke.

"So sad to see the fighting right here in the city." Sister Hoa had appeared beside his bed without so much as a breath warning him.

"Yes, so sad," Mather said as he glanced down at the stump that had once been a foot.

"How is your arm, Sergeant Mather?" she asked softly. "I overheard the nurses talking, that you were having trouble adjusting to the artificial limb."

Mather flexed the shoulder muscles the way they had taught him after days of physical therapy and watched as the metal fingers opened and closed slightly. "My arm is doing fine, Sister Hoa." He forced a smile despite the intense pain that

414

flashed through the muscles and tendons. Mather gritted his teeth as the pain travelled down to where his arm had once been. He could swear he still felt the arm there—"phantom limb syndrome" the other amputees called it. You still sensed the arm's presence, felt the agony of its wound—even though it was no longer there.

"Do you know where you'll be going from here, Sergeant?" Sister Hoa asked, her hands clasped before her like the perfect little saint.

Mather wanted to tell her to get the hell out. Leave him be, so he could drown in his misery and watch the healthy Saigonese below his window rushing about to place their cockfighting bets, buy their lottery tickets or sell "gifts from the U.S.A." on the black market. "I've put in for a transfer to the Military Police Academy. If they don't boot me out of the Army," and he frowned at the probability of this. "I'd like to teach the rookies, the new MPs. Show them what to watch out for on the street, help them survive, survive this. But first I'm going home," he told her. "To see my folks."

His voice choked up when he said the word folks and the tears began rolling down his cheeks. "Can you imagine the surprise they're gonna get when their son's freedom bird touches down?" he asked, bitter sarcasm in the words.

Sister Hoa moved closer, taking the hand he had left and Mather immediately felt the warmth in her tiny, shaking fingers. "I'm sorry, Sergeant Mather." She tried to hold back her own tears as they welled up in her eyes. "I'm sorry you have to come to Vietnam so this can happen to you," and she began sobbing. She stomped her little foot on the floor, angry with herself for the lack of control, but the tears continued and she surrendered to the frustration. "I'm so very, very sorry," she repeated. "If I could take your place. If I could give you my limbs, or if I could—"

"Please, Sister Hoa," he interrupted as he hugged her small, delicate frame with his left arm. "You don't have to do this . . . say all this."

"I'm sorry, Kip," she whispered, as she buried her face in his chest. He stared up at the ceiling in hopes that would stop the flow of tears, but the pain in his soul continued to cry out and he wondered if this was the last woman who would ever hold him again.

XXIX. MISSION: OVERKILL

Rodgers stood in the darkness of the apartment, along the edge of the window, looking down on the four men from the Decoy Squad and trying to hear what was being said across the street. He was rapidly tiring of spending so much time in the dark, his movements restricted, his activities cut to zero, but what was a man in his position to do? The wanted posters advertising a five million-piaster bounty on his head were now turning up nailed to lightpoles throughout the city, and his friend Stryker had broken off contact with him.

He thought about the events leading up to Mai's death—how he had considered himself so normal, so ordinary. Just another MP with a job to do. And when your shift was up it was "catch the fastest taxi home to honey" and make the night last as long as possible. He remembered so many of those nights when he had forced himself to stay awake for hours—just so he could feel the warmth and softness, the curves of her body against his. Something you couldn't experience if you slept. He'd fight off sleep for as long as possible, knowing good and well the less rest he got, the longer the day shift would seem to last. Also knowing the longer he would stay awake, cuddled in her arms, the longer he could breathe in her scent, feel her heart beating against his, listen to her dreams without her knowing it.

He could still compare, in his mind, the way he felt toward

life when Mai was with him and how he lost all desire to continue such life after she was taken from him. Rodgers felt that, as long as he could clearly remember both of these states of mind, he had not gone crazy—the cunning and ability to reason remained, and he would be less likely to make a mistake leading to his capture.

Rodgers did not enjoy being on the run. He did not enjoy the rage that possessed him when all black men began to look like Lance Jackson and he could not rest until they were dead or he had done everything in his power to try and kill them. Rodgers felt that so long as he could clearly remember each death—could consciously retreat from each murder at the last moment if he chose to—then he had not gone insane or totally out of control. He had to maintain the control, the edge. There were just too many younger, ambitious MPs out there with so much less to trouble their innocent minds. So many enthusiastic rookies out there whose first goal in life, in their blooming law-enforcement careers, was to capture the notorious Jeff Rodgers.

He did not like the loneliness of living underground. He clearly recalled the pleasure of working hard each day so that coming home to her would be even that much more rewarding. And so long as he could remember how simple their life had once been, remember how their nights together passed so much quicker than the hell he lived now, remember why he was doing the killing and not just when or where—then he felt confident he had not lost his mind.

Rodgers knew in his heart he did not enjoy stalking the men. He knew some of them were probably innocent of any wrongdoing. He also knew it would only be insanity to continue the killings until one of those ambitious rookies was in the right place at the right time and blew Jeff free of his current tortured existence.

What he did not know was why he could not stop chasing the men who had taken her from him, why the revenge no longer satisfied him when he finally caught them. And why her memory held such power over him. Jeff did not believe he would ever see the jade lady again. He was sure the man who had stolen it from her had either lost, destroyed or long ago sold the tiny Thai dancer. It could be anywhere in Saigon right now, or anywhere outside of Saigon for that matter. And would retrieving the statue be all that important in the end? He had killed so many men who he had not even questioned about the jade lady's whereabouts. He had just stalked and murdered the life in them, and what hurt Jeff and pained him day and night was the knowledge that taking—stealing—that life from the men left him with no feelings about their fate one way or the other. He realized that that was a sign, a signal that it would soon come to an end. And knowing this saddened Jeff even more because, after all the terrible things he had done, even if his death would take him back to Mai, how could such a sensitive, innocent child take back in her arms, against her bosom, such a loathsome monster?

Rodgers slid the glass back ever so slightly so he could hear the conversation in the street below, but the swarm of traffic still being diverted along Bis Ky Dong made it impossible to tell what they were talking about. He didn't realize he was smiling as he looked down on Richards and Broox and Thomas and Bryant. He didn't realize that the arrogance and cunning that possessed him when he stalked the black men now curled his lips as he accepted the Decoy Squad's challenge, and failing to realize these things was what made Jeff Rodgers such a dangerous man.

"I want you to take this kid and get him the hell off the streets before curfew," Sergeant Richards was instructing an MP patrol that had pulled up in front of the Decoy Squad. He handed the driver the boy's dependent ID card. "He lives down on Mac Dinh Chi, behind the U.S. embassy."

The MP behind the wheel looked at his new passenger, down at the photo on the ID, then back at the teenager.

"Nick Uhernik? What kind of name is that?"

The boy shrugged his shoulders as if he'd heard that

question a thousand times. "It's Hungarian," he said. "It means—"

"The soldier from Czechoslovakia," cut in Bryant with a smile, and the members of the Decoy Squad laughed along with Nick.

"Well, did I pronounce it right?" the driver asked.

"No, but nobody ever does," he said, pulling out a pad from his pocket as though, over the years, he had made a game out of it all. He "borrowed" one of the pens out of Bryant's pocket without asking, then scribbled something on the pad. "See, you split it into three syllables and pronounce it just like it looks: You-HER-Nick."

"That's easy to remember," decided Bryant with a grin. "You, her and Nick!"

"Bryant's enthusiastic about anything that remotely sounds like it's connected with sex," Thomas made excuses for his partner.

"I think I'll just call you Nick," the driver grinned and everyone else laughed along as he started the jeep back up.

"Or you can call him the soldier from Czechoslovakia," added Bryant and this even brought a humored nod from the boy.

Sergeant Richards looked the boy over the way he often examined troublemakers in bars: he measured the boy physically, even though he was only seventeen, and decided maybe he shouldn't have come down so hard on the kid. It was something about the pained look in the eyes above the forced grin that gave this boy an air about him that said, "Sure, I'm just a kid, but I've heard it all before—gimme a break."

Richards wondered about his girlfriend—the one he claimed lived over on Nguyen Cong Tru. Whether she was American or Oriental. What his parents thought—how they felt if she was Vietnamese. How Richards would feel if he had a son and that son had an extraordinary childhood in a strange exotic land and chose to love one of the golden, almond-eyed Asian beauties.

420

Hell, the kid even looked Vietnamese, Richards laughed to himself. Dark, shifty eyed. Oh, maybe a little taller perhaps, but skinny. Dark hair kept short, almost like an Army brat. Wearing an MIA bracelet on both wrists like it was the only cause he identified with at this point in his life. Khaki safari shirt and pants like the foreign correspondents all wore, except that he had a patch on one shoulder: "ONE THOUSAND MISSIONS IN A CYCLO." And the blue eyes. Yes, he almost looked Oriental probably because he's been eating rice and fish the entire time his father's been in the foreign service, but the eyes marked his heritage. European.

Richards saw in the boy a lost innocence brought on by spending his youth in Asia. He hoped the kid would perhaps someday return to America and forget Vietnam—leave here before he was old enough to get hurt by the spell that was Saigon. While he was still young enough to remember the city only as a summer adventure and not an experience that would haunt him the rest of his life.

"I been waiting for this all night." The boy smiled from ear to ear as he got in the jeep. "Now this is where the action is. Cruising the streets of Saigon . . . racing under the banners of Tu Do! Can we stop by Tu Do and zip past the banners?" But before the driver could answer, the boy was asking another question, "Did you guys get in on that shoot-out? It sounded pretty hairy from over here. Probably the Cong, don't ya think? Damned jungle slime-suckers."

Richards folded his arms across his chest and sighed. It was too late. He was already talking like a damn GI, like an old Asian hand drinking whiskey on the terrace of the Continental Palace Hotel. The boy would only be an outcast among his own peers, Richards decided, if he returned to the states. America would be so mundane, so boring compared to the Far East. The few friends he'd make would quickly tire of all the stories, about Saigon, of the very background fiber that made him a novelty because of the exotic things he had seen and done. A curio to be displayed at the parties of arrogant snobs who knew little of faraway lands. The depression brought on by his own people and the inability to love his own homeland as much as Asia would force him back to the Orient, where only ruin could await him in the cities of sorrow.

"Now I don't wanna see ya sneakin' down any more back alleys!" Richards called out to the boy in the jeep but he didn't look back, only accorded the sergeant the slightest of waves.

And as Bryant yelled, "We don't want you shooting any more toy rockets at the tower guards anymore, either!" Richards could hear the boy telling the driver, "Someday I'm gonna be a cop too, you wait and see. I'll be back. And I'll be after your job, Specialist." The boy had laughed when he made the mild threat, but the MP laughed even harder when he replied, "Nick, you can *have* it!"

Broox didn't particularly enjoy relief shift. First of all, you had to get up at five in the morning and he didn't like rising before the sun. Sometimes he'd go out for a jog inside the camp perimeter, or if he was staying downtown he'd look out at the street and watch Saigon come alive. Whether breakfast was had downtown in a sidewalk cafe or back alley market, or at the mess hall on camp, the meal always served to energize him for the twelve-hour six a.m. to six p.m. shift. Most of the night shifts worked eleven p.m. to eleven a.m. and day shift just the opposite. The two relief shifts kept men on the streets while the night and day people rotated jeeps and equipment, attended their briefings, and endured the guardmount inspections.

No, Broox didn't particularly enjoy getting up at pre-dawn for relief shift, but the one good thing about that schedule was that it allowed him to volunteer for the Decoy Squad after the sun went back down.

One of the other things Broox could do without was the boredom and routine of the morning patrols. It was like working a regular nine-to-five job except that you went to work three hours earlier than everyone else so you could help funnel the rush hour traffic into the city. And you didn't get off duty till well after they had left for home again.

That's not to say Saigon was like your typical big city. Though the streets became deserted after curfew went into effect, there was a vibrant life and bustle of activity that continued behind the walls of tenements and housing projects spread out and piled atop each other across the downtown area. The suburbs consisted of vast plantations, old French villas or outlying hamlets that straddled the city's outskirts. The Vietnamese usually both worked and lived either in or outside Saigon. Storefront shops that opened entire front walls out onto the edge of sidewalks by day also housed hidden living quarters in the rear that lit up at night and were protected by cast-iron gates drawn across the entrances after dark.

Another thing Broox could do without were the games the GIs played with the MPs. The object to winning was see how much toilet paper, cigarettes and liquor you can smuggle down to the black market.

That's why Broox parked his patrol jeep behind the palms lining the street across from the MACV annex PX. The soldier had given him that guilty look Broox was so good at spotting. When you gave Private Broox any reason to doubt your honesty he usually hung around just to make sure you stayed out of trouble.

From beneath the shade of the palms, Broox watched the soldier leave the PX with a large box, look in both directions nervously as he walked over to the taxi, then duck into the rear seat and direct the driver to take him off post.

Broox followed at a discreet distance, painfully aware it just wasn't practical to believe he could tail a suspicious person while driving a marked military police jeep, complete with siren and red lights on the roof.

But once he entered the crowded city, the American became strangely overconfident, even relaxed, and Broox's only worry would be that the cabbie might be overly alert and mention to his passenger that an MP jeep had been following them for the last five miles from several blocks back.

The taxi eventually crossed the Tran Hung Dao bridge into Cholon and turned onto Minh Mang Street before swerving down a back alley running along behind several villas. It ended along the edge of a bombed-out cliff that overlooked the river. The cab made a U-turn on the little dead-end plateau and stopped beside a line of brick steps that ran up to the rear of one of the dwellings.

The American stepped from the taxi and started up the steps. Broox had secreted his jeep behind an abandoned truck at the top of the hill and watched the GI stumble on a loose brick in the steps. He almost dropped the heavy box but caught himself on one knee at the last second and only a corner of the carton crashed against the ground. As he hustled back to his feet and trotted up toward the rear of the building, Broox noticed something was leaking along the edges of the box near the smashed corner.

The MP waited for the taxi to climb up out of the gully and leave the area, then he walked down to the steps. He bent down where the GI had stumbled and ran his finger through drops of the liquid that had spilled from the broken container in the box. He brought it to his nose—liquor.

Broox avoided the steps and climbed up the hill to the building from behind the cover of trees and bushes. When he got up to the wall running along the rear of the house, he crept over to a window and listened.

"I'm tellin' ya, Bill," a voice came from inside. The soldier Broox had followed. "That's it. My ration card's all punched out. Now how much you gonna give me for the whiskey?"

"One hundred," a different voice answered softly. Sickles. William Sickles. Broox put his hand on his gun out of habit. He wasn't sure what he had here, but he knew a C.I.D. man would probably be armed to the teeth.

"One hundred?" the GI asked, astonished. "It's worth a thousand on the black market."

"One hundred. Take it or leave it."

Maybe Sickles was running a sting, a reverse scam where the cops posed as fences and busted criminals trying to sell stolen goods or rationed items.

"Shit, Bill. You're just gonna sell it on the black market yourself. Okay, five hundred."

"One hundred."

"Jesus H. Christ. Okay, okay—I'll steal some of the guys' ration cards and bring 'em to you tomorrow."

"Here's two hundred bucks," Sickles said and Broox could hear the box being shifted around on the floor inside as if it had just switched owners. "Now get the fuck out."

Broox ducked down behind the hedge groves just as the GI walked out the back door, folding his money and stuffing it in a pocket. After the door slammed shut, Broox overheard the soldier mutter, "Goddamn cops. Can't trust none of 'em."

The MP waited below the window for several minutes, hoping to hear other C.I.D. agents gather from their hiding places to discuss how the undercover operation went, but the back room remained quiet. Broox cautiously peeked through the window, this time hoping to see Sickles filling out a recognizable police form, or pulling the cassette tapes from a hidden recorder. But the man was just sitting at a table, nervously examining his fingernails while a plain-featured Thai woman in her midforties massaged his shoulders from behind. Boxes of liquor and cigarettes were stacked along one wall all the way to the ceiling.

"Daddy! Daddy!" Three little girls had chased each other into the room from the front of the house, but they stopped frozen beside the table when their mother glared at them.

The look on the jaded woman's face demanded silence, but when the oldest child, the girl who had just been a little princess in the school play, looked up at the unsmiling man at the table, she innocently asked, "What's wrong with Daddy?"

The blazing noonday sun beat down on Sgt. Gary Richards as

he led the procession down busy Tu Do Street on foot, and the farther he walked, the redder his face turned. He wore a black robe over army trousers with red sashes around the waist. In his arms was a large, circular tray filled with betel leaves, areca nuts, envelopes of expensive chrysanthemum tea, rice cakes and butterscotch candies wrapped in decorative plastic.

Behind Richards walked Timothy Bryant, also dressed in black with red sashes around his waist. He looked like a man being escorted to the gallows, judging by the expression on his face. A few steps behind him and on either side walked Broox and Thomas, both similarly dressed and leading small goats and pigs on long leashes.

As they neared the entrance to the Xin Loi nightclub, where Bryant's fiancée, Hue Chean, resided with her parents in the living quarters built into the rear of the bar, Richards spotted an MP patrol slowly cruising toward them.

"Oh oh"—he turned back to face Bryant—"here comes some of the troops. Looks like razz time."

"Sorry, Sarge," whispered Bryant, "but Vietnamese customs says we gotta present these gifts to the family before the wedding. And we gotta wear these clothes."

"I gotta admit," Broox told Richards as the MP jeep got closer, "you are a sight—notorious Decoy Squad sergeant traipsing down raunchy Tu Do in a robe!"

"Aw, come on you guys!" Bryant pleaded, "I wanna do this right! Ritual says the groom's oldest relative must lead the procession to the bride's home. And you know Sarge here is the oldest thing I got—I mean the closest thing I got to an oldest relative in Vietnam."

"Thanks a lot," said Richards sarcastically.

"Christ, they're pulling right up to the Xin Loi," observed Thomas. He recognized the men, one white, one black.

"I wonder why," said Broox. "It's only a little after noon— why would they be makin' a bar check in the middle of the day? Half the hookers aren't even up yet."

But the MPs only got out of their vehicle, then leaned

against the side of it, arms folded, smiles growing wider as they recognized the Decoy Squad slowly marching through the dust.

"Hey, you're jaywalking," the white MP called out to them.

"Well, if it ain't the salt and pepper team," declared Thomas.

"You guys workin' undercover or something?" asked Pvt. Craig Davis with a laugh as he took in Richards' long robe.

"I don't wanna hear *no*thing from you clowns," the sergeant replied.

"What you AWOLs doing here, anyway?" asked Thomas. "Isn't your squad on alert duty?"

"Yeah—confined to post," Broox said hopefully.

"Wishful thinking," the white MP said, and Davis calmly reached in under his fatigue shirt and brought out a brightly decorated red envelope. "Hey, we're here by invitation!" He smiled innocently, and the Decoy Squad all turned to stare at Bryant accusingly.

"I needed some moral support," he admitted sheepishly.

"And extra cops to drag his ass up to the altar!" translated the white MP.

"So why the uniforms?" inquired Richards.

"Hey, we're gonna do this with class!" declared Davis as he pulled two long, ceremonial swords from the back of the jeep. "We gonna have us a genuine military marriage today." He unsheathed one of the glittering blades and swished it around wildly, cutting the thick air hugging Saigon like an invading samurai warrior.

"Did you *really* invite these maniacs?" Richards asked Bryant.

"'Fraid so, boss." He was turning red also. After Davis and his partner hooked the swords up to their web-belts, all six men started up the steps to the Xin Loi bar.

When they entered through the swinging front doors, hundreds of firecrackers fell from the roof behind them, crackling, exploding, and sending Davis diving under a table.

Several young women waiting inside the nightclub began giggling at the results of the surprise greeting, and as the Americans' eyes began adjusting to the dark interior of the building, dozens of red, orange and gold Chinese lanterns suspended from the ceiling lit up, and Vietnamese wedding music sounded from the wall speakers that usually emitted blaring rock and roll.

"Too much!" Thomas grinned with sudden excitement as his startled eyes took in all the colorful decorations and the beautiful bride's maids in their attractive gold and black *ao-dai* gowns.

"Now comes the hard part," Bryant warned his friends.

"The hard part?" Thomas lost the smile, growing instantly suspicious and apprehensive.

"Where's Hue Chean?" Sergeant Richards' eyes darted about the huge room but there was no sign of the woman.

"That's the hard part," Bryant explained. "All her girlfriends got her hidden either upstairs or in a bedroom somewhere. It's up to us to find her, pay the ransom if they'll even release her to me, then split before they change their minds."

"Ransom?" Broox swallowed hard. "Hey, Tim buddy. I'm broke till payday."

Richards laughed. "I assume the food and animals here are the ransom," he said.

"And these." Bryant grinned as he pulled several small red envelopes with gold Chinese script on them. "I've already got the gratuities stashed inside. All you guys gotta do is give them to whoever holds their hands out," and then he began passing out the envelopes that contained twenty-dollar bills inside.

"And be sure to *pass* them *out*." Richards eyed each man individually with mock suspicion.

Bryant walked up to the closest bridesmaid, bowed, and asked in Vietnamese where his fiancée was. The woman giggled and briefly hid her face in her hands, then ran off without answering. The other girls in the background were all looking at the American as if he had overdone his entrance and was combining a little too much of the old marriage rites with modern-day customs.

"Okay, where is Hue Chean?" Bryant grinned, but the women all just laughed in return and began talking in hushed whispers among themselves, many producing brightly colored fans to cover their faces.

A vehicle skidded up outside, its wailing siren breaking the tense silence, and in a few seconds Saigon policeman Jon Toi had raced up the steps and rushed into the bar, a huge bible in his hands.

His dramatic appearance set the women to chattering again and the MPs to laughing. "So sorry I'm late, Tim," the Canh-Sat apologized to Bryant, a worried look on his face.

"Hey, we're just getting started, Toi, ol' buddy," Davis told him.

"But why the bible?" Richards smiled again.

"Yeah, I thought this was a Buddhist ceremony," said Broox.

"Just want to make sure everything's legal," Toi said. "You can't ever trust these bonzes too much."

"What the hell is a bonze?" asked Thomas.

"A monk," advised Toi. "And since I'm an official of the Saigon government, we'll just ensure Tim leaves this place in genuine wedlock."

"Thanks a whole bunch, buddy," the groom frowned.

A wave of laughter unrelated to Toi's comments suddenly rolled down from a room upstairs—several girls joking about something or other—and Thomas led the charge up the stairwell. "Let's go!" Bryant was right behind him. "They've got my old lady prisoner up there somewhere!" and the rest of the MPs fell in behind the groom, laughing all the way.

Several more women in the traditional form-hugging *ao-dais* appeared at the top of the stairs, however, blocking their path. "Let us through! Let us through!" Broox demanded, but the women all locked arms and would not back down.

Ten minutes of bargaining in pidgin Vietnamese followed—the women all refused to speak English, making it as hard on Bryant as possible—then several of the red envelopes were handed over, and Bryant and Richards were allowed to pass.

One door to his right was brightly decorated with the Chinese symbols of good fortune and happiness, and Bryant chose this one to knock on. Several giggles came from inside, but the door remained tightly shut. Richards slipped another red envelope under the door and it soon opened slightly, but there was a chain across the latch on the other side, preventing entry. Despite several more minutes of pleading on Bryant's part, the women would not cooperate and their laughter was often drowned out by the bleating of the goats downstairs. When a baby hog began squealing, Richards pointed anxiously down the steps toward the sound for the girls' benefit, trying his sign language to convince them even more ransom waited for the bride's family down on the ground floor. Bryant had been holding a small box behind his back during the entire conversation and he showed it to the girls now.

It was obvious the women behind the door were not impressed with the little red envelopes and didn't intend to surrender their hostage until Bryant's box was opened and Richards said, "See! Gold coins!"

The door closed slightly, and as the two Americans heard the chain sliding off, they gently forced the door open and brushed the surprised women aside as they rushed in, tossing the box in the air for the women to catch.

When Bryant saw Hue Chean standing in the back of the room with flowers clustered in her tiny hands to hide her face, he stopped in his tracks. He had never seen her looking so beautiful, and even Richards was taken aback by her stunning appearance. She wore a shimmering violet *ao-dai* and a purple veil laced with a collage of fresh flowers and colorful ribbons.

The sergeant remained behind as Bryant started walking toward her. When he held out his hands in nervous anticipation, Richards actually felt like the relieved father when she rushed forward into his arms and kissed him lightly against the cheek.

The couple then ran arm in arm out of the room and down the stairs, and Richards was left behind to explain to the irate bridesmaids why the gold coins were only chocolate candies wrapped in gold paper and stamped to look like money.

Scattered applause greeted Tim and Chean as they arrived back on the ground floor.

"What happens now?" Broox was smiling like a proud and honored brother.

"Where's the ring?" Davis asked Thomas.

"Who's got the ring?" Thomas exploded nervously to show it hadn't been his responsibility.

"The rings." Broox looked toward Bryant for guidance. "Who has them?"

"I gave them to Dong for safekeeping," the groom announced.

"You gave them to Dong?" Every MP in the room exploded in shock and disbelief.

"You gave gold jewelry to a shoeshine boy?" Thomas laughed in amazement. "For *safekeeping?*"

"You've lost your marbles, Tim," Davis confirmed. "Bryant's lost his marbles in Saigon."

"Toi, you better put an APB out on Dong." Thomas laughed. "But I'm sure he's—"

Just then little Dong entered the nightclub through the swinging front door. He went directly over to Davis and stuck a hand out, palm up, nervously. "You dropped these," he said. "When I give you shoeshine last week." Three speed-loaders with .38-caliber bullets attached sparkled up at Davis, and before he could grill the boy about the incident where Davis was left out of bullets while three VC charged down on him with bayonets, Dong slipped a thin lacquerwood box from under his miniature tuxedo jacket and solemnly tiptoed up to the couple, the case balanced ceremoniously on outstretched arms.

After Bryant bowed and accepted the rings, a Buddhist monk in bright orange robes was escorted from a back room by Hue Chean's father, while the bride's mother looked on with mixed feelings from the balcony above. She had always hoped her daughter would eventually marry a wealthy Chinese landowner, but her tears were of joy and happiness nonetheless.

The Americans all bowed to the monk reverently but the elderly bonze acknowledged them with only a slight nod of his shaved head. He walked up to the couple, raised his arms before the makeshift altar set up atop the bar counter, and began reciting a flurry of incantations even before the bridesmaids had lit all the incense and joss sticks mounted before the long statue of a golden reclining Buddha.

The ceremony lasted only a few minutes before the bonze disappeared through the smoke into the backroom from which he had come, pausing only a second to speak the customary words of best wishes to the newlyweds.

Bryant and Hue Chean remained frozen before the altar, however, their heads bowed in silent prayer as the bride's father repeated several verses from an ancient scroll he had taken from a tiny jewel-encrusted chest inside the altar.

The entire ceremony had been in Vietnamese, and when a tense silence fell over the room, Broox asked Thomas, "Is that it? Are they married?"

Toi walked up to the couple at that moment and presented them with the official marriage license he had picked up downtown only hours earlier. It was stamped and signed by the chief of police himself as well as the necessary bureaucrats.

"Congratulations." Toi beamed. "It's now official. You are man and wife."

Tim kissed Chean lightly on the lips after slipping the wedding ring on her finger. She took the other ornately carved band of twenty-two-carat Vietnamese gold and placed it on her husband's finger.

"*Ann u emh u lumh,*" she said softly as his lips brushed against her cheek again.

"I love you, too," he responded, and Bryant could not remember a time in his life when he had been happier.

"Outside, to the porch," Richards directed the couple. He knew the second part of the marriage ritual required a trip to the Buddhist temple where another series of prayers were offered to the gods.

After Bryant shook little Dong's hand, he led his new bride to the door but was surprised to see Craig Davis and his partner blocking the exit. Officer Toi suddenly blew his traffic whistle shrilly and the two MPs snapped to attention, paced away from each other sharply until they had left a space between them through which the bride and groom could reach the door. Then they executed an about-face, drew their gleaming swords and touched the tips to create an arch under which the couple would exit their wedding ceremony in the best of luck and good wishes.

"They're doing all this in reverse," Broox whispered to Thomas, "so the drawn weapons won't offend the Buddhists and their priest."

Bryant took Hue Chean's arms in his and ducked through the sparkling archway into the sunlight beyond. A dozen sirens and flashing lights greeted them and Bryant was moved to tears at the sight of two companies of American military policemen standing in formation in the middle of Tu Do Street, saluting him and his bride.

After the couple waved their appreciation and Chean threw the MPs a kiss, the hundred men in full police dress uniform began applauding and cheering.

As the newlyweds waited for their colorfully decorated French Citroën convertible to pull up in front of the Xin Loi, Officer Jon Toi appeared between them and the soldiers standing at parade rest under the bright, fluttering banners suspended between lightpoles across Tu Do Street. "I think we should make sure they're *really* married," Thomas joked at Toi softly, so the other MPs standing in the street couldn't hear. "All that traditional ceremony in there was nice and pretty,

433

but it was all in Vietnamese. How do we know he's *really* married?"

"Yeah," agreed Broox. "What assurance do *we* have this clown can't walk out on Hue Chean on a technicality?"

Bryant laughed, but Chean eyed him with mock suspicion as her eyes narrowed, "You no butterfly me, would you, Timmy?"

Toi took both their right hands gently and said, "Miss Hue, we shall just make sure, right here and now, before you go any farther."

To the applause of the troopers resuming the position of attention out in the street behind him, Toi placed the newlyweds' hands on the badge above his heart and asked, "Timothy Bryant, do you promise to love, honor and protect this woman as her husband, under all circumstanes, harsh or pleasant, so long as you both shall live?"

Bryant looked into his bride's eyes and said, "Of course I do, Officer Jon Toi."

"And Miss Hue, do you promise to love, honor and obey this man as his wife, no matter what crisis may arise in your marriage, so long as you both shall live?"

"I will always love, honor and obey you, Timmy," she answered the question as if her husband had asked it, ignoring Toi.

Toi turned around and faced the MPs out on the street. "I would say that they are definitely, officially and without-a-doubt married forever," he declared, and as Tu Do Street erupted into a clamor of sincere applause, Tim and Chean were escorted over to the ribbon-covered convertible that had rolled up in front of the Xin Loi and ushered into the rear seat.

After Richards and Thomas quietly closed the doors behind them, two MP jeeps activated their flashing lights and blaring sirens and, amidst another downpour of firecrackers from the roof, escorted the newlyweds down Tu Do Street and into downtown Saigon to the Xa Loi temple for the customary prayer service.

"You going over to the Caravelle for the reception?" Richards asked Thomas and Broox after the sirens had faded off in the distance.

"Well, I wasn't planning to," said Broox. "I gotta work tonight."

"What?" Thomas' eyes flashed in surprise. "And abandon Tim in his finest hour? No way, banana breath," and he and Richards proceeded to carry the protesting private over to the nearest MP jeep. "Take his ass over to the Caravelle!" Thomas spoke like he was instructing a Cholon cabbie to take his drunk buddy back to the barracks.

"Yeah, he can help set out the wine and cookies in the reception hall," Richards decided. "With all those cute, little Orientals racing about in their *ao-dais*, we're sure to find *him* a new wife, too."

Broox thought about all the cherry girls that would be attending the reception, and as he envisioned their petite, slender figures accented by the gowns—slit seductively up the sides from ankle to waist and covering tight, black satin pantaloons—he changed his mind.

"The man's got a point there!" Broox leaned over and slapped the driver on the shoulder. "Get me to the wedding on time!" he declared, and the MP jeep accelerated down Tu Do Street, its siren yelping every few blocks just for the hell of it.

Sergeant Richards was mildly upset when the conversation he was having with two waitresses on the rooftop cafe of the Caravelle was interrupted by an excited private who wasn't even a member of his squad.

"Sergeant Richards, I just gotta talk with you!" the private insisted, ignoring the woman standing beside the NCO and the bargirl on his lap.

"Can't you see I'm busy, pal?" he winked, motioning slightly with a facial expression down toward the woman's shapely behind propped across his lap. "We're discussing the

435

finer points of martial law and what effects it's having on the livelihood of these lovely lasses." The private glanced down at the sergeant's hand which was hidden from view—the bargirl was sitting on it.

"Hey, I'm really sorry, Sarge, but I just *really* gotta see you—in private," and he passed a ten-dollar bill to each girl. "Sorry, ladies."

They snatched up the greenbacks with an irritated expression, and the girl on Richards' lap got up, reached under her dress with no embarrassment whatsoever, shifted her panties back in place, and walked stiffly back to the bar.

"This better be damn good, pal," the sergeant gritted his teeth and wiped the fingers of one hand on the tablecloth before lighting up a cigarette. "If you ain't really in the shitter, you can bet your ass you're gonna be."

"Oh yes, Sarge, I'm definitely up to my ass in shit this time, and the guys said you were one of the few NCOs in the battalion a soldier in trouble could safely go to."

"So what's the crisis?"

"I'm gonna level with you from the beginning, Sarge. I got this problem: I'm a junkie."

Richards had always classified the MP as a doper in the first place, but the honesty and frankness surprised the sergeant. *Okay, so I'll listen to the jerk,* Richards told himself. *After all, he is one of the men, even if he is a bad cop.*

"I was over in Cholon a couple weeks ago, hard up for cash, when these two Vietnamese creeps stopped me and asked if I needed an all-nighter, cheap. Said they had some real cherry girls in stock that week. Well, the last thing I needed was a piece of ass, but I guess I was pretty strung out, and before I knew it I was in the sack with some schoolgirl from Thu Duc. A few days later two other guys corner me—they got these real creepy foreign accents, Russian or German or something."

Jesus, this guy can't even distinguish between Russians and Germans, Richards thought to himself. *Got me a real winner here.*

436

"They inform me they know I work at the Information Center beneath MACV. They know I have access to all kinds of secret shit, okay?"

Just like the Army, Richards thought. *Place a doper with all kinds of blackmail potential smack in the middle of your top secret computer terminal nucleus.*

"Well, you know, I'm on restricted status with limited access—certainly nothing any lousy spies want to get their hands on. I mean there's nothing I could steal that would compromise national security, but these goons don't know that. They say they know I've got all the MI access codes."

"Why would they say that?"

"Hell, I don't know—maybe that damn schoolgirl, maybe I brag in my sleep, I don't know."

"Continue," Richards said in a tired tone.

"Well, I think I'm mixed up with the KGB."

Richards shot up in his seat, the obvious sudden interest flashing across his face.

"So they don't really threaten me or nothing. They just ask me if I need some quick cash. Well, as always, I'm hard up for some 'p' but these assholes want some specific computer readouts—they show me a whole list of crap they're after."

Richards gave the private an accusing stare, chock full of disapproval.

"Well, damn, Sarge. Sure, maybe I'm a punk, good-for-nothing pothead, but I ain't no fucking traitor. You see my drift?"

Several drunks, wandering up from the wedding reception downstairs, danced with each other past Richards' table, waving and belching as they glided by, the music from the Vietnamese band on the ground floor swirling up the stairwell like rolling thunder whenever the doors flew open. Richards ignored the private for a few seconds as he concentrated on the woman's voice leading the band. Damn, if it didn't sound like CBC's Hoang Thi Thao. He had asked her to sing at Tim's reception, but, probably because of the scene he had made at the La Pagode bar the night the general caught a grenade in his lap, she declined, saying there were no free nights on her busy schedule. Not enough notice, she smiled sadly, seeming sincere. He was glad she had made time for the newlyweds after all.

A bargirl wearing a see-through blouse and little else sat down at their table, but the private paid her no attention. Richards glanced at her ample chest and wondered if the modest Hue Chean knew the servants were dressed so skimpily. Both men sat in silence until the woman got the message and stood up to leave.

"Sorry, honey." The sergeant smiled at her, but she just shrugged her shoulders and said, "It don't matter, Joe. Maybe next time."

When the woman was out of earshot, the private continued, "So these pricks from Moscow—"

"Moscow?"

"Wherever they're from—hell, Hanoi may have sent some old turncoat Frenchman down even, I don't know. So, anyway, these pricks stick some bucks in my palm and call it a present. They say I don't have to do nothing with it. Buy some dope, buy some cunt, put it in a savings account. They just don't care.

"A week later the amount doubles, but this time they want something in exchange for it—documents, computer discs, MI tape reels. They don't really care again. 'Just something to take back up to the honcho,' they tell me. Hell, they want stuff I ain't got! They demand results and I ain't got nothing to exchange, you know? Well, they threaten to turn over these photos they say they got to my commander."

"Photos?"

"They claim they got some pictures of me getting a skulljob from this underaged teenager they originally stuck me in the sack with. Plus, they say they've got photos of her shootin' me up with H."

"Is it true?"

"Hell, probably. I was so strung out they coulda took snapshots of me humpin' a monkey and I wouldn't have remembered it."

"So how can I help?" Richards asked seriously, now having second thoughts about ever getting involved with a doper tangled in KGB trouble.

"Well, they want the stuff tomorrow night," he said. "Or else they tell my C.O. I'm into drugs."

He probably already knows, Richards thought to himself again, but he asked, "Where's the drop-off point?"

"Rear of the Queen Bee, 106 Nguyen Hu."

"I know where it is located."

"So will you help, Sarge? I don't intend to give nobody no secret type information, but I don't want, 'Traitor' stamped on my tombstone neither."

"Yeah, I'll cover you," Richards decided calmly. *At least this jerk's making an effort to come clean.*

The stake out was in place a couple hours after sunset.

Richards had arranged to have two MPs sitting inside the bar at the counter. Two more occupied a table beside the rear doors. The owner had okayed two more men on the roof and two more, Thomas and Broox, were sitting across the back alley in the Decoy Squad jeep. Bryant and his new bride had left the day before on their honeymoon east to Hong Kong, and wouldn't be back for three weeks—if Hue Chean could put up with him for that long.

All the MPs were armed with pistols and the men on the roof had M-16 automatic rifles. Richards instructed each pair of men to stick close together so they'd have a witness to everything that transpired.

A second unmarked jeep with two additional military policemen aboard was parked three blocks down Nguyen Hu, waiting.

Richards sat in one of the blue and yellow Renault taxis

across the street from the Queen Bee's front doors. He was in civilian clothes, as were the rest of the men in the bar and the Decoy Squad. The MPs on the roof were in full uniform with combat gear.

The private who was being blackmailed sat nervously on the rear steps of the establishment. He was unarmed. Richards had told Staff Sergeant Schell about the mission, an attempt to catch some KGB agents with their hand in the cookie jar, but he bypassed the command officers of PMO because he feared they might not approve of getting involved in matters better handled by MI or the C.I.D.

Immediately after the private had told him of the KGB scam, Richards had purchased six inexpensive walkie-talkies from a pawn shop in Cholon. They would have to suffice as far as communications for the operation went—he dared not approach MPI for a bodytap for fear they would get too suspicious and want to take over the sting. The present setup would have to do.

Staff Sergeant Schell assured Richards he'd have a platoon from the Alert Reaction Force on stand-by at the barracks in case he needed an emergency backup.

Stake outs can be the most boring, tiresome phase of policework. Hours of silence, passive idleness, anticipation. All activity directed at the target subject. Or waiting for the target subject to appear or be located. Then waiting. Waiting for the crime to take place. Waiting to gather enough evidence to make a good, solid bust that would not be thrown out of court later on a technicality.

The stake out Richards had put together was a bit different. It was doubtful anything would go to court. And they didn't have to wait for a crime to go down, although they might be patient, hang back and see how far the target subjects would go. Richards' main objective was to swoop down on the Russian agents with enough show of force that there would be no resistance and he could capture a batch of Soviet spies: overkill. Now wouldn't PMO love that!

The waiting game had lasted nearly five hours until—minutes before curfew—there came a sudden transmission over the portable radios.

"Phantom six, this is phantom one," Richards called into the mike. "Any movement?" The MPs on the roof shook their heads in the negative.

"Phantom four, phantom one, what's your status?" he asked the men inside the bar.

"Phantom one, phantom four . . . just a lot of hot leg in here," answered a wise guy. Sarcastic clicks on the radio followed.

"Phantom one, phantom two," came the transmission from the jeep parked at the end of the block. "One spook type just got out of a black sedan in the two hundred block Nguyen Hu . . . heading toward the target location wearing dark clothing, black bush hat, appears Caucasian, heavy-set."

The eerie silence that followed the warning was broken as charging handles chambered hot rounds into the rifles on the roof.

"Phantom one to all ghosts," said Richards. He was leaning in an alley shadow across the street from the Queen Bee. "I've got an eyeball on the suspects. They're headed around back. Now let's all be cool—I don't want anyone getting trigger-happy. Yet."

Richards followed the man—at a safe distance, careful not to be spotted—down the alley that ran off Nguyen Hu a half block down from the bar, then came up around to the rear of the business. He was disappointed there was only one "spy" walking into his trap, but maybe now that baby-faced Lieutenant Faldwin would get off his back. Pressure on the Decoy Squad to produce more arrests had been increased lately—but the armchair batmen at Puzzle Palace just didn't realize the cowboys were getting wise to the unit's tactics. The quantity of arrests was slightly down, but the quality was still there and they didn't seem to realize that was the important thing.

Richards watched the man, his face kept dark by the wide-brimmed hat, walk up to the doper bait and make contact. The private was handed a small envelope, and he in turn produced a box containing blank reel-to-reel tapes stamped with labels that read, "CLASSIFIED—MI, PROJECT ARCHANGEL."

"It's going down," Richards stated over the radio, but before he could advise his men to move in, the MPs on the roof had already leaped down onto the Russian's back, one yelling, "Halt! Military Police!" and the other, "Geronimo!" Dollar bills flew from the startled private's hands and filled the night air as the reel-to-reel tapes clattered to the ground and began unrolling wildly in all directions.

Richards rushed up and tackled the commie bear from behind, knocking the big man to the ground roughly as a half dozen weapons were trained on him.

"We are American military policemen!" Richards yelled as he jammed his .45 in the agent's neck, below the back of his skull. "You are being detained until—"

"I know who you are," the face-down man answered in fluent, unaccented English. His voice faltered, sounding both embarrassed and ashamed.

Richards grabbed the man by the arm and rolled him over onto his back.

"Jesus Christ!" gasped an astonished Broox. "It's the C.I.D. man. Sickles."

XXX. CITY OF SORROWS

The dead VC soldier—the one with the back of his head missing and his eye sockets blown out—was dragging Stryker down to the bottom of the river. The Green Beret fought to escape toward the surface, but hard as he tried, he could not free himself from the clutches of the corpse that was rapidly sinking deeper . . . deeper. Stryker could no longer hold his breath, and as the last of his air bubbles exploded from his chest, the sound of his lungs deflating was strongly like giant bells pounding against his temples.

When Stryker sprung up in bed, his chest soaked with sweat, he found that the giant bells pounding at his temples were actually his telephone ringing. It took several seconds for him to realize he was safely in his room at Saigon's Miramar Hotel on Tu Do Street and not on that riverbank outside Pleiku where his A-Team had assassinated the sampan-full of Viet Cong cadre five months earlier.

Stryker let the phone ring while he felt along the nightstand for his watch, and as he ran his fingers along the edge of the table beside his bed he noticed his hand was shaking uncontrollably. The nightmares were getting worse, and as he examined the Seiko all he could see was the dead VC rolling over in the river—his hollow and bloodied eye sockets staring back at him above a mocking grin.

"Hello?" He finally lifted the receiver, expecting a dead line with nothing but ghosts on the other end.

"Stryker, this is Bill. Bill Sickles. Did I wake you?"

"Bill?"

"Yeah, Sickles. C.I.D. Uh, I used to be with C.I.D."

"Oh right. Sickles." Stryker's mind was beginning to wake up, and he could remember reading about Sickles in the newspaper the day before. Arrested by his own cops on espionage charges. He was out on his own recognizance, pending a hearing, claiming the MPs had interrupted his own undercover operation.

"Are you awake now, Mark? I have some information for you, but I want to make sure you're hearing me. I don't want you falling back asleep on me."

"I'm awake, damnit. Believe me, I'm awake. What is it, Sickles?"

"The jade lady."

"What?" Stryker wiped more sleep from his eyes, scraping his palms hard against the eyelids until the dark came alive with swirling stars, chased about faster the harder he pressed against the pain.

"The jade lady, Mark. I have the statue."

"Where are you?"

"Home. I'm home. Can you come over?"

"Now?"

"I know it's late. But I've got some other things to discuss."

"Where did you find the Thai dancer?" Stryker asked.

"It's not important. One of my informants located it in a shoeshine boy's box. I'm not even sure it's the one everyone's looking for." Stryker wasn't sure he'd know the statue if he saw it either.

"I don't know if I can get over there." Stryker was trying to focus his eyes on the watch. "Jesus, Sickles. It's three in the morning. There's a curfew out there, you know?"

"Just get over here," Sickles said, a fatal urgency in his voice, and the line went dead.

444

Stryker, still sitting up in bed, replaced the phone on the nightstand and stared across the room at the tapestry of Lai he had brought down to Saigon. It was an excellent likeness, done in bright oils on black felt, and it showed her standing before a field of bamboo, her eyes barely visible below the rim of a peasant girl's conical straw hat. Stryker picked up the letter from Perkins and read it again, hoping perhaps the words had changed overnight to suit his needs:

Mark,

I talked again with all the women in the compound and even had the Strike Force members talk to their relatives in the nearby villages, but no one has seen or heard of Lai. We have no idea what has happened to her. But who can figure women?

Hoa binh,
Alan

Stryker laid the note on the nightstand and rolled out of bed and into a pair of jeans. He wasn't sure how he was going to get past all the security checkpoints and roadblocks between Saigon and its sister city of Cholon, but it couldn't be as difficult as operating behind enemy lines. Might even be fun—a challenge to his rusting insurgency skills.

Rodgers stood beneath the grinning moon, hidden in an alley shadow, licking his lips and holding himself back until the police jeep passed. Then he rushed across the avenue known by many names but labeled Dong Khanh, and slipped into the Cholon Hotel.

He drew his .45 and pulled the slide back to make sure a hollow-point was firmly seated in the chamber. *Thank Buddha for Kim,* he thought, as he moved slowly toward room nineteen. She had spotted the black man with the shaved head and unique tooth at the Nguyen Trai open-air market. Had followed him back to the Dong Khanh address.

He tested the doorknob. Locked. Of course. Anything else would have been unacceptable under the circumstances. *Yes, good ol' Kim,* he decided. *Took a lot of guts for her to trail such a crafty devil all the way back here—even get his room number—then report to him the information and require only a hug as payment.* Rodgers was sure it was Kim who also slipped small envelopes of money under his door at the Bis Ky Dong safe house every other week. Her whoring money. He still couldn't understand her misplaced loyalty to him, so he had stashed every piaster away, refusing to spend it, living instead off the savings he and Mai had managed to set aside. Someday he would be able to return it all to Kim. When this thing was all over.

Jeff Rodgers pulled the M-26 grenade from his pocket and taped it securely to the doorknob. He pulled the pin and dashed around the nearest corner, flattening himself across the floor just before the explosion tore the door and half the wall down with it. He was back on his feet even before the splinters had settled, tossing a second grenade into the room. He could hear the moaning between concussions, and after the second detonation he ran into the room, fanning his pistol from wall to wall, squinting his eyes against the thick smoke.

Lance Jackson was at his feet, unconscious. He rushed over the body, into the bedroom, and found Chilton sitting up in his bed, tiny puncture marks covering his face and chest like measels—where the exploding shrapnel had torn into him. The man was reaching for the shotgun beside the bed and Jeff leveled his .45 at the deserter's chest. "Touch it and you die tonight," Rodgers told him calmly, but Chilton kept reaching for the twelve gauge.

"You gonna kill this nigger anyway!" Chilton screamed. "You gonna make me cut my black pecker off, ain't you!" and the man in the bed grabbed the shotgun and placed it against his throat as if he planned on denying Rodgers his vengeance.

446

"Don't!" Rodgers screamed, and he adjusted his aim to try and take out the man's gun arm and jerked off two quick rounds.

The first hollow-point tore into the man's chest, ripping away his dirty, weeks-old bandage to reveal a layer of maggots and squirming worms covering the infection, slowly eating the man away.

The second round struck the shotgun stock just behind the trigger, shattering the weapon in two, but it discharged just the same and Rodgers watched in disappointment and anger as the nine-mm pellets exploded up through Chilton's lower jaw, shredding the defiant smile off his face as it popped his skullcap off from inside and splattered his gutter personality all over the ceiling.

"You son of a bitch!" Rodgers was screaming now. "Don't die, you son of a bitch!" and he walked over to the man and aimed his .45 at the green, discolored hole scabbing his chest and pulled the trigger.

The impact of the hollow-point came across as a dull, powerless thud, but the result was like dropping a cinder block in a stagnant pond—blood, maggots and undigested food splashed back at him in a revolting wave. Just as he was struck from behind and smashed to the floor.

Lance Jackson kicked Rodgers in the face as hard as he could, two times—was bringing his boot back for a third kick when Rodgers rolled clear and brought up his .45.

But Jackson already had his snub-nosed .38 pointed at the back of Rodgers' head and both men fired at the same time.

Jackson was somersaulted off his feet when the hollow-point found his right shoulder. The black man's aim was just as good, however, and Rodgers felt the dum-dum punch him in the stomach like a sledge hammer, then pass completely through his body like a sizzling, steel rod and crack the wood floor beneath him.

Rodgers, blood oozing between his fingers as he clutched at the gut wound, struggled to his feet and started over toward the

447

moaning Jackson, flat on his back, a thin stream of blood spurting from his shoulder wound like the colored fountains in front of the Rex cinema. The impact had jolted his revolver out of his hand.

"Get up, punk," Rodgers demanded. "Or I'll shoot you where you lie. Get up, you sniveling dog!" And as the man, through anger more than fear, pulled himself rigid with an awkward sit-up maneuver, Rodgers let loose with another round, striking Jackson in the right lung.

"That was for Mai," Rodgers whispered in the black man's ear as he knelt down beside him. "You remember Mai, don't you?" But the only answer was air rushing in and out of the hole in Jackson's chest with a sickening gurgle. Rodgers pulled out his switchblade and flicked it open before the man's dazed, uncaring eyes. "You're gonna die with your prick in your mouth, Lance. I'm gonna carve you up and you aren't going to hell a whole man. I'm going to—"

But Jackson, still conscious though falling into the dark pit of shock, reached up with his good left hand and clamped his fingers around Jeff's throat. It was an iron-tight grip. The kind a man produces when he knows he is going to die and this last effort must be his best, his strongest. Go out fighting, regardless of the consequences.

Rodgers could feel his windpipe being squeezed tightly shut. He could feel the dizziness already coming on as the oxygen no longer flowed freely to his lungs.

In one quick movement, he lowered the .45 to Lance Jackson's groin and pulled the trigger three times, feeling the man's fingers jerked from his throat as the impacting bullets bounced his frame into the floor without mercy. Jackson brought his head back and screamed his pain into the room as Jeff stood up and aimed another round into the man's open mouth.

Jeff watched Lance Jackson's brains slide halfway across the room and he raised his eyes to the ceiling, crying, "Why God? Why can't I feel relief. Satisfaction. Why do you deny me

448

that?" Rodgers stared at the ceiling for several quiet seconds, as though he were listening to his god's answer. "Oh, yes, I see now," he answered the ceiling. "Yes, of course," and he placed the pistol against his temple and pulled the trigger.

Jeff did not realize the weapon's slide was locked back on an empty chamber, and as the door to the hotel room flew open and Kim rushed in, he sat back heavily in the chair behind him, smiling at her as he dropped the .45 to the floor. "I'm sorry," he told her as he leaned back in the chair and closed his eyes, positive he had just blown the top of his head off and would be feeling the rush of pain and death at any second.

The men in the Decoy Squad jeep watched from a distance as the eleven p.m. guardmount drew to a close. The provost marshal had just presented several of the MPs with Army Commendation medals for their involvement in the successful arrest of robbery suspects in a PX heist the week before. Broox and Thomas stood up and clapped when Craig Davis was promoted to private first class and awarded a Bronze Star Medal—America's third highest decoration—for capturing the four Viet Cong who were trying to mortar Third Field Army Hospital. No mention was made when the citation was read that three of the VC were killed in hand-to-hand combat after their capture.

Good ol' Davis, Richards decided. The sergeant had a special place in his heart for black MPs. *They're always catching it from both sides,* he told himself. *From the white bigots, all the arrestees, and the black people who considered him an Uncle Tom for wearing a badge.* "Hell, that's three sides," he mumbled out loud suddenly.

"What's that, Sarge?" asked Broox. "Say again."

"Oh, nothing—just thinking out loud." He blushed as he took the tiger-claw necklace around his neck and rubbed it superstitiously. He was having bad vibes about this graveyard shift all night and had even contemplated calling in sick for the

449

first time in several years.

Broox and Thomas also wore the shiny, gold necklaces with the gleaming tiger claw clasped on the bottom, and when they saw their sergeant rubbing his they both subconsciously checked to make sure they had not lost their own.

Two MP jeeps cruised slowly up to the Decoy Squad just then, as the provost marshal awarded another Good Conduct medal to Sergeant Schell over the loudspeaker in the background. "Well, if it ain't the honorable Lieutenant Faldwin and his leg breakers," Richards muttered sarcastically as he recognized the officer pulling his jeep side-by-side with the new Beast. He was feeling cocky as he watched more flares than usual ringing the city, discouraging the sappers.

"Heard you clowns have been out big game hunting on company time." Faldwin grinned as he motioned to the tiger-claw necklaces everyone in Richards' jeep was rubbing in their fingers.

"Yessireebob!" Thomas stood up and moved his necklace about so that it sparkled in the starlight. "Responded to a see-the-woman call and expected a routine family disturbance. Found a goddamn tiger in her back yard instead. The woman had already blasted it twice with an old musket."

The scene flashed back across the wide-screen picture in Richards' mind: They had rushed through the Vietnamese woman's home to find the Bengal tigress backed up in a corner of the courtyard, breathing heavily beneath a cluster of bushes, blood gushing from two chest wounds. But despite the fatal wounds, the big cat stared back at him with no fear in its eyes as she watched his every move.

When Richards had asked for dispatch to notify the Saigon Zoo they needed some handlers to bring a cage out, the tigress had lunged at the Decoy Squad, claws thrashing with lightning speed as fangs gleamed in the moonlight. Richards did not think he would ever forget the mournful scream the animal unleashed when they cut her down with their M-16 fire. The tigress had lay critically wounded at their feet for several minutes, panting frantically, green glowing eyes staring up at the half moon, ignoring the MPs now. When the rain clouds that rolled into Saigon every night suddenly appeared, covering up the moon, the beast closed its eyes, laid its head back down on the grass, and released its final breath.

"Well, I'll be damned!" Thomas stood up in the jeep as an MP bus pulled up in the dark compound, off-loading new soldiers in-country. Richards was jolted abruptly back from the memory of the tigress and the souvenirs they had stolen from her. "If it ain't the notorious dynamic duo: Schultz and Slipka!"

"The MPs you knew in Colorado?"

"Those clowns finally got their asses shipped to the 'Nam!"

"The short, dumpy guy there is the sergeant who rode around naked on a snowmobile at Fort Carson," Broox reminded Richards. "Except for a gas mask and combat boots. The lieutenant beside him is the watch commander he made the mistake of mooning!"

"I wonder what the both of them could have done to get shipped over to Vietnam—together!" mused Richards.

Thomas fell back in his seat laughing. "Saigon will never be the same, now that those two clowns are here!"

"You shouldn't be calling a lieutenant a . . ." Faldwin began his reprimand, but the three emergency beeper tones came across on the radio, silencing him.

"Attention all Cholon units," the dispatcher came over the air a bit more excited than usual. "Vicinity of number two Dong Khanh, report of shots fired. That's the Cholon Hotel, also known as the Dong Khanh Hotel, shots fired. Have a caller on the line reports two black subjects dead at the scene, American. Also reports the man fleeing the scene, being helped away by a Vietnamese woman, is wounded and appears to be the same American on the wanted posters plastered all over the city."

"That would be Jeff Rodgers!" surmised Lieutenant Faldwin, and he turned to the men in the other jeep across

451

from the Decoy Squad. "You guys head for the Cholon Hotel. See if you can help over there." And as they hit their flashing red lights and flew past the startled guardmount on their way to distant Cholon, Faldwin turned back to Richards as both men started up their jeeps. "You and me'll head for the apartment on Bis Ky Dong and see if we can head him off at the pass!"

"You knew about the safe house on Bis Ky Dong?" Thomas asked in shock.

"I'm your lieutenant. It's my job to know what you guys are up to—where you're at at all times." Then he reached down and pulled a broken, mangled night stick from the floorboard of his jeep. "When I found Broox's equipment in the spokes of that Honda it was only a matter of minutes before I spotted your flower-child Volkswagen parked down the street." Faldwin grinned in wild amusement as Richards turned to give Broox an I-told-you-so frown.

It had been no easy matter for Mark Stryker to race undetected to the C.I.D. agent's home, nearly seven miles away. Twice, militiamen had chased him down back alleys when they spotted him avoiding the roadblocks, and he had to hide in the sewers until they passed or gave up the hunt.

Sickles' house was dark when he arrived a few minutes before four a.m. He tried the locked door, then knocked for several minutes before a fragile-looking woman appeared at the window.

"Mark Stryker," he identified himself, careful to make sure none of the neighbors heard him. "Bill is expecting me." He could see tears streaking the woman's face and he decided perhaps Sickles really might have a good reason for wanting to see him so urgently after all.

The C.I.D. man's wife unbolted the door and bowed her head slightly as she pointed up the stairwell to a room lit by a tiny, yellow light bulb. The look on the woman's face was one of relief that somebody had finally come, and he rushed up the stairs, gun drawn. But it was too late.

William Sickles was hanging by the neck from the ceiling rafters, his slowly winding body turning to look down on him when Stryker swung the door open. Mark jumped up and tore the lamp cord free with the first attempt, but the career military warrant officer was already growing stiff. He must have changed his mind and killed himself right after talking to Stryker on the phone.

The American walked slowly back down to the helpless Thai woman waiting for him at the bottom of the stairs. He wanted to take her in his arms to comfort her, but a little girl ran out from a side room and the woman hugged her tightly instead.

"He wanted me to give this to you," she said several minutes later when she took the jade lady statue from a chest drawer and handed it to him. "He seemed to think it was very important that you received it," and when she handed the precious Thai dancer over to him, he couldn't help thinking— the faces were so similar—that it had been carved in her likeness.

"What will you do now?" he asked her, but before she could answer, Stryker was drawn to the window by the sound of several sirens passing by outside—MPs. He was about to turn back to the Thai woman when he spotted them running down a side street. Jeff, his arm over Kim's shoulder, struggling to flee in the opposite direction the police were headed.

"More trouble?" the woman asked Stryker when she saw the look on his face.

"I'm not sure," he answered. "But it doesn't look good."

Several miles away, on Nguyen Cong Tru Street, the seventeen-year-old American exchange student, whose father was a consular officer and had grounded him the week before for running women's underwear up the MACV flagpole, rushed to the window at his girlfriend's house and brushed the drapes aside, "Wow, look at all the MP jeeps running hot!"

"I wonder where they go?" the girl's father had stepped beside Nick to see what all the sirens were about. Her parents had allowed him to stay far into the night to visit with them since he would be leaving for America the following day. And before they knew it, curfew had been clamped down on the city and he had been given permission over the phone by his own parents to spend the night—on the living room couch.

"And why must you join the U.S. Army?" Angi asked him, ignoring the action racing past outside. "Why must you go to America when you don't have to? Your whole family stays here!" She made it sound like he was going off to a war zone instead of home to the states for the next few months. "*Choi oi!*" she shook her head. "I'll understand you, Nick! You're bookoo *dinky dau, ching!* You *bic?* Bookoo *dinky dau!*"

"It's just for a few months, Angi," he said, turning away from the window. "I've signed up for the Military Police Academy. They're gonna make me a cop, not a grunt. I've got a contract for Vietnam—they'll send me right back to you!"

"They'll send you to Danang or Pleiku!" she said. "The VC will kill you, then what will I do?"

But Nick just laughed. He had never considered the possibility that they'd send him outside of Saigon. "Don't worry, Angi." He smiled. "I'll be OK—you'll see, the army wouldn't shaft me and send me to the boonies."

"They have VC in Saigon, too!" She rose to her feet and clenched a fist like she was going to deck him one. "You will be a target out there, cruising down Tu Do with flashing lights over your head! Why couldn't you just be a clerk or mechanic—something safer. Why do you have to be a cop?" But Nick had returned to the window and was watching another MP jeep scream by, the men inside looking hard core, determined, fearless. Nick could see himself behind the wheel of that jeep, racing toward the unknown, his partners there to back him up if bullets began flying, and he no longer could hear

454

the girl yelling behind him to pay attention or she was going to smack him with a chair.

The maid was not prepared for what she found when she opened the linen closet on the ground floor of the Astor Hotel. Blood was everywhere—in pools on the floor, smeared across stacks of sheets, thick upon one wall. The maid, a very superstitious woman indeed, immediately concluded that only demons could be behind such carnage, and she ran screaming from the hotel out into the street, never to return.

When Officer Toi responded to the scene, he knew instantly that Pham V. had been there. It was one of the few buildings he had not searched top to bottom. It would have meant she doubled back around to the other side of Tu Do Street, and the policeman didn't feel she had the strength to do that.

Toi would have been surprised also if he knew that the woman he sought had kept herself alive on a massive quantity of drugs and self-administered first aid until she could drag herself to one of her past clients who stayed up on the top floor of the Astor. A wealthy doctor, who had several mistresses in several hotel rooms and didn't need trouble.

The physician had treated her gunshot wound despite the voices that told him he should let her die.

Jeff Rodgers would also have been surprised if he knew that pretty little Pham Thi Vien had spotted him fleeing the Palace Hotel the morning of the booby trap explosion. She was so intrigued by a man who could escape her trap that she followed him all the way to his safe house on Bis Ky Dong. She loved games, and this could be one of the best she had ever devised.

Rodgers would have been more than shocked if he were to learn that the woman who tried to kill him with the web of grenade wires wrapped around his bed had rented out the room directly beneath his. That, while he spent his nights standing at his window in the dark, looking out on the street, she spent hers sitting in a corner below him, staring up at the ceiling as his pacing footsteps made the floorboards creak.

"Damn!" muttered Richards as he reached down at his feet and picked up his helmet. Broox took another corner on two wheels and the sergeant pulled the helmet down over his head and strapped it tight, but several letters stashed inside were forced out by the wind anyway and they were soon a block behind, swirling in the speeding jeep's backwash. "Damn, Broox!" he gritted his teeth. "Slow it down!"

"Yeah," said Thomas. "We're not going to do anyone any good if we don't get there in one piece." And then he turned back to Richards, "You lost a couple letters back on that last curve, Sarge."

Richards tore his helmet back off and searched desperately for the blue envelope, but it was gone. "Jesus Christ," he sighed.

"The letter to Anderson's parents?"

"Yeah, I finally got it finished. Shoulda mailed it this morning!"

"Want me to turn back?" Broox asked sheepishly.

"Naw, we're here!" announced Richards as they were the first to arrive at the safe house.

The jeep of four MPs carrying Lieutenant Faldwin was only a half block behind them and closing in fast.

Officer Jon Toi was not thinking about loyalty or being a good police officer when he saw the woman dragging Jeff Rodgers down that back alley. He was thinking more about how the reward money would build an extension onto his private photograph studio, so his wife would not nag him about how he was selfishly covering up all her nice bamboo wallpaper. He had planned to swoop down on them right then and there, at the intersection of Phan Dinh Phung and Bis Ky Dong, but decided to watch and wait after the woman forced some pills down his throat and seconds later the deserter was back on his feet and running again. It would be a simple matter to follow

Rodgers back to his safe house where much valuable evidence would probably be located.

Toi allowed the couple to enter the apartment house through the rear door and gave them ample time to get close to Rodgers' room before the policeman silently crept through the same door, pistol drawn. And was grabbed from behind and disarmed by the deserter. *Holy Buddha,* Toi was thinking, *Not again!*

As Jeff was dragging the trembling Canh-Sat backwards into the ground-floor corridor, a weary eyed Vien emerged from her room and slammed the door shut. Jeff and Kim whirled around to see the woman, draped in a shimmering new crimson gown, staring back at them with an evil glazing her eyes and a straight razor in one hand.

"I want the Canh-Sat!" she whispered in words so soft yet threatening that Rodgers dropped Toi on the ground and backed away. Vien raised the blade over her head and rushed toward the Saigon policeman, yelling insanely as she attacked.

Just then the main entrance doors to the building flew open and all four people turned to see several MP helmets glowing in the doorway. Rodgers instantly raised his automatic and popped off two rounds at the soldiers and they retreated back out into the street. Vien halted, gave both Toi and Jeff a look that said, *This is not the end of it,* then turned and fled for the doors, right behind the MPs.

Lieutenant Jack Faldwin had no idea who the woman was, dashing out of the apartment house behind him, when he reached out to grab her arm. "Hey, slow down, young lady, wait a min—"

But Pham Thi Vien whirled down on him with the sparkling straight razor, neatly severing his hand off at the wrist. She then turned on her heels and ran for the street while the shocked MPs watched blood gush from their lieutenant's wound.

Without really thinking about it, Richards brought up his own weapon and jerked off four rounds at Vien, striking her

457

once in the middle of the back and smashing her off her feet, sending her face first into the gutter beside the parked MP jeeps.

"The woman!" Richards pointed at Vien, and Broox and Thomas started over to her. "The lieutenant!" Richards pointed at Faldwin, and another private went down on one knee and produced a bandage compress. As he started wrapping the stump, Richards took the remaining two MPs and rushed back up to the doorway. He opened it slightly to the sound of voices arguing inside.

"Put down the weapon, Jeff. Please. I'm asking you to put down the weapon." It was Mark Stryker, the ex-Green Beret. Richards recognized the voice immediately, and motioned for his men to remain calm—to wait to see what that crazy Stryker, who must have slipped in through the back door, had up his sleeve.

Back in the street, pretty Pham Thi Vien summoned the energy to raise her face from the leaves and oily water clogging the gutter. She could feel the tear across her chest—the stitches had come loose again. And the MP's bullet had severed her spine this time. She could no longer run from them, but the defiant smile in her eyes when she turned to look at Broox and Thomas told the MPs they had still not won the game. As they reached down to restrain her, Vien used her own straight razor to cut out her throat, silencing the voices that haunted her forever.

"My God," whispered Broox to himself as the woman's lifeblood burst forth across his uniform and into his eyes. Thomas calmly grabbed the dying, paralyzed woman by a leg, dragged her across the stagnant, polluted pool flooding the street to the nearest lightpole and handcuffed her ankle to it. Then he motioned for the frozen Broox to follow him and they both rushed back to help Richards.

"Come on, Jeff, old buddy. It's me—Mark. Let the Canh-Sat go. We can work something out here!" But Jeff Rodgers just kept backing up toward the stairwell to his room, as if only safety awaited him there and nothing Stryker could say would matter anymore. The deserter kept moving his .45 in slow, circular motions from Toi's head to Stryker's chest, then back again.

Stryker searched Jeff's eyes for any sign he might surrender, but all he saw there was the rage over the loss of Mai growing stronger with each labored breath. "How could this woman so influence Rodgers in just a hundred short days?" he recalled Sickles asking the question in one of their many phone conversations. "What did she do to motivate him—shape him into such a revengeful maniac? How could *any* woman have such an effect on a man, especially a cop," the C.I.D. agent had asked, but Stryker remembered back to his college days—that first romantic interlude with the Hawaiian girl, the first woman who had ever taken him to bed, the first to ever dream beside him. Yes—they had even shared some dreams. Woke up the next day eager to find out why they even spent their dreams together, but then six weeks had passed and it was over. She ran out of money, went back home to Honolulu to her parents. Never returned his letters. But she had been his first love, and women after her would always be missing a certain something, that special magic that had made their love more of a spell, and later a curse. Later, when the memories—when missing her—made the pain unbearable.

"Put the gun down, please."

"Yes," Toi agreed anxiously with Stryker. "Please lower the weapon. No one here will harm you." But Jeff's only response was a continuous, low growling in his throat.

"Look." Stryker slowly reached a hand into his jacket even though Rodgers locked his arm out and almost fired when it appeared Mark was going for his own gun. "Look, Jeff. I have her. I have the jade lady." Stryker's palm reappeared in the dim light of the corridor, the tiny, precious Thai dancer statue sparkling back at Jeff in the dark. Stryker started slowly walking toward Rodgers, saying, "I brought it home to you, Jeff. It's what this has all been about, hasn't it? Here, Jeff. Take the jade lady," and Mark reached out his hand until it was within inches of Rodgers' pistol.

Toi could not see the tears streaming down from Rodgers' eyes when the deserter shot Stryker in the chest, point blank. He saw the jade lady fall, as if in slow motion, to the floor where she shattered into a hundred pieces, and he saw Stryker catapulted back into the wall and the muzzle flash inches from his face that sent him there. But Toi could not see the look of overwhelming grief and sorrow that lined the American's face when he brought the .45 back up against Jon Toi's temple and started to squeeze down on the trigger.

"No, Rodgers!" yelled Richards as he and the other MPs rushed in and cornered the deserter and his hostage. Jeff Rodgers stared at Richards for several minutes before he pushed Toi away and fell to his knees, lowering his head out of sight in the gloom of dark that followed the flash of weapons firing.

Richards realized later he should not have delayed in handcuffing the man, but the intense pity and relief he felt required that he allow the surrendering soldier his moment of sorrow.

When Richards finally did walk up the last few steps to Rodgers, the deserter fell over onto his side, the dagger which had sliced open his stomach and pierced his heart lying bloody in an open palm.

Richards was stunned. Stunned and disappointed, yet relieved. He picked up the head of the jade lady and carefully studied it as he walked back out into the street, shaking his head. He looked up to see the men of the Decoy Squad walking back out to their jeep, and he tossed the jade head into the filthy gutter, now running red with the blood of the dead woman handcuffed to the lamp post. Richards frowned as the chunk of jade bounced through the water and landed on the grass on the opposite side of the street. He definitely felt its place was at the bottom of the sewers. Richards watched a shoeshine boy hustle over to the piece of stone, scoop it up on

460

the run, and disappear down a side alley. The Decoy Squad's sergeant frowned even harder at this, and when he started over to join his men, he was cut off by two of Lieutenant Faldwin's MPs, who were hustling Mark Stryker over to one of the jeeps.

"He's alive!" they yelled. "Wearin' a goddamn bulletproof vest! Got a lotta blunt trauma and a hell of a bruise, but he'll make it!"

Richards nodded his head slightly. He didn't care one way or the other if the private investigator made it. Trouble seemed to follow the ex-Green Beret wherever he went.

"Yeah, I'll be back, Gary!" He heard the man laughing despite the injury. "And I'm going after our job, Decoy Sergeant! I'm re-upping!"

Richards just grinned as he continued over toward his men. He didn't really believe anything Stryker said just then, under those circumstances.

The sun had not yet risen over Bis Ky Dong Street. Just a false dawn, but already the sidewalk vendors were setting up their cardboard stalls. A little girl, watching from behind her mother's skirts down the alley, first stared innocently and shyly at the rough-looking MPs, then flipped them the finger and ran off into a leaning, tin-roofed tenement.

From up above, a trashcan came flying off a balcony, scattering debris at the feet of the Decoy Squad and narrowly missing their sergeant. "One, two, three, motherfuck MP!" someone yelled down from the balcony, but the soldier only waved up at them with a smile on his face.

Just then a black sedan pulled up amidst all the arriving MP jeeps and a skinny, red-headed warrant officer stuck his head out and introduced himself as the new C.I.D. agent assigned to their shift. "Where's the shooting?" he asked nervously.

More and more MP jeeps eventually showed up until Richards decided there were enough men present to relieve them. The Decoy Squad members were due to report for duty at their regular assignments within a few hours. "How about a beer over at the Xin Loi?" Broox asked his sergeant.

461

"No, thanks," Richards replied with a straight face. "Gotta get back to Pershing Field. Got an appointment with the career counselor. Going to extend my enlistment another year." Gunships cruised past low overhead. An ARVN convoy rumbled past down the street. Bombs exploded across some distant battlefield. The war went on.

An old *papa-san*, knocked off his bicycle by the reckless convoy of soldiers, sat in the dust for several seconds, then calmly got back up on his feet, brushed himself off, and continued on his way without so much as a word. Behind the ragged group of MPs, a shop owner was swinging back the iron gates of his ground-level store. He waved at them eagerly, as he set out his displays of stolen stereos proudly. Above, on the balconies, the prostitutes were already coming out by the dozens, to see what the commotion was all about.

"You gotta be crazy, Sarge," said Thomas. "This place sucks. It's the asshole of the Earth!"

"You oughta go back stateside, Sarge," another MP suggested. "Or Europe, where it's easy duty."

But Richards just grinned, turned and started for his jeep. Broox watched him for a few seconds as he approached then got in, and the private chose not to say anything just then.

Broox watched Sergeant Richards stomp down on the gas pedal a few times, then twist the starter button until the engine kicked over. When it roared to life, the sergeant gunned it to full capacity and leaned back in the seat enjoying the power under the hood as if he were test driving a new Caddy.

Broox looked past his sergeant's glowing helmet, to the streets. He watched the growing crowds starting the swirl of intense motion and activity that was Saigon. He could feel the excitement, and the pride that came with being a part of it. He polished the dust off his badge, knowing he understood the sergeant now, finally, after all these months.

The streets of Saigon were all that mattered to him anymore. They were all he had left.

NEW ADVENTURES FROM ZEBRA!

THE BLACK EAGLES: HANOI HELLGROUND   (1249, $2.95)
by John Lansing

They're the best jungle fighters the United States has to offer, and no matter where Charlie is hiding, they'll find him. They're the greatest unsung heroes of the dirtiest, most challenging war of all time. They're THE BLACK EAGLES.

THE BLACK EAGLES #2: MEKONG MASSACRE   (1294, $2.50)
by John Lansing

Falconi and his Black Eagle combat team are about to stake a claim on Colonel Nguyen Chi Roi—and give the Commie his due. But American intelligence wants the colonel alive, making this the Black Eagles' toughest assignment ever!

MCLEANE'S RANGERS #1: BOUGAINVILLE BREAKOUT
by John Darby   (1207, $2.50)

Even the Marines call on McLeane's Rangers, the toughest, meanest, and best fighting unit in the Pacific. Their first adventure pits the Rangers against the entire Japanese garrison in Bougainville. The target—an ammo depot invulnerable to American air attack . . . and the release of a spy . . .

MCLEANE'S RANGERS #2: TARGET RABAUL   (1271, $2.50)
by John Darby

Rabaul—it was one of the keys to the control of the Pacific and the Japanese had a lock on it. When nothing else worked, the Allies called on their most formidable weapon—McLeane's Rangers, the fearless jungle fighters who didn't know the meaning of the word quit!

Available wherever paperbacks are sold, or order direct from the Publisher. Send cover price plus 50¢ per copy for mailing and handling to Zebra Books, 475 Park Avenue South, New York, N.Y. 10016. DO NOT SEND CASH.